C000196827

About the Author

Carol Marinelli recently fille[d] ~~~~ job title. Thrilled to be able to put down her answer, she put writer. Then it asked what Carol did for relaxation and she put down the truth – writing. The third question asked for her hobbies and, not wanting to look obsessed, she crossed the fingers on her hand and answered swimming. However, given that the chlorine in the pool does terrible things to her highlights, I'm sure you can guess the real answer.

USA Today bestselling author **Heidi Rice** used to work as a film journalist until she found a new dream job writing romance for Mills & Boon in 2007. She adores getting swept up in a world of high emotions, sensual excitement, funny feisty women, sexy tortured men, and glamorous locations where laundry doesn't exist. She lives in London with her husband, two sons, and lots of other gorgeous men who exist entirely in her imagination (unlike the laundry, unfortunately!)

Mills & Boon novels were the first 'grown up' books **Julia James** read as a teenager, and she's been reading them ever since. She adores the Mediterranean and the English countryside in all its seasons, and is fascinated by all things historical, from castles to cottages. In between writing she enjoys walking, gardening, needlework, baking 'extremely gooey chocolate cakes', and trying to stay fit! Julia lives in England with her family.

Tempted by the Tycoon

Tempted by the Tycoon
The Fake Fiancée

CAROL MARINELLI

HEIDI RICE

JULIA JAMES

MILLS & BOON

First Published in Great Britain 2023
by Mills & Boon, an imprint of HarperCollins*Publishers* Ltd,
1 London Bridge Street, London, SE1 9GF

www.harpercollins.co.uk

HarperCollins*Publishers*
Macken House, 39/40 Mayor Street Upper,
Dublin 1, D01 C9W8, Ireland

ISBN: 978-0-263-31896-8

MIX
Paper | Supporting
responsible forestry
FSC™ C007454
www.fsc.org

This book is produced from independently certified FSC™ paper
to ensure responsible forest management.

For more information visit: www.harpercollins.co.uk/green

Printed and Bound in the UK using 100% Renewable Electricity
at CPI Group (UK) Ltd, Croydon, CR0 4YY

THE PRICE OF HIS REDEMPTION

CAROL MARINELLI

PROLOGUE

'HEY, *SHISHKA*.'

Daniil Zverev stiffened as he walked into the dormitory and heard what his friend Sev had just called him.

It would seem that *shishka* was now his new name.

Russian slang could hit just where it hurt, and tonight it did its job well.

Big gun.

Bigwig.

Big shot.

Daniil watched as Sev put down the book he had been reading.

'We were just talking about how you're going to go and live with the rich family in England, *shishka*.'

'Don't call me that again,' Daniil warned, and picked up the book and held it over his head. He made to rip the pages out but, as Sev swallowed, Daniil tossed it back on the bed.

He wouldn't have torn it—Sev only occasionally had a book to read—but Daniil hoped he would heed the warning.

'Did you find any matches?' Nikolai looked up from the wooden ship he was painstakingly building and

Daniil went into his pocket and took out the handful that he had collected when he had done his sweeping duty.

'Here.'

'Thanks, *shishka*.'

Daniil would do it; he would smash Nikolai's ship. His breathing was hard and angry as he stared down his friend.

The four boys were, in fact, far more than friends.

Yes, Daniil and Roman might be identical twins and Nikolai and Sev no relation, but all four had grown up together. With their dark hair and pale skin, they were the poorest stock amongst the poor. At the baby house they had stood in their cribs and called to each other at night.

Daniil and Roman had shared a crib.

Nikolai and Sevastyan had slept in their own on either side of the twins.

When they had graduated to beds they had been moved to the children's orphanage and placed in the same dormitory. Now, in the adolescent wing, they shared a four-bedroomed room.

Most considered them wild boys, troubled boys, but they were no real trouble to each other.

They were all they had.

'Touch my ship...' Nikolai threatened.

'Don't call me *shishka*, then. Anyway, there is no need to—I've decided that I'm not going to live in England.' Daniil looked over at Roman, his twin, who lay on his bed with his hands behind his head, staring at the ceiling. 'I'm going to say that I don't want to go. They can't make me.'

'Why would you do that?' Roman asked, and turned his head and fixed his brother with the cold grey stare that they shared.

'Because I don't need some rich family to help me. We're going to make it ourselves, Roman.'

'Yeah, right.'

'We are,' Daniil insisted. 'Sergio said…'

'What would he know? He's the maintenance man.'

'He was once a boxer, though.'

'So he says.'

'The Zverev twins!' Daniil was insistent. 'He says that we're going to make it…'

'Go and be with the rich family,' Roman said. 'We're not going to get rich and famous here. We're never going to get out of this hole.'

'But if we train hard we'll do well.' Daniil picked up the photo by Roman's bed. Sergio had brought his camera in one day a couple of years ago and had taken a photo of the twins and, because the others had nagged, he had then taken one of all four boys.

It was the photo of the two of them, though, that Daniil now held up as he spoke to his brother. 'You said that we would make it.'

'Well, I lied,' Roman said.

'Hey…' Sev had got back to reading but, even though he had just teased Daniil, he cared for him and could see where this was leading. 'Leave him, Roman. Let him make up his own mind.'

'No.' Roman sat up angrily. Things had been building for months, since they'd first been told about a family who wanted to give a good home to a twelve-year-old. 'He wants to blow off his one chance because he has this stupid dream that he can make it in the ring. Well, he can't.'

'We can,' Daniil said.

'*I* can,' Roman corrected. 'Or at least I could if I didn't have you dragging me down.' He took the picture of the two of them out of Daniil's hand and tossed it across the floor. There was no glass in the frame, but something broke then. Daniil felt something fracture somewhere deep inside.

'Come on,' Roman said. 'I'll show you who can really fight.'

He got up out of the bed and there was a buzz around the dormitory as the twins eyed each other.

Finally they would fight.

The Zverev twins trained all day.

Sergio put them through drill after drill and they pushed through all of them. The only complaint they ever had was that they wanted to spar. Sergio had refused to allow it until a few months ago, but even then it was always under Sergio's watchful eye. As an ex-boxer himself, he knew better than to start the boys too early.

These boys were beautifully built. Tall and long-limbed, they were fast, light on their feet and hungry.

He knew that with the right training the twins would go far.

What a package!

Two peas in a pod, two pitched minds and two angry youths.

All Sergio had to do for now was contain them.

But he wasn't there tonight.

'Tell the others,' Roman said, and the room started to fill, beds were pushed back to make floor space and the gathering spectators knelt on them.

'Show me what you've got,' Roman jeered, as he came out fighting. He had Daniil straight on the defensive, blocking punches and moving back.

No headgear, no gloves, no money to get them.

Not yet.

Roman gave him nothing, no rest, nowhere to hide, and Daniil, with everything to prove, fought back with all he had.

The other boys were cheering while trying not to, as they did not want to alert the workers.

Roman was at his fiercest, and though Daniil did his best to match him it was he who tired first. He moved in and took Roman in a clinch. He just needed a moment to rest but his brother shrugged him off.

Daniil went in again, holding on to his twin so that Roman couldn't punch him, doing his best to get back some breath before he commenced fighting again.

Roman broke the clinch and the fight restarted, both blocking punches, both taking the occasional hit, but then Daniil thought he was gaining ground. Daniil was fast and Roman rarely needed to rest but it was Roman who now came in for a clinch and leaned on his twin. Daniil could hear his brother's angry breathing but as he released him, instead of giving Daniil that necessary second to centre, Roman hooked him, landing an upper-cut to Daniil's left cheek and flooring him.

Daniil came round to stunned faces. He had no idea how long he'd been knocked out but it had been long enough to have everyone worried.

Everyone except Roman.

'See,' Roman said. 'I do better without you, *shishka*.'

The staff had noticed that some of the dorms were empty and, alerted by the mounting cheers, had started running to the room where Daniil now lay, trying to focus.

Katya, the cook, took him into the warm kitchen, calling to her daughter, Anya, to bring the box of tape. Anya was in there, practising her dance steps. She was twelve and went to a dance school but for now was home for the holidays. Sometimes she would tease the twins and say that she was fitter than them.

Anya still had dreams and thought she would dance her way out of here.

Daniil had none now.

'Hey, what on earth were you doing?' Katya scolded. She gave Daniil some strong, sweet black tea and then she tried to patch up his face. 'The rich family don't want ugly…'

Daniil sat on a bed just a few days later, seemingly a million miles from home.

In the car he had looked at the small houses and shops as they'd passed them and when the car had turned a corner he had seen in the distance a large imposing red-brick residence. They had been driven down a long driveway and he'd stared at the lawns, fountains and statues outside the huge house.

Daniil hadn't wanted to get out of the car but he had, silently.

The door was opened by a man in a black suit who looked, to Daniil, to be dressed for a funeral or wedding but his smile was kind.

In the entrance Daniil stood as the adults spoke over him and then up the stairs he was led by the woman who had twice come to the orphanage and who was now his mother.

At the turn of the stairs there was a portrait of his new parents with their hands on the shoulders of a smiling dark-haired child.

He'd been told that they had no children.

The bedroom was large and there was only one bed, which looked out to vast countryside.

'Bath!'

He had no idea what she meant until she pointed to a room off the bedroom, and then she had gone.

Daniil had a bath and wrapped a towel around himself, just in time, because there was a knock at the door. It opened and she approached him with an anxious smile. She started to go through his things and kept calling him by the wrong name.

He wanted to correct her and tell her his name was pronounced *Dah-neel*, rather than the *Dae-ne-yuhl* she insisted on using, but then he remembered the translator explaining that he had a new name.

Daniel Thomas.

That woman, his mother, had rubber gloves on, and his clothes, his shoes were all being loaded into a large garbage bag that the man in the suit was holding. She was still talking in a language he didn't understand. She kept pointing to the window and then his cheek and making a gesture as if she was sewing and after several attempts he understood that she was going to take him to get his cheek repaired better than Katya had done.

He stared at the case as she disposed of his life and then he saw two pictures, which Daniil knew that he hadn't packed. Roman had slipped them in, he must have.

'*Nyet!*'

It was the first word he had spoken since they had left Russia and the woman let out a small worried cry as Daniil lunged for the photos and told her, no, she must not to get rid of them and neither could she touch them.

His mother had fled the room and the man in the suit

stood there for a while before finally coming to sit on the bed and join him in looking at the photos.

'You?' He had pointed to Daniil and then to one of the boys in the picture.

Daniil shook his head. 'Roman.'

The old man with kind eyes pointed to his own chest. 'Marcus.'

Daniil nodded and looked back at the photo.

Only then did Daniil start to understand that Roman didn't hate him; he had been trying to save him.

Daniil, though, hadn't wanted to be saved.

He had wanted to make his way with his brother.

Not alone, like this.

CHAPTER ONE

TECHNICALLY, LIBBY TENNENT LIED.

She had made it through the gold glass revolving doors and had walked across the impressive marble floor and was just at the elevators when a uniformed security guard halted her and asked where she was going. 'I have an appointment with Mr Zverev,' Libby said.

'Perhaps you do, but before you can take the elevator, first you have to sign in at Reception.'

'Oh, of course,' Libby responded airily, trying to look as if she had simply forgotten the procedure.

Everything about the place was imposing.

It was a luxurious Mayfair address and, even before the taxi had pulled up at the smart building, Libby had realised that getting in to see Daniil Zverev might not prove the cinch that her father had insisted it would be.

Libby walked over to the reception desk and repeated her story to a very good-looking receptionist, saying that she had an appointment to see Mr Zverev, silently hoping that the woman wouldn't notice that the appointment was, in fact, for her father, Lindsey Tennent.

'And your name?'

'Ms Tennent.' Libby watched as the receptionist typed

in the details and saw that her eyes narrowed just a fraction as she looked at the computer screen.

'One moment, please.'

She picked up the phone and relayed the information. 'I have a *Ms* Tennent here. She says that she has an appointment with Mr Zverev.' There was a moment's pause and then she looked at Libby. 'Your first name?'

'Libby,' she said, but then, realising that given the way the security was in this place she was likely to be asked for official ID, she amended, 'Short for Elizabeth.'

Libby tried to appear calm and avoided curling a stray strand of her blond hair around her finger or tapping her feet, as she did not want to appear nervous.

She *was* nervous, though. Well, not so much nervous, more uncomfortable that she had agreed to do this.

Maybe she wouldn't have to because the receptionist shook her head as she replaced the phone. 'Mr Zverev cannot see you.'

'Excuse me?' Libby blinked, not only at the refusal but that it came with no apology or explanation. 'What do you mean, I have—?'

'Mr Zverev only sees people by strict appointment and, Ms Tennent, you don't have one.'

'But I do.'

The receptionist shook her head. 'It is a Mr Lindsey Tennent who has a 6:00 p.m. appointment. If he was unable to make it then he should have called ahead to see if sending a replacement was suitable—Mr Zverev doesn't just see anyone.'

Libby knew when she was beaten. She had rather hoped they might not notice the discrepancy—as most places wouldn't. She was almost tempted to apologise for the confusion and leave, but her father had broken down in tears when he'd asked her to do this for him. Knowing just how much was riding on this meeting, she forced herself to stand her ground. She pulled herself as tall as her petite five-foot-three frame would allow and looked the receptionist squarely in the eye.

'My father was involved in an car accident earlier today, which is the reason that he couldn't make it, and sent me as a replacement. Now, can you please let Mr Zverev know that I'm here and ready to meet with him? He knows very well the reason for my visit, or perhaps you'd like me to clarify that here?'

The receptionist glanced at whoever was standing behind Libby and then to the left of her. Clearly Libby had a small audience. The receptionist must have decided that the foyer wasn't the place to discuss the great man's business because she gave a tight shrug.

'One moment.'

Another phone call was made, though out of Libby's earshot, and eventually the immaculate woman returned and gave Libby a visitor's pass. Finally she was permitted past the guarded barrier that existed around Daniil Zverev.

The elevator door was held open for her and she stepped in.

Even the elevator was luxurious. The carpet was thick beneath her feet. There was no piped music, just cool air and subdued lighting, which was very welcome on a hot summer evening after a mad dash across London to get here.

She should never have let her father talk into this, she thought.

In fact, she hadn't. When Libby had said yes to trying to persuade this man to come along to his parents' fortieth wedding anniversary celebration, it had been a Daniel Thomas she had expected to be meeting.

But just as she had been about to leave her father had called her back.

'Oh, there's something I forgot to tell you.'

Her father, who had been begging Libby to the point of tears, had then looked a touch uncomfortable and evasive. 'He goes under a different name now.'

'Sorry?' Libby had had no idea what he was talking about.

'Or rather it would seem that Daniel Thomas has recently reverted to his real name—Daniil Zverev. He was adopted.'

'Well, if he's gone back to his birth name, clearly there's a serious rift. I'm not going to interfere…'

'Libby, please,' her father begged. 'All Zverev has to do is show up and make a speech.'

A speech? The list of demands for Daniil had again increased. Show up, dance with aunts, be sociable, and now she had to ask him to make a speech!

No, Libby was not comfortable with this at all. She lived in her own dreamy bubble where the role of negotiator didn't exist. She was very forthright, in that she had an expressive face and a tendency to say what she was thinking. She also, to her parents' disquiet, had always refused to quietly toe the line.

'You never said anything about him having to make a speech.'

'Can you just talk to him for me, Libby? Please!'

Why the hell had she said yes?

Of course, she had looked Daniil up on her taxi ride here. Her father had said that face-to-face he was sure that Libby would be able to appeal to his conscience but it would seem, from her brief skim through several articles, that the esteemed financier previously known as Daniel Thomas didn't have one.

It was, one article observed, as if he saw everyone as the opposition and would step over whomever he had to if it meant he achieved his aim.

As for women—well, it would take far longer than a thirty-minute taxi ride to read up on that part of his history! The word *heartbreaker* was thrown around a lot. User. From what Libby could glean, his longest, for the want of a word, *relationship* had been a two-week affair with a German supermodel, who had been left devastated by their sudden ending.

Well, what did these women expect? Libby had thought when she'd read how some considered the break-up to have been cruel.

Why would anyone ever get involved with him?

Libby had never been one for one-night stands but it would seem Daniil Zverev was a master of them. She was cautious in relationships, never quite believing men who said that her dancing wouldn't get in the way and that they had no issue with the hours she devoted to her art.

Always she had been proved right to be cautious. Invariably the reasons for the break-ups were the same—that she was obsessed with ballet, self-absorbed and hardly ever free to go out.

Correct.

She'd told them the same at the start.

Libby got back from dwelling on her disastrous love life to trying to fathom Daniil.

Surprisingly, there had been little made of his name change—it was as if even the press was wary of broaching certain topics around him.

So, too, was Libby. She certainly didn't relish the prospect of asking him to play 'happy families.'

Of course, she felt like David going into face Goliath as she came out of the elevator and walked along a corridor, only to face another seriously beautiful woman who ran her eyes over Libby as she approached the desk.

'I'm here to see Mr Zverev,' Libby said, but her smile wasn't returned.

'Perhaps you would like to freshen up before you go through.'

'Oh, I'm fine, thank you.' Libby shook her head—she really just wanted to get this over and done with.

'You will find the ladies' room just down the hall and to your right.'

To her sudden embarrassment Libby realised that it was being suggested, and strongly so, that she *needed* to tidy herself up.

Could the great Daniil Zverev only lay eyes on perfect people? Was he only prepared to hold court with women at their coiffed best?

She held back the smart retort, though, and instead, blushing to her roots, took herself off to the ladies room. As she stepped inside and saw herself in a full-length mirror she was, though she would never admit it, rather grateful for the advice to take a little time before seeing Daniil.

It was a warm and windy August day and she had the hair to prove it.

Determined to keep practising and to maintain her skills, without the delicious routine of dance class and rehearsals, Libby had been home, warming up, when word had come in that her father had been involved in a car accident. Of course, she had just pulled on some leg-

gings and a wrap over her leotard, grabbed her workbag
and raced to the accident and emergency department.

Her head was still spinning with all her father had revealed that afternoon. The family business was in serious trouble and they needed this anniversary party to go
ahead next month. For that to happen, though, Daniil's
acceptance of his parents' invitation must be secured.

Libby couldn't think about her father's business trou-
bles now.

She went through her huge bag and pulled out a fresh
ivory wrap and put that on over her leotard and changed
from leggings into a grey tube skirt. Her blonde hair was
already tied back but messy so she brushed and retied it
and pinned it up. Her face was devoid of make-up and
she looked far younger than her twenty-five years. Somehow she didn't think fresh-faced would appeal to such a
sophisticated man but Libby didn't have an awful lot in
her make-up bag to work with. Some mascara made her
blue eyes look bigger and she added some lip gloss too.

She'd just have to do.

Libby knew she didn't stand a hope with him. A man
who had cut ties with his family so dramatically that
he'd changed his name was hardly going to want to turn
things around on her say-so.

And, anyway, Libby was the last person to tell someone else what they should do.

She, herself, didn't like free advice.

She'd be working in the family business if she did.

Resigned to being sent away even before she'd got
out the first sentence almost took away the fear of meeting him.

Yes, she'd just say what she had to and then walk away.
She would not allow herself to be intimidated.

Snooty Pants at Reception must have deemed Libby looked suitable now because she picked up the phone and informed him that his 6:00 p.m. appointment was here. 'However, as I said it is—' He must have interrupted her because she didn't finish explaining again that it was Libby rather than Lindsey who was there. 'I'll send her in.'

As Libby *finally* went to head for the door it would seem that she'd jumped the mark.

'You can leave your bag here.'

She was about to decline but again she realised it wasn't a suggestion so she put her bag down and headed for the door. As she was about to raise her arm she was halted.

'Don't knock, it irritates him. Just go straight through.'

Libby felt like knocking just for the hell of it!

And knocking again.

And then knocking again.

The thought made her smile.

Widely!

And that was how he first saw her.

Smiling at some secret joke, because, Daniil knew, nothing his PA would have said would have put her at ease.

She was a dancer.

He knew that not just from her attire but from her posture as she closed the door behind her, and she was fighting her dancer's gait as she walked a little way towards him and then paused.

As she stepped in Libby blinked. She was standing in a postcard view of London. She might just as well have bought a ticket for the London Eye, though there would never have been someone quite as delicious sitting opposite her there!

He had dark hair, dark eyes and pale skin and there was a livid scar across his left cheekbone. He sat straight in his seat at a very large desk, watching her with mild interest.

Despite the huge office, despite the vast space, he looked so formal and imposing that he owned every inch of it.

'Thank you for agreeing to see me, Mr Zverev,' she said, while privately, such was his impact, she rather wanted to turn and run.

'My, my, Mr Tennent,' Daniil said. 'What a high, clear voice you have.'

His own voice was deep and his words were dipped and richly coated in a chocolaty Russian accent, and as she realised he was alluding to the appointment being with her father her smile stretched further and she lost her fear.

'And, oh, Mr Tennent,' Daniil continued, his eyes taking in her slender bare legs, 'what smooth skin you have.'

She stood before him and, no, Libby wasn't scared in the least. Still she smiled.

'I think we both know, Mr Zverev…' she started, and then halted as she properly met those cold grey eyes that pierced her. She sent a silent apology to the women she had so merrily scorned for getting involved with him. She had never understood women who could simply leap into bed with a man but she had to wrestle to hold on to her conscience, for he was so beautiful, his stare so intense and so sexy that he could possibly have had her then.

She had to clear her throat so she could continue

speaking, and she had to recall their words just to find her thread.

Yes, that's right...

'I think we both know, Mr Zverev,' Libby said, 'that *you're* the big bad wolf!'

CHAPTER TWO

SURPRISINGLY, WHEN SHE was so bold as to call him the big bad wolf to his face, Daniil actually smiled. 'Indeed I am.'

Libby caught her breath. Those hooded, guarded features briefly relaxed, that deep red sulky mouth stretched and the cold grey eyes softened. Not a lot, just enough that, for a brief second, he didn't look quite so formidable.

But very quickly that changed and it was down to business.

'Take a seat,' he instructed.

Libby did, crossing her ankles and resting her hands in her lap.

'Would you like some refreshment?' he offered.

'No, thank you.'

'You're sure?' he checked.

'Quite sure.' Libby nodded, just as she realised she was terribly thirsty, yet she felt uncomfortable knowing what she was about to ask him and cross with her father for the position she was in.

Daniil reached across his desk and opened a bottle of sparkling water. It was chilled, she could see that from the condensation on the bottle, and, suddenly *very* thirsty, Libby heard the delicious fizzing sound as he opened it and then the lovely glug, glug, glug as he poured it into a heavy glass.

He didn't offer again.

Bastard.

But then he pushed the glass towards her, and with a slight roll of her eyes she took it. 'Thank you.'

He poured his own and she glanced at his hands—even they were beautiful, his fingers long and slender, his nails short and manicured.

'So?' Daniil said.

Oh, yes. She dragged her mind back to the reason she was there. 'My father is very sorry that he couldn't make it this evening. He was involved in a car accident earlier today.'

'I'm sorry to hear that,' Daniil said. 'He wasn't seriously injured, I hope?'

'Oh, no.' She was surprised at the concern in his voice. 'It's just a mild concussion…'

Daniil hid his smirk as her voice trailed off and he watched as Libby frowned. It was a very mild concussion. In fact, the doctor had come in just as Libby had been leaving and had told Lindsey that he could go home.

If this meeting with Daniil had been so pressing, so vital and urgent, then surely he could have made the effort and come?

'He needs to rest for the next forty-eight hours,' she said, though suddenly she felt as if she was convincing herself instead of him. 'As you know, he's an events planner and—'

'And the event that he is planning will not go ahead unless I attend.' Daniil broke into her chatter.

'Yes.' Libby took a sip of her water. 'Sir Richard is very adamant that without his son there…' She looked at

Daniil and saw the tiny rise of his eyebrows and she had the feeling he was laughing at her, though his lips did not move. 'Well, it's their fortieth wedding anniversary. That's quite an achievement these days.'

'What is?' Daniil checked.

'A forty-year marriage.'

'Why?'

Libby blinked at his question. 'Well, I guess if it's a happy marriage then it's quite an achievement.' She shot out a nervous laugh—he picked up on everything.

'I guess it is something.' Daniil shrugged. 'I have never made it past forty-eight hours...'

His eyes held hers, *really* held hers, and to her astonishment Libby realised that there was a warning there. A delicious warning perhaps, and Libby's own eyes narrowed at something she couldn't quite put her finger on.

One—she pondered, was he flirting with her?

Possibly, she conceded. A lot of work would have gone into honing his technique so he was just idly practising perhaps.

Two—if he could be so direct then so would she.

'There was that German supermodel...' Libby wagged her finger at him. 'You lasted two weeks with her, I believe.'

'You've done your homework,' Daniil said approvingly. 'Ah, yes, Herta. I followed her to a photo shoot in Brazil, not because I was lovesick, more that I had to check something...' His gorgeous index finger went to his Adam's apple.

'Sorry?'

'I kept thinking—she was so tall and that voice of hers was so deep...'

Oh, my God, he was shocking.

'And was she…?' Libby croaked.

'A she?' Daniil said, and nodded. 'She definitely was. Thank God.' He let out a low laugh and Libby forgot what planet she was on. It was Daniil who had to bring her back to earth. 'Go on,' he said.

She had two big guns to use on him and a very impatient target. She could almost sense her time with the great man was about to expire.

'Well, as you know, Lady Katherine is unwell,' Libby said. 'Extremely unwell.'

'Not so unwell that she can't throw a party,' Daniil pointed out.

'No, but…'

'But?'

She tried to trip or even make a tiny jiggle on his guilt switch but he just coolly stared back at her as she spoke. 'Well, there might not be a forty-first.'

'Is that it?' Daniil frowned.

'Sorry?'

'Your attempt to persuade me?'

She swallowed. She did think of her other big gun, that there was a letter awaiting him if he went and something about Sir Richard not giving Daniil's inheritance to his cousin, but, hell, Libby thought, how tacky was that, so she chose not to use it.

'That's it.' Libby sighed and gave in. 'I'm not very good at trying to persuade people. I tend not to bother, in fact.'

'Well, just so you know, your technique is all wrong,' he said. 'First, you should have given me all the shit, just laid it out on the table for me.'

'Such as?'

'You should have told me that I would have to go by

my adopted name if I attended—Daniel Thomas—and
that I would be expected to give a speech...'

Libby sat with her mouth gaping, realising he was
streets ahead of her.

'Then,' Daniil said, 'when you had my emphatic refusal, *then* you should have tried to persuade me and talk
me round by pointing out my mother's declining health
and such things.'

'Would it have worked?'

'Not on me,' he said. 'I'm just letting you know, for
future reference, that you were working backwards with
your technique because, had I dubiously agreed, there
was still more you had to ask of me. You hit me too soon
with the sob story.'

'Well, then, it's just as well this isn't my usual kind of
work,' Libby said, and peered at him. He completely intrigued her. He was a stunning mix—arrogant and hostile yet somehow approachable.

'Tell your father the answer is no—I shall not be attending my parents' wedding anniversary celebrations.'

'Because?' she asked.

'I have no reason to, neither do I wish to share my
decision-making process with you.'

'Was it always going to be a no?'

'Yes.'

'Then, why did you agree to see my father?'

'Well, he insisted that he had something to say that
might change my mind. I notice that you didn't mention
my inheritance going to Cousin George.'

'No.'

'Why not?'

'I have no reason to, neither do I wish to share my

decision-making process with you.' Libby parroted his words but he just smiled.

'You know you want to really.'

She did!

'Well—' Libby shuffled in her seat '—I happen to think that's blackmail.'

'That's my parents' favourite sport,' Daniil said. 'Anyway, I don't need a draughty old mansion on my hands. I loathe the place. I certainly have no wish to ever own it.'

Libby hated that she'd been talked into doing this, she really did. 'Look, I'm very sorry for interrupting you, Mr Zverev.'

'That's it?'

'Yes.' Libby beamed. 'I'll pass on your response to my father.'

'If he is annoyed at not getting his way, know that he would have lasted one minute with me. You can console yourself you did better than he ever could have.'

'Why?'

'I liked watching your mouth.'

'You can't say that.'

'Why not? You demanded to see me, you came into my office without a proper appointment, you don't get to dictate how I behave in here.'

He stood and she just about folded over in her seat as six feet two of heaven gracefully walked across the floor and retrieved his jacket from a stand. Well, he sort of flicked it off the hook and then slipped it on, all in one lithe motion.

'There's water,' Daniil said, 'and over there is a fridge with some nice contents. The bathroom is through there...'

'Sorry?'

'You're still sitting and I'm clearly on my way out so I assumed you were staying.'

'Oh!'

Even standing was a challenge with him in the room. Her legs had forgotten their role, and so had her head because she even bent down to retrieve her bag, which, of course, wasn't there.

'That's right, I left it at Reception.'

He made her seem slightly mad.

She felt slightly mad.

As she stepped out of his office it was like walking out of a ten-hour back-to-back session at the movies and blinking at the light.

Libby picked up her bag and gave Snooty Pants a smile then headed for the elevator but she jumped in quiet surprise when she realised that he was standing behind her.

'I thought that you'd have a special elevator,' Libby observed. 'One that only goes up.'

Yes, she thought, he would take her to heaven.

They stepped in and the doors closed and Libby waited for the most excruciating elevator ride of her life to commence, but instead it turned out to be the best ever.

He was checking his phone and then he looked up to where she stood. She was leaning against the wall, gazing at his stunning face, intrigued by his scar.

'Do you want an early dinner?' he said, and, just like that, he offered her a delectable slice of his time.

'Dinner?'

'Well, I'm hungry and I guess you didn't have time to eat in your haste to get to your critically injured father.'

Libby's lips twitched into a smile.

'And then,' Daniil continued, 'there would have been

all the shock and relief of finding out that he only had mild concussion.'

She laughed. 'No, I didn't have lunch.'

'So do you want dinner?' Daniil checked. 'But on one condition.'

They stepped out and walked across the foyer. She glanced at the receptionist who hadn't been going to let her in and Libby was tempted to poke out her tongue.

'What's the condition?' she asked.

'Know that I shan't be changing my mind.'

'About?' Libby frowned and then answered her own question—oh, yes, the reason she was there. 'I get that.'

They walked out and a car with a driver standing outside was waiting for him.

'How did he know you were on your way out?'

'Cindy would have rung down to alert him that I was leaving.'

Cindy!

Well, yes, she would be called that.

As she climbed into the car, one of the many things that Libby was thinking about was how much money she had on her and what the balance on her credit card was.

Her mother had always warned her to have enough money for a taxi ride home and she also wanted to know she had money enough on her card to pay for dinner.

He was, she had read, prone to walking off in the middle of a meal, or a holiday, or a photo shoot in Brazil. When bored, he did not push through politely.

He could leave at any moment, and she accepted that—this was transient and temporary.

She wouldn't have missed it for the world.

Now they were out of his vast office and in the smaller surroundings of a car, his size was more noticeable. Tall, his shoulders were wide, but as he had put on his jacket she had noted just how flat his stomach was.

She was small but he made her feel tiny as she sat beside him. 'Where are we going?'

'Somewhere nice,' he said.

Nice was a roped-off club that drew a crowd even on a Monday evening.

And it was very nice not to have to queue.

'Did you have a reservation?' Libby asked, as they were shown straight in and through.

'No, I never book anywhere,' he said as they took a seat. She put her bag on the floor and they put their phones down on the table. 'How can you know in the morning what you will want that night?'

Second warning bell.

She glanced around and people were staring at them.

She felt a little like she had when she'd done work experience at the library and the real worker had gone to lunch. Someone had asked her a question and had expected her to know the answer.

'I don't really work here,' Libby had wanted to say as she'd tapped away on the computer.

'I'm not really with him,' she wanted to correct the curious onlookers.

Except, to her absolute delight, tonight she was!

Oh, she knew it was a one-off, that she was here by default only, but it was such a lovely turn of events that she decided to simply enjoy it.

'What would you like to drink?' Daniil asked, as she read through the cocktail menu.

It was overwhelming.

Like him.

Just breathing normally was an impossible feat with him so near.

She gave a slightly helpless shake of her head, which was probably terribly unsophisticated but it was all she could manage.

'Champagne?' he checked, and she nodded, but when he gave the order and she heard just what champagne they would be drinking she knew she had better hold on to that attention span of his because her credit card would not be able to cover it.

The champagne was poured and the ice was truly broken when Libby's phone rang and Daniil glanced down and saw from Libby's caller ID that it was her father calling.

'Answer,' he said.

She did so.

'I'm sorry, Dad, I did speak to him but the answer's still no.'

Daniil watched her as she talked.

His invitation to take Libby to dinner had surprised him. She was nothing like his usual type, which was generally close to a foot taller and quite happy to sit bored and silent, just pleased to be seen out with him.

Libby Tennent didn't sit. She squirmed in the chair as she chatted, one hand was playing with her hair, her eyes were rolling and she was frantically blushing as she spoke with her father. 'No, I'd say that there's no chance of him changing his mind.'

Daniil watched.

'No, I wouldn't try calling him if I were you, Dad,' Libby responded when her father suggested he do just that. She gave Daniil a little wink. 'He's a very cold person.'

Daniil smiled and took a drink of his champagne.

'No, I think you're just going to have to accept that his answer is no. How are you feeling—?' she attempted, but he had already rung off.

She put down her phone and raised her palms in the air then looked up when Daniil started counting.

'One,' Daniil said, and Libby frowned. 'Two…' Just as she was about to ask what he meant, his phone rang. 'I still don't know how he got my private number.'

He took the call from Lindsey and was about to give his usual cold, brusque response, but, maybe because he knew that he'd be sleeping with his daughter in, say, an hour or so from now, Daniil was a touch more polite than he would usually be.

'Lindsey, I am sorry to hear about your accident. I'm blocking your number now. Don't try to get hold of me again.'

He rang off.

'I feel so bad for him,' Libby admitted. 'As well as cross with him for sending me to try to persuade you. I told him I didn't want to.'

'So why did you?'

Libby gave a tight shrug. 'He pointed out that, unlike June, my sister, I do nothing at all for the family business.'

'What does June do?'

'She's a chef.' Libby sighed. 'Who married a chef.'

'A very handy daughter to have for an events planner.'

Libby gave a glum nod. 'Unlike me.'

'What about your mother?'

'She works with my father.'

'Do you get on?'

'We do but…' Libby gave another tight shrug. 'I'm far too demonstrative for the lot of them. You know, sometimes I'm sure that I'm adop…' She swallowed down the most appalling faux pas but Daniil just gave a wry smile.

'At least I knew that I was.'

'I'm sorry.' Libby winced. 'That was thoughtless.'

'What is it with the English and guilt?' he asked. 'It doesn't bother me a bit, and there's no reason for guilt about your father—it's not your fault his business is about to go under.'

Libby shot him a look.

'How?' she asked. How did he know?

'Does he usually chase up every non-attendee with such vigour?'

'No.'

'Clearly this party is very important to him.'

'It is.'

'Guilt and manipulation are terrible bedfellows,' Daniil said. 'My parents must know that your father is desperate, so they used him to get to me. In turn, he knows that he's getting nowhere, so he guilts you into coming to see me, hoping I would not be able to say no to your lovely blue eyes.' He wagged his finger at her. 'Tut-tut, Libby.' Then he gave her a thin smile. 'So are you close to your parents?'

'For the most part,' Libby said. 'I think all families have their issues that drive each other crazy but if you love…' She hesitated as she remembered that Daniil was estranged from his parents. 'Do you care about them at all?'

'No.' He shook his head but offered no elaboration.

'Were you ever close to them?'

'I never let myself get close to anyone.'

She frowned, but said nothing at first. It wasn't for her to correct him, it wasn't for her to say he was wrong. She had stepped into his world uninvited and she didn't make his rules or get to tell him how he should be.

'Why?' Libby asked, and from the blush spreading on her neck both knew she wasn't just discussing his lack of relationship with his parents.

'Because it leads to expectations that it might last and, in my opinion, nothing lasts. Libby…' Daniil was incredibly direct. 'You do understand that whatever happens tonight won't change my mind about attending my parents' party?'

'Yes.'

He didn't believe her for a moment. 'You're sure?' he checked.

She nodded.

'Because,' he warned, 'that would be very foolish of you.'

'I know,' she said, 'and I hope that you understand that your expensive champagne won't buy a night in bed with me.'

'Yes.'

'You're sure?'

'Yes.' Daniil nodded. 'But my charm might.'

Libby laughed.

He was bad but it felt so good.

'What about you?' he asked. 'You know about my two-week record, what's your record in a relationship?'

Libby thought for a moment. 'Eighteen months,' she said. 'Though the last six don't really count.'

'Why?'

'We were seriously limping along by then.' She thought back to that time—the constant knot in her stomach at the juggling of too many balls. It had been a relief when the relationship ball had finally fallen and she could fully immerse herself in dance. 'Apparently I was too focused on my career.'

'Instead of him?' Daniil checked, and Libby nodded. 'That's his issue.'

'Perhaps,' she sighed. 'I keep telling myself that.'

'Then, it's time to start believing it.'

The waiter came and Libby ordered the French onion soup as her main and Daniil asked for two steaks and a green salad.

When they were alone she looked back at him. 'Two?'

'I have a big appetite,' he said, and then admitted that he was curious about her order. 'I'm surprised that you didn't ask for them to leave off the cheese and bread. Isn't that what most ballet dancers do?'

'Ha.' Libby gave a wry smile. 'Unfortunately the only time I'm not hungry is when I'm anxious or stressed. The moment I'm happy I'm constantly starving. How did you know I was a dancer?'

'You were trying very hard to keep your legs parallel and not walk like a duck when you came into my office.'

Oh. Her thighs were definitely parallel now—in fact, they were squeezed tightly together just from the delicious brush of his knees.

'Professional?' Daniil asked.

'Ex.' For the first time he saw that happy smile waver. 'Well, I guess I shall be again soon but in a different way—I'm looking at two rentals tomorrow so that I can start my own dance school. You know the saying, those that can't, teach.'

'That doesn't sound like something you would say to somebody else,' Daniil observed.

'No,' Libby admitted.

'So why do you say it about yourself?'

'I'm guess I'm not where I'd hoped to be.'

'Which is?'

For the first time conversation faltered.

Libby took a large slug of champagne before speaking. 'My biggest part never happened…' She saw his small frown. 'I was understudy once. You know when they say, "Break a leg"? Well, I meant it. But, of course, she didn't.'

'You never meant it.'

'No,' she admitted. 'I'd have loved her to get at least one migraine, though.'

Daniil smiled and now so did she.

'Look, I've accepted that the small roles I get aren't going to lead to anything bigger. I love ballet, seriously I do, but it's not *everything.* It's almost everything but if you want to go far then that's what it has to be. I've also had a couple of injuries that I haven't come back from…'

'Such as?'

'You never want to see my feet,' she said.

'Oh, but I do.'

Said feet's toes were curling at another press of his knee, so much so she was almost tempted to flick off her shoe and place it in his lap.

Help!

'Anyway, the last fracture I had demanded rest and you just can't. You have to push through but I realised that I can't keep doing it any more. I know I'm not going to go far, at least not anywhere that's going to pay more than my rent, so I've been studying to teach. I'm actually excited about it now. I've had my depression.'

'You thought that your life was over?'

'Oh, yes,' she readily agreed, because for months she had not been able to imagine leaving her dream behind, but now, well, she was happy with what she'd achieved and excited for all that was to come.

Almost.

There was an ache there—that she would never be a part of a big production again, never audition—but she avoided touching it for now.

'And so tomorrow you look at places to open your own dance school?'

'I do.'

'Good luck, then.' He raised his glass and they chinked them.

The soup was sublime, the crust perfect, and she poked a hole to get to the lovely brown broth beneath.

'Tell me about the places you are looking at tomorrow,' he said.

'Well, there's one not very far from where you work and it has the rent to prove it. Then there's one in the East End, which I can afford and it already has mirrors...'

'So it was once a dance studio?'

'Yes.'

'Why did it close down?'

Her spoon paused midway to her mouth. 'Don't spoil my appetite.'

'No, these are the questions that you need to ask. Trust me, I know these things.'

She gave him a tight smile. 'I don't think teeny-tiny dance studios are your area of expertise...'

'Business is business.'

'Perhaps, but it's very personal to me.'

'There's nothing wrong with being personal,' he said. His knees did not dust hers now, they were there touching hers and pressing in a little and, yes, they were officially flirting, and if he could be nosey then so could she. 'How did you get your scar?'

He gave a tiny shake of his head as a response.

Just that.

No evasiveness, no excuses, just a tiny shake of his head that told her not to go there.

It intrigued her, though.

The scar was jagged and raised and, given his billions, Libby wondered why he didn't get it tidied up.

His teeth were beautifully capped—well, she assumed that they were because no genes were *that* good—and clearly, from everything else she could see, from his immaculate hair to his exquisitely cut suit, Daniil took care of his appearance.

Apart from that scar.

They chatted, or rather she did. He was extraordinarily good at getting information out of her. Where she lived, where she'd gone to school, where she'd danced.

And as he went to top up her glass and only a trickle came out, she realised most of the conversation had been about her.

'I'll get more,' he said, about to call for a waiter, but Libby stopped him.

'Not for me—I'd pass out.'

'Dessert?'

He saw the wrestling in those lovely blue eyes. Libby knew their time was up, yet she simply couldn't walk away.

'Please.'

The menus came again and she looked through her choices, tempted to order the chocolate soufflé, just to prolong the inevitable end.

'Crême brulée,' Libby settled for instead. 'You?'

'Just coffee.'

It was eight twenty-seven when her dessert was served and it was already over.

'Nice?' Daniil asked.

'Very.' Libby nodded, yet she could more than sense his distraction. He glanced out to the street and once more she saw him check the time.

Thank him for dinner and go home, Libby told herself, but instead she dragged things out a tiny bit by going to the loo. Then she had a coffee and little chocolate mints but all too soon their drinks were done and all that was left for Libby to do was slip a serviette into her bag as a memento of the evening.

A few moments later they walked out into the street and there, waiting for him, was his driver.

'I'm going to get a taxi home,' Libby said.

'Why would you do that when I have a car waiting?'

A car that, from the way she was feeling, would only lead to his door. She looked up at him. 'I think we both know why.'

'Well,' he said, 'it was very refreshing to meet you, Ms Tennent.'

'It was very daunting to meet you.' Libby smiled. 'Well, it was at first.'

'And how about now?'

His hands went to her hips, the move sexy and suggestive as he framed where their minds were. Libby had a sudden urge to be lifted by him, to wrap her legs around him.

'I'm very daunted,' she admitted, 'though the middle bit was fun.'

It *was* daunting only because she was about to be kissed by the devil.

Why the hell did I order French onion soup, she thought, wondering if she could press Pause on him and scrabble in her bag for mints.

Oh, that was right, she'd had those chocolate ones with her coffee.

'What are you thinking?' Daniil said, because her eyes were darting and it was as if she was having a conversation with herself.

'I'm not going to tell you.'

He didn't test the waters, he didn't start slowly, he just lowered his head from a great distance and Libby got the most thorough kissing of her life. His lips parted hers, his lips, not his tongue, and he held her so firmly that even as she went to rise onto her toes still he held her down. And when her lips were opened his tongue tipped hers and he explored her, not particularly softly. His jaw was rough and delicious, and when she tried to kiss him back she was met by a refusal.

This was his kiss to her, his mouth said. It wasn't a dance of their mouths. He didn't even lead, he simply took over, tasting her, stilling her, making her body roar into flame with his mouth. So solid was he Libby felt as if she were leaning against a wall. Even when someone knocked into them they were barely interrupted, such was the shield of him.

His kiss had her hot, right there in the street, but the only movement he allowed was to let her hands reach for his chest. She slid her fingers over the cool fabric of his shirt and found the nub of his nipples. Yes, she was hot and aching for more, her hips were pushing frantically against his hands so their bodies might have more contact. But then, when he coiled her so tight, he released her mouth. He'd let her glimpse a fraction of what being held by him felt like and then he cruelly removed the pleasure.

She sucked in the summer night air while craving his mouth again.

'Bed,' Daniil said.

'I don't…' Libby halted. What had she been about to say—that she didn't want to?

Well, yes, she did.

Since the age of eight, dancing had come first, which had meant self-discipline.

In everything.

How nice to stand here on the brink of making a decision based purely on now, on her own needs and wants right at this moment.

And she did want.

So she chose to say yes when the wisest choice might have been to decline.

'Bed.' Libby nodded and then blinked at her response. She didn't retract it but her voice was rueful when she spoke next. 'I am so going to regret this in the morning,'

'Only if you expect me to love you by then.'

Third warning bell.

She could turn and walk away now.

'Oh, no,' Libby said, and in that at least she was wise. 'Then, there's no reason for regret.'

CHAPTER THREE

THE SECURITY TO get past for his penthouse apartment rivalled that at Daniil's office.

First his driver spoke into an intercom and gates opened that led to an underground car park. From there they walked to another elevator that was only opened when Daniil typed in a code and gave his name in his low sexy drawl.

Up into a foyer they went, where they were greeted, and then it was another elevator up to his place.

Once inside, he threw his jacket over a couch and poured them both a drink and then sat on one of the large sofas, leaving Libby standing for a moment, taking it all in.

Daniil was very used to having women in his home. He didn't like going to theirs. Here, he was in control.

What he wasn't used to, though, was a woman like Libby. Her flat shoes made no sound on his marble tiles as she went over and looked out at the view and, Daniil was sure, she had another conversation going on in her head.

He lived above the clouds, Libby thought, or at least that was how it felt. They were so high up that she could be flying now, or in a hot-air balloon.

'You don't sound like a pony clipping around,' he observed.

'Ah, yes, noise irritates you.' Libby smiled as she nursed a brandy and stared out at a dusky London, the sky flaring orange and promising that tomorrow would be another hot day, and she thought about the lead-up to tonight. 'I was going to knock on your office door just to annoy you. And then knock again.'

'Is that why you were smiling when you came in?' Daniil asked, as he recalled thinking that she had been laughing at some private joke.

Now she shared it.

'It was.' Libby turned from one delicious view to another.

Him.

'Do you know that I was sent off to clean myself up before Cindy would let me in to see you?'

'Of course.'

'I felt like I was at school and they were doing uniform inspection,' she said, and then got back to peering at Big Ben and wondering if you could hear the chimes from in here, but her question never got asked because he spoke first.

'Do you have your navy panties on?'

She wanted to lift her skirt and flash her bottom at him and she laughed out loud as she imagined doing so. 'I'm most unlike me tonight,' she admitted.

'In what way?'

She thought for a long moment, wondering how best to describe the sheer heady pleasure of self-indulgence, how, till today, she had contained herself, unless she was dancing. Instead of saying so, though, she shook her head, just as Daniil did when there was something he would rather not discuss.

He accepted her silence.

'I'm most unlike me, too,' he said.

Usually he'd be just about on his way out.

Dinner with Libby had been very civil and certainly it was early to be home. More pointedly perhaps, they hadn't kissed their way up in the lift, neither were they in bed already.

Instead, she wandered around and, rarely at ease with that, he let her.

It was a vast floor space; the walls, to the sides of the glass one, were brick, and the effect was amazing against the night sky. There was a storm rolling in and it was a sight to behold, the sky lighting up pink in the distance with each strike, yet there were no rumbles of thunder to be heard; rather she felt them. Looking out, it was almost as if you were on a very high balcony, suspended there on the outside. In fact, it was a little dizzying, as if you should be able to feel the breeze. After a few moments of taking it in, Libby stepped back and, as she did so, she felt she should be closing doors behind her. 'Your home is stunning.'

It was.

The dark leather sofas were so wide and inviting she could happily sleep on a quarter of one of them, and naturally there were all the mod cons.

Except there was something missing.

There was no artwork on the walls, no photos on the shelves.

'No books!' Libby exclaimed.

'I read online.'

'But what about all your old ones?'

'I dispose of them when I'm done.' Daniil shrugged as Libby almost fainted in horror at the thought of him callously tossing them out.

Well, there's your lesson, she warned herself. She'd be shivering in the recycle pile tomorrow, with all evidence of her ever being here tidied away by his maid.

Yes, it was somehow, despite the beauty, sterile.

The kitchen was something that would have any serious cook weeping with envy but, unlike her sister, Libby wasn't a cook by any stretch of the imagination so she passed by quickly.

'You don't like the kitchen?' he called over his shoulder as she walked past it.

'It's a kitchen,' she said.

She hesitated as she approached the master bedroom, where she would be performing later, but was surprised at her lack of stage fright.

They might not even make it to the bedroom, Libby sighed, because right now she was fighting the temptation to turn around and run over and do him on the sofa.

She could feel his eyes on her and she had a prickly, excited feeling that at any moment he might choose to pounce.

What a bedroom, she thought as she peered in.

Just a bed.

That was it.

There was one perfect, vast, four-poster bed, which was dressed in white and was up against a huge brick wall.

No art on the walls, no mirrors…

It was curiously beautiful in its simplicity because there was nothing and nowhere to hide.

'Where do you put your clothes?' she called from the doorway.

'There is dressing room behind the wall to your right.'

There were no bedside tables, either.

'Where do you put your glass of water?'

'I get up if I want a drink.'

'Condoms?'

'Ha!' He laughed at her brevity. 'I have a woman who hands one over at the necessary moment...'

She turned and rolled her eyes.

'Under the pillow,' he said.

'Oh.' Libby felt curiously deflated. 'I thought you'd at least have a button to push or something for that.'

Again, it was very sterile, almost clinical, but terribly, terribly sexy too. She was incredibly turned on and almost ached for him to come over but still he sat, quietly watching her.

She let out a breath and chose not to enter the bedroom for further inspection; instead, she wandered some more.

There was a large, very neat study; again, though, there were no books, no photos and no clutter.

It was all so beautiful and yet so empty.

She came to another door and went to open it.

'Libby.'

She turned and he gave a slight shake of his head, the same one he'd given when she'd asked about his scar.

No excuse, no explanation, just a warning as to what was out of bounds.

Now he stood and moved in that same lithe way he had in the office and she felt suddenly nervous as he took off his tie.

It was a delicious nervousness that started between

her legs and worked up to her stomach and then caused a blush to spread on her neck.

'Come on,' he said, and walked towards the bedroom.

No kiss, no 'whoops, how did we end up here,' no words of endearment even.

This was sex, possibly at its most basic. Really, she should hot tail it out of there, Libby knew, and yet his lack of affection, his cold instructions turned her on rather than off. She had never felt so drawn to anybody. The ease and unease she felt with Daniil was a heady combination. She would possibly have followed him to the moon right now and so she chose not to refuse this rare invitation.

'Can anyone see in?' she asked, looking out of the vast windows and noting the lack of drapes or blinds.

'No.'

'You're sure?'

'Quite sure,' Daniil said, and gestured for her to come to the window, where she had the same giddy sensation of stepping outside. 'See there...' He pointed to the left and she saw the soft glow behind a large window. He told her it was the home of a rather promiscuous junior royal and above that lived a film star. 'Like an ambulance,' Daniil said, 'you can see out but not in.'

'Have you ever been in an ambulance?' she asked.

'A few times.'

She turned and looked at his cheek, wondering if now she'd find out how he'd got that scar. 'For?' she fished.

'For...' Daniil said, and moved his mouth to her ear as if to reveal a secret. Libby stood there, tense in anticipation, but no words were uttered. There was just the soft sensation of his lips on her lobe, a decadent hush as his mouth worked its way down her neck, her skin alive to

his touch but her mind sparking in frustration at his refusal to connect with her.

She jerked back and he raised his head and saw the
glitter of frustration in her eyes.

'You don't need my life story, Libby.'

She wanted it, though.

She walked off towards the bed and sat there, her
legs dangling over the edge as she tried to pull herself
out of a sulk.

One night, she reminded herself, but already she was
in over her head—how could one night ever be enough
of this man?

She watched as he removed his shirt, and when he
took it off she felt her jaw clench.

She knew bodies; it was her job to after all.

His was seriously beautiful—his abdomen, which she
had already gauged as flat was toned and taut, his chest
was so powerful and defined she was reminded of a huge
butterfly spreading its wings. His arms were muscled,
though long and slim, but she frowned at the dark bruise
on his rib cage. She was about to ask what had happened
but then saved herself from another rebuff and delivered
an instruction instead.

'Turn around,' she said, and blinked at herself, finding it a little odd that she'd dared to ask, but there was a
thrill when he obliged.

His back was like art; she could see the muscles beneath the white skin, and her colleagues would have
fainted in pleasure just to see this.

She watched as he removed the rest of his clothing
and then when he turned and she saw him naked she
didn't pretend not to look, she just stared at his growing erection, as dangerous and as beautiful as him, ris-

ing from straight black pubic hair, and for tonight this pleasure was hers.

'Get undressed,' he said, and he took her hand and pulled her to a stand, but instead of leaving her there he held her and her exposed skin was on fire against him. She pressed her cheek against his chest and, as direct as he was, she inhaled him, feeling him under her hands. She ran her hands over his hips and to his buttocks and she wanted her fingers on his spine.

Later.

Her eyes still glittered, but now it was with the plea-sure to come, and when he released her she started to undo her ivory wrap.

'Wait.'

He went and lay on the bed and stretched out that long body and then nodded for her to continue.

She had a little trouble with the knot, only because she was watching him and feeling his eyes carefully take in any flesh she exposed. She was too small to worry with a bra but her breasts felt heavy and her nipples were swol-len and jutting out of her pale leotard.

She went to take down her skirt.

'Slowly,' Daniil said, and then he gave the same in-struction she had. 'Turn around.'

Libby obliged.

First she kicked off her shoes and then rolled the skirt down over her hips, bent and took off her skirt, and heard his low moan of approval and knew he was stroking himself.

She stood and lowered one strap of her leotard and fought not to turn around.

She lowered the other one and slid it down past her shaking thighs and then bent to take the leotard over her feet. Without instruction, she held that position a little longer than necessary before coming back to a stand.

'Turn around.'

Naked, she stood and she loved the examination of his eyes, over her tiny bust, down her stomach and to her small blond mound.

Yes, she hadn't waxed in a while but, thank God, she'd shaved her legs that morning. Then she stood, legs a little crossed and one ugly foot on top of the other as his eyes went there.

'I love your feet,' he said. 'You know pain.'

'Is that what you're into?' Libby swallowed.

'No,' he said. 'I'm just saying I like it that you persisted. Don't be embarrassed by them.'

'Phew.'

'Worried I was going to spank you?'

'No.'

Technically, Libby Tennent lied.

In truth, he could put her over his knee this minute and she'd be delighted, and *that* worried her because she'd never thought like that in her life.

Yes, she was most unlike herself tonight.

And yet, when he called her over, when he said, 'Come here,' she was more herself than she had ever allowed herself to be, for she did as she wanted and went easily to him.

She climbed onto the bed but now she did not await instruction or summons. She knelt over him and kissed him, and he went to move his head but, no, she persisted, for it was her turn to kiss him now.

His lips were relaxed and accepting and she caressed them with hers, slipping in her tongue between them to get the lovely soft taste as his fingers took care of the ache in her breasts.

Usually Daniil did not care to linger, but tonight he dared to.

It was a night of firsts for both of them—for Libby it was a night of pure self-indulgence, for Daniil a brief break from resistance. Tonight he let himself feel—the softness of her lips and the breath that was sweet, the moans of her pleasure just from his taste and the soft shape of her breast that warmed and swelled to his palm.

Yes, it was a night of indulgence. Her lips never left his as she moved over him, sat naked on his stomach and kissed him more deeply. His hands left her breasts and slid down her waist but their ache was soon sated as he moved her higher and, pulling her down, took one breast in his mouth.

She pushed up on her knees, leaned forwards and gave him the full taste of her breast and the freedom to let his hands roam over her buttocks.

She felt incredible to Daniil—no silicone, no wobbly bits, just hard muscle beneath his fingers—and he pressed in as his mouth sucked harder.

She wanted more of the press of his fingers and the suction of his mouth, then he eased into her cold, long fingers, and she had a heady memory of his beautiful fingers caressing a glass and they were now inside her.

'Cold hands,' Libby breathed.

'Cold heart,' Daniil mumbled, with a mouthful of breast.

'I don't care…'

Her face was a furnace, her moans were ones of reproach as she berated herself for being so easy, so loose, and it had nothing to do with their fleeting time together, more that she was fighting not to come.

Daniil loved a fight; he stroked her so deeply, he got right up and into her oiled, heated space till she gripped tight on his fingers, and still he did not relent, stroking her down till she knelt on him breathless.

'I'd be a terrible male,' Libby said. 'It would all be over...'

'You'd be snoring,' he said, looking up at her shuttered eyes. 'And I'd be lying all tense and frustrated.'

He laughed at his own joke and lay with his fingers inside her, laughing when usually sex was a serious pursuit for him.

And then, because this night was more pleasurable than expected, he rested on the ropes and planned the next round, for he would take her to the limit; he would enjoy the lithe body that came so easily to his hand.

He lifted her so she sat high on his chest, her legs astride him, but he moved them so that her legs were over his shoulder and then he sat up.

'What...?'

Her eyes snapped open as she was lifted up.

God, he was strong.

His hands held her hips, and when she was sure she would topple he secured her with his mouth, burying his face in her sex.

Her legs were over his shoulders and down his back, and it took a moment to balance, but when she did, oh, my. He just held her and sucked her and there was nothing to hold on to, just mid-air and his hands on her hips and the bliss of his mouth. He moved her as he wanted, he tasted her absolutely, he drew from her words that she'd never uttered with each probe of his tongue.

'Never stop,' Libby begged as she came, loving the way he pushed her to the limit.

He had to stop, or he'd be coming to mid-air.

Daniil loved sex, for his own pleasure, but feeling her flicker to his tongue, that musky scent had him giddy and right on the edge himself.

He dropped her.

And she loved that he did.

The slam of the mattress on her back, the slight disorientation as she tried to locate the pillows, just to sheath him, but she was upside down in his bed.

'I'd better warn you...' He didn't need to. She saw he was more than ready as he slipped the condom on and he could come now and he'd still be her best lover.

His lips were shiny from her as he came over her and kissed her, and had she had any manners she'd have parted her legs, but she loved the roughness of his hairy thigh as he dealt with that.

She lay, a lazy, drunk-on-lust lover, hazy and giddy from two orgasms and trying to find brief pause, but there was none. There was a shrill of nervousness in her as she looked into ice and then surly lips spread into a ghost of a smile and she knew that she was about to find out what it was to be taken.

'Oh...' Libby said, as she was rapidly stretched, and she looked up into those cold grey eyes that were open to hers and she didn't need kissing, she just drowned in his pleasure and chose to enhance it—her arms raised as she gripped the wooden slats at the foot of the bed.

Rough were the hands that pulled her down but she held on firmly.

'Libby,' he said, and tugged her down again but she

did not let go, holding on as he took her, shackled by their thoughts, and it was a decadent bliss.

Oh, one night was not enough. It was her only tangible thought as he swelled within her, but still he did not give in.

'Come…' she begged, because she would at any moment. The noise alone signalled the end, he was so fast and so pumped, but still he would not unleash. He slowed and she clenched around his thick tip, gripped and released and watched his lips part as she played him at his own game, a game where both won, for he drove fully into her then, a punishment for daring to goad him, a delicious internal wrestle to take the lead.

Beneath him, she still came out on top, for Libby arched into him, pressed her hands into his buttocks, urged him and fully partook, but then, as her legs went to wrap around him, as she went to cling to him and share in the journey home, he took the lead.

His legs came to the sides of hers, halting their progress to his hips. Still he thrust as he trapped her thighs in his.

She went to protest, but his mouth smothered hers.

She lay there immobile and let out a sob as his pelvis opened and aligned fully with hers, his length sliding in so deep, the friction of him so relentless she lay there pinned, trying to remember to breathe, then deciding she didn't even need to because she was floating and sinking at the same time as he said something, presumably in Russian, presumably very bad, and he unloaded within her.

'Oh…' It was all she could manage.

It was an orgasm so deep that she cried.

Real tears.

And Libby, during a very difficult year, had refused to cry.

Best of all, he didn't comfort her afterwards.

He simply let her be.

It was exceptional bliss.

CHAPTER FOUR

'*NYET.*'

Daniil was half-asleep when her fingers set to work on his back.

'Shut up,' Libby said. She had promised herself a little dalliance with that back. 'It's my one-night stand, too.'

He frowned at her words for usually women were only too eager to please him and yet she made it sound as if she was pleasing herself.

Libby was.

As he rolled onto his stomach she climbed on and sat on his lower back and found herself in heaven.

His back was truly beautiful and his shoulders were just so wide that she could work for hours and never unravel all the knots, but feeling some of them dissolve beneath her fingers she carried on.

'What was that?' he asked as one minute in he realised it wasn't some sensual massage he was getting but a deep-tissue one. Right into his deltoid her slender fingers burrowed.

'You'll be in agony the day after tomorrow,' Libby promised. 'And the next day, but maybe by Friday you'll remember me fondly.'

Daniil did not like massage but her hands were so precise and expert that he let himself sink into it.

They were both in bliss.

Libby loved feeling his neck loosen and how he moaned with the pleasure of pain at times as she located a tense area. Down she slid and went to his buttocks and sustaining the pressure with her thumb did a muscle-stripping technique and he let out a small curse but did not tell her to stop.

In fact, he spoke, trusting her enough to let her get on as he asked her the question she hadn't answered.

'Why are you most unlike yourself tonight?'

Her hands paused for a moment and she found she was frowning as she worked out her answer. 'Maybe I'm just working out who I am without...'

Libby didn't finish. She didn't need to; they both knew she had been consumed by the dancing world for a very long time. She pressed her palms into Daniil's loins, lifting up a little so that more of her weight was on him, and shifted the conversation away from herself. 'So why are *you* most unlike yourself tonight?'

Daniil gave a low laugh that she felt in her hands before he answered, 'Because I'm still awake.'

She gave him a light slap between his right buttock and thigh for his response but she laughed, too, and they both paused a moment. She felt him shift a little to get comfortable, felt the resurgence of desire, but it wasn't sex that drew her closer to him in that moment—it was the shared moment of laughter and being herself.

Her most honest self.

She turned her head and looked out of the window and never again would she look at even a photo of Big Ben without remembering her time with him.

Today was supposed to have been the hardest day.

She had been warming up, at home alone, when her father had rung.

It had been her first day without dance class and now, when all the white noise had gone, everything she'd told her family, her flatmate, her colleagues, her friends, *herself* even, hushed. There, twenty minutes before the close of the day, she watched the storm over London and thick drops of water sliding down the windows, and she told him the *real* reason behind leaving the dance company she had loved.

'I jumped before I was pushed.' Libby voiced her truth. 'I wasn't even getting the small roles anymore.'

He didn't turn and kiss her, he didn't dim the pain with sex, he just let her fingers work his back. 'At least you jumped,' Daniil said. 'Most people have to be prised kicking and screaming from something they don't want to let go of.'

'That was almost me—I took forever to read the writing on the wall,' she admitted. 'I should have gone six months, maybe a year ago but I clung on to the bitter end. I'm crap at dignified exits—I can't even end a text conversation gracefully, let alone my career.'

'It must have been hard to let it go.'

And let it go she finally had, yet it hurt so much to have done so.

He heard her sniff and tears came again and he felt the drops of her tears on his skin. He let her cry awhile before speaking on.

'So now you fly solo,' Daniil said.

'I don't want to, though.'

'No choice sometimes.'

She liked it that he didn't fob her off, that he didn't tell

her, as others repeatedly had, that as one door closed…
when the simple fact was that she'd loved being on that
side of the door. Neither did he tell her how the greatest
opportunities were often born from the darkest times…
Being a part of a dance company had been a lifelong
dream and it was an opportunity that was now gone.

She carried on with his back and then there was silence, a lovely silence that Daniil usually only achieved
when he was here on his own. And it was better than
being alone because he really wasn't thinking about
where he was. Instead, he was thinking of where he'd
come from, which was a place in his mind he rarely visited from the vantage point of calm.

He'd never wanted to leave the orphanage. It had almost killed him to be prised from his friends and his twin
and thrust into a world that he hadn't wanted to inhabit,
and then she spoke again.

'I wanted to work with what I had,' she said.

In that moment he understood her and she understood
him; in that moment they were both pushed reluctantly
through the same portal of change and he remembered
his resistance. Daniil recalled with clarity how he had
wanted to be back with his brother and friends and a
world he had been told he should be happy to have left.
He thought of Sergio and how they'd raced from school
to the makeshift gym. Of Katya and strong, sweet tea
and a kitchen that had been big and always warm. Of
nights spent talking into the darkness and how the four
of them would speak with certainty about the world they
were going to change.

Instead, he'd had to learn to somehow coexist with a
family he could never be a part of, a headmaster who had

done all he could to quash rebellion and a cousin who had goaded and bullied him.

He, too, had had to make his way in a place he would have preferred not to be.

Libby knew there was nothing he could say that might make this better and was certain that he could never understand but then, as he spoke, she realised he did.

'Being resourceful sucks.' His response was sleepy but it hit the mark and Libby smiled unseen.

'It truly does.'

She worked his neck till it was pliant and then ran her hands down a very loose spine and then, tired now, bent and gave his shoulder a kiss and moved off him to lie down, liking the feel of his arm over her chest as he pulled her a little bit closer.

Neither moved all night.

In fact, Libby woke up exactly as she'd fallen asleep, on her back with his arm across her chest, and she turned to steal a look at him.

He was starting to wake up and he needed a razor and she'd never woken to such male beauty before.

Regret?

God, no.

Her whole body felt…well, it felt as if she'd been in for a tune-up.

He woke to her stretch and smile.

'Bad girl,' he said.

'I know.' She rolled her eyes. 'Whatever must you think of me?'

'Only good things.'

He adored that she was unashamed of her body and the pleasure that they'd had last night.

And Libby adored it that he did not mention her big revelation about her career or her possibly rather red eyes.

He reached for his phone and raised an eyebrow in surprise when he saw that it was after eight. Usually he would be at work by now.

'I'm late,' he said.

'Well, it's very lucky that you're the boss, then.'

'True.' He turned and looked at her. 'Are you late?'

'No. I'm meeting one agent at ten to be shown through.'

'Near here?'

'No, that's not till one.'

'You should have booked them the other way round.'

'Ah, but I didn't know I was going to be sleeping in your bed!' She gave him a smile. 'Goldilocks.'

'I don't know that one so well.'

'Well, I guess you'd have grown up on Russian ones.'

Daniil nodded and he thought for a moment of Sev reading to them, or Katya, the cook, who, when they had been little, would sometimes tell them a tale.

Nice memories, Daniil thought.

'I did,' he said, 'though where I come from the wolf is the good guy.'

'Really?'

'You've seen *Firebird*?'

'I've heard about it, of course, but, no, I've never actually seen it performed…'

'It's on in London now,' he said, and he waited for her to jump as most women would at the tiny line he'd just thrown them.

She didn't.

She lay there her in a state of self-imposed anxiety. Rachel, her flatmate, had been to see it twice and had suggested that Libby join her many times, until Libby had broken down and admitted that, no, she just couldn't face a full-scale production yet. Her head had let go of the dream, her heart just wasn't ready to, and it would hurt: it would be agonising to sit and watch what she now knew she would never be a part of again.

Daniil was relieved when she didn't jump. For a moment he considered taking her to the ballet but soon decided against it. He didn't want to give the false impression that this was about anything other than sex.

Still, it surprised him that he'd even considered it so he quickly changed the subject.

'Tell me more about your studios.'

'There's not much more to tell.'

'Have you spoken to the bank?'

Libby gave a small grimace. 'I'm doing that this afternoon.'

'Are you prepared for them?'

'I think so,' she said, and went a bit pink. 'Actually, last night I was going to sit down and work out figures.' She let out a sigh. 'I'd far rather talk about wolves...'

'I know that you would but you need to sort this out.'

'Do you always hold a business meeting with your lovers the next morning?'

'The scatty ones, yes,' he said, and didn't reveal that *any* conversation was rare the next morning. 'You are too vague. I think you are leaning towards the one in the East End and that would be a mistake.'

'Er, I have given this some thought. The one near here charges four times the rent. I can hardly quadruple my prices.'

'No, but if you can double your number of students you only have to charge double the fee. It's maths.'

'Perhaps but there's only one of me.'

'So you might get a senior to take some of the juniors.'

'Oh, so you're an expert in ballet?'

'No,' Daniil calmly responded to her slightly sarcastic tone. 'I'm an expert in business.'

She frowned. She'd have thought he only knew about massive conglomerates but as he spoke on, more and more it seemed that he understood what she would be dealing with if she opened her own dance school.

In fact, he hit several points that Libby had been hoping she could gloss over when she spoke with the bank.

'The poorer suburb that you are talking about—I doubt there would be a lot of spare money for dance classes and costumes.'

'Dance should be available to everyone.'

'Please.' Now it was Daniil who rolled his eyes. 'If that's your aim then go and hire a hall and give it away for free. What if you get a child with real talent and her parents can't afford the extra classes?'

Libby lay there.

She didn't have to tell him her answer. Of course, she would give the child free lessons—how could she not?

'Now,' Daniil continued, 'around here they could afford it. Even for the fat kid with no talent the parents will pay through the nose...'

He was cruel, he was abrasive but, damn him, he was right.

'Here you could hold adult classes during the day, lunchtime ones—people are trying to squeeze exercise into their days. What were the premises used as previously?'

'The one near here was used for yoga and the other a ballet and jazz school.'

'Ask the agents why they closed down. I know you

dismissed that yesterday but it is a very important question you must ask and take careful note of the answer.'

'I shall.'

'Are you putting your own savings into it?'

Libby's snort told him that she had none. 'No, just my talent and enthusiasm...' She let out a sigh. 'I haven't a hope with the bank.'

'Go and have a shower,' he said. 'I'll make a drink.'

He didn't join her.

Deliberately.

There was something about sex in the morning that was a touch too intimate for Daniil, but as she climbed out of bed and stretched again he wanted to break his own rule.

Even his bathroom was sexy, Libby thought as she stepped inside.

It wasn't warm and inviting, but it was decadent all the same.

It was tiled in white and one wall was a mirror, set back in the middle and angled so that she could see her body from every direction. No, it wasn't ballet exercises she envisaged as she stood there—instead, it was her and Daniil in this space.

Behind a glass wall were towels as thick as pillows. He had an array of toiletries and Libby spent a few giddy moments opening lids and inhaling his scent. At first she wondered where the shower was but when she flicked a button she soon found out that water came from a long rod set in the ceiling and shot in strong jets at her from every direction.

It was utter bliss and she stood for perhaps a while longer than one usually would in the circumstances and then she turned the water off and wrapped herself in one of his fluffy towels. She would have loved to have simply padded out and back to his bed.

Instead, she used all his lotions, not just for the luxurious feel of them on her skin and in her hair, more that for the entire day she would have a little of the scent of him.

'That,' Libby said, as she came into the kitchen, dressed as she had been last night but now all damp and pink, 'was the nicest shower I have ever had.'

'Good,' he said, handing her a drink.

He had made her a frothy coffee and Libby added sugar and saw that Daniil drank black tea with the bag still in the cup.

As she perched on a bar stool he stood leaning against a counter, and it was awkward between them for the first time.

'You should have take-out cups so that you can avoid the small talk,' Libby commented, and he even managed a small smile.

'I don't normally do coffee.'

'Well, I'll consider it a compliment, then,' she said. She made it halfway down her mug before the awkwardness became too much for her, and deciding that it really was time to go she hopped down from the bar stool. 'If I want to get there before ten, I'd better head off.'

Daniil waited for one of two questions—for Libby to ask if he'd given any more thought to attending his parents' anniversary celebration.

Or if they might see each other again.

'I can have you driven or a taxi,' Daniil offered.

'No, thanks,' she said, because that would mean she wouldn't need to leave for a while and it was already tense between them.

Why did it have to be like this? she wondered.

It just did.

She'd heeded the warnings and had gone into it with her eyes wide-open, if a touch dilated by lust. No, she didn't want him down on one knee, begging her not to go, but the ending of them was, for Libby, harder than she could ever have anticipated when she had accepted his invitation to bed.

'Thank you for a lovely evening,' she said. She came around the kitchen bench and whether he wanted one or not she gave him a kiss on his cheek.

Even his clenched jaw was sexy, she thought. She wanted to rub her lips over his rough chin but she restrained herself.

A bit.

Well, no, she didn't, she did exactly that. She wanted to coil around him and live on his hips, she thought as she inhaled his heady scent. She'd be no trouble at all, he could carry on with his day and just give her the odd glass of water and bar of chocolate.

'What's funny?' Daniil said, as she pulled her head back.

'The things that I think.'

She walked out with barely a sound and gave him a half-wave as she let herself out of the door and he stood there, waiting for her to turn around.

Oh, I was just wondering if you'd given it any more thought...

She didn't.

You know you mentioned Firebird, *well, maybe we could...*

She didn't suggest that they see each other again, either.

He heard the door close and at fifteen minutes to nine,

some fourteen hours and forty-five minutes after they had met, Libby Tennent was gone.

Libby sat on the underground on the way to her appointment with the estate agent.

She was back to reality but after last night she knew she was changed forever.

Oh, she knew her mother would faint if she told her what she had got up to and her sensible older sister probably would, too. Then again, they'd always thought she had her head on backwards.

And her father?

Well, he'd thoroughly disapprove, of course, and then after ten minutes of sulking would be wondering how it might benefit the family business.

She was sick of it.

Guilt ridden with it, too.

Yes, she had begged for extra lessons, for private tuition, and the business had, of course, funded that, but did it mean she now had to work for him, doing something she didn't love?

Had it all been conditional on her making it to number one for their investment in her to count?

Couldn't she just love what she did?

Coming out of the underground her phone rang and Libby saw that it was her father. She would have preferred not to have answered but given his accident yesterday she felt she ought to. 'How are you this morning?' Libby asked.

'Pretty bruised,' Lindsey said. 'Did you get anywhere at all with Zverev?'

'Nowhere,' she answered. Well, yes, technically she lied, but she was hardly going to let her father know just how far she'd actually gone! 'Dad, I think you've just got to accept that he isn't going to go…'

'But—'

'It's not up to us to persuade him, Dad,' Libby said, and she was firmer than she usually was with him. 'And if your entire business is reliant on him attending then I think you've got bigger things that need to be faced.'

'Elizabeth!'

'Well, it's true,' she said.

'If things go well with this then I'll be back in the game. And if you came on board…'

She closed her eyes as the same old argument was raised. They had never taken her dancing seriously, they had considered it a phase, an expensive hobby that they had indulged her in, and now it was time to pay them back.

'Libby, what are you doing, looking at dance schools when you're needed here? We've done all we can to support your dancing but clearly it hasn't worked out…'

The tiny paper cuts her family delivered over and over hurt.

Okay, maybe she hadn't made it to the top, maybe she'd never been cut out to be a soloist, but didn't any of her career count to them?

'Dancing still is my career.'

'Even when your family needs you? Look, if you can't help us out there then at least go and speak with Zverev again…use your charm, smile that smile.'

Now at least he was being a little more honest, though it had taken Daniil to get her to fully see that her father had been hoping that a woman might make more headway with Daniil than he could.

'It's not going to happen, Dad—I shan't be seeing

Daniil again. So maybe you should contact the Thomases and let them know that their son isn't going to be attending their anniversary celebration.'

Libby turned off the phone and got back to daydreaming about Daniil and trying to fathom how at twenty-five she'd possibly already had the best night of her life.

His little pep talk about business, however unwelcome at the time, did help today though.

The first studio she saw was perfect! There were huge mirrored walls and the floor space was amazing. There was a small kitchenette, a nice-size changing room…

'What happened to the last business?' Libby asked.

'I'm not sure.' The agent was evasive. 'I think she retired.'

Hmm.

Back to the Land of Daniil she went and met with the second agent.

This studio was smaller but the floor space was enough and there was also a little waiting area that hopefully she could lock the parents into so they didn't interfere!

'What happened to the last business?' Libby asked.

'Yoga,' the agent said. 'They moved to new premises, a converted warehouse, as they needed more space.'

Oh, it made sense to go there, but the bank wasn't going to listen to her, Libby was sure.

'I've got another woman coming for a second look tomorrow,' the agent said. 'She's very keen.'

Libby shrugged but her heart leaped in her throat.

She wanted this place very badly.

She thanked the agent and he locked up and got into his car and she stood awhile longer, peering through the window, desperate for her dream to live here.

'Well?'

She jumped at the sound of that gorgeous, low, chocolaty voice.

'Daniil!' She turned and gave him a wide smile. 'Shouldn't you be at work?'

'I have been,' he said, and then handed her a large creamy envelope with the Zverev name embossed in gold on the corner. 'This is for you.'

'Oh, God, did you mark my performance last night?' she exclaimed. 'Did my knees crack…?'

She made herself laugh but he didn't join her. 'It was a joke…' she started, but then her voice trailed off as she opened the envelope and read what was written.

'Oh, my!'

She had a business plan.

A real one.

It went into demographics of the area, mean ages, average incomes and things she'd never have thought of. He'd even put things like expected revenue from the vending machine that it looked as if she'd be getting and the cost of hiring mirrors.

Everything had been taken into account.

'I'm not asking for this much!' Libby yelped when she saw the figure he had suggested the bank give her for a loan.

'You don't have to spend it, but it is something to factor in if you get sick or you get so busy that you have to hire another teacher.'

There were pages and pages of it.

All the little throwaway stuff she'd told him, about her career, her study, was all neatly referenced and then he'd added that in his opinion the proposed business model was an extremely viable one and it was signed with his lovely expensive signature.

And that if they required more information, they could contact him.

Oh, my!

This would have cost her thousands to have done privately. In fact, it wouldn't have happened, because there was no way Daniil Zverev would have done this for her if she'd stepped in from the street.

Which she had.

Sort of.

'You'll get the loan.'

He sounded so sure that Libby was starting to believe that she would. That he had spent the morning doing this for her almost blew her away, but instead she put her arms around his neck and held on tight to the lovely anchor of him.

'I have to kiss you!'

He lifted her up so she could do so. He was just so big and strong and sexy as hell and his jaw less rigid than this morning as she ran her lips over it. His mouth was receptive, taking her kiss, returning it fiercely, but only for a moment because, though holding her, he peeled his face back from her liberal display of affection.

'Thank you,' Libby said.

'You're welcome.'

She didn't want to come back to planet earth but he placed her back on it.

'I have to go now.'

And just like that he did, leaving her standing there, reeling.

Excited, elated and back to the agony of his leaving, which was worse the second time around.

He'd broken their unspoken rule.

Libby had been set to get on with her life, to determinedly not contact him and to expect nothing more from their one night.

He'd given her more than a business plan, Libby thought.

Daniil Zverev had given her hope for them—that she might see him again, that last night had meant more to him, too.

And that was scary.

CHAPTER FIVE

DANIIL STARED AT the phone.

His mind was finally made up.

Almost.

He was leaning towards going to his parents' anniversary party, which was being held next weekend.

The ongoing pressure from Lindsey Tennent had had nothing to do with his change of heart. Lindsey had today called Reception twice, using different names, in an effort to be put through to him. One call had made it as far as Cindy but she had quickly seen through him.

Daniil re-read the invitation: *To Daniel Thomas*.

Reverting to his own name had been the final straw that had caused his parents to disown him. They had taken it as a personal affront and had said that, in doing so, he not only shamed them but it was a smack in the face for all they had done for him. They had refused to listen to his reasoning and, for Daniil, it had actually come as a relief when they had said that they wanted nothing more to do with him.

It had suited him, in fact.

The occasional visits he used to make at Christmas and for birthdays were excruciating at best, for all concerned. He could feel the strain from the moment he walked in and there was a sigh of relief that had reverberated from everyone when the duty visit was over and done, till the next time.

No, it wasn't a moral debt or his conscience that had Daniil changing his mind. He had a question for his parents and he wanted an honest answer. He might not get one, but he would be able to know if they were lying if the question was asked face to face.

Did you mail the letters I wrote to Roman?

He was sure that they hadn't, but that realisation had come a long time after the letters had been penned. At first Daniil had believed his parents when they had said that the post was very slow. They had also suggested, when still no letter had come, that maybe his brother was still angry at him and they would point to Daniil's cheek. That had made no sense because Daniil was quite sure now that the fight had been Roman's attempt to force him to leave the orphanage.

Only when he had left home and gone to university had Daniil considered that his parents may have lied and simply not mailed them. Of course, by then Roman had long since left the orphanage—to where, no one had been able to tell him.

Daniil actually felt as if a part of him was missing. A vital part—his identity.

He had been back to Russia on several occasions but had always drawn a blank. He was going again, for another attempt at finding out what had happened to his twin, after the anniversary.

He knew how much he missed his twin, and surely it must be the same for Roman. Daniil knew he would spend the rest of his life searching for him.

Yes, he had decided that he would go to the anniversary party and make the speech, just for the chance to get to the truth, but as he went to make the call his intercom buzzed and he heard his receptionist's resigned voice.

'There's a Ms Tennent in Reception, asking to see you. It's been explained to her that she doesn't have an appointment. She insists that we ask for ten minutes of your time.'

Daniil let out a slight curse.

Of course Libby was here.

No doubt Lindsey was sending in the big guns again.

Well, Libby could hardly be called a big gun.

'She can have five minutes.'

'Oh.'

Cindy was clearly expecting him to offer his usual refusal, and possibly he should have, but he had been waiting for a week for her to make contact and ask that he reconsider about the anniversary celebration.

There was, Daniil believed, always a hidden agenda and so far he had never been proved wrong.

'Cindy, you can go to lunch once she is here. Tell Libby that she can come straight through.'

He leaned back in his chair and waited.

It was almost a relief that her true colours would now reveal themselves because he hadn't been able to get her out of his head.

The business plan had been a spur-of-the-moment thing, and by that evening he had regretted it.

He had arrived home from work and as promised his back had felt as if he'd been run over by a bus.

It had felt the same for the next two days but on the third...

Yes, he had remembered fondly.

Extremely fondly, in fact, because he had had his first weekend in in very long time.

'Whoops!' Libby said as she burst into his office in a blaze of colour. 'I nearly knocked.'

Daniil sat there.

She was wearing a bright red wraparound dress that looked rather like a very tight T-shirt, bright red lipstick and her smile was wide.

She also had her huge leather bag over her shoulder.

'Guess where I've been?' Libby said.

'I have no idea.'

She made a great show of going into her bag, opening her purse and taking out a pale pink business card, and then she came around the desk and handed it to him.

Libby Tennent School of Dance

Beneath that was a photo of two lower legs in the same blush pink and the dancer was *en pointe*.

'Do you like it?' she asked. 'It took me hours, no, *days*, to sign off on it.'

He had never seen anyone so delighted with a business card. Daniil could fill a room with all the cards that had been handed to him over the years.

'You can keep it if you like,' she said, as he went to hand it back. 'I've got hundreds.'

As soon as she'd gone he would do his usual and toss it in the bin and for now he gave a polite nod, but the examination of the business card hadn't finished yet because she was standing over him, peering at it.

'It's gorgeous, isn't it?' she sighed, and then Daniil looked a little closer and, yes, it actually was because…

'That's you.'

There was a certain disquiet in Daniil that he could recognise her from the knees down!

'It is! Well, it's me two years ago. Are you going to guess where I've been?'

'No,' he said, because he didn't partake in games.

'Then, I'll tell you—I've just picked up the keys to the studio.' She beamed. 'And the mirrors are coming this afternoon. I've had a poster printed for my information evening… I'm just so happy and excited that I wanted to come and say thank you for all your help.'

Daniil stared as again she went into her bag.

'Here.' She pulled out a present, beautifully wrapped and tied with a pale pink satin bow, and there was a card addressed to him.

'What's this?'

'Well, if you open it you'll find out.'

Daniil didn't like gifts.

Birthdays at the orphanage had meant an extra piece of fruit with lunch and knuckles on the head from his peers. He had never received a wrapped gift, chosen specifically for him, until he had come to live in England and had quickly found out that always, *always*, they came with guilt or conditions attached.

He remembered getting a tennis racket when he hadn't liked the game and finding out later that their late son, Daniel, had been a gifted tennis player.

There had been clothes, books, instruments, computers and electronics, too, that had supposedly been chosen for him, but Daniil had known the thought had been with their late son.

At eighteen he had stood awkwardly as he'd been handed a bunch of keys and taken out to the drive where a luxury navy car sat wrapped in a bow. He had caused tears when he had refused to perform for the video camera and take his gift for a drive.

It hadn't been a gift in the true sense.

Daniil had known that again it would come at a price.

How grateful he should be, he had often been told. Didn't he understand just how lucky he was?

Lately his gifts had been of the serious corporate kind but they, too, had come with their own quiet sway.

He looked up to Libby, who was waiting expectantly for him to open her gift.

'Come on…' she urged, as he undid the ribbon.

'Too much pink,' he commented.

'You can never have too much pink,' she said, as he peeled back the paper. 'It's not very exciting,' she warned as he opened the box. 'Well, it's exciting to me but I just…' Her voice trailed off as her gift was revealed.

It was a porcelain, hard *thing*. A bit like a grey-silver bear with pieces of glittery wool stuck to it, and it had a smiling face and eyes.

He removed it from the paper and saw that it had very long legs with the ends dressed in pink ribboned ballet shoes.

He tried to stand it on his desk but Libby laughed.

'It sits on your bookshelf,' she explained, and put it at the end of the desk so that its long legs dangled over the edge. She looked around his office. 'You, Daniil, are lacking in knick-knacks.

He didn't like pointless things.

Daniil had never been attached to a thing for the sake of it.

And, yes, this was possibly the most pointless thing that had ever graced his desk.

'I've ordered loads,' Libby explained. 'I might give them as little prizes.'

'I see.'

He didn't.

'Well, I have to go,' Libby said. 'I've got to get back for my mirrors arriving…'

'What else did you want?'

'Nothing.' Libby beamed. 'Just to say thank you. I know now that I couldn't have done it without you. I tried by myself at the bank and I truly believe he was about to laugh me down the street when I produced your business plan. Honestly, almost the moment I did he offered me a coffee *and* I got two chocolate biscuits.'

Daniil looked at her and smiled. She, like the *thing*, was now sitting on his desk, only she was chatting away happily.

'How's your back?' Libby asked.

'Well, for a couple of days I struggled even to put a shirt on and if your ears were burning that was me, cursing your name every time I moved…'

'But then?' she said.

'Amazing,' Daniil said. 'If your ballet school flops you can—'

'Don't even say it!' she said. 'I'm terrified.'

'There's no need to be,' he said. 'I wouldn't put my name to any business plan that I didn't consider had every chance of succeeding.'

'Really?' She frowned. 'You weren't just being nice?'

'I don't lie about business,' he said. 'I was just being nice to you…'

'I didn't think you played nice,' she said, as he pulled her from the desk and onto his lap so that she was facing him.

'Occasionally I do,' he said, arranging her legs so she was half kneeling on the chair with her arms resting on his shoulders.

'I'd love to kiss you—' she sighed '—but I have far too much lipstick on for that.'

'Poor excuse.'

'Valid excuse,' she said. 'I really came just to give you your present. If they weren't going to let me up then I'd have left it with the misers at Reception. You haven't opened your card.'

'I will,' Daniil said. Right now, though, his hands were on her hips. 'Before you arrived I was about to call your father.'

'My father?' Libby blinked. 'And tell him what a bad girl his daughter is?'

'No.' Daniil smiled. 'To say that I will go next weekend.'

He waited for her smile to widen, for a dart of triumph in her eyes now that she had got her way, but he was slightly taken aback when instead she frowned.

'But you said that you didn't want to go.'

'I know that I did, but I've given it some thought and...' He wasn't about to tell her about the letters—that was way too personal to him—so he shrugged and was vague instead. 'Maybe it is the right thing to do.'

'Not if...' She was clearly uncomfortable with his choice. 'Daniil, I knew, almost the second I said I'd do it, that it was wrong to try to persuade you...'

'You didn't persuade me,' he said. 'I decided to go by myself.'

'You're sure?' she checked.

He nodded.

She was like no one he had ever met. He could tell that she was uncomfortable with her part in it all.

Up till that moment he had thought she might be playing a game and that the reason for her visit would contain another attempt to change his mind.

He moved her up his lap, just slithered her unresisting body closer to his.

'Someone might come in,' she said.

'No one ever comes in without Cindy's say-so.'

'Even so.'

But remembering that he had sent Cindy to lunch, Daniil went into his drawer and pulled out a tiny remote and there was the *thunk* of the door locking.

She wanted him but hadn't expected this.

For a week there had been nothing. No phone call, no flowers, no anything and now here she was, sitting on his lap facing him.

Their one night Libby could never describe as a mistake but, despite her bravado, it had rattled her.

A lot.

She had found it hard, no, impossible, to believe that was it and, guiltily, even if the present had been left at Reception she had hoped it might serve as a prompt, to remind him about what she could not forget—their night.

'I can't kiss you,' Libby said, revelling at the feel of his solid legs between her thighs. 'I'm not walking out of here with my face all smeared.'

'Don't…' He was about to say, 'Don't come here wearing red lipstick next time, then,' but changed his mind. 'Don't kiss me, then, but I can still kiss you.'

She closed her eyes in bliss as his lips met her neck and her skin nearly wept in relief as finally Houston made contact again. His lips brushed her tender skin and then there was the warm wet slide of tongue. As he kissed her neck he undid the wrap of her dress and then lowered the little cami she wore so one breast was exposed, and he kissed her there. He swirled round her nipple with his tongue, making little nips with his teeth.

'Oh...' Libby squirmed in his lap at the pleasure and held on to his shoulders. His tongue was cool on her breast at first and then warm, the tiny nips and sucks were making her feel faint and she was incredibly, rapidly, turned on, especially as he slid down in the seat enough so that his hands moved her hips over his erection.

'This could go far too far...' she breathed, as his fingers burrowed into her panties.

'Good.'

It did go far too far because he took a letter opener and dealt with the lacy threads of her underwear so she was completely naked to the hand that stroked her.

'Daniil...' she whispered into his ear, 'I'm not on the Pill...'

'Get yourself on it, then.'

She blinked.

She wanted to dash out and find where Cindy kept the fire extinguisher just so she could put out the sudden hope in her heart that flared. The hope that said that there would be more, that he and she...

'What?' he said, as he felt her still.

'I went to the doctor this morning. It's okay, I wasn't hanging out for you to call me or anything...' She hesitated and then, what the hell, she chose honesty. 'Well, of course I was, but really I was a little worried by my lack of morals the other night. I don't regularly fall into bed...'

'You didn't fall,' he said. 'I wouldn't let you.'

In between words he was flicking her nipple with his tongue and it felt as he was doing the same to her clitoris as she remembered her legs resting on his shoulders as he'd made magic with his mouth.

'The other night was…' Libby attempted to explain that it had been an exception but it was hard to form a sentence as his fingers moved faster inside her and the suction of his mouth around her breast had her frantic in his arms.

'Precious and rare,' Daniil finished the sentence for her in the nicest of ways.

'It was,' she said. 'So I am getting myself on the Pill the very second I can…'

'Come,' Daniil said, his fingers working her, 'and then we will see what you can do with that red mouth.'

She unbelted him just to feel him, and then his hand discontinued the delicious probe of her and her sob of frustration turned into a moan of pleasure as she freed him. Hard, erect, there was a bead of moisture at the tip that had her longing to lower her head, but instead she rose up a little, not just to his hand, which was back where she felt it belonged and bringing her closer to the boil, but her legs raised to have him nearer her heat.

Again he removed that skilled hand and guided her so that she hovered, and he stroked her now with the head of his cock and her lips twitched from the absence of his kiss.

'Condom…' she breathed, because she was fighting not to lower herself.

'I don't have any here.'

'Please.' Libby let out a half laugh of disbelief.

'Why would I have them at work?'

He surprised her.

Always.

He pulled her down onto him just a little way. 'I want to feel you come around me.'

'You might, though.'

'I have a lot of self-control…'

It was a risky game, but they were way past reading the fine print of the rule books. Yes, somewhere it would state that this was foolish at best, but the thought of him inside her unsheathed had Libby licking her lips. She'd never done it without a condom and she told him so.

'Nor me.'

'Just for a moment, then.'

He lowered her down, not all the way, and she let out a moan of both bliss and want.

He raised her and then lowered her again, watching his naked length being swallowed up and feeling the blissful wet warmth of her.

Then he pulled her hard down and watched her grimace.

'Come on, baby,' he said, thrusting into her. 'I won't last long.'

'Talk about pressure…' she said, but the only real pressure was building in her. He just moved her at his will. She was limp and compliant and then suddenly her spine felt rigid and she was shaking and her orgasm was so deep, so intense she cried out.

For Daniil, feeling her pleasure, her concentrated tightness around him was rapturous. Yes, he had self-control but even Libby felt the final swell and jerk of him just before he lifted her off. She held his shoulders and they both watched as he shot over her and her desire flickered back to life as he stroked himself empty, her hand coming down over his and their fingers mingling.

She'd never seen anything more sexy, never felt more adored, and in that moment she truly was.

His tongue was cold as he ignored the rule that had got them to this point and kissed her slack mouth and then they rested their foreheads on each other's.

'I want to curl up and go to sleep...' Libby admitted, but what she didn't admit was that she wanted to do that right there on his lap. She wanted the door to stay locked and the rest of the world to disappear and leave them alone.

Libby had never had such intense feelings for anyone—no man had ever moved her in the way that he did—but already he was peeling her off.

Her jelly legs moved to a stand and she looked down at her panties where they lay shredded on the floor.

'Come on,' he said, and at first she thought she was being shown the door but instead he took her into the adjoining bathroom and it was the lipstick he dealt with first because they were both wearing it. He wetted a cloth and discarded the evidence from her face and then he stripped her and they showered, kissing, kissing, kissing, washing each other, caring for each other. Then he turned off the taps and it was time to dress.

Now it was time for Daniil to pretend it was simply sex.

God, but he'd prefer that it was.

He loathed having somebody in his headspace, he dreaded letting another person get close.

She could feel the awkwardness descend and there was no frothy coffee this time, her marching orders were given.

'I am expecting a client...'

'Please don't make excuses,' she said, pulling on her

dress and trying to get her arm in, which wasn't very easy with a body that was damp. 'I'm going.'

Now there was regret.

There was embarrassment on Libby's part that she'd practically handed herself to him and also the knowledge that their behaviour had been risky.

On Daniil's part, there was unease that he might care about her.

It hurt to care and he avoided that at all costs.

She went through her bag, where thankfully she had fresh underwear and she pulled it on as Daniil selected a fresh shirt and suit.

She tied up her hair and, even though she could feel his impatience, she took her time putting on her lipstick so she could at least look as if nothing had taken place.

She did that odd little wave at the door and got his grim smile in return.

She had that same feeling of having stepped out of a movie theatre as she came out of his office. Cindy's desk was empty. Presumably she was at lunch and there was no sign of the client he was waiting for.

The worst thing about seeing him was the parting.

She never knew if this was it.

CHAPTER SIX

DANIIL DIDN'T CALL HER.

He woke one morning, more than a week after she had stopped by his office, and lay in his bed, thinking. He didn't like how at any given hour his mind drifted to her, how he worried about whether or not she was okay, how he lay there wondering what she was feeling and also how he had to fight himself not to get in touch.

So after several moments doing his best not to think about Libby he went out and poured himself a long glass of water and checked his phone and scrolled through contacts.

Tonight he would go out, he decided.

Libby Tennent had occupied way too much of his headspace of late.

He pulled on some shorts and went into the room he hadn't allowed her to go into.

No one came in here, not even his domestic. This was strictly his space and he took care of it himself.

It was more than a gym, it was his sanctuary. There were training mats, punch bags and weights. This morning he did consider going to the club that he went to on occasion—they knew nothing about him, there he was Dan the moody Russian.

There, he taught kids drills and could spar with others, but he didn't feel like seeing anyone today.

He warmed up and then took a rope and skipped till he would usually be panting for breath, then he worked on some rhythm drills but he could not focus.

His mind was elsewhere.

He looked at the ledge and there was the *thing* she had brought him and next to it… Daniil took a drink and then walked over and picked up a very old photo.

Twenty years old, because he had been ten when it had been taken.

There he was, a slight smile on his mouth, excited that Sergio had brought in the camera, and that he was having his first photo taken.

Roman was next to him, unsmiling, and Daniil could remember every word of the conversation.

'Come on, Roman,' Sergio had said. 'Smile, you're going to be famous. This photo will be worth a lot one day—The Zverev twins.'

'When do we get to fight?' Roman had asked. That had been all he'd wanted to know.

'Soon,' Sergio had said.

For it had been a case of drills, more drills.

Daniil put down the photo and then picked up the card Libby had given him. He hadn't read it while she'd been there, instead it had remained unopened after she had gone, but curiosity finally won and he opened the envelope.

Thank you for making my dreams a reality.
Libby

He read it several times, searching for the inference, the little trip of guilt, a demand for more.

Was she talking about the dance school or their night together?

He closed the card and went to put it back on the shelf and then he saw a little postscript she had written on the back of the card.

Both...

She had answered his question.

He could almost see her chewing her pen before adding it.

Yes, he wanted to call her.

Instead, he put on gloves and went to the punch bag and reminded himself why he would not.

He thought of the upcoming anniversary party.

His cousin would be there, of course, smarming up to them.

Daniil didn't give a toss about the inheritance, more it was the thought of that greedy, cruel man getting a free ride that galled him.

'Face it, Daniel,' George had often said. 'You just don't fit in.'

Daniil could hear his cousin's voice as he took his anger out on the punch bag.

From the day you got here Aunt Katherine realised her mistake.

Oh, the punch bag earned its keep this morning as he recalled George's words.

Have you noticed how she blanches when she introduces you as her son?

But the worst one, the one that still hurt even now, especially now, was the one that held him back from pursuing a relationship—*This used to be such a happy home until you came on the scene.*

Daniil well remembered the toxic atmosphere of home—his mother's frequent tears and his father berating him for not living up to their son's ghost. He believed to this day what George had said—that the house, until he had arrived, had been a happy one, that it had been he who had caused all the pain.

He took out his anger on the punch bag till he was physically exhausted but with his mind still racing. He could not stand the thought of dimming the light in the star that Libby was.

He drove to work and took a slight detour. Slowing down, he saw a large pink poster and discovered that between four and seven she was holding an information evening.

Tonight.

Fortunately he had a very important dinner meeting tonight because still, despite a workout, despite the knot of dread at going to his parents' at the weekend, there was the temptation to make contact.

Getting too close to anyone was something he avoided at all costs and yet Libby had simply stepped over the walls he had put up. Direct as she was, he never felt invaded and, he thought, she made him smile.

He made her smile, too, Daniil realised as he drove on. She had walked into his office, and the closer she had got to his desk the wider her smile had become.

She seemed happy when she was with him.

For the first time Daniil was considering that he might make somebody happy.

Libby should be at her happiest, she well knew.

The turnout for the information evening had surpassed her expectations—parents had brought their children, lots of women had come to find out about classes during the day and some had suggested she hold a class once or twice a week later into the evening, so that they could come once the children were in bed. A young girl called Sonia, Libby was particularly impressed with. She was fifteen years old and very talented, and was looking for an opportunity for part-time work.

Libby had thought it would be a very long time before she could even consider hiring someone but, given the impressive turnout, she had told Sonia to come along next week so that she could speak to her one on one. For now she took out the garbage and came back in and smiled when she saw that she had only three little pink cupcakes left. She had bought loads but at first, not wanting to look presumptuous, she had only put out a small plate. The rest of them she had hidden in the little kitchenette.

Presumptuous.

Yes, that word was the reason why, even during her busiest most exhilarating week, she couldn't quite hit happy.

Oh, she'd tried not to get her hopes up, or to assume that he'd call, but such was their chemistry she just couldn't believe how easily he could let her go.

She'd given him a business card, for God's sake, so it wasn't as if he didn't have her number.

Worse, Libby knew that she had made things far too easy for him.

She should have left the present at Reception. Yes, she had practically handed herself to him with a pink satin bow on top.

Maybe he thought she was easy?

Well, so was he!

She angrily pulled down the blinds, terribly cross with herself.

The writing had been on the wall from the start and she had chosen to ignore it.

What had she expected? For man like Daniil to send flowers with a little love note?

Hell, yes!

As she turned Libby saw a broad shadow at the door and realised it was him. He'd startled her so much that instead of opening up Libby pulled down the blind on the door.

'We're closed,' she said. 'The information night finished at seven.'

'Libby...' He opened the letterbox and spoke through it. 'It's me.'

She said nothing.

'I think we both know that I'm not here for a ballet lesson,' he said.

She shouldn't open the door—it was as simple as that, she knew. She should tell him to go away. While she was thrilled that he had turned up, a week between meetings was far too long.

'Libby?' Daniil pushed open the letterbox and his voice was as if he was there in the studio. 'Are you going to let me in?' His answer was hearing the lock release on the door.

Libby thought, *Why does he have to be so beautiful?* With just one look at him she felt like melting but she remained firm with herself.

'I assume you're not here for a cupcake? I have three left,' she said, rabbiting on as he stepped in. 'Honestly, I thought I'd have to freeze them and that Rachel and I would be living off them for weeks.'

'Rachel?' Daniil checked.

'She's my flatmate,' Libby said.

'Another dancer?' Daniil checked, and she nodded.

'So if you're not here for a cupcake then what are you here for?' Libby said. And then answered her own question. 'Oh, I know—sex!'

'What the hell is that supposed to mean?'

'Well, given that this is almost within walking distance from the office, I guess it might make things easier for you. If you suddenly get bored in your lunch break...'

'Stop right there,' he said, and looked at her. She was wearing a dark purple dance outfit, with leggings over the top, and though similar to the woman he had met just a couple of weeks ago she looked tired now. He could see that there were dark circles under her eyes and that she was paler than she had been before.

He knew that she had been busy and had every right to look tired but he acknowledged the certain fact that some of the sleeplessness might be down to him.

He wasn't being arrogant. Daniil had spent many hours awake himself, willing himself not to get in touch, not to tarnish her world, and now he was here, about to ask a favour—for her to come to his parents' with him.

He couldn't do it, though.

'I was just wondering how your information evening went,' he said instead.

'Well, if you want to discuss my business, you can make an appointment,' Libby said, stuffing all her belongings into her bag, determined to just lock up and go home.

'Libby...'

He came over and she was on her knees, looking up at him. 'I don't for one minute believe that that's the reason you're here.' She looked up at his groin. 'Are you disappointed that you didn't get everything you wanted the other day?'

He had the gall to laugh. 'I'm actually on my way to a dinner meeting. I'm already running late.'

'Oh, I'm sure they'll wait for *you* to suddenly appear!'

He heard the barb, and one of the things he adored about her was that, just in case he'd missed it, she made very sure he got her point.

'I mean, we're all supposed to be happy to idly wait for you to drop by. Am I not even worth a single bunch of flowers?' she asked, as she angrily stood up.

'Libby,' Daniil said. 'I have never sent flowers in my life.'

'If I hadn't come to your office I'm quite sure that I'd never have seen you again.'

'Exactly. *You* came by *my* office! You took it further.'

Libby furiously shook her head. 'Daniil, you broke the rules. You were the one who turned up out of the blue the next day with a business plan for me. If you'd just left it at one night then I'd have known where I stood. Now I don't have a clue. You don't call me, you don't text...'

'What is it with women and texting?' he asked.

'It's nice to know that you're being thought of.'

'I never took you for needy.'

'I never took myself for a slut,' Libby said. 'But when you frogmarched me out of the office after we'd had sex, that was what I became.'

'Please.' He scoffed at her exaggeration, but he did relent just a touch. 'I was uncomfortable,' he admitted. 'I never bring my personal life to work.'

Libby was dubious. From what she'd read, he was at

it all the time but then she did remember that there had been no condoms to hand.

'What about Cindy?' Libby asked.

'Her husband is twice my size and three times as miserable.'

'What about your clients?' She simply had to know more about him, about his world, about what she was dealing with.

'Most are portly middle-aged businessmen.' Daniil shrugged. 'If I want sex I go out. I don't bring my personal life to work.'

She got that what had happened had been a rarity but, still, the endless stretches of silence from him galled and she told him that.

'I said from the start—'

'You did,' she responded, 'and maybe when you offered your little warning about not expecting you to love me I should have offered you a warning of my own—if you're involved with me, then you're involved. I'm not dangling on for weeks, wondering if you're going to call.'

'Fine,' Daniil said. 'I won't be calling. So now you know.'

'Or drop in on me unannounced.'

'Very well,' Daniil said. 'I shan't do so again.'

She wanted to stamp her feet in frustration as he complied with wishes she didn't really want and so she pushed him instead, pressing one hand up against his broad chest. She might as well have been a fly for all the impact she had. 'You make me so cross.'

'I know I do.' He shrugged. 'Tell you what, why don't you come with me tonight?'

'To dinner?'

'No.' He shook his head. 'It's going to be a very long,

boring meal and there are no partners allowed given that all we'll be doing is talking business. I do, though, have a suite booked.'

'Oh, I bet that you do,' she sneered.

'I won't lay a finger on you,' Daniil said. 'You could have a sleep or order room service, maybe have a massage or even just spend the night in the bath.' He smiled as her rapid blink indicated that the last suggestion was the one that tempted her most. 'They have a bath menu...' Daniil said.

'Really?'

'Really.'

'Is that what you came here for?' Libby asked. 'To ask me to come with you tonight?'

'No.'

'Then, why are you asking me now?'

'You bring out the niceness in me,' he said. 'You look tired. It might be pleasant to be spoiled. My driver can take you home or back here tomorrow.'

Libby stared back at him and thought of the frozen meal waiting for her in the freezer at home after a long ride on the underground. And then she thought of another long ride on the underground to get back here tomorrow.

Then she thought of a bath in a luxury hotel suite, room service and the bliss of having his driver in the morning.

And then she thought of one more night in his arms.

She didn't for a second believe that he wouldn't touch her.

He watched her eyes as all those thoughts raced through her head and he guessed exactly the moment she decided to accept, because she gave him an angry look.

How she wished she could be a little more haughty

and aloof and say no to him, but instead her shoulders sagged in defeat. 'Yes,' she said, and gave his chest another push. 'I'm still cross, though.'

'I know you are.' He didn't try to change her mind. 'You lock up and I'll wait in the car.'

Yes, she was cross, Libby thought, but there she went dreaming and hoping again because after all he had come around.

The drive was a short one and they were soon at the hotel. Of course, Daniil didn't have to worry about checking in the way mere mortals did. He was greeted with a handshake and taken straight up to his suite.

As she stepped in it wasn't the huge bed or the luxurious surroundings that made a shiver run down her spine—yes, things in Daniil's world certainly moved quickly because he picked up, from a walnut table, a huge bouquet of the palest pink peonies, roses and calla lilies and handed them to her.

There was even a card!

It took a week to find the perfect blooms—Daniil

'I don't believe it took a week,' she said, but gave a little *humph* noise, because the blooms were so perfect and her favourite colour. Possibly she could pretend it had taken him a week to find them and that he hadn't ordered them from the car while she'd locked up.

'I can be thoughtful when pushed,' he said, and she buried her face in the flowers when she wanted her hand back on his chest, but for different reasons this time.

She put the flowers in the huge vase that had been put on the table but she moved them through to the stunning bedroom and placed them by the side of the bed.

'You shouldn't sleep with flowers in the bedroom,' Daniil said.

'Sleep out there, then,' she said, because she wasn't letting the flowers out of her sight. She sat on the bed and it was like sinking into a marshmallow, and she watched Daniil as he quickly went through some notes on his computer.

'I was supposed to be doing this on the way here,' he admitted, and then glanced over to where she sat happily watching him, content to let him do whatever he had to. 'Will you be bored?' he checked.

'I hope so,' Libby sighed. 'That's my ambition.'

'Right,' he said. 'I'm going to go down. Wish me luck?'

'For a business dinner?'

'More than that,' he said. 'I want to buy this place.'

'Don't I get a kiss?' she asked, as he went to leave.

'I promised not to lay a finger on you.'

'Just your lips, then.'

'Nope,' he said, and then he was gone.

Libby lay back on the bed, breathing in the scent of the flowers, with the feeling that the world seemed in better order now.

She looked out of the window. There was her friend Big Ben and she remembered giving Daniil a massage, wishing she could freeze the hands of time.

And here she was again.

She had a bath and she deviated from the menu with a request of petals of her own—pale pink peonies and roses and calla lilies.

Damn the man. Till now anemones had been her favourite flower, which had been good because they were cheap.

Now, as she lay in her lovely bath with room service on

the way, she pictured a life with half her wages spent on luxurious flowers just so she could remember this bliss.

Daniil had spent a lot of time trying to convince himself that it was because the sex was good between them that he kept going back to her.

But as dinner dragged on his theory worked less and less.

He could not stop thinking about her, wondering what she was doing in the suite, thinking back to their conversation and her demand for a text. He was actually considering sending one; he had her business card in his wallet and he could easily pause the conversation and do just that.

No.

He was seriously considering buying this place—he should have his mind more on the conversation.

It usually was.

Daniil never mixed business with pleasure—his mind was only ever on one thing at a time.

Tonight, though, his thoughts kept drifting several floors up. He was glad that he had brought Libby and it felt good to know that after this very long dinner meeting he could simply head upstairs to her.

No, he did not want a brandy. In fact, he drank his coffee down in one and wished the current owners goodnight.

Just after midnight he arrived at the penthouse suite.

The maid was wheeling away the trolley and he halted her. He lifted the lid on the plates and there were the dark remains of a chocolate soufflé and also another dish that looked as if it had once held ice cream.

Good for her, Daniil thought. He was glad she was making the most of the night.

He stepped quietly into the suite and the air smelled fragrant, even more so in the bedroom. For a small moment he thought she must have gone home because in the darkness the bed, though unmade, looked empty, but there, he soon realised, she was—curled up in a ball and sound asleep.

No, Daniil knew for certain then that it wasn't sex that kept leading him back to her. She needed to sleep; he had seen how tired she'd looked tonight and for the first time in his life he undressed with the sole intention of not waking someone up.

He got into bed and the sigh she gave as she turned and curled into him was one of pure pleasure. He took her into his arms.

'I had the very best night…' Libby mumbled.

She had. It had been a completely indulgent night and it was better for knowing that he would soon join her. She was floaty and relaxed for the first time in… As his arms wrapped around her Libby lay there in a sugary haze, trying to remember how long it had been since she had felt this content and peaceful.

Since he had arrived in her life and turned it upside down?

No, because before then she had been grappling with the end of her dancing career and coming to terms with the fact that her performing days were over.

Before then, perhaps? No, because she had been grappling with her career just to stay in it.

And before then?

She had never known peace as if it was the answer.

'Go to sleep,' Daniil said, and kissed the top of her head, and she did just that.

It was a deep and dreamless sleep for both of them until just before dawn when Libby awoke in slight panic as his arms pulled her closer into him.

It didn't reassure her.

He'd be gone soon.

Libby had considered herself fully warned.

She hadn't thought that she might fall in love.

It was then she was honest with herself and admitted that she had done just that.

She was in love with Daniil Zverev, heartbreaker to the stars.

'You're okay,' he said, as if he understood a sudden panic.

He did.

Daniil had woken on many occasions thinking of Roman and wondering where the hell he was in this world and how he himself could even stand to be on the planet without him.

In more recent days he had lain filled with dread at the thought of a night back at his parents'.

He could barely stand the thought of going there—he knew that it would be hell. He felt her start to relax in his arms and her breathing evened out. She rested her head on his chest. He thought how much more pleasant the evening had been, simply knowing that she was near and that when the meeting was over she would be there.

Yes, it was far more than sex.

Daniil had never asked for help with anything in his life. In fact, he considered it selfish that he was even considering putting her through the misery of Saturday night just to make things easier on him.

But, selfishly, he was.

He needed her there.

'This weekend,' Daniil said into the darkness, 'does your father have to be there?'

Libby frowned as she pondered the question. 'I guess.'

'Could he stay away?'

'Why?'

'I want you to come with me.' He felt the flutter of her eyelashes on his chest as her eyes opened and he was grateful that she did not lift her head to look at him.

He couldn't quite admit just how much he wanted her there or how important it was to him, so he tried to keep things light.

'I want to take you because you know about my name change and things...'

'Of course,' she said, and then nodded. 'I'll speak to my father.'

Hope, foolish hope wasn't just unfurling in her chest, it ran like magical ivy through her body, and she tried to contain it, to tell herself he wasn't exactly taking her home to meet the parents, but she was sure there was more to it than that she knew of his name change.

'You'll go?' Daniil checked.

'I shall.'

It was then that she lifted her head and he lowered his and their mouths met and the kiss that they shared was different from any either had known—slow at first and then gently building...

Yes, it wasn't just about sex because, on this morning, they made love.

CHAPTER SEVEN

'I THOUGHT THAT you weren't going to get your hopes up,' Rachel commented as Libby packed her brand-new overnight bag. Her blond hair was in ringlets, her smile painted wide and every sentence seemed peppered by the word *Daniil*.

'Well, I'm trying my best not to,' Libby admitted, and then said to Rachel what she kept trying to tell herself. 'I don't think that this is a meet-the-parents night. I know that I'm just there because I...' She gave a little shake of the head rather than carry on speaking. Usually she told Rachel everything. They were very close friends, but she didn't feel quite right sharing Daniil's life. He was so intensely private that there wasn't much she knew, but the little he had told her felt like a gift.

'So it's an overnight thing?' Rachel asked, but Libby shrugged.

'I don't really know,' she admitted.

'Can't you call him and find out?'

'I don't have his phone number,' Libby sighed. 'Which is probably wise of him. I'd have found ten million reasons to text or call.'

Still, she lived in a state of suspension.

She knew she had gone a little bit overboard for tonight. She'd had her hair done and had bought everything new—right down to her toothbrush, which she was packing in her new toiletry bag.

'You know his reputation,' Rachel said.

'I do,' she called over her shoulder as she popped into the bathroom to grab her pills. 'I'm choosing to ignore it and just live in the now.'

And right now she was happy.

Terribly so.

Hopefully, Libby thought as she swiped her pills from the shelf, her period would wait until after the weekend was over and then she could start on them. It had been his comment about going on the Pill that had first given her hope and now that she was going to meet his family.

The one-night stand had spread over days and was starting to run into weeks. 'It's lasted far longer than I expected it to,' Libby said, as she wriggled into neutral sheer stockings and put on her brand-new dress.

'But you still don't have his number?'

'No.'

She headed to the lounge where the flowers he had bought her held prime position. They weren't exactly in pristine condition—the roses were open and splendid and, yes, the lilies were dropping pollen, but they were still a sight to behold.

'You should play it a bit more aloof,' Rachel warned, as Libby sat on the window ledge like a cat, watching the street and waiting for his car to appear.

'I know that I should but then I'd be lying to us both,' Libby said. 'Anyway, I've tried to play it all cool with him but I simply can't—the very second that I see him my self-control is shot. I've decided that I'm just going to be myself,' she said. 'It's all I can be.'

'Well, don't say I didn't warn you…' Rachel said, as a low silver sports car pulled up and a male model got out.

Actually, it was Daniil!

No, there was absolutely no such thing as playing it aloof where he was concerned. Libby answered the door before he had even knocked and as it opened Daniil, who was not looking forward to tonight, smiled at her effusive greeting.

'You look amazing,' Libby said, running her hands over his jacket simply to feel him. He was always immaculately dressed but tonight his black suit sat so beautifully on his shoulders and his crisp white shirt and gunmetal tie enhanced his beauty. Above his right eye was a small bruise and she ran a finger over it.

'Fighting again,' she commented, as she remembered the bruises on his chest the night they had met.

'Maybe I walked into a door.'

'Poor door,' she said, and his smile made her melt because she could feel that he was pleased to see her, also.

Of course, his greeting wasn't quite as over the top. 'You look very nice, too,' he said.

She would hope so!

'It's all new!' She gave him a twirl to show off her lovely moss-green dress. He then watched as she picked up some black court shoes and peeled the labels off before putting them on her feet.

'New shoes, too!'

'I told you it's *all* new.' She grinned and wrapped her arms around his neck. 'Now I can reach you.' His hands moved around her waist, stealing kisses between her words. 'New toothbrush, new overnight bag…'

'The loan went in, then?'

'It did!' Libby grinned again. 'However, this was a necessary expenditure...'

'Very necessary,' he agreed, because had her flatmate not been standing scowling at them he'd have been asking which way her bedroom was.

She was just so scented and dressed up and excited to see him and Daniil had never stepped into a home and felt so welcome.

Not once.

His home was always his chosen venue and hotel rooms, however luxurious they were, were bland at best.

Home had never been where the heart was for him and yet he could tell that happiness resided here and he was being welcomed in.

'Come through,' Libby said. 'This is Rachel.'

'Hi, Daniil,' Rachel said, and then looked straight at her friend. 'I hate you.'

'I know you do.' Libby smiled and led him through a door. 'This is the living room.'

He had a look around. They certainly did a lot of living in here—there were books and magazines and more *things* on every shelf space than he had ever seen.

The tour wasn't over yet.

'Kitchen.' Libby gestured as they passed it, though didn't stop to let him peek in. 'And there's the loo just in case you get lost in the dark at night.'

Oh, stop it, she told herself, but she could not contain her joy at having him there.

'And this,' Libby said, as they approached a door, 'is my bedroom.' As she went to open it he halted her hand.

'I'm guessing there's a theme,' he said. 'Pink?'

'Nope,' Libby said, and it was he who opened the door and stepped in.

There was no room for it to be pink.

He stepped into the chaos.

Usually he didn't like clutter, he didn't like anything out on display, and yet here in this room her whole life was on show.

There was a huge mirror where no doubt she exercised and there were endless pictures of her that had been taken through her dancing years. There were certificates on every wall—so much stuff he wondered how she ever found anything.

'I'm such a narcissist,' Libby said, as he looked closely at a huge framed photo of her.

'You're too nice to be one,' he said. 'Too thoughtful.'

'Well, I did tidy up for you,' Libby said.

'Really?'

'And I changed the sheets.'

'Are they new, too?'

Libby nodded. 'There was a selfish motive there, too, though...'

'Come on.' He smiled and released her. 'We had better go.'

He made no attempt to kiss her, Libby thought. Instead, he picked up her overnight bag and they headed out to his car.

'No driver?'

'Not at weekends.'

Into the passenger side she went and sank into the leather seat. The traffic was quieter than Daniil had allowed for and they were soon pulling into the parking basement of his office.

'Why are we here?' Libby asked.

She really didn't know anything about tonight.

'Because,' Daniil explained, 'on the rooftop there is a helipad.'

'Oh!' She had never been in a helicopter before. 'Are we flying back tonight?'

'I think we are expected to stay but I am going to keep the pilot on standby all night. I really don't know how it is going to go.'

They took the elevator to the foyer, Libby's shoes clipping away, making a noise on the marble floor, and, no, it didn't annoy him.

'We just have to stop in my office for a moment. I need to pick up the gift.'

'What did you get them?' she asked. He didn't answer at first and when they were in his office Libby blushed as she remembered what they had got up to at the desk.

'I'm not sure what Cindy got for them,' Daniil answered, and pointed to a large beautifully wrapped gift and picked up a note beside it. 'A ruby vase apparently.'

'A ruby vase?' Libby groaned. 'Have you no imagination?'

'I don't. Well, at least not where my parents are concerned, and Cindy certainly doesn't have one.'

'You sent her out to get your parents their gift?'

'Of course I did.'

Libby, who could happily spend a day thinking about the perfect gift for somebody, was appalled and suddenly terribly concerned about what had happened to the present she had bought him. 'Where's the present that I got for you?' she asked.

'I think it's in my drawer,' he said, and then watched as she opened it up and rummaged through for a full minute.

'No, it isn't.'

Daniil stood there as she opened his drawer, surprised

by his own non-reaction. Had anybody else done the same he might possibly have had their hands off.

'I don't know where it is, then,' he said. 'The cleaner must have moved it.'

Libby pouted. She didn't believe him for a moment. 'Should we go up?' she asked.

'We'll just wait here,' he said. 'I'll get a text when he's ready for us.'

Daniil walked over to the window and looked out at the bright late-afternoon sunshine and Libby could see the tension in his shoulders. 'Are you nervous about tonight?'

'I'm not nervous…' he said in a rather scoffing voice, but then he checked himself. It wasn't her fault how he felt right now. He had woken early this morning and taken himself to his club in the East End, where he had trained hard and then sparred, yet it had done little to relieve his mounting tension. That was the reason for the bruise over his eye and he was glad that Libby hadn't demanded answers. No, *nervous* wasn't the word and he tried to find the right one. He did not turn and look as he told her exactly how he felt. 'Dread.'

Libby, who was perched on his desk, felt the happy bubble she was floating on deflate on his behalf. 'I'm such a selfish cow,' she said, jumping off the desk and going over to him. 'I was so excited to see you that I never stopped to think just how hard this—'

'It's fine,' he interrupted. There was no need for an apology and he told her another truth. 'Despite how things are, I was looking forward to seeing you, too.'

For Libby, his open admission was unexpected.

It felt like opening the kitchen cupboard and finding a bar of chocolate when you were quite sure that you didn't have any.

And then Daniil elaborated on why he was dreading tonight and that, too, was unexpected. 'I'd better give you some background.'

'You don't have to,' she said, because she could sense his reluctance. 'I'm very good at winging it.'

'I'm going to be making a speech tonight so you will hear some of it anyway and I want you to know, before we arrive, why the evening might not be an easy one,' he said. 'As you know, I'm adopted.'

Libby nodded.

'I lived in an orphanage until I was twelve years old. Apparently my parents had tried for a very long time to have a baby and eventually they did—they had a son and his name was Daniel. He was their only child but he died when he was twelve and they missed him so much...'

Libby bit her tongue.

'They had hoped I would be like him. The trouble was, not only did I not speak the language—' he gave an extremely uncomfortable shrug '—I was very institutionalised when I arrived in England. I liked routines. Even though I was used to sharing a room, we all had our privacy. No one really touched anybody else's things. If someone was quiet, that was respected. It was very different when I came here. My parents felt they could come uninvited into my space, that they, or their maids, could touch my things. I wanted my meals at a certain time, that was all I knew. I didn't want their lavish food and to be grateful for the nice things they gave me. I didn't want to play tennis...'

He had wanted to box; that had been all he had wanted to do. If they had taken in Roman, he would have picked up a racket and shone at tennis, he would have been the perfect *Daniel*—but that part was too hard to share. And so, leaving his twin aside, as he had been forced to do for close to two-thirds of his life, Daniil told her a little more.

'I think that within a couple of days of me arriving they understood the mistake they had made. They wanted to love me but they couldn't and I don't blame them for that…'

Libby had kept hold of her mounting horror till now, but, as she had freely admitted, she had no self-control where Daniil was concerned. That someone could do that to him had her blood boil, and her voice was harsh when she spoke. 'They were never going to love you, no matter what you did. Instead of working through their grief and facing it, they did this to you.'

'I made their lives hell,' Daniil said. 'They simply couldn't understand how I wasn't grateful for all the opportunities they gave me. Earlier this year we had a major falling out when I told them I wanted to change back to my birth name.'

'Of course you did,' Libby said. 'After all they did—'

But he interrupted her, and when he did so Daniil nearly blindsided her with something she had never considered.

'I think they think that I changed my name to spite them—it wasn't about that, though. I changed my name in the hope that my past could find me.'

'And has it?'

'No.'

'I feel even worse now that I tried to persuade you to go.'

'Libby, you could never have persuaded me to do this. Believe me, I have my own reasons for going tonight.' He had revealed more than he ever had and certainly more than he had expected to, but her acceptance was sooth-

ing and that she was angry with his parents on his behalf helped. So a couple of hours before he would enter
the house that should have been home, he told her a little
of his real one.

'There were four of us,' he explained. 'We were the bad
kids. By the time you get to be six or so you know that you
are unlikely to be adopted. We never wanted to be anyway.
We were going to make our own way in the world. Sev—
Sevastyan—would read all the time, and he was clever
with numbers. Then there was Nikolai and he wanted to
work on the ships. I'd love to know if he ever did.'

'Who was the fourth one?' Libby asked innocently.

'Roman.'

It hurt even to say his name out loud.

'And what was he going to do?' Libby asked, but
Daniil just gave the same shake of his head that he
did when things were off limits, and finally his phone
bleeped a text and they could head to the roof.

But Libby halted him.

'You can still change your mind about going tonight.'

Not going was no longer an option. 'I have a question
for them,' he said. 'I hope that if I do the right thing by
them tonight they will give me an honest answer.'

'Isn't there a risk that they won't?'

'There are always risks,' he said. 'I only take them
if I am prepared to weather the consequences, and tonight I am.'

He was.

He wanted to know what had happened to the letters
he had sent, and if attending tonight gave him a chance
to find out, it was a price he was willing to pay.

Even if killed him to do so.

CHAPTER EIGHT

LIBBY KNEW THAT the view from the helicopter would be amazing but as it lifted into the sky she found that she was holding her breath. It was nerve-racking, dizzying and very unsettling. The buildings were getting smaller but, for a moment, she felt as if the ground was slamming upwards towards them. As the helicopter lurched a touch, so, too, did her stomach, and Libby discovered that possibly she wasn't suited to helicopters at all.

She swallowed the gathering saliva and then dragged in air and closed her eyes, appalled that she might be sick, but then Daniil placed his hand over hers and when next she opened her eyes the ground was back where it should be. The houses and flats were tiny and the landscape was becoming a deep gorgeous green as the helicopter headed towards Oxford. Libby looked over at Daniil and he mouthed that she would fine and she gave him a nod of thanks.

Would *he* be fine, though?

She was somehow trying to get her head around all that Daniil had told her. She tried to imagine arriving here, not knowing anything about the country and being unable to speak the language. She tried to understand how he must have felt, being sent in as some sort of replacement for a deceased child. For all her family's faults, for all the problems they might have, their love for each other had never been brought into question.

Through the headphones Libby heard the pilot announce their imminent arrival and saw Daniil staring out of the window, looking down to the vast expanse of land that held his home. His face was unreadable and her hand had been long forgotten. She glanced down and saw that he had clenched fists.

He was so closed off now that she might, Libby thought, just as well not be here.

Daniil couldn't really process that she was with him—till now he had always taken this journey alone. Yes, his new parents had sat beside him in the car the first time that his new home had come into view but they had been strangers then.

They still were.

For family occasions, his cousin's weddings included, he had never considered bringing a date. Through his teenage years and university not once had he thought of bringing somebody to the family home.

The sinking feeling he felt had nothing to do with the helicopter that was now hovering just before landing. He looked at the familiar red-brick mansion and the immaculate grounds that could all be his.

No, thank you.

He'd never once wanted to be here.

Daniil was almost tempted to ask the helicopter pilot to return them to London—in fact, he was seriously considering it—but just then he felt Libby's hand close over the top of his fingers and as he had sensed her nervousness earlier and reassured her, now she did the same to him. Daniil turned to smiling blue eyes that told him she was there, and that in a few short hours it would all be over and duty would be done.

It was he who nodded his thanks now.

They disembarked and the grass was so thick and lush that Libby wished she'd had the foresight to wear flats. Instead, she sank into the green carpet with each and every step till she gave in and took her heels off.

'Next time—' she started, but Daniil offered a swift retort.

'There won't be a next time.'

She tried to tell herself he was referring to the fact that they wouldn't come back to his parents' home but his comment still jarred. Daniil could be so brusque with his words that she never quite knew how they applied to her, or even if they did.

He didn't hold her hand as they walked up the stone steps, which she took as an affront, but Daniil was so tense he knew that if he did he might well crush her fingers. Everything about the place made him feel ill, from the growling stone lions to the fountain.

There was one familiar face that drew a pale smile from him—Marcus, the old butler who had been with the family since before his parents had married, opened the door. 'It's good to see you here, sir.'

'It's...' Yes, Daniil's response was initially sparse, he could hardly say that it was good to be here, but, determined to keep to his side of the deal, he pushed on. 'It's good to see you again, Marcus.'

'I'll have your luggage taken to your room,' Marcus said, and Daniil felt his stomach clench.

'I'd prefer—'

'Naturally, I'll leave it for you and your guest to unpack.'

Daniil gave a small nod of thanks, grateful that there was one person in this place who had, over the years, listened to his repeated requests that his belongings be left alone.

The entrance hall was as uninviting as it had been his first time here. At twelve he had been used to being surrounded by people and sparse furnishings. He would never forget first seeing this vast, imposing space, the walls lined with tapestries and portraits and the daunting Jacobean oak staircase. Most confusing of all had been that there were so few people.

'Daniel!'

Libby turned when she heard the *wrong* name and saw a small, busy-looking woman, with wiry hair and cold blue eyes, approach. She was wearing a deep red dress, which did nothing for her flushed complexion.

'Finally!'

Libby watched as she forced a smile, even though her lips seemed to disappear as she did so, and then a tall bearded man with a glass in his hand came and joined them.

'This is Libby,' Daniil said. 'Libby, this is my mother, Katherine, and my father, Richard.'

'It's lovely to meet you.' Libby beamed as they were introduced and no one, not even Daniil, could have guessed just how well she was acting right now, because from everything he had told her about them, there was no reason to smile.

Katherine ran her eyes over Libby, from head to toe and back again, and to Libby it felt as if she was being checked for lice. 'Libby?' Katherine frowned. 'Short for...?'

'Elizabeth.' She beamed again and when they just stood and openly stared she attempted conversation.

'We had a wonderful helicopter ride here. Your home is beautiful from the sky.'

Daniil watched as his mother fought not to step back from the warmth of Libby as she carried on with her observations. She dazzled and smiled when he was unable to and she filled the strained silence that usually ensued whenever he and his parents were together.

'Mind you, I should have worn flat shoes,' Libby continued. 'I'll be able to find my way in the dark—just follow the holes in the lawn—'

'Yes, well, guests are already arriving,' Katherine interrupted. 'Daniel, why don't you take Elizabeth to freshen up, but don't take too long. You've kept us waiting for quite long enough already.' A bell rang and Katherine looked around. 'Where the hell is Marcus?'

'He's taking our luggage up,' Daniil replied.

'Well, that's him gone for a week,' Katherine huffed, as she realised she might have to greet guests herself for a few moments. 'Why I offered to keep him on after retirement is beyond me. Go on, you two, get ready.'

Oh, she was completely awful, Libby thought as they went up the stairs. Her father only ever called her Elizabeth when he was telling her off.

They walked up the imposing staircase just as Marcus limped down, and Libby stiffened on the turn as a huge photograph came into sight. There, standing with the family, was a young Daniil, and it just about broke her heart to look at it. He was wearing a private school uniform and his eyes were hostile and it looked as if the effort of smiling for the camera might just be killing him.

Daniil refused to give it a glance.

'Daniel…' They both turned and there was Katherine,

who, Libby thought, looked a little like a fox terrier with her clipped hair and solid body. 'Charlotte just arrived.'

'And?'

'I'm just letting you know.'

He said nothing, just turned and carried on walking, but Katherine didn't leave things there. 'You'll be delivering a speech.'

'Of course.'

'It might be better if I skim through it...'

'No need,' he responded.

She had the tenacity of a terrier, too, Libby thought, as his mother followed them up the stairs.

'There's every need,' Katherine said. 'Daniel, our guests tonight, well, they're important...'

'Then, you'd better get back to them,' Daniil said, and taking Libby's arm he guided her down a corridor. Finally Katherine gave up and slunk back down the stairs.

'*Tupa shmara*,' Daniil cursed, as the bedroom door closed.

'I'm going to assume that you just said something terribly rude,' Libby said.

'Just the truth,' he responded, and looked around. Their cases sat closed, waiting to be unpacked, and he was grateful to Marcus for that.

To most the space would be inviting. The room was light and airy, the panelled walls were cream and offset by the dark wooden floor and door. The bay windows offered magnificent views of the estate and the furnishings, though antique, were peppered with modern touches. Daniil could well recall lying on the vast bed, watching television and not understanding more than a few words.

'It's beautiful,' Libby said, looking up at the plasterwork on the ceiling.

'If you like museums.' Daniil shrugged. She looked at the photos on the mantelpiece over a fireplace of Daniil holding a tennis racket and another of him sitting, scowling, on a horse. 'I was a poor replica of Daniel.'

'He'd have been a poor replica of you,' Libby said. 'I'm sure the guests would be terribly disappointed if I stepped into my sister's restaurant tonight and took over the kitchen. It would be like asking her to be my understudy—unthinkable! And we've got the same genes.'

She went over and wrapped her arms behind his neck as he looked around the bedroom he hated so much.

'Did you bring a lot of girls home?' Libby asked.

'I've never brought anyone here.'

'Till now,' Libby said, and she watched his eyes shutter, but she refused to be closed out and she stretched to reach his mouth, but he pulled back.

'Libby...' She could almost see the keep-out signs he held up.

'No.' She would not. She would enter at her own risk because that was where her heart led.

His jaw was like marble, his lips like ice, and one hand came up and went to unwrap her from his neck but she simply ignored him, pressing into those lips that she craved.

He was tense and reluctant yet she refused to be perturbed but then, just then, it was like cracking a safe, because she felt him give in to her mouth and he was pulling her closer, letting her in to a deep kiss.

Yes, she may not have his number but his mouth was familiar now, the way he led their kiss, the feeling that nothing and no one could reach them. His hands felt like silk, wrapping them tighter in the delicious cocoon they made.

'Not here,' he said, which was contrary to his actions, for his hand was pulling at the hem of her dress while at the same time pulling her in.

'Yes, here…' she breathed, disengaging her hand from around his neck and moving it down to between them, feeling the hard outline of him and running her palm over the swollen tip.

Yes, here, Daniil thought, for he was back in his old bedroom but he felt different this time, and his kiss was rough now, leading her to the bed. But suddenly there was a knock at the door and without waiting for a response it was opened.

Now she understood why he loathed people knocking at the door so much—it meant nothing, because, completely uninvited, in walked his father. Libby jumped back, embarrassed and shocked, ridiculously grateful that Daniil held one of her hands as the other smoothed her dress.

'*Se'bis*,' Daniil said.

'*Se'bis*,' Richard said, and a very flushed Libby frowned at the slight smirk on Daniil's face at his father's response. 'I've just been speaking with your mother about your speech,' Richard said. Daniil released Libby from his arms and she stood there, breathless, embarrassed and very, very angry at the intrusion, but she tried not to show it as Richard spoke on.

'I thought I might just take a quick look through it,' Richard said, but Daniil shook his head.

'There is no need for that.'

But his father was insistent. 'I just want to check that you've covered all bases.'

'I have.' Daniil refused to give in to him.

'Your mother's worried, Daniel. She's under a lot of

124   THE PRICE OF HIS REDEMPTION

stress about tonight and isn't feeling well.' His hand moved to his chest and Libby thought the gesture was clearly meant to provoke a reaction.

'If she has chest pain then call an ambulance.' Daniil's response was calm and measured, unlike Richard's, whose hand balled in frustration as his son remained unmoved. 'Anyway—' Daniil shrugged '—there's nothing for you to see. I have my speech prepared here.' He tapped the side of his head. 'Now, if you will please excuse us, Libby and I would like to get ready. We'll be downstairs shortly.'

'Very well,' Richard said, but at the door he turned. Clearly, Libby thought, his father had to have the last word. 'But, Daniel, when you do come down, can you please lose the accent?'

They didn't get back to their kiss. Libby put on some make-up and tried to make sense of what she had just heard. It wasn't just an accent. Daniil's voice was one of the many beautiful things about him, and the thought they would censor that had tears sparkling in her eyes, which wasn't ideal when you were trying to put on eyeliner.

She simply didn't know what to say.

At first.

'Tupa shmara,' Libby hissed, and Daniil smiled.

'Nice try, wrong gender,' he said.

'Well, if we're having a Russian lesson, what does *se'bis* mean?' she asked, remembering the slight smirk when Daniil had greeted his father. Daniil laughed as he realised that Libby was far more perceptive than most.

'It means *get out*,' Daniil said. 'They always assumed I was saying it as a greeting when they came into my room. Soon enough they started to say it back to me! I took my victories where I could get them.'

'Ah, you can take the boy out of Russia…' Libby said, and even as they smiled, there was sadness there, for that, she realised, was exactly what his parents had done—they hadn't just taken him from his home, they had tried to erase his past, too.

'Your ambulance trips…' Libby said, and Daniil nodded.

'She would get chest pain or faint or whatever any time that she didn't get her way. It was always my fault, of course, but we had a lesson at school when I was fourteen about emergencies and first aid. The next time she collapsed I called an ambulance…'

'And?'

'I did the same the next time then the next time and the next…'

Libby looked into his cold grey eyes and could well picture him standing calm and detached as chaos surrounded him, but it didn't unsettle her. She knew, or was almost sure of, the warmth behind that guarded gaze.

'I can't be manipulated, Libby. Tears don't move me. Neither does drama.'

'What does, then?'

'Nothing.'

And therein lay a warning. This time, though, she was choosing not to heed it.

She didn't believe him.

'Let's do this,' he said, and they headed downstairs.

It was a supremely difficult evening.

Not for everybody else—after all Lindsey had seen to it that everything had been done to ensure that the celebration ran smoothly. The surroundings were sumptuous—the grand hall glittered, not just from the chandeliers but from the huge red pillar candles dotted around the room. The air was heavy with the scent of the deep red roses that were on each table, which, Katherine told anyone who listened, had been cultivated by their gardener just for this occasion. Yes, the caterers were fantastic, the band amazing; the whole kit and caboodle was brilliant.

'Your father did a good job,' Daniil commented, and then shook his head at a passing waiter as a drink was offered. Yes, everything was perfect—even Daniel Thomas, the wayward son, behaved beautifully and spoke with friends and family in a very schooled voice.

Didn't they get, Libby thought, *that when he had to think about what he was saying just to appease them, so much conversation was lost?*

No, she realised, they just cared about appearances. It wasn't Daniil that they wanted to know. He was merely a replacement for the Thomases' dead son.

'Daniel…' Libby bristled as a glossy brunette came over. Terribly glossy from her gleaming hair right to her blushing cheeks. 'It's been a long time.'

'Libby—' Daniil gave a tight smile '—this is Charlotte Stephenson. We were at school together. Charlotte's father was headmaster.'

'Still is,' Charlotte said, and then pointed across the hall. 'He's over there. You should go over and say hello.'

'Since when have I done as I should?' he replied.

Libby watched as Charlotte flounced off and she waited, waited for Daniil to explain, to tell her where Charlotte slotted in to his past, but, of course, he was supremely comfortable with silence, leaving Libby and her overactive imagination to fill in the gaps—of course, they'd been lovers.

Ah, and then they all paused for the wonderful speeches! Libby's throat was tight as Daniil walked to the front.

There was no fumbling in his pocket for his speech or hiding behind notes. He would speak, seemingly off the cuff, but Libby was quite sure of the hours of practice that must have taken place for him to be able to deliver this speech with apparent ease.

She glanced over at Katherine, who stood, eyes bulging and with a sheen of sweat on her upper lip. Richard, too, was tense, taking a hefty belt of his drink and then steeling himself as if preparing for bad news.

Would it be?

She looked at Daniil and for a moment wondered if he was about to wreak revenge for close to two decades of wrongs.

He'd thought about it.

For the first time in his life Daniil had the family stage, unmanaged. He looked at his parents and saw the tense warning in their eyes. He looked at his cousin George and his slight expectant smile, because wouldn't venting his spleen serve George's purpose well?

There was no need for the truth, though, Daniil thought, for there was no one here that he cared enough to explain it to.

And then his eyes met Libby's and possibly he would amend that thought soon.

For now he accepted her tight smile and the look that told him that whatever he chose to say was fine by her.

There was a slight heady relief that came when somebody accepted you, Daniil thought.

Whatever he might choose to do.

First, in perfect, clipped English, he thanked all the guests for coming, particularly those who had travelled from afar, and then he addressed his parents.

'Of course, the people who I really want to thank are the reason we are all here tonight.'

Libby heard the happy sigh trickle through the room and watched as both Katherine and Richard visibly relaxed. A smatter of applause paused Daniil's speech and she felt ashamed of herself, furious that she might have played any part in procuring this hell for him.

He went through his parents' marriage and spoke of their achievements, which were plenty, and the charities they supported, and then she watched Katherine's shoulders stiffen as Daniil brought the white elephant up to the front of the room.

'As you will all know, twenty years ago my parents suffered the devastating loss of their only child. For two years they were bereft but then, being the generous people that they are, they came to realise that they still had so much love to give.'

Libby wanted to stand up and clap. Not in applause. She wanted to stand and clap and call attention to herself. 'No, they didn't,' she wanted to say. 'They didn't want to deal with the death of their son so they simply did their best to get another one.'

Instead, though, she listened as he spoke on.

'As most of you will know, two years after their insufferable loss my parents brought me into their family. I was twelve years old at the time and—' he gave a wry smile '—far from easy, yet they opened their home to me and gave me opportunities that I could never have dreamed of.'

He spoke of the school they had sent him to, one where Richard was still on the board of directors.

'I see that Dr Stephenson is here tonight.' Daniil nodded to his old headmaster. 'You were right,' Daniil said, and it took everything he could to keep the malice from his eyes as he looked at man who had wielded his draconian power so mercilessly in an attempt to whip him into suitable shape. 'I had no idea just how lucky I was.'

Libby could feel the tension from her jaw right to her shoulders. Possibly she was the only person in the room who was reading between the lines, for Dr Stephenson was smiling as if he'd been thanked as Daniil continued.

'I know that without my parents' endless support and encouragement I would not be where I am today.'

Those present knew that financially Daniil was head and shoulders above everyone here and so, when he gave his parents the credit, there were oohs and aahs and applause from the crowd, and Katherine gave a small beatific smile and put her hand up to stop people, as if saying that she didn't deserve the praise.

She didn't, Libby thought savagely.

Yet Daniil saw it through.

He borrowed the line Libby had used on the day they had met, which he had at the time questioned, and said what an achievement forty years of marriage was. He wished them well for the future and said that their marriage was a shining example and one he could only hope to emulate.

As everyone raised their glasses, Libby was a few seconds behind. The expensive French champagne tasted like a dose of bitters on her tongue as Richard gave his first ever appreciative nod to his son.

Finally Daniil had toed the line.

I just sold my soul, Daniil thought as he returned to Libby's side.

But he had done it for a reason.

CHAPTER NINE

THE RED VELVET cake was cut and it looked amazing but sat like sand in her mouth as Daniil performed several duty dances.

Clearly she wasn't the only one who found the cake tasteless because the table she sat at became littered with discarded plates of half-eaten cake, but finally Daniil made his way over and now it was Libby he held in his arms.

'Your speech went down well,' she commented.

'The downside to that is they're now talking to me,' Daniil said. 'I preferred their silence.'

He glanced over Libby's shoulder and saw that his cousin was watching them. Libby had noticed him, too.

'Your cousin seems overly interested in you,' she observed.

'He's hoping I'll disgrace myself just to shore up his inheritance,' Daniil said. 'You know, sometimes I consider smarming up to my parents just for the dread it would cause him…'

'But you don't?'

'Nope,' Daniil said. 'I just amuse myself with the thought at times.' He looked down at Libby. His hands were on her waist and her spine was rigid and he missed the fluidity of her movements, the ease between them that they usually enjoyed.

'I'm sorry to have left you alone for so long.'

'It's fine.'

'We'll be out of here soon,' he said. He just wanted this night over so that he could speak with his father and find out a vital part of his past. He had no plans after that. His thought process had always stopped at the moment his father revealed the truth about the letters.

'We're not staying, then?' Libby checked, and then smiled. 'Or when you say out of here...'

She meant the bedroom, she meant a door between them and the rest of the world, and, for the first time ever, he realised that might be enough. He looked down into clear blue eyes and the thought of staying the night was appealing if it meant that they could be alone sooner.

'You've seen for yourself how my father had no compunction about knocking and not waiting to be asked in...'

'We could cure that annoying habit very easily,' Libby said into his ear.

'It didn't work this evening.'

'I wasn't naked and on top of you then,' Libby said, and Daniil found himself smiling at the thought of his father's hasty retreat if he found them in such a compromising position.

'You wouldn't duck under the covers, would you?'

'Of course not,' she said. 'I'd ask him to pour me a glass of water. He'd never not knock again.'

'What are you doing?' Daniil asked, as she smiled and gave a small wave to someone over his shoulder.

'I'm annoying George for you,' she said. 'I just smiled at your mother.'

Here at the family home, when he had never thought there could be, there was the first glimpse of ease. With Libby, there was a sense of togetherness—nothing and no one could touch them.

'What are your family functions like?' Daniil asked.

'Catered for by my sister, micromanaged by my father...'

'And your mother?' Daniil asked, because she rarely mentioned her.

'Frowned on by her.' Libby's response was resigned. 'I don't think she's ever been truly happy. She simply doesn't know how to enjoy the moment.'

And that was exactly what they did.

Right now, in the midst of so much history, a sliver of pleasure was found—the beat of the music, the feel of each other.

Was this what a relationship made possible? Daniil pondered.

A hellish visit made bearable simply by having her there.

Always there was the next thing to aim for, the race to be run, but right now, in a place that held no happy memories, where he had least expected to find it, he started to glimpse a future, a constant that could remain.

The dance had turned into one of pleasure, an unexpected treasure that he had never expected to find this night, though it unnerved Daniil, rather than bought comfort, for he knew better than to get used to such a thing.

Nothing lasted—that much had been proved long ago.

As the music shifted he released her from his arms and Libby excused herself to visit the ladies' room. Daniil went and got another glass of sparkling water—he was very deliberately not drinking tonight.

He stiffened as George came over to him—he was all smiles as he congratulated Daniil on his speech.

'Very nicely said.' George gave a nod of approval that Daniil did not need but, because he *had* sold his soul tonight, just to find out about the letters, he seemingly accepted the praise and shook his cousin's hand.

'It's true what you said about a forty-year marriage being an achievement...' George sighed. 'I doubt it will ever happen to either of us.'

'Yes, I heard about your divorce,' Daniil said. He really was on his best behaviour tonight, for he omitted to mention that this divorce would be George's third.

'Yes, the cow is taking me for all I haven't got,' George hissed. 'The last two saw to that. Relationships are bloody hard work if you ask me.'

Daniil hadn't.

'So how long have you been with Libby?' George asked. 'She seems like a very lovely lady.'

'She is.'

'How did you meet?'

'We...' Daniil started, and then he realised there was no reason to lie. 'We met through Libby's father. He organised tonight.'

'So you only got together recently, then?'

Daniil nodded.

'I thought as much.'

'Excuse me?' Daniil checked.

'She still seems happy,' George said, and walked off.

Daniil's jaw gritted but he told himself to ignore what had just been said. As he went to walk away it was straight into Charlotte, who was standing, talking with his mother and her father.

'For old times' sake?' Charlotte said.

It was a duty dance or make a small scene, Daniil knew, so he held his ex in loose hands and, had Libby not been here tonight, she'd have sufficed.

Charlotte didn't do it for him now.

'My father's looking very displeased,' Charlotte whispered, and twelve years or so ago that would have turned him on.

Hell, a few weeks ago it might have been enough for Daniil to make his way to her room later tonight for the simple pleasure of screwing her under her father's nose.

'I'm coming down to London next week,' Charlotte purred.

'I'll be away on business.'

'I'll be there again next month.'

And he knew then he'd changed because next month was an eternity in the relationship stakes for him and yet he was starting to envision the weeks with Libby— imagining that, weeks from now, months from now, years from now, they two might remain. Yes, Charlotte was like the cake, perfect to look at yet something was lacking. There was no temptation to taste now.

'Why don't you give me your number?' Charlotte asked. 'I tried calling a while back but your receptionist wouldn't put me through. If I had your—'

'I don't give it out to just anyone,' Daniil interrupted.

'I'm not just anyone.'

And he looked into eyes that were playing the game he had played for so long, yet he was over it now.

'Oh, but you are.'

Yes, he was the bastard she told him he was, and as Libby returned to the grand hall it was to the sight of Charlotte walking rapidly away from his arms.

No, Libby wasn't secure enough not to notice or care.

The evening was winding down and Daniil just wanted to get out of this toxic place but he still hadn't spoken with his father and as Richard came over, he decided to deal with that now.

'We're going riding in the morning,' Richard said. 'It will be an early start and then back here for breakfast...'

'Not for me,' Daniil said. 'We need to head off before nine. I was wondering if I could have a word, though.'

'Now really isn't the best time.'

Libby was by his side, watching the terse exchange, feeling Daniil's hand tighten around her fingers.

'It will only take a few moments.'

Richard gave a very stiff nod and as he walked off Daniil went to follow him. Given he was holding her hand, Libby walked with them, but as they reached the entrance hall Daniil seemed to remember she was there and let go.

'I need to speak with my father.'

'I could come with you.'

He shot her a look that told her she had overstepped the mark and she didn't know her place here.

'Go to sleep. I'll be up later.'

'Sleep?' Libby said. 'People are still dancing, the party hasn't finished...'

'It has for us.' Already he had gone and she stood there, trying to comprehend such a dismissal. She gave a wide, though incredulous smile as Marcus the butler came over.

'I think I've just been sent to bed.' Libby shook her head in bewilderment. One moment they had been dancing and together, the next she had been packed off to bed.

Daniil stood there as Libby flounced up the stairs and then followed his father into the dark bowels of the house—Richard's study. As they walked in and his father took a seat at his desk Daniil remembered standing here, handing over his report cards. But he wasn't a teenager now and he stood taller than the man who had so badly bullied him.

'I can guess what you're here for,' Richard said. 'Your mother and I have spoken at length about the inheritance—'

'I am not here about your estate,' Daniil interrupted, and he watched his father press his lips together as his son's public school voice fell away and Daniil stood, menacing, challenging and defiant. 'What you do there is your business. I've never had an interest in your money.'

Air whistled out of Richard's nostrils in frustration. One of the many things that irked him was that Daniil could buy and sell him several times over.

'The letters.' Daniil had known exactly what he planned to say, but in the courtroom of his father's study for a moment he felt as if he was back to being a teenager and the words did not flow. 'I want to know—'

'Ah, yes.' Richard went into his desk. 'A deal's a deal. Though there was only one.'

Daniil frowned as his father took out an envelope. He did everything not to display need but his hand was shaking as he took it from his father. The writing was in English but it had been written by a Russian, Daniil could tell that from the curve of the letters and the numbers.

It must be from Roman!

He wanted to rip it open there and then but he just stared at it, looking at the stamps from home and the faded writing and trying to read the postmark as hope started to rise in his chest—finally he had contact with his twin.

'When did this come?' Daniil asked.

'Oh, it would be five or six years ago now.'

'What?' Daniil growled, glad he had asked his father about the letter now, rather than earlier in the evening. If they'd had this exchange then, the only speech he would have been capable of delivering would have been his statement to the police when they arrested him, such was the temptation to lash out.

Instead, he contained it.

He still had questions.

'Why didn't you give me this at the time?' Daniil asked.

'We didn't want you raking up the past.'

'It's *my* past,' he said. 'You can't take that from me. God knows, you've tried, though.' A little of his temper unleashed. 'Why did you give it to me now?'

'I told Lindsey it might persuade you to come.'

Did Libby know?

It was irrelevant, Daniil knew. This letter had lain hidden in a desk for years. A few weeks made no difference; he just wasn't thinking logically now.

He wanted out.

'Will you answer one question?' Daniil asked, and Richard gave a nod. 'The letters I gave you to post to my brother—were they ever sent? I'd really appreciate the truth.'

Perhaps Richard knew it might well be the last time they came face-to-face, perhaps he accepted this man would never be his son because he tapped in the final nail.

'They weren't sent.'

'Can I ask why?'

'All the advice we got was that if you were to successfully integrate…'

'No,' Daniil said. 'You disposed of the advice you were given and sought puppets who would tell you what you wanted to hear.'

'You'd be on the streets without us, Daniel, or locked up. The temper you had—'

'Richard,' Daniil interrupted. He would never go through the farce of calling him Father again. *'Otyebis ot menya.'*

He told his father to get the hell away from him, though rather less politely than that, and then he told him, in Russian, to *stay* the hell away.

He could not stand to be in a room with him a moment longer. He wanted the door between himself and his family that Libby had alluded to, their privacy, but as he walked to the stairs, unable to resist, he tore open the letter. All he could see was that it wasn't from Roman but Sev.

It said that he was in London for one day and could they meet?

The letter had been sent five years ago!

He saw the portrait of his so-called family on the turn of the stairs and felt like ripping the picture off the wall and putting his foot through it, or calling his pilot and leaving now, but then he remembered he'd told Libby to get some sleep and tearing her from her bed in some angry display didn't appeal.

Instead, he walked out onto a balcony and watched the partygoers leave, staring out into the black countryside as he had done so many times growing up, and finally he took out the letter and read it properly.

Hey, *shishka*!

Daniil's jaw still clenched when he read that name but there was a smile, too, at the memory and he read on painfully.

I met a woman who wanted me because I was Russian; she was hung up on a guy she once slept with—Daniel Thomas.

That didn't sound very Russian to me and so I looked him up.

You've done well.

I am going to be in America for a month making some rich man richer but I will be in London on the twelfth of November. I don't know where to suggest we meet, all I know there is a palace? Midday?

I hope my writing to you doesn't cause you embarrassment.

Sev

There was nothing about Roman, or Nikolai, no hint about their lives, and he ached to know something, anything about the past he had been forced to leave behind.

He was, though, five years too late to find out.

He looked out at the sky that was black to match his mood.

There were no stars.

Despite the warmth of the day it was now one of those crisp nights that heralded the end of summer.

The end of them?

In the same selfish way that Daniil had wanted Libby here tonight he wanted to head back to his bedroom. He wanted it to be just the two of them and the uncomplicated world that was there, but he was more than aware of his own dark mood.

George's comment was like a worm in his ear. He tried to shrug off his cousin's words—he knew just how poisonous he could be—and yet, as always, there was an element of truth.

How long would Libby be happy for?

How much would he put her through before that perpetual smile disappeared from her face for good?

He had no experience with relationships, no hook to hang hope on, nothing to recall. There were vivid memories of yesteryear, and look how that had worked out.

Roman had made no effort to contact him.

Neither had Nikolai.

One letter five years ago from Sev was all he had from his past.

It wasn't much to go on. It didn't instil the necessary confidence it would take to tell her the hollow disappointment he felt tonight.

She was surely better out of it.

CHAPTER TEN

LIBBY WASN'T SLEEPING.

As she stepped into Daniil's old bedroom it would seem that it wasn't just helicopters that Libby was averse to because she had the strange feeling again of the floor coming up to meet her. She sat, a touch dizzy, on the bed and wondered if maybe she'd eaten something that hadn't agreed with her.

Or drunk something, perhaps?'

But that didn't work because even the glass of champagne she'd taken to toast his parents had tasted bitter and she'd struggled to swallow a sip down.

She was overtired, Libby decided.

Of course she was. After all, she'd been busy with her new business and rushing around with the banks and open nights and things.

That made no sense, either, because what might seem an exhausting few weeks to some felt like a holiday to Libby—she was used to being up at six and warming up, ready to start her first dance class at eight. Rehearsals had commenced at ten, then there had been matinee and evening productions, and, even if she'd been playing the smallest of roles, it had still been well after midnight before she'd got into bed. And as well as all that she'd had to rehearse for roles she'd been understudying.

So, no, despite feeling drained, there was no real reason to be tired, or was she simply in turmoil from falling head over heels for a man who had warned her from the get-go not to get too attached?

Perhaps he should have been more specific; perhaps he should have also told her not to go and do something as foolish as to get pregnant!

Libby voiced it for the first time in her head as she lay there, staring up at the intricate plasterwork on the ceiling, and then she chided herself for her complete overreaction.

She wasn't even late.

Well, barely.

Amenorrhea was the dancer's curse, Libby told herself.

It just didn't ring true tonight.

She jumped when she heard a knock at the door, knowing Daniil would never knock and wondering if Richard or Katherine was about to burst in.

There was another knock on the door.

'Come in,' Libby said, and as the door opened she saw that it was Marcus with a tray. She let out a sigh of relief.

'I thought you might like some tea.'

'I would.' Libby smiled. 'That's very kind of you.'

There wasn't just tea, there were biscuits and a slice of cake, too, as well as a jug of iced water. It was rather nice to have supplies while she was shut away!

'Is Daniil still speaking with his father?'

'I'm not sure,' Marcus said, as he poured her tea, and then he gave a tight smile that spoke volumes. 'I expect they shan't be too long.'

'Is it always this tense when Daniil is home?' Libby asked, as she took her cup. Oh, she knew she was talking out of turn but she simply couldn't help herself. She expected to be chastised or for some vague, polite, dismissive answer but the cup rattled in the saucer as Marcus, far more directly than Libby was expecting, responded.

'It's *always* this tense.'

She looked up at Marcus's kind lined face, surprised at his indiscretion, wondering if he would retract or attempt to cover up what he'd said. She saw that he was looking directly at her, almost inviting her to speak.

'And yet you're staying on after your retirement?'

'Oh, no,' Marcus replied. 'Sometimes we just say things to appease, though, of course, Daniil has never mastered that art.' He looked around the room. 'I remember the day he arrived here. I was just about to hand in my notice—the last thing I needed was another spoiled preteen telling me what to do—but then he arrived and...' He shook his head. 'Well, there was so much damage...'

Libby swallowed and then opened her mouth to speak. It hurt to hear Daniil described as that but her protest died on her lips as Marcus carried on talking. 'Far too much damage to leave a child to deal with, especially one who spoke no English.'

It was the biggest insight she had ever had.

'So you stayed?'

'Yes, I chose to stay for a few weeks to ease him in and that turned into a few months, then years. I decided to leave when Daniil started university.'

'But you didn't?'

'A new cook started.' Marcus smiled and he glanced at the tray he had brought up and saw that the cake was untouched. 'Shirley. You have no idea how many times she tried to get that cake right...' He didn't elaborate. 'Of course, we've never told the Thomases about us— they'd have had us moved to couples accommodation on half the wage.'

'Why are you telling me this?' Libby was as direct as ever with her questions.

'You asked,' Marcus said. 'That's very rare around here. Anyway, suffice it to say, in a few weeks' time Shirley and I shall retire, and it can't come a moment too soon.'

He said no more than that, just gave a smile and wished her goodnight.

After he had gone Libby undressed and climbed into the vast bed and flicked out the side lights. Noise filtered through and she longed for the thick double-glazed windows of her little flat, which kept the sound of the buses and cars out. Here the windows were old and allowed her to listen to the guests leaving and the crunch of cars on gravel and the sound of helicopters lifting into the sky and even, at one point, Sir Richard's voice, laughing at something someone had said and then wishing them a safe journey home.

She heard George guffaw at something and, no, her straining ears told her that Daniil wasn't locked in conversation with them.

And she lay there, alone, and as it edged towards three in the morning she wondered if he had gone already. She didn't know if he'd simply upped and left. Maybe he'd forgotten she was there, like some discarded bag on a train that he'd suddenly recall at midday tomorrow, and make a few half-hearted calls to retrieve.

She remembered only too well how cautious she had been when she had accepted his invitation to dinner that first night. Then she had ensured that she'd had enough money in her purse to offer an escape route.

Tonight she had none.

All she could do was wonder why he would prefer to be alone than with her.

If he *was* alone.

Doubts were as long and black as the shadows that were cast in the room.

Fear that she could be pregnant did not foster restful sleep. There was a need to accelerate things, to know exactly what she was dealing with, so her eyes were wide-open when, well after four, the door opened and Daniil came in.

'Where were you?' she said, as she listened to him undress.

'I've never answered that question in my life and I don't intend to start now.'

'So I'm supposed to just lie here, waiting…'

'I never asked you to wait up for me.'

It disconcerted him that she had. Daniil had assumed that Libby would have been asleep long ago. He was used to operating on his own hours and he wasn't used to accounting for his time.

'I hope she was worth it.' Libby closed her eyes in regret as soon as that sentence was out. It sounded jealous, suspicious, needy, but, hell, four hours waiting for the master to return and that was exactly how she felt. 'Were you with Charlotte?'

'Grow up!' Daniil said. 'Do you really think I've spent the past few hours flirting with some ghost from my past? Making out with Dr Stephenson's daughter to get my kicks…?' His voice trailed off and she listened to him undress.

'Is that what you used to do?' Libby asked. 'Was she a part of your rebellion?'

'Yep.' Daniil's response was blithe.

'Any other ex-lovers here tonight?' she asked, as she lay there bristling.

'Many,' Daniil answered. 'The village pub closes at eleven—which was far too early to come back to this hellhole.' He climbed into bed and she could feel the cool come in under the sheets and it dawned on her that he had spent all that time outside.

Rather than be here with her.

'All I know is…' Libby started, but didn't finish.

'All you know is what?' he said, pushing her to complete whatever it was she had been about to say.

'Nothing,' she admitted. 'I have no idea where we are or where we're going…' She turned and looked at him. He was lying on his back, staring up at the ceiling, with his hands behind his head, and though sharing a bed he might just as well have been in another room.

'Nowhere,' Daniil said. 'I told you the night we met—we're going nowhere.'

'Bastard.'

'You have no idea the bastard I can be, Libby.'

'I'm starting to find out,' she said. 'I don't understand what's happened. I know that something has, but rather than tell me you'd leave me lying here, wondering where the hell you were.'

'I was out on the balcony, if you *must* know.'

'I *want* to know.'

She was demanding. It was all or nothing with Libby—that was how she lived her life. With Daniil she felt she was supposed to hold back, to restrain herself, to feign nonchalance, but that wasn't who she was.

'Did you know anything about a letter for me?'

'Yes, about your inheritance, I think…' Libby was vague.

'Actually, no, it was a letter to me.'

'Well, how would I know that?' she said.

'Go to sleep,' he said.

'If only it were that easy. I'm sorry if I'm not laid-back enough for you. I apologise if I can't sleep the sleep of the dead when I've no idea where you are.'

No one had ever waited up for him.

Occasionally Marcus had let him in if he'd had arrived home late minus his keys. That was the sum of concern in this place.

He recalled one Christmas Eve, when he'd been about seventeen, and a night at the local pub had seemed more palatable than a night spent with his parents, George and Dr Stephenson and family.

He'd been unable to get a taxi from the village and had rather foolishly decided to take the long walk home in the snow. He hadn't counted on the lack of landmarks, or that a few drinks on a stomach of dread might make for a difficult journey. He had given in and holed up in a barn, waking to a weak silvery sunrise before tackling the last mile home.

Marcus had let him in and, following voices, Daniil had walked into the drawing room to see his parents opening their presents, along with George.

They had all turned as he had stepped in, his black hair white with snow, his clothes damp from a night sleeping out, but what had truly frozen out that Christmas morning had been his mother's slight shrug. 'Oh!' she had said. 'We thought you were still in bed.'

Daniil looked over to where Libby lay. He knew that his anger was misplaced.

'I thought you would be asleep.'

'Well, I wasn't.'

'I know that now.'

He'd entered the room determined to stay away but now he rolled towards her, his cold mouth seeking hers, his hands everywhere, but she slapped them off.

'You'd rather screw me than talk to me.'

'Tonight, yes.'

'Well, tough,' she said. 'You can't ignore me for half the night and then expect peak performance...'

He rolled away from her and she lay regretting her stance and yet refusing to relent.

She lay facing away from him perhaps as lonely and scared as Daniil had been all those years ago in this very room. After all, her problem was the same as his had been—it was hard to accept that you weren't really wanted.

CHAPTER ELEVEN

LIBBY MUST HAVE drifted off to sleep because she woke to the sound of Daniil in the shower and the recollection of their row.

Maybe she had been too harsh. Libby knew from the little he had told her that coming back here would prove hard but, hell, she was tired of numbing their issues with sex.

She watched as he walked out of the en suite, still sulking.

He dried himself and she looked at his beautiful, toned, sensual body and really she should give herself a gold star for managing to say no to that last night.

She was tired of the roller-coaster ride, though.

For the best part of a year she had lived on one, courtesy of her fading career. Having stepped off that one, she had promptly climbed into a carriage named Daniil, yet she had forgotten to strap herself in.

It was time to rectify that.

'Are we going down for breakfast?' she asked, as her stomach declared it would like some.

'No,' Daniil said.

'Well, thanks for keeping me informed.'

She headed into the en suite and looked at her pale

complexion and white lips and prayed her pallor was down to the fact she was getting her period.

Her breasts certainly felt as if she was, Libby thought as she showered and felt them swollen and sensitive beneath her fingers.

She simply couldn't be pregnant.

Apart from the fact that it would mean the father was possibly London's most notorious rake, there was a little thing called the Libby Tennent School of Dance to consider. It was the summation of her life's work and her entire future. The dance school had felt for a while like a last resort but it was where all her hope resided now.

Yes, maybe her anger last night and this morning was a touch illogical and misdirected, yet that was how she felt—*illogical* and *misdirected* were apt words to describe her behaviour since Daniil had come into her life.

She stepped out of the shower and looked into the mirror, barely turning as Daniil, dressed in black jeans and a black crew-neck, came and stood behind her.

Apart from naked, she had never seen him out of a suit and she was angry that he looked better, if possible. Unshaven, scowling, his expression matched her mood.

'You didn't knock.'

'You know how I feel about knocking,' he said. 'What's wrong, Libby?' He gave a hollow laugh at his own question. 'Aside from me not coming back last night, but we were fine until then.'

'No,' Libby corrected. 'We weren't.'

She was naked but she never felt that with him and unabashed she turned and faced him.

'Has there been anyone else since me?'

He blinked at her forthright question and, guessing this was still about Charlotte, he just shrugged. There was no need to be evasive or to think so he simply answered, 'No.'

'So we've been seeing each other for a month?'

'I don't think it's been a month.'

Now he was being evasive.

'Yes.' Libby nodded and then proceeded to tick off their encounters on her fingers. 'It has been—we had dinner and then the next week I came by your office and then the next week you came by my studio and then the next week here we are.'

'And tonight I am going overseas on business for a few nights,' Daniil said. He didn't like a numbers game; he didn't want it confirmed but they had been together a month. 'I don't get your point.'

'Then, I'll explain it.'

She had nothing to lose, not even her pride—that had long since gone out of the window where Daniil was concerned. She was tired of things being one-sided, tired of expending emotion on a man who was so reluctant to give it back.

'I don't have your phone number,' she said. 'Your apartment is like Fort Knox and your receptionist is so intimidating I can't imagine myself popping in...'

'I don't get where you're going with this.'

'Then, listen,' Libby said. 'I want flowers, I want conversation, I want phone calls and texts and presents...' He went to open his mouth but she got there first. 'And before you accuse me of demanding expensive gifts, that's not what I mean. I'm tired of living on a knife edge. It's not all about whether you want to see me again, Daniil. It's about whether or not I want to see you, too, and if you can't be bothered to pick up your phone and ask about my day then I don't want you to be a part of it anymore.'

She was through with prolonging endings. If they were over, if he couldn't offer more than a weekly visit, then they were done.

'Is that it?' he said.

'That's it,' she replied, and brushed past him to the bedroom, where she opened the overnight bag that she had packed with such hope and, of course, that wasn't quite it.

'Don't think you can return from your business trip and pick up where we left off.'

'Why would I want to pick up where we left off? From what I recall, last night wasn't exactly—'

'It's not all about sex.'

'Actually, for me, it is.'

'Then, you *really* did bring the wrong date last night.'

'I don't like pushy—'

'Same answer,' Libby responded. 'You're with the wrong person, then. I'm affectionate, I'm demonstrative, that's who I am. If you want some nonchalant lover then you're with the wrong woman. I'm not going to pretend I don't care just because that's what you'd prefer.'

'Have you finished?'

'Yes.'

She had.

Libby was as lovely with his parents as she had been on arrival and as Marcus came from the helicopter where he had deposited their luggage she gave him a fond hug.

Yet as the helicopter lifted off there was no touching hands this time. Instead, she closed her eyes and dozed for the journey home.

Even on the car ride back to her flat she was silent.

'When I get back maybe we could...' Daniil started, but she was already climbing out of the car.

She could see the curtain flickering and knew Rachel would be waiting for an update and would scold her for not playing it cool. But where Daniil was concerned there was no such thing as lukewarm; there was no question now of sitting on the fence and waiting to see what his next move would be.

Libby delivered her ultimatum.

'I don't do well with maybes so if you leave it till then don't bother calling—it will be too late,' she said. 'I mean it.'

His car didn't sit idling until she was safely inside.

And neither did Libby turn and wave.

He was in or out and so was she.

She just hoped that some time this century her heart would catch up with that fact.

To her shame, that night Libby took her phone to her bed *and* plugged it into its charger.

Just in case.

But she woke to no calls or texts and no flowers, either.

He's on a business trip, she reminded herself, though it was a poor excuse because he could probably have a koala bear delivered to her if he so chose.

And on Tuesday, again nothing.

Even her period refused to make itself known. That evening, Libby came in the door and tried to pretend to Rachel that she wasn't scanning the hall, kitchen and lounge for flowers and she asked, oh, so casually, 'Any phone calls?'

'Only your parents call you on the landline. I warned you…'

'He might still be flying…'

'Oh, so his personal pilot would have told him to turn

his phone off? You shouldn't have pushed so hard,' Rachel said, because Libby had told her some, if not all, about the weekend she and Daniil had shared.

'Why not?' Libby said. 'I'd be being ignored now whatever I'd said. At least this way I know he's not interested.'

On Wednesday she played good toes, naughty toes with a group of very wriggly four-year-olds and listened to the sound of babies crying in her tiny waiting room.

She couldn't possibly be pregnant, Libby thought as she pointed her toes down.

'Good toes,' she said, deciding that she was lovesick, that was all.

'Very, very naughty toes,' Libby said, wondering why the hell she'd been foolish enough to do it without protection.

Eight little girls blinked at the deviation from the script and the sound of their ballet teacher's slightly strange laughter.

'Good toes,' Libby said, because, hell, he hadn't come inside her.

But they were soon back to naughty toes and dark thoughts that maybe he was so potent that his sperm would be the same, brutally tapping away at her poor egg just as he had at her heart.

As she waited for her older students to arrive Libby went into her locker and looked at the pregnancy test kit she had bought but hadn't had the courage to use.

She was scared to find out.

There was the temporary distraction of a young adult class later that evening. For now it consisted of three— Sonia, a girl called Oonagh and a young man called Henry, who had so much talent it both thrilled and scared her to have a hand in moulding it. But her fears caught up with her as she made her way home.

A broken heart she could deal with.

Possibly, an unexpected pregnancy, too.

It was Daniil Zverev who had her stomach somersaulting.

He was the most remote, distant man she had ever met.

The antithesis of her.

A man who had told her from the very start he didn't get close to anyone, and now with every day that passed it was more and more likely he was going to be the father of her child.

'You look like death,' Rachel said, as she came in the door. 'Your father called…'

'I know,' Libby said. 'I just spoke to him.'

Dr Stephenson was retiring and had asked Lindsey if he could organise the party, and he also wondered if Libby might consider travelling to Oxford to discuss it.

'He was most impressed,' Lindsey had said.

'I'm not meeting with him, Dad.'

'You're a point of contact.'

'No,' Libby had said. 'I'm not.'

The last thing she wanted now was a trip to Oxford and a trip down memory lane when it looked as if the next few months would be taken up getting over Daniil.

Getting bigger by him.

Libby looked over at Rachel, wondering if she should tell her friend just what was on her mind.

Rachel would be brilliant; Libby knew that. She'd dash off to the chemist and in half an hour or so…

She'd know.

Maybe she already did.

'You didn't ask if there had been any phone calls or deliveries,' Rachel observed.

'You'd have told me if there had been,' Libby sighed. 'Please, don't say you warned me.'

'I shan't.'

'Maybe I should have done what you said and—'

'No,' Rachel interrupted. 'If you had, then he'd have been in for a very rude shock a few weeks or months down the line. You're right, it's better to be yourself from the start.'

'Even if that self is pushy and demanding?' Libby checked.

'Yep, I'm proud of you for standing firm.'

'You know, he warned me not to go falling in love, I should have—' She never got to finish. Instead, she jumped as the one moment she wasn't looking at her phone it bleeped with a text.

'Oh!' Libby let out a shout of joy when she read it. 'It's from Daniil.'

'What does he say?' Rachel checked as Libby started tapping away.

Hi. Daniil.

'That's it?' Rachel checked, and then jumped up and tried to wrestle the phone from her friend but was already too late—Libby's response had been sent.

Hearts, flowers, kisses, she had used every emoticon at her disposal and Rachel was appalled.

'I thought you were proud of me for being myself,' Libby said, as she chewed on her nails. She knew her response had been over the top and wondered if it was possible to retrieve a text.

Even if it was possible, it was way too late for that, she thought as she saw the little tick beside her message that meant it had been read. 'I should have just said hi.'

'You should have waited two hours before saying hi,' Rachel reprimanded.

'I know, I just—'

Then it rang.

'Daniil!' Libby exclaimed.

He smiled at the obvious delight in her voice and could compare it to nothing else—it was unchecked, without agenda and simply her.

'I missed you,' Libby said, and Rachel cringed.

'I miss you, too,' he admitted. 'And I'm ringing to tell you that I lied.'

'I'm quite sure you did,' she said, waving to Rachel as she headed into her bedroom. 'About what? Charlotte?'

Daniil laughed at the edge to her voice.

'I don't lie about things that don't matter. I'm not away on business, I'm in Russia.'

'Oh.'

'I'm trying to find out what happened to the others.'

'Have you had any luck?'

'Not really,' he said, and then with that hopefully out of the way he changed the subject. 'How are you?'

Libby hesitated. She wanted to tell him she was floating on air just to hear from him, she wanted to tell him that her period was AWOL and she had never been more scared in her life, but somehow she managed to find the off switch.

'Busy,' she said. 'The classes are filling up.'

'That's good.'

'Why did you call?' she asked.

'I didn't like how we left things. I was a bastard the other night…'

'I know that you were,' she said.

'I didn't mean to be. I really thought you would be asleep.'

'I know that now,' she said. 'So what's this letter your father gave you?'

'Do we have to talk about it?' Daniil asked.

'No,' Libby said, but it was like being told not to push a button or knowing that her parents were out and her Christmas presents were in the wardrobe. 'Yes.'

'You have no patience.'

'Not a scrap.'

'Okay, I got a letter from Sev.'

'One of your friends from the orphanage?'

'Yes, he must have found my parents' address and sent it to them. He was asking to meet me outside Buckingham Palace. I guess it was the only place he had heard of in London but they never gave it to me till that night. My father said they didn't want to rake up the past.'

'How long ago was it sent?'

'Five years ago.'

'What does it say?'

'Just that.'

'Tell me.'

Daniil sighed and picked up the letter he had just been looking at.

'He says, "Hey, *shishka*."'

'*Shishka?*'

'It's slang for big shot. They started to call me that when they found out that I was going to be adopted.'

'What else does it say?'

Daniil wasn't sure he should translate the next part verbatim but he did so and read it out loud, telling her about the woman Sev had nearly slept with, and about meeting outside Buckingham palace at midday in November.

'What else?'

'Nothing,' Daniil said. 'Well, he says that he hopes his writing wouldn't embarrass me.'

'Why would his writing embarrass you?' she asked.

'He would think I wanted nothing to do with him.'

'At least it's something to work on,' Libby said, but he disagreed.

'There's nothing—no contact address in the letter, no surname. There's no more information than that. We didn't do much schooling in letter writing.'

Daniil had scanned every part of his memory to try to recall the surnames of Sev and Nikolai. They had never used or needed them where they had lived.

'Have you been to the orphanage?'

'It's a school now,' he said, 'but I've been asking around. Sergio, he was the maintenance man, has since died but I spoke to his wife this afternoon. Sev got a scholarship to a good school and Nikolai left when he was fourteen.'

'For where?'

'He ran away,' Daniil said and was quiet for a moment. 'He drowned.'

'Oh, no,' Libby wailed but Daniil carried on speaking in his low voice.

Last night he had cried.

'Katya—she was the cook—apparently left to follow her daughter, Anya, to St Petersburg.'

'Roman?'

'Nothing. I'm trying to find out if he did his military service but apart from that there are no more leads.'

'Well, November is just a couple of months away. Why don't you try to meet Sev then?'

'I'm five years late,' Daniil pointed out.

'Well, it's still worth a try. I know if I'd written that letter that I'd be there every year, like some sad old thing, holding a rose…'

She made him smile.

'Can we start again?' Daniil said.

'Can we?' she asked, wishing it were that easy.

'I thought we might go out on a date, a proper date. I've bought tickets for *Firebird*. I could pick you up and go out to dinner…'

Libby lay on her bed in silence. She hadn't watched a ballet production since she had made the decision to end her career and she didn't know if she was ready to go and see beauty unfold and not be in it. She knew she would be aching to take part and yet he really was making an effort to give them a new start.

'I don't know…' she said, but Daniil spoke over her doubt, quoting *A Winter's Journey* by Polonsky, on which the ballet was based.

'"And in my dreams I see myself on a wolf's back
Riding along a forest path
To do battle with a sorcerer-tsar
In that land where a princess sits under lock and key,
Pining behind massive walls.
There gardens surround a palace all of glass,
There Firebirds sing by night
And peck at golden fruit."'

His voice made her shiver.

'Sev used to read to us at night,' Daniil said and thought back to that time. 'Come and see a nice wolf for once.'

'Is there such a thing?'

'Maybe it's time to find out.'

After the call ended Libby wondered if she'd done the right thing in agreeing to go.

It had to be the right thing, she decided, swinging her legs off the bed and standing up.

A date.

A proper one.

Their first.

'Well?' Rachel said, when she came out of the bedroom.

'He's taking me to see *Firebird* on Saturday.'

'That was thoughtful of him.' Rachel rolled her eyes. 'What an insensitive jerk.'

'He doesn't know.'

'Then tell him what you told me just a couple of weeks ago, that you're dreading going to see a full production.'

'That was a couple of weeks ago,' Libby said.

'You're sure?'

Libby nodded and headed over to the calendar that they kept on the fridge so that they would loosely know each other's comings and goings.

'Firebird,' Libby wrote boldly, even if she felt sick at the thought of it, but then again she felt sick all the time anyway…

She flicked the calendar back and remembered the last week she'd spent with the company, blaming her up-and-down mood and tears on the time of the month.

She was going on her *first* date with Daniil and there was no getting away from it now—she was five days late.

Libby stepped away from the calendar as if closing the stable door.

The horse might already have bolted.

CHAPTER TWELVE

LIBBY DRESSED IN a simple black dress and shoes and took extra care with her make-up and this time, as she waited for Daniil to arrive, she didn't sit on the window ledge, looking out for him.

It had nothing to do with playing it cool, she simply couldn't relax.

'When did he get back from his business trip?'

'I'm not sure,' Libby said.

There had been one text and one phone call in total. It had taken a herculean effort not to call him back each night, not to text and ask when he would be home, or for confirmation of times for tonight.

No flowers again, no cyber displays of affection.

Still, she lived in a state of suspension, courtesy of the man who was taking her out tonight.

'I am looking forward to it,' she said to Rachel. 'It's just...'

'I know.'

'I'll probably enjoy it once I'm there,' she said, though it was more to convince herself. She wanted to see Daniil; tonight was important for so many reasons. It was their first date, a new start for both of them.

It wasn't just seeing *Firebird* that weighed heavily on

her mind, though, and she excused herself for the second time in an hour and fled to the bathroom. She was just about over convincing herself it was nerves that accounted for the constant feeling of nausea.

How could she tell him? she wondered.

She couldn't, she decided, even though she wasn't one for keeping her emotions or feelings in check.

At least till she was sure.

'Daniil's here!'

Rachel's voice came down the narrow hall and as Libby brushed her teeth and topped up her lipstick she forced out a smile. There was so much pinned on tonight and she truly wanted to focus on the two of them, aside from everything else.

She walked down the hall. Rachel had let him in and he stood in her hallway and back in her life. The trouble with seeing so little of him was that each time she did, Libby was reminded in detail of his beauty.

The last time he had been in jeans and unshaven, his hair a touch too long. Tonight said hair was smoothed back but longer than she remembered. He still had the designer stubble and his skin was as pale as hers but without that English trace of peaches and cream. Even his scar seemed devoid of colour now.

'When did you get back?' she asked.

'A couple of hours ago.'

His beauty, his demeanour, his guarded approach—she had not even known what country he was in till now—all daunted her.

No kiss, Daniil noted as she went for her bag.

No leaping into his arms, no guided tour of the house.

Just a scowl hurled at him by Rachel as a rather tense Libby wished her goodnight.

'Your flatmate doesn't approve of me,' Daniil said as they drove to the restaurant.

'She's just…' Libby shrugged. Maybe now was the time to tell him how hard tonight would be for her but then she glanced over and decided against it, quite sure that he wouldn't understand.

It was strained, it was awkward and yet it had absolutely nothing to do with him. As she took her seat in the restaurant Libby didn't know if it was the thought of watching *Firebird* or the scent of garlic coming from the kitchen that had her stomach hovering close to her throat.

'Are you looking forward to the ballet?' he asked.

'Of course.' She pushed out a smile as she read through the menu. 'The costumes are supposed to be fantastic.'

The waiter hovered and Daniil wanted to tell him to give them ten minutes but if they were going to make it in time for the show then they needed to order now. He skimmed the menu as Libby deliberated.

'I'd like the scallops…' she started, and then stopped when she saw that the dish she'd chosen would be served on a butter bean sauce—from the tightening of her throat clearly her stomach didn't approve. She wanted something plain and so changed her mind and chose the risotto but then read it had goat's cheese and that made her want to gag too. 'Actually—' Libby called the waiter back '—I'll have consommé.'

'And for the main?' the waiter asked, but Libby shook her head. 'Just the consommé for me.'

'Clear soup for dinner?' Daniil frowned, remembering her comment about her appetite fading whenever she was anxious or stressed.

'Please, don't lecture me about eating.' Libby's response was tart.

He was trying not to, but she looked very pale and he saw the flash of tears in her eyes and he was quite sure it was down to him. Daniil had seen the cautious look on Rachel's face when she had opened the door to him and George's words were still like a worm in his ear. It would seem that Libby Tennent was no longer happy.

No, it wasn't a brilliant dinner.

And despite the most sumptuous company, and chocolates to boot, as well as the very best seats at the ballet, as Libby stared at the curtain that would soon part all she felt was that she was on the wrong side of it.

It had been a mistake to come tonight, she knew as she looked through the programme. The biographies made her want to weep, the sound of the orchestra taking their seats, the air of anticipation all made her want to run for home.

She turned to him, to tell him that this was possibly the worst place on earth that she could be right now.

'Can we just…?' Libby's words were halted by an announcement, telling the audience that the part of the Firebird would tonight be performed by the understudy Tatania Ilyushin.

It was like rubbing salt into the wound for Libby. She looked through the programme and saw that the dancer usually played one of the thirteen princesses. Tonight Tatania had her chance to shine—it was the breakthrough Libby had long dreamed of as her career had started to fade.

Daniil, on best first-date behaviour, though wondering how long it would go on for, stifled a yawn and glanced down at his own programme. The second he turned the page his head tightened as he looked into pale green eyes and remembered a little girl being sent by her mother to get the box that held the tape.

It couldn't be Anya, surely?

Yes, it could.

Tatania might be her full name, or a stage name perhaps. He had never known Anya's surname. Sergio's wife had told him that Anya had done well and had moved to St Petersburg and that Katya had moved there to be closer to her daughter.

He glanced at Libby but her attention was now on the stage, watching as the curtain drew back.

It was stunning, Libby thought as she saw the smoke swirling around the trees on the stage.

And far, far too late to leave without making a small scene.

She peered into the dark forest, waiting for the lights to lift further, but they didn't and she strained to see, wondering if there was a problem. But then a streak of burnt orange flew across the stage, and the audience gasped as Tatania's entrance was made. Graceful, reed thin, Libby knew that if she never ate another piece of cheese in her life and exercised and trained for every minute of every hour she could still never achieve the amazing lines that this dancer made.

She was surely too tall, Libby thought as she attempted a critical eye, yet her arms were like wings without feathers, and it was as if Tatania was truly flying. She spun in the prince's arms—fragile, tiny and seductive—and Libby sat grieving for her own dreams. She had been wrong to come. It was far too soon, a torture of her own making. Yes, it might sound selfish and self-absorbed but that was what it took to make it as far as Tatania had. For Libby it had killed her to leave it behind.

It was a relief when the interval came.

For ten seconds.

'She's amazing,' Daniil said, as did the people standing behind them. As did the people to the left.

'Do you know…?' he started, but how could he tell Libby here? How could he say that possibly the leading lady might know something about his twin?

If it even was Anya.

And if it was, would she even remember him?

Libby could sense his distraction and chewed on the slice of lemon that had come with her water—she didn't dare risk gin, not just because she might well be pregnant, more for the hopeless tears it might produce. Still, the lemon matched the sourness in her mouth and she was about to bite the bullet and suggest that they leave when Daniil drained his drink and spoke.

'I'll be back in a moment.'

He might never have been to the ballet but he was very used to getting his demands met and after a few enquiries he was told that, certainly, they would relay a message to Tatania, asking her to meet him afterwards.

As Daniil went to give his name, he hesitated, wondering if Anya would remember him, given that he had left the orphanage when he was twelve. She had only really come in on her school holidays, he thought.

She would remember the Zverev twins, though, surely?

It was his best chance of being allowed backstage.

'Tell her that one half of the Zverev twins is here and would like to congratulate her personally.'

'Would you like us to organise flowers?'

Daniil accepted. He had not a clue as to protocol in the dancing world and nodded grateful thanks for the suggestion.

Libby stood, biting down tears as the bell went and it was time to take their seats again. Tonight was supposed to be about them, about working things through. Yes, she was well aware that she hadn't been the best company, but did she deserve him walking off and leaving her alone? She looked at the happy couples, all hand in hand, heading back for the second half. Yes, Libby thought as she saw Daniil approaching, gesturing for her to hurry up, she had been a fool to come.

'Where the hell were you?' she asked, but there was no time for a reply as they were being ushered to take their seats quickly.

'I'll tell you later,' Daniil said, just as the curtain went up.

'Do you get a thrill out of keeping me waiting?' she whispered.

'I said that I—' he started, but was shushed by a woman behind them.

Yes, he had left her standing, and as soon as he had a proper chance he would explain.

All of it.

Tatania truly came into her own in the second half.

Maybe next month, or next year, Libby would be delighted that she'd witnessed such an amazing performance, that she'd been there the night Tatania Ilyushin had been discovered by the world.

She was holding back tears as she clapped and Tatania curtsied, scooping up flowers, and Libby didn't like the jealous part of her but, yes, here it was, sitting on her shoulder and whispering dark thoughts.

She couldn't get out quickly enough.

She took her bag, but as she turned to go Daniil was speaking with one of the ushers.

'Come on,' he said.

'Where…?'

He didn't answer and they were led down stairs and through a rabbit warren of corridors, pausing so that he could pull a hefty tip out of his wallet and collect a huge bouquet of flowers.

She wanted to stop him. Really! Was this supposed to be some sort of special treat?

Meet the cast!

Come on, Libby, come and see, up close, exactly what you didn't achieve.

'Daniil…' She stopped dead outside a dressing room, like an angry donkey refusing to budge. When she saw Tatania's name she wanted to turn and run but it was simply too late.

He pushed the door open and there, about to remove her make-up, was, she presumed, another ex-lover of Daniil's.

Libby knew that for certain as Tatania looked into the mirror and saw him and let out a small keening cry as if she had mourned Daniil forever.

That sound had come from her soul and Libby watched as Tatania jumped up and turned around and ran to his arms.

Oh, they'd been lovers, Libby knew, because the dancer's arms wrapped around him and her mouth did not seek, it just homed in, but possibly the words said in Russian by Daniil warned her of the company they were in and Tatania's shoulders drooped briefly and she rapidly stepped back.

'Libby,' Daniil said, 'this is Tatania…'

As if Libby didn't know.

'Excuse me,' Tatania said in a husky voice, 'but I have not seen Daniil in a very long time.'

What was she supposed to say here? Libby wondered.

Not that they would notice—they were back to speaking in Russian, voicing low urgent words until Libby could stand it no more.

He was cruel.

Unnecessarily cruel.

No, Russian wolves weren't kind, she decided there and then. Russian wolves were beautiful and beguiling and the most dangerous of them all.

She had started to believe in him.

And though she'd been warned both about him and by him, she had chosen to believe in good. She knew that she hadn't been at her sparkling best tonight, but she also knew that she didn't deserve this. Was this Daniil's idea of a good night out, to bring her backstage, to point out what she could never be and throw in one of his ex-lovers to boot?

She walked out of the dressing room, salty rivers of tears falling down her cheeks as she turned and looked at the empty corridor behind her. She didn't need to run. Daniil was so locked in conversation with Tatania that he hadn't even noticed that she had gone.

CHAPTER THIRTEEN

IT WASN'T JUST because she was unable to face Rachel and her 'I told you so' that she asked the taxi to take her to the studio.

It was more that she had to know.

Letting herself in, Libby locked the door behind her and, without turning on the main light, raced through to the back, opened her locker and took out the pregnancy test kit.

In the tiny loo she flicked on the light and read the instructions. In three minutes she'd find out, if her shaking hand could just hold the stick steady. She kicked off her panties and did the deed and then stepped out.

She couldn't watch.

Instead, she headed to the dark studio and paced but, really, it wasn't the result that had her heart in her mouth and her nerves in shreds, it was being in love with a consummate bastard. It was the next forty or fifty years, or however long she had left on this planet, to get through without him.

Oh, but she would, she vowed.

And she'd listen to Rachel and have acting lessons if she had to just so she could address him airily if the need arose.

'Yes, it's your baby but not your problem…' She would practise those words till she could look him in the eye and say them, she would…

And then she had the most horrible vision of arriving in Reception with his screaming baby and being pointed in the direction of a creche…a creche filled to the brim with dark-haired, dark-eyed babies and all the other harried mothers who'd succumbed to that devilish charm.

And yet, despite visions and fears, there was want there, too, for that little pink cross and a baby that was his, for a piece of him she could keep, because he had her heart. From the moment she'd walked into his office she might as well have tied up her heart in a pink satin bow and placed it on his desk.

A baby was the only gift he'd ever give, Libby thought.

She'd had to practically beg for flowers.

And then she heard him.

Or rather she heard the purr of his car and the pull of the handbrake, and just as Daniil had been disconcerted to recognise her legs on a business card, that she knew the sound of his car and the way he slammed the door just about brought her to her knees.

Her heart recognised his footsteps and so did her body because it wanted to run to the door and fling it open and leap to him.

Instead, she sat on the floor, curled into the wall, and hugged her knees not just so that he would not see her—more so that she would not succumb, so she would not give in and hit the snooze button on warning thoughts just for ten more minutes with him.

He was the diet that started tomorrow.

The hope that refused to die.

'Libby.'

His voice was low and rich and annoyingly calm.

Bored even?

'I know you're in there.'

He opened the letterbox and started to speak and she put her fingers in her ears so as not to hear that chocolaty voice that lowered her guard and could make her believe she was mad not to give them a try.

'I know that you're there,' he said through the opening. 'I can see you in the mirror.'

'We're closed!' Libby shouted. 'Go away.'

'If you don't want to talk, fine, you can listen. I'm sorry for what happened back there. It was never my intention to ignore you—'

'It just comes naturally to you, does it? Did it give you a kick?' she shouted, forgetting that *she* was supposed to be ignoring *him* now. 'Were you hoping for a threesome?'

'For God's sake—' Daniil didn't sound so calm now '—open this door.'

'No,' she shouted. 'I just want you gone. Tonight was a huge mistake—I didn't even want to go to the ballet. I knew how much seeing *Firebird* was going to hurt but that you'd do that to me, that you'd take me backstage and introduce me to one of your ex-lovers. Have you any idea how much it hurt, how badly I wanted...?' She could barely get the words out. 'Everything that happened to her tonight I dreamed of for myself and you can call me childish and selfish, I don't care. Tonight hurt, but what you just put me through doesn't even compare...'

Daniil closed his eyes. It had never entered his head that she might not be ready to go to the ballet.

Not for a moment.

Now, though, he could see how hard tonight would have been.

'We're not lovers,' he said. 'We never have been.'

'Liar!'

'I mean it,' he said. 'I knew Anya from the orphanage where I was raised. You know I left there when I was twelve.'

She was so about to be glib, about to ask if that was how they'd all kept warm or passed the time, but decided against it.

'Open the door, Libby.'

'No,' she said, though she did move over to the letterbox. 'I know what I saw, Daniil. She ran to you like…'

Just like I would, she thought.

She ran to you with hope in her heart, just as I would if you dropped into my life ten years from now. And Libby loathed herself for being so weak.

So weak because she was at the closed door and trying hard not to open it.

Instead, she peered through the letterbox and saw that delicious mouth.

'Go,' she said. 'You hurt too much.'

'No.'

'Yes.'

'You're the one who always wants to talk,' Daniil pointed out.

'Well, I don't now.'

'You should have said you weren't ready to go the ballet. That was all you had to do.'

Yes, Libby knew that, but it wasn't just the ballet that had had her emotions in turmoil all week.

'If you had just told me…'

'That's fine, coming from you,' she snapped. 'King of boundaries.'

All that was visible of him was that lovely sulky mouth

and she watched as it stretched into a smile. 'I'm here to talk, Libby.'

'You might not want to hear what I have to say, though.'

Oh, they had a whole lot of talking to do but there was something she had to get off her chest first.

'You remember that you said my technique was all wrong, that I should just lay it all out on the table upfront?'

'I do.' Daniil frowned. He had no idea where this was leading. He had raced through the night to tell her his truth and was instead being asked to listen to what she had to say.

'I haven't been feeling well,' Libby said.

'Okay?'

'My period…'

'Is that why you're teary and irrational?'

'No,' she whispered. She'd deal with his presumption another time. 'It's late.'

She watched as his tongue ran over his lips and then closed her eyes, too scared to look.

'How late?'

His voice sounded very normal, much the way it had when he'd asked her if she'd be using her own savings for the ballet studio, only the stakes were far higher now.

'A week,' Libby said, and when she got no response elaborated, 'That's a lot for me.'

'And how do you feel?'

'Sick,' Libby said.

'Sick with nerves, or sick?'

'Both,' Libby admitted. 'I'm scared.'

'Never, ever be scared when you're near me.'

'You're not cross?'

'Why would I be cross? We were both there when

it happened, we both took the chance. I've told you—I never take risks unless I'm prepared to weather the consequences.'

'You thought about it.'

'Not really,' Daniil said, and now she had the courage to look at his beautiful mouth and see his slight smile. 'But I've never taken such a risk with another woman. Libby, whether you are pregnant or not, you don't need to be scared.'

'But I do. I've just started my own business…' Tears were taking over again and Daniil listened to them. He could step in, tell her she had nothing to worry about, that even if she didn't want him, the money would be taken care of, yet he knew that right now it was about her.

That Libby needed to know that she would be okay.

Herself.

'I'd have to employ someone or close and I was just getting started, it's too soon…'

'Libby!' He broke into her mounting panic. 'Do you know why my business plans work so well, why the banks always say yes to me?'

'No.'

'Because I'm a pessimist. The bank knows that I don't put a positive spin on things. I factor in things like illness and pregnancy and women who leap to the worst possible conclusion and shut up shop because their soon-to-be ex might have slept with a ballerina a decade or so ago…'

She started to smile because she had been thinking exactly that—wondering how she could work while her heart was breaking, how she could dance and smile if she found she had a baby on board and no longer had him.

'You really think I can do it?'

'Of course. I wouldn't have put my name to it otherwise.'

She was calm, not as calm as she had been in that sugary haze in his hotel suite, but the panic was fading.

'You're very good in a crisis.'

'I am,' Daniil said. 'It's the normal stuff that I don't do so well with—like flowers and calling and letting you know the day-to-day stuff in my life. Will you let me in?'

She stood there.

'You're asking the same of me, Libby,' Daniil pointed out. 'You're asking me to let you in, and I can't do that from the other side of a door.'

She turned the lock and stepped back, and though she wanted to go into his embrace she remembered how Tatania had and she folded her arms in defence, confused and raw and hurting yet wanting him all the same. 'I don't believe for a moment that you and she weren't lovers.'

'We never were.'

'Daniil, can we move past the lies? I saw the way she ran to you.'

'Did you notice the way her shoulders sagged?' he demanded. 'Did you see her recoil, or her expression when I stepped out of the shadows and she saw my scar?'

'I don't understand.'

'She thought that I was Roman.'

'Roman?' Libby blinked. 'Why would she…?' Even as she asked, she knew the answer.

'Roman is my twin.'

She felt as if all the air had been sucked out of the room as he spoke on.

'My identical twin,' Daniil said. 'For a moment, Anya, I mean Tatania, thought that I was him. I think you're right. I think something must have gone on between them after I left the orphanage.'

'They separated you?' Libby could hear the horror in her voice as she struggled to comprehend what had happened. 'They didn't let you keep in touch?'

'My parents never sent him the letters I wrote.'

Libby stood there, her head spinning, and Daniil mistook her silence.

'I messed up tonight,' he said. 'When I saw—'

'No, no,' she said, for she understood now. 'I'm surprised you didn't storm the stage and demand answers.'

'I had other things on my mind, too,' Daniil said.

'Like?'

'A very unhappy date. I thought I was making you miserable.'

'No.'

'You could have told me it was too soon for the ballet.'

'I'm glad I've been now,' she said. 'And Tatania was amazing. Why would you think you made me miserable? You know I'm crazy about you, I've never attempted to hide it.'

'I listened to my cousin. He reminded me how miserable I made the family.'

'Rubbish!' Libby said. 'They were miserable and messed up long before you arrived.'

'You don't know that.'

'Oh, but I do,' she said. 'Marcus has been with them for thirty years…' And she told him that Marcus had been ready to leave until a twelve-year-old orphan had arrived in a very unhappy home. 'He felt he couldn't leave you to deal with them.' Her eyes filled with tears. 'I can't believe they didn't send your letters, that they took you from him.'

'It's okay,' Daniil said to her obvious upset. He'd had many years to get used to the facts that Libby was only now trying to understand.

'No, it's not okay!' she said, furious and hurting on his behalf, and then she told him not what perhaps she should say, just exactly what she felt. 'We'll find him.'

They were the best three words he had ever heard for they were delivered with the same urgency and passion that he felt. Whether finding Roman was possible or not, it was the priority she afforded it that sealed his love. For the first time since the orphanage there was *we* rather than *I*, and it meant she would reside in his heart forever.

'We'll find him,' Libby said again, and she didn't try to fight her feelings anymore—she simply flew to arms that lifted her, accepted her. And she had been right that first morning. She *could* live on his hips because her legs coiled around him and his face was near hers and it was better than being home. 'We're going to find him,' she said, with the hope he'd been starting to lose.

'I've tried.'

'We'll keep trying.' And it hit Libby then, the *we* word, because she knew they were the future, as easily as breathing; somehow her mind accepted they were in each other's lives forever. 'Who's the eldest?'

'We don't know,' Daniil said.

And with that answer Libby glimpsed a world without a foundation.

'We were going to be boxers—that was going to be our ticket out of poverty—but then the Thomases made enquiries about me. I didn't want to be adopted but Roman insisted that I go. We had a fight… He said he would do better in the ring without me. I know now he was just trying to ensure I took my chance…'

CAROL MARINELLI   181

'That's how you got the scar?' she asked, and Daniil gave no shake of his head to warn that that question was out of bounds. Instead, he nodded.

She put her fingers up to the jagged flesh and understood now why he had kept it as it was—it was the mark of his brother's love for him and he wore it with pride.

'We'll find your family,' she said.

'I have a family now,' Daniil said. 'You.'

Then Libby forgot; she forgot they had problems, she forgot all that was wrong with the world because all was right in hers as he held her in his arms and they kissed. It was a different kiss from any of their others. This kiss was theirs, nothing held back and no leader—they were in this race together. She kissed him back and he kissed her forward, deep, hungry kisses that had waited too long.

'You turn me on...' Libby breathed into his mouth, wrapping herself around him even tighter.

'I thought I couldn't ignore you all night and expect...' He stopped because as his hand slipped up her dress he felt naked buttocks. 'No underwear...' He was at her neck, marking it; she could feel it and she wanted his mark.

'I was...'

Oh, she'd forgotten everything—even the most important thing had flitted away.

'I was doing a test...'

Between hungry kisses she pointed and he carried her through to the tiny area and the light went on but Libby didn't see it. Her face was buried in his neck as her hands worked his zipper and the only thing that really mattered was the two of them.

'You are.'

He told her she was pregnant and then kissed her

hard enough to chase away any thoughts of too soon, too much. It was good news and they sure as hell deserved it.

Oh, didn't becoming a parent make you suddenly responsible? Instead, she was back in a dance studio with her shoulders against a mirror and her hands holding the barre in a way she never had before.

There was nothing other than the sound of desperate sex and Libby could no longer hold on. He pulled her flush to his torso and she wrapped her arms round his head and sobbed as he started to come.

Yes, naughty toes, because hers curled as every muscle squeezed to his tune yet he was no puppeteer—there were no strings, and she danced free in his arms.

'You're pregnant.' He said it while still inside her. When they should have been coming down from a high, they just stepped from one cloud to the next. 'Are you happy?'

'So happy,' she said. 'You?'

'More,' Daniil said, because his family had just got bigger.

They shared the sweetest kiss and then he tried to put her down but she refused. 'I don't want to let you go.'

She was over-the-top, way too affectionate, yet everything he hadn't known he needed.

'I'm going to love you so much,' Libby said.

'Then, I'd better take you home.'

CHAPTER FOURTEEN

'WHEN DID YOU first know you loved me?' Libby asked as they stepped into his home.

'I haven't told you I love you.'

'Oh, please...' she dismissed. 'So come on, when?'

She was nothing like he was used to but then again he wasn't used to smiling, either, but he was doing that now as she prowled around his home.

Yes, he smiled at the slight sag in her shoulders as she looked at his bookshelf and he knew she was annoyed that the *thing* she had brought him wasn't there.

And neither was it in the bedroom when she peered in.

'Did the cleaner move it?'

'Move what?' he teased.

'I can't believe you got rid of my first present to you.' She pouted. 'I've the napkin from our first dinner.'

'Seriously?'

'Yes...and I've pressed three of the flowers you gave me and...'

She went into her handbag and produced a little bar of very exclusive soap.

'That's from my bathroom.'

'I know. I went through your cupboards and took one. I

wanted a memento of our *one* night.' She almost stamped her foot. 'You really are the most unsentimental man.'

'There's something for you in the kitchen.'

That put a smile on her face and for the first time in living memory Libby ran into a room she usually tried to run from and there on the bench was a box.

'You got me a present.'

'I did,' Daniil said. 'I got it in Russia and I had it wrapped, but it was opened at customs. I was going to have Cindy rewrap it on Monday. As you can see, I tried…'

There was more sticky tape than one box could handle, and Libby rightly guessed that choosing presents and wrapping gifts wasn't something he'd done much of in his life.

'Can I open it?'

'Do.'

Daniil was as tense as she'd been when he had opened her gift, and he glimpsed then how things like this mattered, how choosing something for someone you loved meant you so badly wanted them to love it, too.

'There aren't any gift shops where I come from and I didn't want to just get something from the airport.' He could hear the rare tension in his own voice as she opened it. 'Sergio's wife knew someone who was an accomplished glassblower. I watched this being made.'

Her hand was shaking as she opened the box and there was her *thing* from him—a slender ballet dancer in glass, with blue eyes and a wide smile.

'And she has a hole in her head for a flower!' Libby cried out in delight. 'I love it, I love her, it's the best gift I've ever had and you must have loved me then…'

'Maybe,' he relented. 'Or maybe a bit before that.' He guided her to the room she hadn't been allowed to enter before, and just as he had opened her bedroom door, Libby opened this one and entered his private space.

'You did keep it.' She smiled, because once her eyes had taken in all the gym equipment, she looked over to a shelf and there that glittery porcelain ornament sat.

She placed her glass ballerina next to it and then saw she belonged beside the only other possessions that mattered to him.

She reached up and took the picture down and Daniil stood behind her, looking at the photo of four young boys.

'You look like brothers,' Libby commented, because they all had dark hair and pale skin and solemn eyes.

'I know, but only Roman and I are related. I didn't even know I had these with me when I came. Roman must have slipped them into my case. I had copies made and sent them to him but, of course, they were never posted.'

How cruel, Libby thought.

'My parents tried to throw these out,' he said, 'but Marcus retrieved them and kept them for me.'

And then she said it.

'They're not your parents,' Libby said. 'They don't deserve that title.'

'You don't hold back, do you?'

'I'll try…'

'Never hold back,' he said, and then he looked down at the photo. 'That's Sev.' He pointed to a serious-looking child.

'The one who the letter was from?' Libby asked, and she turned her head and he nodded.

'You'll find him.'

'Maybe.'

'So that must be Nikolai.'

There was a long stretch of silence and then he ran a

finger over the image of a young life lost and his voice was a husk.

'Yes.'

'How did he drown?'

'He was found in a river,' Daniil said. 'He ran away because he was being abused.' He closed his eyes and she was patient with his silence and then he opened them again. 'And there's Roman,' he said, but he did not point. Daniil waited for her to try to guess which one of the twins he was. 'You won't be able to tell us apart, no one was ever able to.'

'I can.'

She pointed to the boy on the left. 'That's you.'

'Fluke,' Daniil said. 'Look at this one.'

He took down the other photo and she looked at two serious boys with black hair and dark eyes, and it had been taken before the scar on his cheek…

Again she chose correctly.

'How do you know?'

'I just know,' Libby said. 'I guess that's love.'

She watched as he put the photos down beside the letter. The *thing* she had given him seemed to smile and say it would keep them safe.

'Come on,' he said.

This time when they moved to the bedroom it was hand in hand, and as she walked into the vast space another question she had was answered.

She stilled as she heard through the night the chimes as Big Ben struck midnight. It made her shiver low in her stomach. The room that had looked so empty seemed to fill with the low and beautifully familiar noise and Libby wondered how she had missed it their first night.

Daniil watched her mouth open as it did and he saw

that tiny frown and he knew her question without her voicing it.

'On a still night you can hear them,' he said. 'I had the glass modified so that sometimes you can hear them chime. It is very nice to fall asleep or wake up to.'

'You *are* sentimental,' she said.

'I am,' Daniil said. 'And the answer to your question is nine o'clock.'

'Sorry?' Libby frowned.

'Fifteen hours after you walked into my office, and fifteen minutes after you walked out of my home, the clock struck nine and I guess I was already in love with you because I called Cindy and told her to cancel my morning so I could work on your business plan. So,' Daniil asked, curious now, 'when did you know you loved me?'

'What's the time, Mr Wolf?'

Daniil frowned at her game.

'Six o'clock.' Libby answered with the truth.

The moment I saw you I knew.

EPILOGUE

'I HATE YOU,' Rachel said, as she added the last curl to Libby's hair.

'I know you do.' Libby smiled.

In half an hour's time she would be marrying the man of her dreams and Rachel was going to be a witness.

Wrapped in her dressing gown, Libby took one last look around the flat. It was a lot emptier now as over the past few weeks her things had been moved over to Daniil's, but now she gave her flatmate and friend a hug before she finally moved out.

'You've been the best friend…'

'Don't get all sentimental,' Rachel warned. 'I've just done your make-up.'

'I know.' Libby smiled but then it wavered. 'I'm so nervous…'

'Why?' Rachel asked. 'You're head over heels and not afraid to show it.'

'I know. I'm just worried what everyone's going to say when they find out we're married and…' Libby screwed her eyes closed. 'I don't care what they say.'

Oh, she did.

A bit.

Her father would freak at the missed opportunity to

organise such a potentially prominent wedding. After all, the press were going to go crazy when they found out that Daniil Zverev was married and that his bride was pregnant.

'It wouldn't be fair to Daniil to have a big family wedding when his own brother can't be there.' Rachel reminded Libby of the reason they had chosen the quietest of celebrations. 'Do you feel as if you're missing out?'

'Missing out?' Libby's mouth gaped. 'This is my idea of a perfect wedding.'

It was.

Libby looked in the mirror once she had put on her dress—it was very simple, a soft ivory and more like a silk slip than a designer gown, but to her it was perfect.

She put on new soft ballet shoes and she had a bunch of palest pink peonies, roses and calla lilies, and she'd added anemones, too, because she'd loved them first.

'Am I showing?' Libby asked, because she was desperate to get a bump but it was still way too soon.

'You're only ten weeks,' Rachel pointed out.

They had been the happiest weeks of both hers and Daniil's lives.

'Do you think he's guessed about your surprise?' Rachel asked.

'No.' Libby smiled as they got into the car and Rachel drove them to the registry office.

They wouldn't be getting some random witness. Instead, Libby had called Marcus, and he and his own new wife Shirley were coming to the wedding today before they headed off on a cruise.

They were family, Libby had decided as the car pulled up and there, waiting, was Daniil.

'You don't look nervous,' she said, as he took her hand.

'Wolves are never nervous,' Daniil said. 'Anyway, why would I be anything other than happy today?'

Why indeed?

They walked into the old building and he stilled and the calm, always composed Daniil was at a loss for words when he saw Marcus and Shirley waiting for them.

'Thank you,' Daniil said to the man who had stepped in, who had guarded his precious photos for him and had respected his space.

'We wouldn't miss this for the world,' Marcus said.

It really was the tiniest of weddings, but it was loaded with love.

The least sentimental man put a ring on her finger, dotted with pink argyle diamonds, just because it was her favourite colour in the world.

'I love you.' He said words he'd never thought he would. 'And I will make sure you know that every day. You will always be my leading lady.'

It was her favourite role and one she could only have dreamed of till now. There in the spotlight of his love Libby felt she could fly.

'And I love you,' she said. 'I always will.'

There was cake for everyone, made by Shirley again, only this time without resentment so it tasted divine, and there was champagne for everyone except the bride, who didn't need bubbles to be fizzing with joy.

And then it was just them, husband and wife checking into a lavish London hotel with a different view, one that looked out at the palace where tomorrow they would sit at midday and wait and see if Sev came.

'I don't think he'll be there,' Daniil said, because tomorrow was five years to the day he should have met him.

'He might be,' Libby said. 'It's worth a try.'

'It is,' Daniil said.

Love was *always* worth the try, he'd now found out.

Love was the most precious gift and, Daniil found, with love had come hope.

He closed the drapes on the view and the possibilities of tomorrow as he focused on this special night.

He took his bride in his arms and Libby lifted her face to meet his kiss.

Tomorrow they would look for answers.

Tonight, though, for Daniil and Libby there were no questions, just the tender celebration of their love.

* * * * *

HOT-SHOT TYCOON, INDECENT PROPOSAL

HEIDI RICE

To Bryony, for knowing when the Elvis impersonator needs to be kicked out of the manuscript.

With special thanks to Eilis, who made sure Connor didn't sound like an extra from *The Quiet Man*.

CHAPTER ONE

'YOU can't do this. What if you get caught? He could have you arrested.'

Daisy Dean paused in the process of scoping out her neighbour's ludicrously high garden wall and slanted her best friend, Juno, a long-suffering look.

'He won't catch me,' Daisy replied in the same hushed tones. 'I'm practically invisible with all this gear on.'

She looked down at the clothes she'd borrowed from her fellow tenants at the Bedsit Co-op next door. Goodness, she looked like Tinkerbell the Terminator decked out in fourteen-year-old Cal's sagging black Levi's, his tiny mother Jacie's navy blue polo neck and Juno's two-sizes-too-small bovver boots.

She'd never been this invisible in her entire life. The one thing Daisy had inherited from her reckless and irresponsible mother was Lily Dean's in-your-face dress sense. Daisy didn't do monotones—and she didn't believe in hiding her light under a bushel.

She frowned. Except when she was on a mission to find her landlady's missing cat.

'Stop worrying, Juno, and give me the beanie.' She held out her hand and stared back up at the wall, which seemed to have grown several feet since she'd last looked at it. 'You'll have to give me a boost.'

Juno groaned, slapping the black woollen cap into Daisy's outstretched palm. 'This better not make me an accessory after the fact or something.' She bent over and looped her fingers together in a sling.

'Don't be silly.' Daisy shoved her curls under the cap and tugged it over her ears. 'It's not a crime. Not really.'

'Of course it's a crime.' Juno straightened from her crouch, her round, pretty face looking like the good fairy in a strop. 'It's called trespassing.'

'These are extenuating circumstances,' Daisy whispered as a picture of their landlady Mrs Valdermeyer's distraught face popped into her mind. 'Mr Pootles has been missing for well over a fortnight. And our antisocial new neighbour's the only one within a mile radius who hasn't had the decency to search his back garden.' She propped her hands on her hips. 'Mr Pootles could be starving to death and it's up to us to rescue him.'

'Maybe he looked and didn't find anything?' Juno said, her voice rising in desperation.

'I doubt that. Believe me, he's not the type to lose sleep over a missing cat.'

'How do you know? You've never even met the guy,' Juno murmured, wedging the tiniest slither of doubt into Daisy's crusading zeal.

'That's only because he's been avoiding us,' Daisy pointed out, the slither dissolving.

Their mysterious new neighbour had bought the double-fronted Georgian wreck three months ago, and had managed to gut it and rehab it in record time. But despite all Daisy's overtures since he'd moved in two weeks ago—the note she'd posted through his door and the message she'd relayed to his cleaning lady—he'd made no attempt to greet his neighbours at Mrs Valdermeyer's Bedsit Co-operative. Or join the search for the missing Mr Pootles.

In fact he'd been downright rude. When she'd dropped

off a plate of her special home-made brownies the day before in a last ditch attempt to get his attention, he hadn't even returned the plate, let alone thanked her for them. Clearly the man was too rich and self-centred to have any time for the likes of them—or their problems.

And then there were his dark, striking good looks to be considered. 'All you have to do is look at him,' Daisy continued, 'to see he's a you-know-what-hole with a capital A.'

Okay, so she'd only caught glimpses of the guy as he was striding down his front steps towards the snazzy maroon gas-guzzler he kept parked out front. At least six feet two, leanly muscled and what she guessed most people would term ruggedly handsome, the guy was what she termed full of himself. Even from a distance he radiated enough testosterone to make a woman's ovaries stand up and take notice—and she was sure he knew it.

Not that Daisy's ovaries had taken any notice, of course. Well, not much anyway.

Luckily for Daisy, she was now completely immune to men like her new neighbour. Arrogant, self-absorbed charmers who thought of women as playthings. Men like Gary, who'd sidled into her life a year ago with his come-hither smile, his designer suits and his clever hands and sidled right back out again three months later taking a good portion of her pride and a tiny chunk of her heart with him.

Daisy had made a pact with herself then and there—that she'd never fall prey to some good-looking playboy again. What she needed was a nice regular guy. A man of substance and integrity, who would come to love her and respect her, who wanted the same things out of life she wanted and preferably didn't know the difference between a designer label and a supermarket own brand.

Juno gave an irritated huff, interrupting Daisy's moment of truth. 'I still don't understand why you haven't just asked the guy about that stupid cat.'

A pulse of heat pumped under Daisy's skin. 'I tried to catch him the few times I spotted him, but he drives off so fast I would have had to be an Olympic sprinter.'

She'd suffer the tortures of hell before she'd admit the truth. That she'd been the tiniest bit intimidated by him, enough not to relish confronting him in person.

Juno sighed and bent down, linking her fingers together. 'Fine, but don't blame me if you get done for breaking and entering.'

'Stop panicking.' Daisy placed a foot in Juno's palms. 'I'm sure he's not even home. His Jeep's not parked out front. I checked.'

If she'd thought for a moment he might actually be in residence the butterflies waltzing about in her belly would have started pogoing like punk rockers. 'I'll be super-discreet. He'll never even know I was there.'

'There's one teeny-weeny problem with that scenario,' Juno said dryly. 'You don't do discreet, remember.'

'I can if I'm desperate,' Daisy replied. Or at least she'd do her best.

Ignoring Juno's derisive snort, Daisy reached up to climb the wall and felt the skintight polo neck rise up her midriff. She looked down to see a wide strip of white flesh reflecting in the streetlamp opposite and caught a glimpse of her red satin undies where the jeans sagged.

'Blast.' She dropped her arm and bounced down.

'What's the matter now?' Juno whispered.

'My tummy shows when I lift my arms.'

'So?'

Daisy frowned at her friend. 'So it totally ruins the camouflage effect.' She tapped her finger on her bottom lip. 'I know, I'll take off my bra.'

'What on earth for?' Juno snapped, getting more agitated by the second.

'The material's catching on the lace—it won't rise up as much.'

'But you can't,' Juno replied. 'You'll bounce.'

'It'll only be for a minute.' Daisy unclipped the bra and wriggled it out of one sleeve. She passed the much-loved concoction of satin, lace and underwiring to Juno.

Juno dangled it from her fingertips. 'What is this obsession you have with hooker underwear?'

'You're just jealous,' Daisy replied, turning back to the wall. Juno had always had a bit of a complex about her barely B-cups in Daisy's opinion.

She put her foot in Juno's sling and felt her breasts sway erotically under the confining fabric. Thank goodness no one would get close enough to spot her unfettered state. She'd always been proud to call herself a feminist, but she was way too well endowed to be one of the burn-your-bra variety.

'Right.' Daisy took a deep breath of the heavy, honey-suckle-flavoured air. 'I'm off.'

Grabbing hold of the top, she hauled herself up, her nipples tightening as she rubbed against the brick. Throwing her leg over, she straddled the wall with a soft grunt.

She peered through the leaves of a large chestnut tree and scanned the shadows of their neighbour's garden. Moonlight reflected off the windows at the back of the house. Daisy let out the breath she'd been holding. Phew, he definitely wasn't in.

'I still can't believe you're actually going to do this.' Juno scowled up at her from the shrubbery.

'We owe this to Mrs Valdermeyer—you know how much she adores that cat,' she whispered from her vantage position on the wall.

The truth was Daisy knew she owed her landlady much more than just a promise to find her cat.

When her mother, Lily, had announced she had found 'the one' again eight years ago, Daisy had opted to stay put.

She'd been sixteen, alone in London and terrified and Mrs Valdermeyer had come to her rescue. Mrs Valdermeyer had given her a home, and a security she'd never known before—which meant Daisy owed her landlady more than she could ever repay. And Daisy always paid her debts.

'And don't forget,' Daisy said urgently, warming to her subject, 'Mrs V could have sold the Co-op to developers a thousand times over and become a rich woman, but she hasn't. Because we're like family to her. And family stick together.'

At least Daisy had always felt they ought to. If she'd ever had brothers and sisters and a mum who was even halfway reliable she was sure that was how her own family would have been.

She looked back at the garden, gulped down the apprehension tightening her throat.

'I don't think Mrs Valdermeyer would expect you to get arrested,' Juno whispered in the darkness. 'And don't forget the scar on that guy's face. He doesn't look like the type who can take a joke.'

Daisy leaned forward, ready to slide down the other side of the wall. She stopped. Okay, maybe that scar was a bit of a worry. 'Do me a favour—if I don't come back in an hour, call the police.'

She could just make out Juno's muttered words as she edged herself down into the darkness.

'What for? So they can cart you off to jail?'

'Forget it, I'm not conjuring up a fiancée just to keep Melrose sweet.' Connor Brody tucked the phone into the crook of his shoulder and pulled the damp towel off his hips.

'He went ballistic after the dinner party,' Daniel Ellis, his business manager, replied, the panic in his voice clear all the way down the phone line from New York. 'I'm not joking,

Con. He accused you of trying to seduce Mitzi. He's threatening to lose the deal.'

Connor grabbed the sweat pants folded over the back of the sofa and tugged them on one-handed, cursing the headache that had been brewing all day—and Mitzi Melrose, a woman he never wanted to see again in this lifetime.

'She stuck her foot in my crotch under the table, Dan, not the other way around,' Connor growled, annoyed all over again by Mitzi's less-than-subtle attempts at seduction.

Not that Connor minded women who took the initiative, but Eldridge Melrose's trophy wife had been coming on to him all evening and he'd made it pretty damn clear he wasn't interested. He didn't date married women, especially married women joined for better or worse to the billionaire property tycoon he was in the middle of a crucial deal with. Plus he'd never been attracted to women with more Botox and silicone in their body than common sense. But good old Mitzi had refused to take the hint and this was the result. A deal he'd been working on for months was in danger of going belly up through no fault of his.

'Come on, Con. If he backs out of the deal now we're back to square one.'

Connor walked across the darkened living room to the bar by the floor-to-ceiling windows, Danny's pleading whine not doing a damn thing for his headache. He rubbed his throbbing temple and splashed some whiskey into a shot glass. 'I'm not about to pretend to be engaged just to satisfy Melrose's delusions about his oversexed wife,' he rasped. 'Deal or no deal.'

Connor savoured the peaty scent of the expensive malt—so different from the smell of stale porter that had permeated his childhood—and slugged it back. The expensive liquor warmed his sore throat and reminded him how far he'd come. He'd once had to do things he wasn't proud of to survive, to get out. The stakes would have to be a lot higher than a simple business deal before he'd compromise his integrity like that again.

'Damn, Con, come off it.' Danny was still whining. 'You're blowing this way out of proportion. You must have a ton of women in your little black book who'd kill to spend two weeks at The Waldorf posing as your beloved. And I don't see it being any big hardship for you either.'

'I don't have a little black book.' Connor gave a gruff chuckle. 'Danny, what era are you living in? And even if I did, there's not one of the women I've dated who wouldn't take the request the wrong way. You give a woman a diamond ring, she's going to get ideas no matter what you tell her.'

Hadn't he gone through the mother of all break-ups only two months ago because he'd believed Rachel when she'd said she wasn't looking for anything serious? Just good sex and a good time. He'd thought they were both on the same page only to discover Rachel was in a whole different book—a book with wedding bells and baby booties on the cover.

Connor shuddered, metal spikes stabbing at his temples. No way was he opening himself up to that horror show again.

'I can't believe you'd throw this deal away when the solution's so simple.'

Connor heard Danny's pained huff, and decided he'd had enough of the whole debate.

'Believe it.' He put the glass down on the bar, winced as the slight tap reverberated in his sore head. 'I'll see you the week after next. If Melrose is bound and determined to cut off his nose to spite me, so be it,' he finished on a rasping cough.

'Hey, are you okay, buddy? You sound kind of rough.'

'Just fine,' Connor said, his voice brittle with sarcasm. He'd caught some bug on the plane back from New York that morning and now there was this whole cluster screw-up with Melrose and his wife to handle.

'Why don't you take a few days off?' Danny said gently. 'You've been working your butt off for months. You're not Superman, you know.'

'You don't say,' Connor said wryly, resting his aching forehead against the cool glass of the balcony doors and staring into the garden below. 'I'll be all right once I've a solid ten hours' sleep under my belt.' Which might have worked if he hadn't been wired with jet lag.

'I'll let you get to it,' Danny said, still sounding concerned. 'But think about taking a proper break. Haven't you just moved into that swanky new pad? Take a couple of days to relax and enjoy it.'

'Sure, I'll think about it,' he lied smoothly. 'See you round, Dan.'

He clicked off the handset and glanced round at the cavernous, sparsely furnished living room in the half light.

He'd bought the derelict Georgian house on a whim at auction and spent a small fortune refurbishing it, thanks to some idiot notion that at thirty-two he needed a more permanent base. Now the house was ready, it was everything he'd specified—open, airy, clean, modern, minimalist—but as soon as he'd moved in he'd felt trapped. It was a feeling he recognised only too well from his childhood. And he'd quickly accepted the truth, that permanence for him was always going to feel like a prison.

He turned back to the window. He reckoned a therapist would have a field day with that little nugget of information, but he had a simpler solution. He'd sell the house and move on. Make a nice healthy profit—and never be stupid enough to consider buying a place of his own again.

Some people needed roots, needed stability, needed for ever. He wasn't one of them. Hotels and rentals suited him fine. Brody Construction was all the legacy he wanted.

He dropped the handset on the sofa.

His shoulder muscles ached at the slight movement. Damn, he hadn't felt this sore since he was a lad and he'd woken up with the welts still fresh from dear old Da's belt. He squeezed his eyes shut. *Don't go there.*

Forcing the old bitterness away, he lifted his lids and spotted a flicker of movement in the garden below. He blinked and squinted, focussing on the shadowy wisp. Slowly but surely, the wisp morphed into a figure. A small figure clad suspiciously in black, which proceeded to crawl over one of the flowerbeds.

He jolted upright and braced his palm against the glass, his head screaming in protest as he strained to see. Then watched in astonishment as the intruder stood and dipped under one of the big showy shrubs by the back wall—a light strip of flesh flashing at its midriff.

'What the…?' The whisper scraped his throat raw as fury bubbled.

Damn it all to hell and back, could this day get any worse?

A surge of adrenaline masked his aching limbs and exploding head as he stalked across the living room and down the wide twin staircase. Whoever the little bastard was, and whatever they were about, they'd made a big mistake.

No one messed with Connor Brody.

For all the trappings of wealth and sophistication that surrounded him now, he'd grown up on Dublin's meanest streets and he knew how to fight dirty when he had to.

He might not want this place, but he wasn't about to let anyone else nick a piece of it.

CHAPTER TWO

'HERE, kitty, kitty. Come to Daisy. Nice kitty.' Daisy strained to keep her voice to a whisper as sweat pooled in her armpits and the coarse wool of the beanie cap made her head itch.

She scratched her crown, pulled the suffocating cap back over her ears and peered into the pitch dark under the hydrangea bush. Nothing.

Why hadn't she brought a torch? She huffed. And gave up. This was pointless. She'd almost broken her neck getting over the wall and had then spent ten long minutes searching the garden, gouging her thumb on one of the rose bushes in the process, and she still hadn't seen a blasted thing.

She crawled out from under the bush, her fingers sinking into the dirt as she tried to avoid squashing any of the plants in the flowerbed.

Raucous barking cut the still night air like a thunderclap. She clasped her hand to her throat and swallowed a shriek.

Her heartbeat kicked in again as she recognised the excited yips. Trust Mr Pettigrew's Jack Russell, Edgar, to give her a flipping heart attack—it had to be the most annoying dog on the planet.

She puffed out her cheeks and sucked on her sore thumb. Well, at least she could go back home now knowing she'd done her best to find the invisible Mr Pootles. Wherever he'd got to, it wasn't Mr Hot-Shot's back garden.

She stood, ready to walk back to the wall when the yapping cut off. The sound of a soft pad behind her had her glancing over her shoulder. She spotted the dark silhouette looming over her and had a split second to think. 'Oh, crap.'

A muscled forearm banded around her tummy and hauled her off her feet. Her breath whooshed out as her back connected with a solid wall of hot, naked male.

'Gotcha, you little terror,' muttered a deep voice.

She sucked in a quick breath ready to scream her lungs out, when a large hand slapped across her mouth—smothering her with the scent of sandalwood soap.

'No, you don't, lad,' the voice murmured, the hint of Irish in it only making it more terrifying. 'You're not calling your mates.'

She struggled against the band around her waist. It didn't budge.

Lifting her as if she weighed nothing at all, her captor hefted her back towards the house. The soap smell overwhelmed her as she listened to the grunts of her own muffled screams through the powertool now buzzing in her ears.

Daisy's head began to spin as tomorrow's tabloid headlines flashed across her mind. WOMAN SMOTHERED TO DEATH OVER MISSING CAT.

She kicked clumsily, connecting with thin air, and the baggy jeans slipped off her hips. Then the arm released and she landed hard on the ground, pitching head first onto the grass. As she scrambled up a hand grasped the waistband of her jeans and yanked.

'Hey, what's with the satin panties?' came the shocked shout from behind her.

She gasped, blood surging into her head as she lurched round and hauled the jeans back up to cover herself.

'Who the hell *are* you?' he yelled.

Silhouetted by the porch light, all she could make out of her captor were acres of bare chest, ominously black brows, waves of dark hair and impossibly broad shoulders.

Her whole body vibrated with fury as embarrassment exploded in her cheeks, but all that came out of her mouth was a pathetic yelp.

He reached forward and whipped the beanie cap off her head. She tried to grab for it but her hair cascaded down.

'You're a girl!'

She swiped her hair out of her eyes as outrage over-whelmed her. How dared he manhandle her and scare her half to death? She snatched the cap back. 'I'm not a girl,' she snapped, her voice returning at last. 'I'm a fully grown woman, you big bully.'

He took a step forward, towering over her. 'So what's a fully grown woman doing breaking into my house?'

She stumbled back, now holding the trousers in a death grip. Outrage gave way to common sense. What on earth was she doing arguing with the guy? He was twice her size and not in a very good mood if that threatening stance was any indication.

Forget standing her ground. Time to get the hell out of Dodge.

She turned to bolt. Too late—as strong fingers clamped on her arm.

'I don't think so, lady. I want some answers first.'

The forward momentum pulled her off her feet. 'Let me go,' she squeaked, tugging on her arm. His grip tightened as he dragged her backwards up the porch steps.

Panic welled up as he marched her through sliding glass doors into a massive open-plan kitchen. The smell of fresh varnish assaulted her nostrils and light blinded her as he snapped on a switch.

He hauled her past polished oak work surfaces and gleaming glass cabinets to a sunken seating area and shoved her, none too gently, into a leather armchair. 'Take a seat.'

She went to leap up but he grabbed the arms of the chair, caging her in. Heat radiated from his naked chest like a furnace, as did the heady scent of soap and man. She flinched at the fury in his face, which was now illuminated in every shockingly masculine detail.

A drop of water from his damp hair splashed onto her sweater. She shrank into the cool leather as the moisture sank into the fabric and touched her naked breasts.

Ice-blue eyes dipped to her chest and her traitorous nipples chose that precise moment to draw into excruciatingly hard points. Heat flared in her face. Why had she taken off her bra? Could he tell?

'Stay put,' he snarled, his laser-beam gaze lifting back to her face. 'Or, so help me, I'll give you the spanking you deserve.'

She began to shake, her heart wedged in her throat. Up close and rather too personal, the stark male beauty of his face was staggering. Dark slashing brows and angular cheekbones rough with stubble did nothing to detract from the cool, iridescent blue of his eyes, nor the livid white scar twitching against the tensed muscles of his jaw. As his gaze swept over her she noticed he had the longest eyelashes she'd ever seen.

They ought to have made those arctic eyes look girly. They didn't.

'You can't spank me,' she whispered, then wished she hadn't as his eyes darted back to hers.

'Don't tempt me,' he rasped.

Daisy's heartbeat sped up to warp speed. *Do not antagonise him, you silly cow.*

He straightened and raked a hand through his hair, pushing the thick black waves back from a high forehead. His gaze slipped to her chest again.

Her cheeks got several crucial shades hotter.

'You can stop shaking,' he said at last. 'You're in luck. I don't hurt women.'

The contempt in his voice was too much. Her temper flared, destroying the vow she'd made moments before. 'You just scared the crap out of me, Atilla. What the heck do you call that?'

'You were in my garden. Uninvited,' he sneered. Not sounding anywhere near as apologetic as he should. 'What did you expect, a red carpet?'

Before she could come up with a decent comeback, he turned and stalked over to the kitchen's central aisle. She noticed a curious hitch in his stride. Why was he walking as if he were on a swaying ship?

He bent over the double sink. Her eyes lifted to his back and she stifled a gasp, the question forgotten. A criss-cross of pale ridges stood out against the smooth brown skin of his shoulder blades. Daisy swallowed convulsively.

Whoever this guy was, he was not the rich, pampered, narcissistic playboy she'd assumed.

Coupled with the mark on his face, the scars on his back proved he'd lived a hard life, marred by violence. Daisy bit into her bottom lip, clasped her hands to stop them trembling and dismissed the little spurt of pity at the thought of how much those wounds must once have hurt.

Do not make him mad, again, Daisy. You don't know what he might be capable of.

He filled a glass with water, then turned back to her. Propping his butt against the counter, he crossed his bare feet at the ankles and stared. She shivered, suddenly freezing in the heat of the late-July evening.

He downed the water in three quick gulps. Daisy swallowed, realising her own throat was drier than the Gobi Desert. Probably the result of the extreme emotional trauma he'd put her through. She wasn't about to ask him for a glass, though. Keeping her mouth firmly shut at this juncture seemed like the smart choice.

He put the glass down on the counter. The sharp snap made her jump. He coughed, the sound harsh and hollow as it rumbled up his chest, and rubbed his forehead against his upper arm. Bracing his hands against the counter, he dropped his chin to his chest, gave a weary sigh.

Daisy let a breath out between her teeth. With those broad shoulders slumped he looked a little less threatening. When he didn't speak for a while, or look up, she wondered if he'd forgotten her. She eased out of the chair. The treacherous leather creaked, and his head snapped up.

'Sit the hell down,' he said, the huskiness of his voice doing nothing to disguise the snarl. 'We're not through.'

She sat down with a plop. He still looked enormous, and she suspected he was doing his level best to intimidate her, but she could see bruised smudges of fatigue under his eyes.

She ruthlessly quashed another little prickle of sympathy. Whatever was ailing him, he'd terrified her, threatened her and quite possibly let poor Mr Pootles die a long and painful death.

She'd be better off reserving her sympathy for the Big Bad Wolf.

'What exactly do you want?' she asked, pleased when her voice barely wavered.

He crossed his arms over his chest and cocked an eyebrow, saying nothing.

Completely of their own accord, her eyes zeroed in on the dark curls of hair on his chest, which tapered down a washboard-lean six-pack and arrowed to a thin line beneath the drooping waistband of his sweat pants. The worn grey cotton hung so low on his hips, she could see the hollows defining his pelvis. One millimetre lower, and she'd be able to see a whole lot more.

The errant thought had Daisy's thigh muscles clenching.

Her gaze shot back up to find him watching her. The heat flared across her chest and up her neck. Did he know where her thoughts had just wandered?

He rocked back on his heels, still studying her in that disconcerting way, and tightened his arms over his magnificent chest. Her heart gave an annoying kick as his biceps flexed, and her eyes flicked to a faded tattoo of the Celtic cross on his left arm.

She gulped, struggling to ignore the long liquid pull low in her belly. What was wrong with her? The guy might have the tanned, sculpted body of a top male model, but Daisy Dean did not get turned on by arrogant, self-righteous bullies, however buff they might be.

'So let's hear it,' he said, his soft, but oddly menacing tone cutting the oppressive silence at last. 'What were you about in my garden?'

She thrust her chin up, determined not to feel guilty. Her mission had been innocent enough, even if it now seemed somewhat suicidal. 'I was looking for my landlady's cat.'

He coughed, the dry rumble making her wince. 'How much of an idiot do you think I am?'

She bit back the pithy retort that wanted to pop out of her mouth.

'His name's Mr Pootles. He's a large ginger tom with a squinty eye,' she hurried on, despite the sceptical lift of his eyebrow. 'And he's been missing for two weeks.'

'And you couldn't come to the door and ask me if I'd seen him? Because why exactly?'

'I did, but you never answer your door,' she said, righteous indignation building. If he'd answered his damn door in the last two weeks she wouldn't be in this predicament. In fact, now she thought about it, this was all his fault.

'I've been out of the country this past week,' he shot back at her.

'Mr Pootles has been missing for two. And anyway I left messages with your housekeeper—and brownies,' she added.

His eyebrows shot up. Why had she mentioned the brownies? It made her sound like a stalker.

'Look, it doesn't matter.' She stood up, forcing what she hoped was a contrite look onto her face. 'I'm sorry I disturbed you. I didn't think you were in and I was worried about the cat. It could have been starving to death in your backyard.'

His eyes swept her figure again, making her pulse go haywire. 'Which doesn't explain why you dressed up like a burglar to come look for it,' he said wryly.

'Well, I…' How did she explain that, without sounding as if she were indeed a lunatic? 'I really should be going.'

Please let me get out of here with at least a small shred of my dignity intact.

'The cat obviously isn't here and I need to get back…' She stumbled to a halt, edging her way round the chair.

'Not yet, you don't,' he said, but to her astonishment his lips quirked.

She blinked, not believing her eyes. Was that a smile?

'I got the brownies, by the way. They were tasty.' He rubbed his belly, his lips lifting some more. The smile became a definite smirk.

'Why didn't you answer my messages, then?' And what was so damn funny all of a sudden?

'They probably got lost in translation,' he said easily. 'My cleaner doesn't speak much English.'

He straightened, swayed violently and grabbed hold of the work surface.

'What's wrong?' Daisy stepped towards him. His face had drained of colour and looked worn and sallow in the harsh light.

He put a hand up, warding her off. 'Nothing,' he growled, all traces of amusement gone.

She could see he was lying. But decided not to call him on it. After the way she'd been treated he could be at death's door for all she cared.

He let go of the counter top, but didn't look all that steady. 'I know what happened to your cat.'

It was the last thing she'd expected him to say. 'You do?'

'Uh-huh, follow me.'

Gripping the edge of the centre aisle, he made his way across the kitchen. He moved with the fragile precision of someone in their eighties, his bare feet padding on the floor.

Daisy tramped down on her instinctive concern as she followed him. She hated to see people suffering, and for all his severe personality problems this guy was obviously suffering. But he'd made it clear he didn't want her sympathy, or her help.

He shuffled to a small door in the far wall and opened it. Leaning heavily on it, he beckoned her over with one finger.

As she stepped forward he pulled the door wide. She heard the soft mewing sound and glanced down. Gasping, she dropped to her knees. Nestled in an old blanket beneath a state-of-the-art immersion heater was Mr Pootles—and his four nursing kittens.

Make that Mrs Pootles.

'The cat showed up after I moved in.' She glanced up at the husky voice, saw the hooded blue eyes watching her. 'She had no collar and didn't want to be petted so I took her for a stray.'

Daisy studied the cat and her kittens. A saucer of milk had been placed next to the blanket. She reached out a finger and stroked one of the miniature bodies. The warm bundle of fluff wiggled. Daisy sat back on her haunches.

Maybe the Big Bad Wolf wasn't as bad as he seemed.

A little of Daisy's anger and indignation drained away, to be replaced by something that felt uncomfortably like shame.

'She had the kittens ten days back,' he continued, the hoarse tone barely more than a whisper. 'The cleaner's been looking after them. They seem to be doing okay.'

'I see,' she said quietly.

Daisy stood, resigned to eating the slice of humble pie she'd so cleverly served herself by climbing over his garden wall in the middle of the night.

Still, she took a few seconds to collect herself, brushing invisible fluff off Cal's jeans and then folding down the waistband so they'd stay up without her having to cling onto them. Humble pie had always been hard for her to swallow. Having delayed as long as possible, she cleared her throat and made eye contact.

He was studying her, his expression inscrutable. She might have guessed he wasn't going to make this easy for her.

'I'm awfully sorry, Mr...?'

'Brody, Connor Brody,' he said, a penetrating look in those crystal eyes. Her pulse skidded.

'Mr Brody,' she murmured, her cheeks flaming. 'What I did was unforgivable. I hope there are no hard feelings.'

She held out her hand, but instead of taking it he glanced at it, then to her astonishment his lips curved in a lazy grin. The slow, sensuous smile softened the harsh lines of his face, making him look even more gorgeous—and even more arrogant—if that were possible.

Daisy held back a sigh as her heart rate kicked into overdrive.

How typical. When Daisy Dean made an idiot of herself, it couldn't be in front of an ordinary mortal. It had to be in front of someone who looked like a flipping movie star.

'So are your cat burgling days behind you, now?' he said at last, the roughened voice doing nothing to hide his amusement. He tilted his head to take in every inch of her attire, right down to Juno's Doc Martens. 'That'd be a shame, as the outfit suits you.'

She dropped her hand. Make that a movie star with a warped sense of humour.

'Enjoy it while you can,' she said dryly, trying hard to see the humour in the situation—which was clearly at her expense. She knew perfectly well she looked a complete fright.

'And what would your name be?' he asked.

'Daisy Dean.'

'It's been a pleasure, Daisy Dean,' he said, still smirking as if she were the funniest thing he'd ever seen.

'I'll come back tomorrow to get the cats, if that's okay?' she said stiffly, clinging to her last scrap of dignity.

'I'll be waiting,' he said. The hacking cough that followed wiped the smirk off his face, but only for a moment. 'I've a question, though, before you go.'

'What is it?' she asked warily, the teasing glint in his eyes irritating her.

Honestly, some men would flirt with a stone.

He didn't say anything straight away. Instead, his gaze roamed down to her chest and took its own sweet time making its way back to her face. 'Did you lose the bra on your way over the wall?'

Colour flared in her cheeks and her backbone snapped straight. That did it. 'I'm glad you find this so hilarious, Mr Brody.'

'You have no idea, Daisy,' he said, coughing out a laugh, his pure aquamarine eyes sparkling with mischief.

'I'm off,' she said through clenched teeth, not even trying to keep the frost out of her voice.

She might have been wrong about the cat, but she hadn't been wrong about him. He was an arrogant, overbearing, insufferable, full-of-himself—

A hissed expletive interrupted her cataloguing of his many character flaws.

She turned, watching in astonishment as he stumbled and then collapsed. The thud of his knees hitting the laminated floor made her wince.

She crouched beside him, her resentment fading fast as she took in his pallid complexion and the tremors racking his body. 'Mr Brody, are you okay?'

'Yes,' he hissed, a thin sheen of moisture popping out on his forehead.

She pressed the back of her hand to his brow, felt the scorching heat as he jerked back. 'You're burning up, Mr Brody.'

'Stop calling me that, for Christ's sake.' His head snapped up, the headache clear in his bloodshot eyes. 'The name's Connor.'

'Well, Connor, you've got yourself a very impressive fever. You need to see a doctor.'

'I'm okay,' he said, gripping the work surface. She offered her hand, but he shrugged it off as he struggled onto his feet, the muscles in his arms bulging as he hauled himself upright.

She could see the effort had cost him as he stood with his hands braced on the polished wood. His chest heaved in ragged pants and the fine sheen of sweat turned to rivulets running down his temples.

'You can leave any time now.' He grunted without looking round.

She came to stand next to him, could feel the heat and resentment pulsing off him. 'What? When I'm having so much fun watching you suffer?'

The tremor became a shake. 'Get lost, will you?'

She rolled her eyeballs. Men! What exactly was so terrible about asking for help? Propping herself against his side, she put an arm round his waist. 'How far to your bedroom?'

'There's a spare room across the hall.' The words had the texture of sandpaper scraping over his throat. 'Which I can get to under my own steam.'

She doubted that, given the way he was leaning on her to stay upright. 'Don't be silly,' she said briskly. 'You can hardly walk.'

To her surprise, he didn't put up any more protests as she led him out of the kitchen and across a hallway. The spare room was as palatial as expected, with wide French doors leading out into the garden. She eased him down onto the large divan bed in the dim light, his skin now slick with sweat. He shivered violently, his teeth chattering as he spoke.

'Fine, now leave me be.'

He sounded so annoyed she smiled. The tables had certainly turned. She didn't have long to savour the moment though as brutal coughs rocked his chest.

'I'm calling the doctor.'

'It's only a cold.' The protest didn't sound convincing punctuated by the harsh coughing.

'More like pneumonia,' she said.

'No one gets pneumonia in July.' He tried to say something else, but his shadowy form convulsed on the bed as he succumbed to another savage coughing fit.

She rushed back into the kitchen, spotted the phone on the far wall and pumped in the number for her local GP. Maya Patel lived two streets over and owed her a favour since the mother-and-baby club fund-raiser she'd helped organise a month ago. Her friend sounded sleepy when she picked up. Daisy rattled out her panicked plea and Connor's address.

'Fine,' Maya said wearily. 'You need to get his temperature down. Try dousing him with ice water, open the windows and take his clothes off. I'll be there as soon as I can,' she finished on a huge yawn and hung up.

Daisy returned to the bedroom armed with a bowl of ice water and a tea towel. The hideous coughing had stopped, but when she got closer to the bed she could feel the heat pumping off her patient. He'd sweated right through the track pants, which clung to his powerful thighs like a second skin.

She flipped the lamp on by the bed to find him watching her, the feverish light of delirium intensifying the blue of his irises.

'The doctor said to try and get the fever down,' she said.

She took his silent stare as consent and dipped the cloth in the water. She wrung it out and draped it over his torso. He moaned, the sinews of his arms and neck straining. She wiped the towel over his chest and down his abdomen. Her heart rate leaped as he sucked in a breath and the rigid muscles quivered under her fingertips.

The cloth came away warm to the touch.

'Dr Patel's on her way,' she said gently. 'Is there anyone you want me to call? Anyone you need here?'

He shook his head and whispered something. She couldn't hear him, so she leaned down to place her ear against his lips.

Hot breath feathered across her ear lobe and sent a shiver of awareness down her spine. 'There's no one I need, Daisy Dean,' he murmured, in a barely audible whisper. 'Not even you.'

She straightened, looked into his face and saw the vulnerability he was determined to hide.

He might not want to need her, but right now he did and Daisy had a rule about people in need—you had to do your best to help them, whether they wanted you to or not.

She rinsed the cloth, wrung it out and placed it on his forehead. He tensed against the chill, his big body shivering.

'That's a shame, tough guy,' she said as she stroked his brow. 'Because I'm afraid you're stuck with me until you're strong enough to throw me out.'

Connor closed his eyes, the blessed cool on his brow beating back the inferno that threatened to explode out of his ears.

Every single muscle in his body throbbed in agony but those cool, efficient strokes, over his cheeks, across his chest, down his arms, doused the flames, if only for a short while.

He'd always hated it when his sisters had fussed over him as a kid, trying to tend the wounds their father had inflicted in one of his drunken rages. Even then he'd hated to be beholden to anyone. Hated to feel dependent. But as his eyes flickered open he was pathetically grateful to see his pretty little neighbour leaning over him. He stared at her, taking in the clear, almost translucent skin and the serene, capable look on her face as she soothed the brutal pain. She reminded him of the alabaster Madonna in St Patrick's Church, which had fascinated him as a boy, when he'd still believed prayers could be answered.

But then his Virgin bit into her full lower lip and shifted on the edge of the bed to dip the cloth back in the water bowl. His gaze dropped, taking in the enticing movement of her breasts and the outline of erect nipples against her skintight top. Despite the heat blurring his senses and the pain stabbing at his skull, Connor felt the rush of response in his loins.

He shifted uncomfortably and she turned towards him. Flame-red curls outlined her head like a halo and the vivid jade-green eyes grew larger in her gamine face.

She placed gentle fingers on his forehead, pushed back the hair that had fallen across his brow. 'Try to get some sleep, Mr Brody. The doctor will be here shortly.'

The desperate urge to take back what he'd said, to ask her not to leave, overwhelmed him. He opened his mouth to say the words, but nothing came out other than a guttural murmur. He grasped her wrist, grimacing as his shoulder cramped. He had to get her attention, make her stay, but however hard he tried he couldn't make a coherent sound.

'Don't talk, you'll only tire yourself out.' She took his hand in hers, folded her small fingers round his palm and squeezed. 'It's okay, I won't leave you,' she said, as if she'd read his mind.

He shut his eyes, let himself fall into the fiery oblivion, his mind clinging onto one last disturbing thought.

Would wanting to see his angel of mercy naked send him straight to hell?

CHAPTER THREE

DAISY placed Connor's hand carefully by his side, listened to the harsh pants of his breathing as he fell into a fitful sleep and then ran all three of Maya's instructions back through her mind—one of which she'd been pretending she hadn't heard.

She nipped over to the room's French doors, unlocked the latch and flung them wide. Maybe two out of three would do the trick. But the evening air was suffocatingly still, creating no respite from the heat.

Daisy sat back on the bed. She chewed her lip and concentrated on wiping the cloth over the contours of Brody's upper body. She applied the cooling linen to his arms and shoulders, and listened to the low groans as he struggled with the fever.

After five agonisingly long minutes, it was clear the fever had no intention of abating. If anything it seemed to be getting worse, the ice water now lukewarm in the bowl. Daisy wiped her own brow, cursing her smothering outfit for the umpteenth time that night.

Where was Maya? Shouldn't she have been here by now? But even as she registered the thought she knew it was a delaying tactic.

Brody shifted on the bed, his movements stiff and uncomfortable.

What was her problem? She should just take off Brody's sweat pants and be done with it. She was being ridiculous, behaving like a silly schoolgirl, when she was a mature, sensible and sexually confident woman.

Good grief, she'd seen naked men before. She'd lost her virginity at nineteen, to sweet, geeky Terry Mason. She wasn't exactly prolific when it came to partners and some of them had definitely been more memorable than others. But none of her relationships had been disastrous enough to give her a complex about nudity. Hers or anyone else's.

Until now.

Okay, Brody was a stranger, and his physique had affected her rather alarmingly already. But she could hardly let the poor bloke suffer because she'd had a sudden, inexplicable attack of modesty. And anyhow, this wasn't remotely sexual, she was only trying to get his temperature down until Maya arrived. Plus, he probably had underwear on. There was absolutely no need to worry.

That vain hope was crushed like a bug when Daisy peeked under his track pants and spotted the dark, springy wisps of hair.

She let go of the damp waistband so fast it snapped back into place. Brody moaned, sweat beading on his forehead in the lamplight.

Calm down, Daisy, stop being a ninny. You can do this. You have to.

She'd just ignore her pounding pulse and her quivering ovaries.

Right. She got up to look for some fresh linen, reasoning she'd need a sheet once she got the sweat pants off, to preserve his modesty. Not that she thought he had a great deal from his cheeky remark about her bra, but it seemed she had more than enough for both of them.

It took her approximately two seconds to find the brand-new bed linen in the dresser drawer. After spending a full minute undoing the packaging and snapping out the sheets, she was all out of time-wasting tactics.

Perching on the edge of the bed, she shook Brody's shoulder.

'I have to take your sweat pants off, Mr Brody. They're soaked and we need to get the fever down.'

No response, just another hoarse groan. Fine, she wasn't going to get his permission. She'd just have to hope he didn't sue her when he woke up and found himself naked.

She hooked her fingers in the waistband, pressed her thumbs into the damp fabric and sucked in a breath. She turned her face away, heat pumping into her cheeks as she eased the garment over his hips. Almost immediately, something halted its progress. She tugged harder, he grunted and the fabric bounced over the impediment.

A few moments more of give, and then the sweat pants got stuck again.

She fisted her hands and tried the same trick twice, but this time the pants weren't budging. Anchored, she guessed, under his bottom. She huffed, not ready to look round. Whatever that bump had been a moment ago, she knew she'd got the pants far enough down now to afford her more of an eyeful than was good for her blood pressure.

She squeezed her eyes shut, gripping the band of elastic harder, when he mumbled something and rolled towards her. As the trousers loosened Daisy sent up a quick prayer of thanks and gave them a swift yank. They slipped down before he flopped onto his back again. She was leaning so close to him now, she could feel the heat of his skin against the side of her face, and smell the musky and oddly pleasant scent of fresh male sweat and sandalwood soap.

Do not turn round. Do not turn round and look at him.

Daisy repeated the mantra in her head, staring at the open doorway and trying not to picture long, hard flanks roped with muscle as the silky hair on his thighs tickled the backs of her fingers. She gave a huff of relief as she peeled the sweat pants over his knees, inching along the edge of the bed as she went. The effort to keep her balance and resist the urge to look at him had sweat beading on her own brow. Concentrating hard, Daisy nearly toppled off the bed when her patient groaned again.

Daisy noticed the difference in sound immediately, her ears attuned to even the slightest change in tone. This groan didn't sound like the others, more a low, sensual moan than a painful grunt. Daisy puffed out a breath, damning her overactive imagination as her thigh muscles clenched and the sweet spot between them began to throb in earnest.

Get serious, woman. This situation is not erotic. Pretend you're undressing a sick child.

But however hard she tried, Daisy couldn't think of Brody as anything other than a man. A man in his prime. An extremely sexy, naked man who had something nestled between his thighs that had produced that resilient bounce.

As she was busy conjuring up some extremely inappropriate images to explain that damn bounce Daisy's luck ran out. The heavy, confining folds of the track pants locked around Brody's ankles. No matter how hard she tugged and pulled and yanked she couldn't unravel the sodden fabric and get the pants the rest of the way off.

Blast, it was no good, she'd have to look to sort out the tangle.

Keep your eyes down. Remember. Eyes on toes.

Muttering the new mantra, she swivelled her head and her eyes instantly snagged on something they shouldn't. Something that had her jaw dropping, her eyes widening and the liquid between her thighs turning to molten lava.

Wow!

She'd found the source of her bounce. And it was more erotic than anything she could have imagined on her own. Brody, it seemed, despite his fever, his delirium and his earlier exhaustion, was sort of turned on. His partial erection sat proud and long, angling towards his belly button.

Daisy swallowed past the rock lodged in her parched throat. She'd always been a firm believer that size didn't matter, but that was before she'd seen Connor Brody naked. Everything about the man was quite simply magnificent.

The sudden urge to run her fingertip along the ridge of swollen flesh was so all-consuming, Daisy had to fist her hands and force her gaze away. She stared at the ceiling and gritted her teeth. Utterly disgusted with herself.

How could she have admired his private parts like that? How could she have even considered touching them? How had she gone from frightened schoolgirl to raging nympho-maniac in the space of a few minutes?

What she'd almost done was unconscionable and unethi-cal, a gross invasion of his privacy and against everything she'd ever believed about herself. She had absolutely no right to take advantage of the poor man when he was deliri-ous and burning up with fever and needed her help.

She grabbed the sheet she'd laid out at the bottom of the bed and whisked it over him. It settled in a billowing wave over his lower half, but did nothing to disguise what was underneath. If anything, veiled in the expensive linen—the stark white standing out against his tanned skin—Connor Brody's naked body looked even more awe-inspiring.

She spent several seconds grappling with the sweat pants, finally freeing his feet, struggling to forget what she'd seen. But she couldn't.

Her eyes drifted back up and she noticed the small scar on his hip, which disappeared beneath the sheet. Her breath gushed out.

She'd always thought Gary had a beautiful body. Fit and perfectly proportioned, with that tantalising sprinkling of hair that had made her mouth water. Of course Gary had always thought he had a beautiful body too, which had taken the shine off a bit. But there was no getting round the fact that Gary compared to Brody was like Clark Kent compared to Superman.

Brody's long, lean limbs, toned muscles, the deep and, she now knew, all-over tan and that arresting face made quite a package all by themselves—not to mention his actual package, the memory of which was making Daisy feel as if she were the one with a fever—but even more tantalising was the hint of danger about him, of something not quite tame.

One thing was for sure, Gary naked had never had the physical effect on her Brody was having right this instant—and the man wasn't even conscious.

She couldn't catch her breath. Her skin felt tight and itchy and nothing short of a nuclear explosion had detonated at her core. And her ovaries weren't just quivering, they were doing the rock-a-hula—with full Elvis accompaniment.

Daisy frowned, contemplating what her unprecedented reaction to a naked Connor Brody might mean—none of the options being good—when the doorbell buzzed.

She leaped off the bed so fast she tripped on the carpet and almost fell flat on her face.

Brody must have heard her, because his eyelids flickered and he grunted before turning onto his side. Unfortunately, he took the sheet with him, flashing Daisy the most delicious rear end she'd ever set eyes on. She yanked the sheet back to cover his bare butt before her blood pressure shot straight through the roof.

Her heartbeat racing and her pulse pounding in her ears, she headed down the corridor to the front door. She took several deep breaths as she fumbled with the latch.

Get a hold of yourself. He's just a good-looking bloke and, from his rough, arrogant behaviour earlier, not a very nice one at that.

She tugged the door open to see her friend and local GP Maya Patel on the other side.

'This had better be good, Daze.' The harassed doctor marched past her with a loud huff, toting her black bag under her arm, her usually immaculate hair falling in disarray down the back of a two-piece track suit. 'I hope you realise I can't actually treat this guy as he's not registered with our practice. I could end up getting sued if any—'

She stopped in mid-sentence to gape at Daisy. 'Blimey, that's a new look for you. What are you? In mourning or something?'

Yes, for my nice, sensible, discerning libido, Daisy thought wryly.

'It's a long story,' she said as she led the way down the hall. The less Maya knew about the situation, the better.

'Who is this bloke anyway?' Maya asked, following Daisy into the darkened room.

'I told you, my new neighbour.' *And the harbinger of nymphomania.* 'I called round to ask about Mr Pootles and he collapsed in front of me.' *Sort of.*

'Let's take a look at him.' Maya sat on the edge of the bed, and plopped her bag on the floor. 'What's his name again?'

'Connor Brody.'

Maya touched his shoulder. 'Connor, I'm Dr Patel. I'm here to examine you.' She moved her hand to his brow when he failed to reply. 'He's certainly got quite a temperature,' she said, lifting her hand. 'How long has he been out?'

Daisy glanced at her watch, and realised he'd only collapsed about fifteen minutes ago, even though it felt like a lifetime. She relayed everything she knew to Maya, who began rummaging around in her bag.

'Would it be okay if I popped next door while you examine him?' Daisy asked. 'I'll be right back as soon as I tell Juno what's going on.'

'Sure, it shouldn't take long,' Maya replied, fishing a thermometer and a stethoscope out of the bag. 'Looks like this nasty twenty-four-hour flu bug that's been doing the rounds to me, but I'll check his vitals to make sure it's nothing more serious.'

Daisy high-tailed it out of the room. She did not want any more flashes of Connor Brody's anatomy just yet. She'd had enough already to keep her in lurid erotic fantasies for weeks.

'Have you completely lost your marbles?'

Daisy ignored Juno's pained shout as she walked past her down the corridor to her bedsit, the towel wrapped tight around her freshly showered body. 'I've got to go back there. He's really ill. I can't leave him to fend for himself.'

'Why not? You don't know the first thing about him.' Juno followed her into her room and slumped down on the bed. Her brows lowered ominously. 'What if he gets violent?'

'Don't be melodramatic. I told you, that was a misunderstanding,' Daisy said, riffling through her wardrobe. Connor Brody getting violent was one of the few things she wasn't worried about. 'He looked after Mrs Valdermeyer's cat. I think I've misjudged him. He's not a bad guy.' *Well, not in that way.*

She pulled out her favourite dress, a simple bias-cut cotton sheaf printed with bright pink blossoms. 'Once the fever's broken and I'm sure he's okay, I'll leave.' She certainly didn't want to be around the guy when he had all his faculties back. Brody unconscious was quite devastating enough, thank you very much.

'But it's the middle of the night, he's a stranger and you'll be in the house alone with him,' Juno whined.

Daisy paused in the act of slipping on her hooker underwear. 'I'll be perfectly safe. Apart from anything else, he's unconscious.' She presented her back to Juno after tugging on her dress. 'Here, zip me up. I told Maya I'd be back straight away.'

Juno continued to grumble about personal safety as she

zipped Daisy into her dress. Daisy tuned her friend out as she spritzed patchouli perfume on her wrists, put on her bangles and brushed the tangles out of her newly washed hair.

She knew why Juno was a pessimist, why she hid behind baggy dungarees and a scowl, and why she always saw the cloud instead of the silver lining. Juno had been hurt badly once, very badly. She didn't trust men. Which really was rather ironic, Daisy thought as she stared at herself in the mirror. After Daisy's grossly inappropriate behaviour in their neighbour's spare bedroom, Brody wasn't the one who couldn't be trusted.

'Why are you getting dolled up?'

Daisy stopped dead, her lip gloss in mid-air. 'What?' She met Juno's censorious gaze in the mirror.

'You're all dolled up. What's that about?'

'I am not,' Daisy replied, mortally offended. But as she focussed on her reflection she could see Juno had a point. The figure-flattering dress, the sparkle of bangles and beads, the signature scent of patchouli, not to mention the make-up she'd been applying, made it look as if she were planning a night on the town, not a night spent nursing a sick man. Shocked and a little dismayed, she shoved the lip gloss back in her make-up bag.

She most definitely was not dressing up for Brody's benefit; the very thought was ludicrous. She didn't even like the guy.

Daisy slipped on her battered Converse, forgoing the beaded Indian sandals she'd already pulled out of the closet. 'I'm not dressed up—this is me getting comfortable,' she said lamely.

She pretended she didn't hear Juno's grunted, 'Yeah, right,' as her best friend trailed after her.

'Don't wait up,' Daisy said, closing the door to her bedsit. 'I'm not sure when I'll be back.'

'Be careful,' Juno said, giving her one last considering look.

The crooked banisters of the old Georgian house creaked as Daisy made her way down the stairs. She noticed the peeling paint as she opened the front door, the patched plaster on the stoop. The house's imperfections had always made her feel comforted and secure. As she walked the few steps to Brody's door she couldn't help comparing Mrs Valdermeyer's cosy wreck of a house to the sleek, impersonal perfection of its neighbour.

Daisy sighed as she walked in.

The sight of Brody's naked body might have short-circuited her hormones, but she was not going to allow it to short-circuit her brain cells too. The very last thing she needed was for anything to happen between her and her arrogant new neighbour. He might be dishy, but she'd only needed to spend a few minutes in his company—and his home—to know he was so not right for her it wasn't even funny.

'He'll probably drift in and out until the temperature breaks,' Maya Patel announced, slinging her black bag under her arm. 'Keep dousing him with ice water. And if you can, get some more paracetamol down him in four hours' time.'

Daisy nodded, the butterflies having a ball in her stomach at the thought of the long night ahead.

'Are you sure it's not serious?' Daisy asked. Like most doctors, Maya didn't seem to think anything short of double pneumonia was worth getting excited about.

'I'm sure he'll be fine once he's sweated it out of his system. His temperature's hovering around one hundred and two, but that's to be expected. If it gets any higher give me a call. But his breathing's okay and he's a young, healthy guy.' Maya smiled at Daisy. 'Actually, if I wasn't here in a professional capacity, not to mention married and a mother of three children—I'd say he was a total hunk.'

Daisy dropped her head to concentrate on undoing the front door latch, her cheeks boiling.

'He's been in the wars a few times,' Maya continued. 'But he seems to have come through them surprisingly well.'

'You mean the scars on his back?' Daisy asked as she yanked the heavy door open.

'Yeah, do you know where he got them?'

'No, I hardly know the guy,' Daisy replied. Then her curiosity got the better of her. 'What's your professional opinion?'

'Old, probably from before he hit puberty would be my guess, but I'm no expert,' Maya said matter-of-factly, then chuckled as she stepped onto the stoop. 'And why, might I ask, do you care if you hardly know the guy?'

Daisy struggled to come up with an answer that wouldn't sound totally suspicious. She might as well not have bothered.

'Ah-ha.' Maya pointed an accusing finger at her. 'I thought so. Seems I'm not the only one who thinks our patient is a hunk.'

'He's okay,' Daisy replied flatly, praying her rosy cheeks weren't a total giveaway.

Maya jogged down the front steps. 'Let me know how he's doing tomorrow if the fever still hasn't broken.' She turned by the kerb and wiggled her eyebrows at Daisy. 'And keep an eye on your own temperature, Daze. Being in a room with a guy that hunky and that naked all night long can be hard work.' She winked. 'But I'm sure you're up to the job.'

She laughed as Daisy's cheeks shot from rosy to beetroot, and climbed into her car.

Daisy locked the front door and leaned back against it, focussing on the room down the hall where her hunk of a patient awaited.

A platoon of butterflies dive-bombed under her breastbone.

Hard work indeed. Maya didn't know the half of it.

CHAPTER FOUR

CONNOR awoke with a start to the dazzle of morning sunlight. The shadows from the long, traumatic night still lingered at the edges of his consciousness.

He squinted, threw his arm up to ward off the glare, and noticed several things at once. The hammer in his head had quit banging, his muscles had stopped throbbing in time with it and he was no longer sleeping in a sauna. He eased his arm down as his eyes adjusted to the light, gazed out at the leafy old chestnut in his back garden, and the last of the dark disappeared.

Hell, it was good not to feel as if he'd gone six rounds with the champ any more.

How long had he been out? He didn't have a clue. He caught a whiff of perfume: flowery, spicy and wildly erotic. Recollections from the night before washed over him: the pain, the heat, the terror. But more vivid was the recollection of calm words, of whispered reassurances, of firm hands soothing him back to oblivion when the cruel flashbacks had wrenched him to the surface. And all the good memories were wrapped in that enticing scent.

She'd stayed with him. Just as she'd promised.

He pushed up on his elbows as panic sprinted up his spine.

Where is she? Has she left?

His heartbeat slowed when he spotted her curled up in the armchair across the room. He drank in the sight of her—like the icy water she'd made him sip through the night—then felt like a fool.

When had he turned into such a girl? The nightmares had stalked him on and off throughout his life, always catching him at a weak moment, but he'd learned to handle them a long time ago. They didn't bother him now the way they once had. It was good of her to stay last night, to see him through the fever and the familiar demons it had brought with it, but he didn't need her here.

But as he gazed at her a smile curved his lips. He might not need her, but she was still grand to look at in the daylight.

He folded his arms behind his head, relaxed into the pillows and indulged himself.

She'd changed her cat-burglar outfit, which was kind of a shame. The creased summer dress did amazing things for her figure, but the hint of satin at the plunging neckline, which he guessed matched her panties, meant her nipples were no longer clearly visible. Still, the pale, plump flesh of her cleavage was some compensation.

Her rich red hair, which had been springing out all over her head last night as if she'd had an electric shock, fell in soft unruly curls to her shoulder, framing high cheekbones. His lips quirked as his gaze wandered to her feet, which were folded under her bum, and he spotted a pair of battered blue basketball boots tied with lurid green laces.

The funky mix of styles suited her. From the little he could remember of last night, before he'd passed out, she'd been headstrong and prickly as hell—with a surprisingly soft centre when her angel-of-mercy tendencies had come charging to the rescue.

He sat up and swung his legs off the bed, glad that they didn't even wobble as he stood up. He wrapped the sheet around his waist, and his smile widened as he spotted his sweat pants neatly folded at the end of the bed. She must have stripped him. The smile became a grin. What he wouldn't give to have been conscious at that moment.

He stretched, yawned and rubbed his throat—pleased to discover the rawness gone—but kept his eyes on his angel of mercy.

Jesus, but she was pretty, in a cute, off-the-wall way. Not his usual type for sure, but then he considered himself very flexible where women were concerned.

Despite the horrors of the previous night, desire stirred. Then his stomach growled, interrupting the erotic direction of his thoughts—and reminding him all he'd eaten in the last twenty-four hours was her brownies.

The memory of the rich chocolate squares—crusty on the outside with a luxuriously moist centre—had his senses stirring again and his stomach giving another loud rumble of protest. She didn't move, her breasts rising and falling in steady rhythm. Connor's heart stuttered. She really had exhausted herself on his behalf. No one had ever done that before.

Once you factored in the gift of the brownies and her mad mission to save her landlady's cat, it occurred to Connor his sweet and captivating neighbour was quite the little Good Samaritan. Definitely not his type, then. But he still ought to thank her for being so neighbourly. At the very least he should show her there were no hard feelings for sneaking over his garden wall.

He chuckled. What he'd like to do was scoop her up and give her a long, leisurely kiss to show his appreciation. He resisted the urge. He doubted she'd thank him for the attention until he'd had a shower.

He strolled to the French doors, and closed the drapes. He'd let her sleep a while longer. Once he'd cleaned up and staved off starvation he'd wake her. He could offer her breakfast and then maybe they could get to that thank-you kiss if she wanted. No harm in seeing if they couldn't celebrate his recuperation together before she took the cat and its kittens and headed home. If he remembered correctly she hadn't been completely immune to him before he'd fallen on his face.

He began to whistle softly as he left the room. He felt a little shaky, probably from lack of food, but his other symptoms were as good as gone. It looked like another scorcher of a day outside, the morning sun making the garden's showy blooms look bright with promise. He'd call the French deli round the corner, get them to send over some fresh pastries and coffee and they could eat on the terrace. He fancied finding out a bit more about the intriguing Miss Daisy Dean before he sent her on her way.

All the stresses and strains of the last few days, the torments of the night, lifted as he bounded up the wide sweeping staircase to his bedroom suite. It felt good to be alive and back to his usual self. Anticipation lightened his steps, making him feel like a kid let loose from school on the first day of summer.

An hour later, Connor had indulged in a scalding hot shower, pulled on his favourite worn jeans and Boston Celtics T-shirt and stuffed down the last two brownies and a cup of steaming black coffee.

He peeked into the spare room and frowned. Angel Face hadn't moved. He padded into the room and squatted in front of her. Thick lashes rested on her pale cheeks and her breath scythed out in the gentlest of snores.

He caught a curl of hair that had fallen over her face, breathed in the spicy scent and then tucked it behind her ear. He skimmed his thumb over her cheek, felt the soft downy skin as smooth as a child's and fought the urge to kiss her awake. Still she didn't budge.

He cocked his head. Damn, but that position had to be

uncomfortable, she'd have a crick in her neck when she came round and probably wouldn't thank him for it. She'd be better off sleeping in his bed. The sheets were fresh and she could lie down flat. It was the least he could do after all she'd done for him.

Never a man to second guess himself, Connor threaded one hand under her bum and the other beneath her shoulders and hefted her into his arms. She murmured something, then cuddled into his chest, her flyaway hair tickling the underside of his chin. Her scent drifted up and he breathed it in. She smelled delicious. So delicious he had a hard time controlling the rush of blood to his groin as he walked from the room.

She was surprisingly light, even in his weakened state it took him less than a minute to carry her up to his bedroom. As he placed her gently in the middle of the deluxe king-size bed it struck him how tiny she was. Probably no more than five feet two or three. Funny he hadn't noticed that the night before—no doubt the indignant scowl on her face had made her seem taller. He grinned again, his hands braced on his hips. He certainly hadn't managed to intimidate her much—and he'd been in a bad enough mood to give her a very tough time.

She stirred, squinting in her sleep. He strolled to the large floor-to-ceiling windows, where sunlight flooded the room, to close the curtains.

'Where am I?'

He turned at the soft murmur, to find his guest propped up on her elbows. She gazed at him out of those large mossy eyes, looking confused and wary—and good enough to eat.

'You were out cold,' he said as he finished closing the curtains. 'I figured you'd be better in bed.'

Her eyes popped wide. 'Mr Brody! What are you doing up?'

He sat on the edge of the bed, and smiled, touched by her

concern. 'I'm right as rain, thanks to you.' He traced his thumb over the pulse in her throat, resting his fingers on her collarbone, and felt her shiver of response. 'And seeing as you've seen me naked, Daisy Dean, I think you best be calling me Connor, don't you?'

Colour flooded her cheeks, giving her pale skin a pretty pink glow. He chuckled, desire stirring again, but a lot more forcefully this time. No, she wasn't immune to him at all.

What the hell? Why not let breakfast wait until after that thank-you kiss?

Daisy blinked, the last of the sleepy fog clearing from her brain. Goodness, those eyes, that face were even more devastating spotlighted by the shaft of daylight beaming through the curtains.

And his comment had brought back dangerous memories: of how delicious he'd looked naked—and just how thoroughly she'd assessed all his assets.

She pulled back, sat up. Did he know about that? Maybe he hadn't been as delirious as she'd thought.

'I'm so glad you're feeling better,' she said. She breathed in the scent of freshly washed male and was hit by another alarming jolt of memory. 'Sorry to pass out like that but it was a long night.'

'It was,' he said, the confidential curve of his lips doing very strange things to Daisy's heart rate.

'Right, well…' she edged back '…I should shoot off. You obviously don't need me here any more and I—'

He leaned over and grasped her upper arm, halting her retreat in mid-scramble.

'You'll not be running off,' he said, 'before I've a chance to thank you.' The mesmerising blue gaze dipped to her lips as the Irish in his voice became more pronounced. 'Properly.'

Heat flooded between her thighs. But instead of saying

the polite denial her mind was screaming at him—something else entirely popped out of her mouth. 'How do you intend to do that?'

His eyes flared and he cradled her cheeks in his palms. His hands felt rough but unbearably erotic as he threaded his fingers through her hair, pushed the heavy mass back from her face. 'How about we start here?' he murmured, still smiling that devastating smile, his breath feathering her cheeks.

Then he slanted his lips across hers. The warm, wet heat was so shocking, and so unexpected, Daisy gasped. His tongue probed, firm and possessive, and her mind disengaged completely as the reckless thrill, the spike of adrenaline shimmered through her bloodstream.

He tasted of coffee and chocolate and danger. Forgetting everything but the feel of his lips on hers, Daisy sank shaking fingers into the silky black curls at his nape and drew him in as a drowning woman draws breath.

He didn't need any more encouragement. The kiss went from coaxing to demanding as he hauled her against him, his palm sweeping down her back. The weight of his long, strong body pressed her into the mattress as he pushed her down. She gave a staggered moan. This was madness, supreme folly and she couldn't summon the will to care.

As his lips stoked her into a frenzy she heard the hiss of her zipper. He reared back, breaking the kiss. Their eyes locked, his stormy with passion, the gleam of desire so intense she felt as if she'd been branded.

'You're beautiful, Daisy Dean,' he said, his thumbs stroking her nipples through the fabric as his eyes met hers. 'I want you naked.' The gruff statement was both question and demand.

She drew in ragged breaths, her arousal painful, as he tugged down the bodice of her dress, unsnapped the hook of her bra and bared her breasts.

She should have been shocked; she should have pushed him away. This was all wrong and she knew it. She'd been telling herself all night, she didn't even like this man—that he was not her kind of guy. But the time spent tending him, caressing fever-drenched flesh, hearing the broken cries of his nightmares, had formed a strong bond of intimacy that she couldn't seem to shake.

She'd looked into his soul last night, was looking into it now. They'd connected on some primal level and this was the only way to break the spell.

She wanted him naked too. She wanted him inside her.

His legs straddled hers and she looked down to see the ridge of his erection pressed against faded denim. Her fate was sealed as all her common sense dissolved to leave nothing but raw need clawing at her gut.

She shifted, but couldn't budge, pinned to the bed under him.

'You'll have to get off me if you want me naked,' she said.

'Good point.' His grin dazzled her. 'I'll race you,' he said, bounding off the bed.

She lurched into a sitting position, and watched mesmerised as he whipped his T-shirt over his head and his six-pack rippled. She looked away, determined not to be distracted from the task at hand by the muscular chest she'd spent most of the night memorising by touch. Anticipation surged through her. She was going to win this race.

She grappled with her shoelaces, cursing her choice of footwear. If only she'd stuck with the sandals. Finally she freed her feet, toed off the boots and flung them off the bed. She heard the thud as his jeans hit the floor, concentrated on wriggling her dress over her hips.

Heat blasted through every nerve ending as she looked up to see him standing before her, gloriously naked and his erection looking even more magnificent than she remembered it.

She bit into her bottom lip; her breath clogged her throat

as excitement and trepidation seared her insides like a flash-fire. He mounted the bed, grasped her ankle and gave a sharp tug. 'Come here,' he said, dragging her beneath him.

'Wait.' She braced her hand on his chest. 'I want to touch you.'

'Same here,' he said, cupping her chin. 'Let's negotiate.'

Then he kissed her, moulding their mouths together and crushing her body into the mattress. The coarse hair of his chest abraded swollen nipples. She dragged in a breath, let it shudder out as his lips trailed over her collarbone. His tongue slid fire across the swell of her breast and then his teeth nipped at the rigid peak and tugged. Rough hands kneaded her buttocks as his lips found hers again, the kiss so wildly erotic she thought she might be consumed by the flames.

She reached down, shaking with suppressed desire, and cupped his powerful erection in her palm. He shuddered as her fingers wrapped around the pulsing length.

She revelled in the feel of him, everything she'd imagined and more. His forehead touched hers, his whole body vibrating, his breathing harsh as she stroked and caressed him, learning the shape and texture as she had yearned to do all through the night. Velvet over steel. So solid, so warm, so responsive to her touch.

She ran her thumb over the thick head, felt the tantalising bead of moisture. He cursed softly and grasped her wrist, jerking back.

'You'll have to stop, or this'll be over before it's begun,' he rasped.

'I don't want to stop,' she cried, desperation edging the words.

Don't make me stop. Don't make me think, her mind screamed.

I don't want to think, I just want to feel.

'Are you sure?' he asked. 'I don't want to rush you.'

She'd never been more sure of anything in her life.

'I want to rush. I'm ready,' she said, alarmed, need over-whelming her. She had to do it now, before the delicious fog of sensation cleared.

'Let's see how ready, then,' he murmured.

Before she could figure out what he meant, his fingers delved into the curls at her sex. She shuddered as he circled her clitoris and probed. She cried, gripped his shoulders, slick juices flooding out as she bucked against those knowing fingers, primed to explode.

He chuckled. The sound deep, husky and self-satisfied. 'Hell, you're incredible.' His fingers pushed inside her, his thumb grazing the hard nub. She moaned, clinging to the edge of control. 'But you're a bit tight, Angel Face,' he said, sounding regretful.

'What?' The question shuddered out on a breath of need—and confusion. Why was he still waiting?

He groaned, holding her buttocks as he pressed his erec-tion against the slick folds of her sex. 'I don't want to hurt you.'

'You won't,' she gasped. 'I want you inside me.' How much more encouragement did he need? 'Now.'

'You're sure?' he asked again, making her want to scream.

She nodded, lifting her knees, angling her hips to accom-modate him, so frantic she'd lost the power of speech. If he didn't get on with it, she'd die of need.

She was about to tell him so when he stilled, cursed under his breath and then, to her complete astonishment, pulled away from her and climbed off the bed.

She bounced up on her elbows. Horrified.

'Where are you going?' she cried out on a thin wail of exasperation. Had he lost his mind?

He bent to get something out of his bedside table. 'What's the hurry, angel?' he murmured.

Her eyes drifted down to that perfect rear end. Lust and

frustration surged through her. She wanted to scream the house down. He'd worked her up to the point of meltdown and now he'd decided to rearrange his dresser!

'What's the hurry? Are you joking?' she squeaked, embarrassed by the desperate quiver in her voice.

He turned back gripping a telltale foil packet between his fingers and heat flooded into her cheeks. Even in her rampaging nymphomania, how could she have forgotten about protection?

'No joke,' he said, sounding ever so slightly smug. 'We wouldn't want any surprises.'

He knelt back on the bed, grinning at her as he ripped open the packet with his teeth and rolled the condom on. He put his hands over her shoulders, forcing her back on the bed, caging her in.

'Hasn't anyone ever told you, patience is a virtue, angel?' His eyes dipped to her tightly peaked nipples. 'Although, it should be said, there's not a lot of virtue in what I'm thinking right at the minute.'

Daisy's caustic reply caught in her throat as his lips covered hers. She rose up to kiss him back, letting the need, the sensation take over. But as she wrapped her arms round him, her fingers found the ridges on his back and tenderness welled up right beside the need.

His fingers gripped her hips and in one smooth move, he thrust inside her.

She sobbed, the fullness shocking her, the fury of sensations making her cry out. Then he began to move. Slow, heavy, insistent strokes that had the orgasm coiling ruthlessly inside her.

A staggered moan wrenched from her throat as the intense pleasure sent shock waves rocketing up from her core. She anchored her legs round his waist, sweat slicking her skin as she moved to meet each of his deep thrusts with thrusts of her own, and he drove deeper still. Her high-pitched pants matched his harsh grunts. Everything clamped down, her whole body glowing and pulsating as it rode the crest of a magnificent wave. The broken sobs echoed in her head as she burst free and exploded over the top—and heard his muffled shout as he crashed over behind her.

'That was amazing. You're amazing,' Connor murmured, stroking Daisy's cheek, then winced at the cliché.

But what else was he to say? Hell, if he hadn't been horizontal already he would have fallen over. He'd never had a stronger, more satisfying orgasm in his life. The experience had been literally mind-altering.

Using every last ounce of his strength he braced his arms to stop himself from collapsing on top of the woman responsible and crushing her. Her eyelids fluttered open as he stared down at her. He grinned as she focussed on his face. She looked as shattered as him, those round expressive eyes wide with amazement.

Then her vaginal muscles squeezed around him in the final throes of her orgasm.

'God, sorry,' she whispered as the pink in her cheeks darkened to maroon.

She looked horrified.

He had no clue what the problem was—but with her still wrapped tight around him he was finding it hard to give a damn. Feeling the blood rushing back to his groin, he did the decent thing—with not a small amount of regret—and lifted off her. The next round would have to wait. Something had spooked her—and he didn't want to scare her off.

Propping his elbow beside her head, he leaned over her. His gaze swept her lush little figure and came to rest on her face. The flush of afterglow warmed her skin and dilated her pupils, darkening the deep green of her eyes, while the sprinkle of freckles across her nose defined those impossibly high cheekbones. She really was gorgeous.

She coloured even more, then looked away and tried to scoot out from under him. He locked his arm round her waist. 'Now where would you be going? We're not half finished yet.'

She wiggled, he held firm. Finally she looked at him, her cheeks now a deep and very becoming shade of scarlet. 'There's no time for anything else. I really have to be going, Mr Brody.'

His eyebrows shot up at the formal address. Then he simply couldn't stop himself. He threw back his head and roared with laughter.

When he finally got his amusement under control, she'd stiffened like a board, her bottom lip puffed up in a defiant pout as she glared at him.

He grinned. What *was* she about?

Women! He gave his head a rueful shake. They really were a whole different species. But didn't that make them all the more fascinating?

'Angel Face,' he murmured, loving the way her eyes narrowed, 'as we've just made love like a couple of rabbits, I think you'd best be calling me Connor.'

CHAPTER FIVE

DAISY was utterly mortified. But she couldn't decide if she was more annoyed by her own behaviour or the patronising look on Connor Brody's face as he held her trapped by his side.

'I don't feel comfortable calling you by your given name,' she blurted out. And then realised how prim and ridiculous it sounded.

Thank goodness he didn't bust a gut laughing at her again. But the twinkle in his eye made it clear it was a struggle not to.

'Should I make you more comfortable, then?' He pulled the sheet over her, flattening his open palm on the expensive linen and lifting his eyebrow as if willing her to share the joke.

Daisy felt the warm weight of his hand on her belly and turned away, feeling so exposed she wanted to die on the spot.

When she'd surfaced a moment ago to find him gazing at her, his face flushed, those sexy blue eyes intent on hers and his erection still gloriously firm inside her, the hideous truth had dawned on her.

She'd ravished a complete stranger. Had as good as begged him to make love to her.

Which meant she was her mother's daughter after all. Her

mother, who had spent her whole life latching on to any guy who could give her a decent orgasm.

Daisy didn't know the first thing about Connor Brody. And he knew nothing about her. For all he knew she could be the sort of woman who made rabbit-love every chance she got. He couldn't possibly know she'd never ravished anyone before in her life.

The fact that the orgasm they'd shared had been the most incredible she'd ever had only made the situation that much worse.

When the muscles of her sex had clenched in response to the feel of him inside her, she'd been mortally embarrassed. Knowing she'd been tricked by her pheromones into believing they shared an intimacy, a connection, that they actually didn't.

Whatever way you looked at it, she'd used this man and his mouth-watering body to slake a temporary physical thirst—and fallen victim to her own libido. In so doing she'd broken the solemn promise she'd made to herself as a teenager, that she would never be like her mother. That she would never let her libido rule her life.

A calloused thumb skimmed down her cheek. 'What's the problem? Tell me and we'll see to it.'

Daisy swung round to face him. The tenderness in his eyes surprised her, but the lazy, confident, let's-humour-her smile on his lips contradicted it rather comprehensively.

Daisy felt her misery being replaced by irritation.

It really was a bit much of him to find the biggest identity crisis of her life so hilarious.

She sat up abruptly. She had to stop wallowing. Letting a total stranger witness her having a breakdown was not going to help matters. 'I'm absolutely fine,' she said, her voice as matter-of-fact as she could manage.

She grasped the sheet to her breasts, pushed her hair behind her ears, and felt a tiny bit better. She'd always been a woman of action. Once she saw a problem she set about fixing it. She'd have more than enough time later to analyse her wanton, irresponsible behaviour and what it all meant. Right now she needed to get the heck away from her studly neighbour before anything else happened.

The way he'd been studying her—all that smouldering intent in his gaze—suggested he was planning a repeat performance. And she wasn't entirely sure she could trust her body not to take him up on his offer. Given what this little liaison had already cost her, another frenzied encounter with Mr Sex-On-A-Stick was the very last thing she needed.

'This is a little awkward,' she said. 'But could you pass me my dress? I need to be off.'

He made no move to get her dress, so she scooted down the bed, intending to lean over him and get it herself.

But as she did so he stroked a hand down her hair. 'What's the rush?' he murmured, his voice husky but firm. 'Let's talk about it. Whatever it is, we can fix it.'

She gaped at him over her shoulder. Would you credit it? The only time in her life she'd rather gnaw off her own tongue than talk about her feelings and she'd found the one man on the planet willing to share and discuss.

'Mr Bro…' She paused when his eyebrow lifted again. 'Connor, we had sex. It was great sex. So thank you. But I don't think there's anything else to say.'

Both his eyebrows lifted at that one. Clearly, her no-nonsense approach had shocked him but she soldiered on. 'We have absolutely nothing in common,' she continued, slipping off the bed. 'We're obviously totally wrong for each other.' She dropped her end of the sheet and whipped on her dress. 'This was strictly a one-shot deal after a difficult night.'

They both knew the score here, and if he thought they were going to have another quickie for old times' sake he could forget it—the first one had been quite devastating enough to her peace of mind.

She pulled on her knickers, scouted around for her bra, grabbed it off the floor and shoved it into the pocket of her dress. 'So why don't we call it quits and leave it at that?'

She straightened, holding one baseball boot as she scoured the luxurious deep-pile carpet for the other.

'Are you serious?' he asked. He hadn't moved, the sheet resting tantalisingly low on his hips as he stared at her.

'Absolutely,' she said, forcing a smile.

Noticing the way the thin wisps of black hair curled around his belly button, she swallowed and averted her eyes. To her immense relief she spotted the other boot peeking out from under the bed. She grabbed it and stood up.

He'd propped himself up on the pillows, and was still studying her, looking stunned.

No doubt with those dark, dangerous good looks and the masterful way he made love, having the woman do a runner was a new experience for him. Daisy couldn't muster much sympathy. He'd have to learn to deal with it. She had her own problems.

He slid his feet to the floor, the sheet now barely covering him.

Daisy threw up her hand to stop him going any further. 'Please don't get up. I can see myself out,' she squeaked. The last thing she needed was another full-frontal view of that mouth-watering physique.

Before he could say another word, she dashed out the door, barefoot.

Connor gaped at the open bedroom door and listened to the pit-pat of Daisy's footsteps as she hightailed it down the stairs.

The muffled slam of the front door echoed at the bottom of the house.

He flopped back on the bed, stared at the ceiling and frowned at the fancy light fixture his interior designer had insisted on shipping in from Barcelona.

What the hell had that been about?

He might as well have set her tail on fire, she'd shot out of the room so fast. Either he'd been hallucinating, or he'd just been treated to the female equivalent of the 'wham-bam thank you, ma'am' routine.

He guessed he ought to be hurt, but first he'd have to get over the shock.

Not that he hadn't been dumped before, mind you. Of course he had. He could still recall Mary O'Halloran, slapping him down in front of all his mates when he'd been thirteen and full of the carelessness of youth. He'd snogged her and forgotten to call her the next day so he figured he'd deserved it. In fact, he still felt a little guilty whenever he thought about Mary.

But even Mary, riled to the hilt, hadn't dumped him without chewing his ear off first for twenty minutes about all his shortcomings. And he'd never met a woman since who wouldn't talk you to death about 'the state of the relationship' as soon as look at you. God, when he thought about all the times Rachel had insisted on 'having a little chat about where they were headed' his stomach sank.

So why should he care that Daisy had brushed off his offer to talk? Sure, he hadn't really meant it. All he'd wanted to do was calm her down, get her to stick around.

He lay on the bed, the ripples of sexual fulfilment making him feel lethargic, and tried to convince himself it was all for the best. He should be overjoyed. It made things a lot less complicated. He wasn't looking for anything serious and neither was she.

He rubbed his belly, stretched his legs under the sheet, contemplated taking another shower, then caught the heady whiff of her scent. Heat surged into his crotch. He frowned and sat up, staring at the tent forming in his lap.

The damn problem was, he wasn't pleased. Because he wasn't finished with her yet. Okay, they had nothing in common, and their one-night stand, or one-morning stand or whatever the hell it was didn't have any future. But still, he hadn't wanted it to end, not yet. He'd had plans for today. Fine, so them getting naked and having mind-blowing sex hadn't been a definite part of it, but he didn't see why they shouldn't go with the flow there. They might not be compatible out of bed, but they sure as hell were in it. In fact they were more than compatible. She'd been as blown away as he had by the intensity of…

He stopped, his brain finally catching up with his indignation. Had she been spooked by how good they were together? He relaxed back into the pillow, the pounding heat in his groin finally starting to subside.

That had to be the problem. Daisy might be the most pragmatic, forthright woman he'd ever met, but she was still a girl. And wasn't it just like a girl to analyse everything to death? To worry about what great sex meant instead of just enjoying it while it lasted.

He huffed out a laugh.

And now he thought about it, he didn't have to feel hard done by either. Little Daisy might turn out to be his ideal woman. Someone sexy enough to turn him inside out with lust and smart enough to know he wasn't a good bet for the long haul. Hell, they'd only just met and she'd already figured that out. Now all he had to do was show her that just because they weren't going to spend the rest of their natural lives together, didn't mean they couldn't spend the next little while exploring their potential in other areas.

He whipped back the sheet and leaped out of bed—his faith in the wonder of womankind restored. He'd have that shower after all, get dressed and then head to her place and invite her back for breakfast. Whatever she had planned for the next couple of days he'd persuade her to drop it.

Daisy seemed to be remarkably susceptible to him—whether she liked it or not. Getting her over this little hump so they could finish what they'd started shouldn't be too tough. He strode into the bathroom, his whistled rendition of 'Molly Malone' echoing off the tiles.

CHAPTER SIX

CONNOR was feeling a lot less jolly two hours later as he stood on Daisy's doorstep. He braced the box under his arm, heard the furious feline hiss from inside and stabbed the door buzzer, impatient to see Daisy again and get at least one thing sorted to his satisfaction.

It had taken him an eternity to chase her landlady's cat down and get it in the box—and he had a criss-cross of scratches on his hand for his trouble. Unfortunately the cat wasn't the only thing that had mucked up his morning. After a panicked call from the architect on his Paris project, he'd had to book a Eurostar ticket for this afternoon.

As soon as he'd put the phone down to his PA, Danny had been on the line from Manhattan, begging him to bring his trip there forward a week to stave off the now apparently imminent possibility of the Melrose project going belly up. He really hadn't needed another conversation about Danny's ludicrous 'fake fiancée' solution so he'd ended up agreeing to fly over there from Paris at the end of the week.

All of which was going to stall his plans to get the delicious Daisy Dean back in his bed any time soon. But once he'd finally wrestled the cat into the box, he'd made up his mind he wasn't prepared to write the idea off completely. Not yet.

He glanced at his watch. He knew a cosy little four-star restaurant in Notting Hill where he and Daisy could discuss their next moves over a glass of Pouilly Fumé and some seared scallops before he grabbed a cab to St Pancras International. He didn't see why he shouldn't stake his claim before he went. A three-week wait would be a pain, but he could handle it if he had something tangible to look forward to when he got back.

He pressed the buzzer again. Where the hell was she? It was ten o'clock on a Saturday morning and she'd been up most of the night—surely she couldn't have gone out?

He noticed the ragged paint on the huge oak door and glanced up at the house's elegant Georgian frontage. Crumbling brickwork and rotting window sills proved the place had been sadly neglected for years. She really did live in a dump.

The thought brightened his mood considerably.

Maybe he could persuade her to housesit while he was gone. He'd had a call back from the estate agent while he was having his spat with the cat. Even if he got an offer straight away as the guy seemed to think, it would take a bit to do all the paperwork. And he liked the idea of Daisy being there, waiting for him when he got back from his trip. He was just imagining how much they could enjoy his home-coming when the door swung open.

'Well, if it isn't the invisible neighbour.' The elderly woman standing on the threshold stared down her nose at him, which was quite a feat considering she was at least a foot shorter than he was. The voluminous silk dressing gown with feather trim she wore looked like something out of a vintage Hollywood movie. Her small birdlike frame and the wisps of white hair peeking out of her matching silk turban would have made her look fragile, but for her regal stature and the sharp intelligence in her gaze. Which was currently boring several holes in his hide.

'What do *you* want?' she sneered, eyeing him as if he

were a piece of rotting meat. 'Finally come to introduce yourself, have you?'

As Connor didn't know the woman, he figured she must have mistaken him for someone else. 'The name's Connor Brody. I've a cat with me belongs to the landlady here.'

He put the box down in front of her, the screech from inside making his ears throb and the slashes on his hand sting.

She gasped and clutched a hand to her breast as her face softened. 'You've found Mr Pootles?' she whispered, tears seeping over her lids. She bent over the box—the anticipation on her face as bright as that of a child on Christmas morning.

He stepped forward, about to warn her she was liable to get her hand ripped off, but stopped when she prised open the lid and a deep purr resonated from inside. He watched astonished as she scooped the devil cat into her arms. Lucifer rubbed its head under her chin, gave another satisfied purr and slanted him a smug look. The little suck-up.

'How can I ever thank you, young man?' The old woman straightened, clutching devil cat to her bosom as if it were her firstborn babe. 'You've made an old lady very happy.' The joyful tears sheening her whiskey-brown eyes and the softening of her facial features made her look about twenty years younger. 'Wherever did you find him? We've been searching for weeks.'

'The cat's been bunking in my kitchen,' he said, stuffing his hands in his pockets, not sure he really deserved her thanks. 'I should warn you. There's more than one cat now.'

The elderly lady's eyes popped wide. 'Oh?'

He nodded at the creature, who was gazing at him as if butter wouldn't melt in its mouth. 'Your Mr Pootles became a mammy eleven days ago. I have four kittens at mine.'

'Four…' The lady gasped and then giggled, sounding for all the world like a sixteen-year-old girl. She held the cat up in front of her and nuzzled it. 'You naughty cat. Why didn't you tell me you were a girl?'

Connor figured it probably wasn't his place to point out the cat couldn't talk. 'Here.' He pulled out a spare set of keys from his pocket. 'You'll want these to get the kittens now, as they're too little to be on their own for long.'

'Why, that's awfully sweet of you,' she said, taking the keys.

'They're in a cupboard in the kitchen,' he added. 'Is Daisy around?' he asked, awkwardly. 'I need to speak to her.'

The old lady's eyes widened as she put the keys in the pocket of her gown. 'You know Daisy?' she asked, sounding a lot more astonished about that than she had been about her tomcat's kittens.

'Sure, we're friends,' he said, colour rising in his cheeks under the old woman's scrutiny. It wasn't a lie. If what they'd got up to that morning didn't make them friends, he didn't know what did.

'Well, I never did,' she said. 'After all the nonsense Daisy's said about you in the last few weeks.'

What nonsense? She hadn't even met him until last night.

'Daisy's such a dark horse.' The old woman gave him a confidential grin, confusing him even more. 'I always thought she might have a little crush on you, the way she could not stop talking about you. Little did I know she'd been fooling us all along. So, did you two have a lovers' tiff? Is that why she said all those awful things?'

'No,' he said, totally clueless now. And not liking the feeling one bit. 'What things?'

The old woman waved her hand dismissively. 'Oh, you know Daisy. She's always got an opinion and she does love to voice it. She told us all how you were rich and arrogant and far too self-absorbed to care about a missing cat. But we know that's not true now, don't we?'

Connor's lips flattened into a grim line. So she'd bad-mouthed him, had she, and before she'd even met him. Wasn't that always the way of it? As a boy it had driven him insane when people who barely knew him told him he'd never amount to a thing. That he'd turn out no better than his Da.

But Daisy's bad opinion didn't just make him mad. It hurt a little too. Which made him more mad. Why should it bother him what some small-minded, silly little English girl thought?

Was that why she'd bolted? Because she'd decided he wasn't good enough for her? If she thought that she was in for a surprise.

'Is Daisy in her room? I need to speak to her.' *Make that yell at her.*

'Of course not, dear,' the old lady said quizzically. 'Daisy and Juno are working on The Funky Fashionista.'

'The what?'

The woman gave him a curious look. 'Her stall in Portobello Market.'

'Right you are,' he said hastily. Not knowing what Daisy did for a living probably made his claim to be a friend look a bit suspect. He took a step down the stairs, keen to get away.

Portobello Road Market was round the corner. It shouldn't take him too long to track her down—and give her a good piece of his mind.

'But, Mr Brody…' The elderly woman called him back. 'How will I get your keys back to you?'

'Don't worry about them,' he said, a smile playing across his lips as the kernel of an idea began to form. 'You keep them. If I lock myself out, it'll be useful for you to have a set.'

He waved and hopped down the last few steps to the pavement.

He mulled his idea over as he strode down the street

towards the Bello. And the more he mulled, the more irresistible the idea became. Sure what he had in mind was outrageous, and Daisy wasn't going to like it one bit, if her disappearing act that morning was anything to go by. But if ever there was a way to kill two birds with one stone, and teach a certain little English girl how not to throw said stones in glass houses, this had to be it.

After the shoddy way she'd treated him, it was the least she deserved.

Daisy Dean owed him. And what he had in mind would make the payback all the sweeter.

CHAPTER SEVEN

'NO WONDER you're knackered. It's called compassion fatigue.' Juno scowled as she placed the last of Daisy's new batch of silk-screen printed scarves at the front of the stall. 'You didn't need to spend the whole night there looking after him. You don't owe that guy a thing. And I bet he didn't even thank you for it.'

Oh, yes, he did.

The heat suffused Daisy's cheeks as she recalled how thoroughly Connor Brody had thanked her. She ducked behind the rack of cotton dresses and prayed Juno hadn't noticed her reaction.

'Why are you blushing?'

Daisy peeked over the top of the rack to see Juno watching her. Did the woman have radar or something? 'I'm not blushing. I'm rearranging the dress sizes.' She popped back behind the rack. 'It never ceases to amaze me how out of order they get,' she babbled, shoving a size fourteen in between two size eights.

'Daze, did something happen I should know about?' Juno asked quietly, appearing beside her. She placed her hand over the one Daisy had clutching the rack. 'If he did something to you, you can talk to me—you know that, right?'

The concern in Juno's eyes made Daisy's blush get a whole lot worse as embarrassment was comprehensively replaced by guilt.

It had taken her less than twenty minutes of angst after bolting out of Connor Brody's house that morning to get over her panic attack. She wasn't even sure what she'd got so worked up about now. Okay, so she'd jumped him, but who wouldn't in her situation? She'd been exhausted. She'd spent the whole night in close proximity to that beautiful body of his. She'd seen him at his most vulnerable plagued by those terrible nightmares and it had created a false sense of intimacy. So what? He hadn't exactly objected when she'd demanded he make love to her. And she'd never be idiotic or delusional enough to fall in love with a man like Connor Brody. A man who was so totally the opposite of the nice, calm, settled, steady, average guy she needed.

All of which meant she could rest assured that what had happened in Connor Brody's bed that morning hadn't suddenly turned her into her mother. Because that had always been her mother's mistake—not the pursuit of good sex, but the belief that good sex meant you must have found the man of your dreams. Daisy knew that good sex—even stupendous sex—had nothing whatsoever to do with love.

The relief she'd felt had been immense.

But the one thing Daisy hadn't been able to get past—or to justify—was the scurrilous way she'd treated Connor Brody. Not just after they'd made love—but before she'd ever met him. Was it any wonder Juno thought something bad had happened at Brody's house when Daisy had spent the last few weeks assassinating his character to anyone who would listen?

And on what evidence? None at all. She'd judged him and condemned him because he was rich and good-looking and, if she was being perfectly honest with herself, because she'd fancied him right from the first time she'd laid eyes on him and she'd resented it.

She'd broken into his home, all but accused him of killing a cat he'd actually been looking after and then—after trying to make amends during the night by nursing him through his fever—she'd ruined it all by seducing him first thing the following morning and then freaking out and running off.

Thinking about the way she'd brushed off his perfectly sweet attempts to calm her down made her cringe. He'd been a nice guy about the whole thing—had even offered to talk about it, and how many guys did that after a one-night stand? And what had she done? She'd told him to get lost. The poor guy probably thought she was a total basketcase and frankly who could blame him?

Daisy gave a deep sigh. At the very least she owed the man an apology. What was that old saying about pride going before a fall? She might as well have hurled herself off a cliff.

'Daze, you're really starting to worry me.' Juno's urgent voice pulled Daisy out of her musings. 'Tell me what he did. If he's hurt you, I'll make him pay. I promise.'

Daisy gave a half-smile, amused despite everything at the thought of Juno, who was even shorter than she was, going toe to toe with Brody. She shook her head. 'He didn't hurt me, Ju. He's a nice bloke.'

She paused. Maybe *nice* was too tame a word to describe Connor Brody, but it served its purpose here. 'If anything, it's the other way around—I hurt him.'

She knew she hadn't done more than dent his pride a little, but that still made her feel bad.

Walking round the stall, Daisy pinged open the drawer on the antique cash register. She lifted out the rolls of change and began cracking them open.

'How?' Juno asked, picking up a five-pence roll and ripping off the paper wrapping.

Daisy blew out a breath. 'I've been a complete cow to him. All those things I said to you and Mrs V and everyone else, all the assumptions I made. They all turned out to be a load of old cobblers.' The tinkle of change hitting the cash drawer's wooden base couldn't disguise the shame in her voice.

'What makes you think he'd care?' Juno scoffed, but then she'd always been willing to think the worst of any good-looking guy. Daisy wondered when she'd started to adopt the same prejudices.

'That's not the point,' Daisy said. 'I care.'

'All you really said was that he's rich and arrogant. What's so awful about that?'

'He may be rich, but he's not arrogant.' As she said it Daisy recalled the way he'd kissed her senseless before she'd even woken up properly. 'All right, maybe he is a little bit arrogant, but I expect he's used to women falling at his feet.' She certainly had.

'So what? That doesn't give him the right to take advantage—'

Daisy pressed her fingers to Juno's lips. 'He didn't take advantage of me. What happened was entirely consensual.' Just thinking about how consensual it had been was making her pulse skitter.

'What exactly *did* happen?' Juno's eyes narrowed. 'Because it's beginning to sound as if more than rest and recuperation were involved. You're not telling me you slept with him, are you?'

Daisy's flush flared back to life at the accusatory look in Juno's eyes. How on earth was she going to explain her behaviour to Juno when it had taken her so long to explain it to herself? She opened her mouth to say something, anything, when the rumble of a deep Irish accent had both their heads whipping round to the front of the stall.

'Hello, ladies.'

Daisy's heartbeat skipped a beat. He looked tall and devastating in the same worn T-shirt and jeans he'd stripped out of that morning—and amused. His lips twitched in that sensual smile she remembered a little too vividly from the moment she'd woken up in his bedroom.

'While I hate to interrupt this fascinating bit of chit-chat—' he gripped the top of the stall's canopy and leaned over the brightly coloured scarves and blouses '—I'd like to have a word, Daisy.' His forefinger skimmed her cheek. 'In private.'

Daisy swallowed, feeling the burn where the calloused fingertip had touched.

'Daisy's busy. Buzz off.'

He dropped his hand and shifted his gaze to Juno, still looking amused. 'Who would you be, then? Daisy's keeper?'

'Maybe I am?' Juno blustered, standing on tiptoe and thrusting her chin out—which made her look like a midget with a Napoleonic complex next to Brody's tall, relaxed frame. 'And who the hell are you? Mr High and—'

Daisy slapped her hand over Juno's mouth.

'It's all right, Ju,' she whispered, desperate to shut her friend up. 'I'll take it from here.'

All she needed now was for Brody to get an inkling of what she'd said about him to pretty much the whole neighbourhood. This apology was going to be agonising enough, without Juno and her attitude wading in and making it ten times worse.

'I'll explain everything later,' she said into Juno's ear, holding her hand over her friend's mouth. 'Can you look after the stall on your own for half an hour?'

Daisy took Juno's muffled grunt as a yes and let her go.

'Fine,' Juno grumbled. She shot Brody a mutinous look. 'But if you're not back by then I'm coming after you.'

Daisy gave Juno a quick nod. Great, she guessed she'd owe Juno an apology too before this was over. She picked up her bag and rounded the stall to join Brody. Right at the moment, though, she had rather bigger fish to fry.

'I know a café round the corner in Cambridge Gardens,' she murmured, walking through the few milling shoppers who'd already made it up to the far end of the market under the Westway where The Funky Fashionista was situated.

He fell into step beside her but said nothing.

'Why don't we go there?' she continued, not quite able to look at him. 'They do great cappuccinos.'

And Gino's cosy little Italian coffee house was also off the tourist track enough that it shouldn't be too crowded yet. The last thing she wanted was an audience while she choked down her monster helping of humble pie.

It took them less than five minutes to get to Gino's. Not surprising given that Daisy jogged most of the way, clinging onto her bag with both hands and making sure she kept a couple of steps ahead of Brody's long stride. As soon as they'd walked away from the stall she'd been consumed by panic at the possibility that he might touch her or speak to her before she'd figured out what she was going to say to him.

And how ridiculous was that? she thought as they strolled into Gino's and she grabbed the first booth by the door. He'd been buried deep inside her less than three hours ago, given her the most earth-shattering orgasm of her life and now she was scared to even look at him.

She slid into the booth and hastily dumped her bag onto the vinyl-bench seat beside her, blocking off any thoughts he might have of sitting next to her. Casting his eyes at the bag, he slid his long body onto the bench opposite. As he rested his arms loosely on the table she noticed the Boston Celtics logo ripple across his chest.

Her eyes flicked away.

Don't even go there, you silly woman. Hasn't that chest got you in enough trouble already?

She raised her hand to salute Gino, who was standing behind the counter. 'Would you like a cappuccino?' she asked as she watched Gino wave back and grab his pad.

'What I'd like is for you to look at me.'

The dry comment forced her to meet his eyes.

'That's better,' he said, the low murmur deliberately intimate. 'Was that so terrible now?'

Daisy decided to ignore the patronising tone. She supposed she deserved it.

'Look, Mr Brod... I mean, Connor. I've got something to say and I...' She rushed the words and then came to a complete stop, her tongue stalling on the apology she'd worked out.

Then Gino stepped up to the booth. 'Hello, Daisy luv. What'll it be? The usual?'

Daisy stared blankly at her friend, struggling for a second to remember what her usual was. 'No, thanks, no muffin today.' She'd probably choke on it. 'Just a latte, not too heavy on the froth.'

'As always, my lovely,' Gino said as he jotted the order on his pad, his broad cockney accent belying the swarthy Italian colouring he'd inherited from his mother. 'What's your poison, mate?' he asked, addressing Brody.

'Espresso.'

'Coming right up,' Gino replied. Then to Daisy's consternation he tucked his pad under his arm and offered Brody his hand. 'Gino Jones, by the way. This is my place,' he said as Brody shook it. 'Haven't seen you in here before. What's your name?'

Daisy rolled her eyes. She'd forgotten what a busybody Gino could be.

'Connor Brody,' Brody replied. 'I moved in next door to Daisy a few weeks back.'

Gino frowned, releasing Brody's hand. 'You're not the bloke who—'

Daisy coughed loudly. Good God, had she blabbed to Gino about Brody too? Why did she have such a big mouth? 'Actually, we're in a hurry, Gee,' she said, slanting Gino her 'shut up, you idiot' look. 'I've left Ju alone on the stall and the market will be heaving soon.'

'No sweat,' Gino said carefully. 'I'll go get your drinks.' Then he shot her his 'don't think I won't ask you about this guy later' look and left.

'You know, it's funny,' Brody said, although he didn't sound at all amused, 'but people around here don't like me much.' The statement sounded slightly disingenuous, but Daisy suspected that was wishful thinking on her part.

Her stomach sank to the soles of her shoes as guilt consumed her.

Time to stop messing about and give the man the apology she owed him. And she better make it a good one.

'Mr... Sorry, Connor.' She stalled again, forced herself to continue. 'I've behaved pretty badly. Climbing into your garden, accusing you of...' She paused. *Don't say you thought he killed the cat, you twerp.* 'Of not helping to find Mrs V's cat. And then...' The blush was back with a vengeance as he watched her, his face impassive. 'This morning I forced you to make love to me. And then I ran off without saying good-bye. I feel completely ashamed of my behaviour... It was incredibly tacky and I'm awfully sorry. And I'd like to make it up to you.' She stumbled to a stop, not sure what else to say.

His expression had barely changed throughout her whole rambling speech. Maybe he'd looked a little surprised at first, but then his face had taken on this inscrutable mask.

'Hmm,' he said, the sound rumbling up through his chest. For some strange reason, Daisy's knees began to shake. She crossed her legs.

He cocked his head to one side. 'That's a lot of sins you've to make up.'

'I know,' she said, hoping she sounded suitably contrite.

To her surprise, he reached across the table and took her hand in his, threading his fingers through hers. 'What makes you think I was being forced, Daisy Dean? Did it seem to you I wasn't enjoying myself?'

She gulped past the dryness tightening her throat. How

had they got onto this topic? 'No, it's not that. It's just. I was rather demanding. I don't think I gave you much of a choice in the matter.'

She ought to tug her fingers away, but somehow they'd got tangled up in his. Just as her stomach was now tangled in knots.

He rubbed his thumb across her palm, making her fingers curl into his. 'You'd be wrong about that,' he said. 'You gave me a choice and I took it. With a great deal of enthusiasm.'

His thumb began stroking her wrist, doing appalling things to her pulse rate. She was just about to muster the will to pull her hand away when he let her go and sat back.

Gino cleared his throat loudly and slid their coffees onto the table.

'Here you go, folks.' Gino sent Daisy a searching look, raising his eyebrows pointedly, before leaving them alone.

No doubt Gino was as confused as she was. Why had she been holding Brody's hand? Letting him caress her like that? It wasn't as if they were intimate. Well, not in the proper sense.

She wrapped her hands around her coffee mug to keep them out of harm's way. 'I'm so glad there are no hard feelings,' she said.

At least she would be glad, once she'd got away from that penetrating gaze.

'Not about making love to you, no,' he said, the Irish in his voice brushing over her like an aphrodisiac. 'There are no hard feelings about that. I enjoyed it, a lot. And, I think, so did you.' It wasn't a question. 'But as to the rest,' he continued. 'There you've more explaining to do.'

Her cup clattered onto the table and coffee slurped over the rim. 'I do?'

'Why did you run off?'

'I don't know,' she lied, and then felt guilty again when he lifted one dark brow. He wasn't buying it.

'It was a bit too intense,' she said. 'And I don't usually jump into bed with men I hardly know.' She clamped her mouth shut. Half the truth would have to do. Because she was getting the weird sensation she was being toyed with, lured into some kind of a trap. Which was preposterous, of course, but Daisy never ignored her instincts.

'That's good to know,' he said.

She took a gulp of the hot coffee and then reached for her bag. 'I'm so glad we got all this settled. I'd hate for us not to be friends. Especially as you live right next door.'

Which made the whole thing even more awful. How was she going to face him every day if her hormones went into meltdown every time she looked at him? She'd have to get that little problem under control and quickly. But for now she decided distance was probably the best medicine. Slinging her bag over her shoulder, she slid out of the booth and offered her hand. 'I'll see you around. The coffees are on me. I'll tell Gino to put them on my tab. Thanks for being so understanding.'

He clasped her hand, the warm, rough feel of his palm sending little shivers up her arm—and held on. 'Sit down. We're not finished.'

'We're not?'

He nodded at the booth seat. 'There's still the matter of the making up to settle.'

'What?' She plopped back in her seat, not at all sure she liked the commanding tone.

'The making up.'

Finally he let her hand go. She tucked it under the table, her fingers tingling.

'You said you wanted to make up for what you'd done,' he said calmly. 'And we're going to have to sort it now, because I don't have much time.' He looked at his watch. 'I'm catching the Eurostar to Paris in a little over an hour. I've got eight days there and then I'll be two weeks in New York.'

Daisy's shoulders slumped with relief. Thank you, God. She had no idea why he was telling her his itinerary, but at least she'd have over three weeks before she had to see him again. She should be well over this silly chemical reaction by then. 'That's wonderful. I'm sure you'll have a lovely time. I'll miss you,' she added, a tad concerned to realise it was the truth.

'Not for long, you won't,' he said, the predatory smile that tugged at his lips concerning her a whole lot more. 'Because when I get to New York you'll be meeting me there.'

She choked out a laugh. 'You lost me,' she said, but she could have sworn she heard the sound of a trap snapping shut.

He relaxed back in his seat, the picture of self-satisfaction. 'You want to make things up to me,' he prompted. 'It so happens I need a girlfriend in New York for those two weeks. It has to do with a business deal.' He tapped his fingers on the table in a rhythm that sounded like the tumblers of a lock clicking into place. 'And that girlfriend's going to be you.'

He could not be serious? Was he insane? 'Don't be ridiculous. I'm not going to New York. When I said I wanted to make things up to you, I was planning to bake you another plate of brownies. Not take a two-week trip to New York as your fake date. Are you nuts?' He was still looking at her with that cocksure, you'll-do-as-you're-told expression on his face. It was starting to annoy her. 'Even if I wanted to go.' Which she most definitely did not. 'I couldn't possibly. I've got my stall to run.'

He sighed. 'If your little bodyguard friend can't run the stall on her own you can find someone to help her. I'll pay any wages due. My PA will sort out your travel plans.' He looked pointedly at his watch again, as if to say, *I don't have time for this.*

Daisy's temper kicked up another notch. 'You're not listening to me, Brody. I'm not doing it. I don't want to. You'll have to find someone else.' She did not want to spend two weeks alone with him in New York. She already knew how irresistible he was—what if she had another lapse in judgment brought on by extreme hormonal overload and jumped him again? Things could get very complicated indeed. 'I don't owe you that much,' she finished, indignation seeping from every pore.

'Oh, but you do, Daisy Dean.' He leaned forward, those icy blue eyes chilling her to the bone. 'You told half of London I was selfish, arrogant and not to be trusted. That's known as slander.'

The blood seeped out of her face. How did he know about that?

'There happen to be laws against that sort of thing. So unless you want me to be calling my solicitor, you'd best be on that plane.'

He got up from the booth. She drew back, but he caught her chin in his fingers and tilted her face to his. 'And, Daisy,' he murmured, the warmth of his breath making her heart go into palpitations. 'Who said anything about a fake date?' he finished, his lips so close she could all but feel them pressed against hers.

'But I'm not your girlfriend,' she managed to say as her heart pounded in her throat. 'I certainly don't love you. And right now I don't even like you.'

His gaze swept over her, making her notice the length of his lashes again, before his eyes fixed on her face. If she'd hoped to wound him she could see by his expression she'd failed.

'Make no mistake. This is only a two-week deal. I'm not in the market for anything more and neither are you.'

She thought she could hear a tinge of regret in his voice and cursed her overactive imagination. She doubted he had the emotional capacity for regret. The rat.

'But we don't have to love each other for what I have in mind.'

With that, his lips came down on hers in a hard, fast and sinfully sexy kiss. She tried to twist away but he held her firm until she felt the pulse of response, the throb of heat. And before she knew what was happening, she was kissing him back.

He pulled his mouth away first and straightened. 'You like me right enough, Daisy Dean.' He brushed his thumb across her bottom lip. 'And we both know it.'

She jerked back, mute with anger and humiliated right down to her knickers—which were now soaked with need.

'There will be lots we can see and do in Manhattan—and I've a mind to show it to you,' he continued, that devil-may-care charm not the least bit fazed by her furious glare. 'So, you can spend the two weeks in your bed alone, or make the most of the experience. The choice will be yours.' He gave her a mock salute. 'I'll see you in New York, Angel Face.'

Daisy glared at his back as he strolled out of the café, heard him whistling some off-key Irish ditty as he disappeared down the street.

The overbearing, conceited, blackmailing jerk.

She flung her bag on the seat. How dared he steamroll her like that?

She glowered at the booth opposite, sure she could feel smoke pumping out of her ears. To think she'd actually felt sorry for what she'd said about him. He wasn't just arrogant. He was a megalomaniac—with an ego the size of his precious Manhattan.

If he thought she was going to step into line, he could forget it. And whatever happened she was not going to sleep with him again. No way, no how.

But even as she made the promise she knew it was going to be next to impossible to keep.

CHAPTER EIGHT

BY THE time Daisy had packed up the stall with Juno that evening and trudged back to her bedsit, she'd decided the conversation with Brody in Gino's café had been his crazy idea of a joke. Either that or she'd been dreaming.

He couldn't be serious about blackmailing her into a trip to New York. This was the twenty-first century—people didn't do that sort of thing. Well, not people with any semblance of decency.

She turned on the light and toed off her shoes, every cell in her body weeping with exhaustion after a virtually sleepless night and ten solid hours on her feet—not to mention the day's emotional trauma. Thank you so very much, Connor Brody. Pulling off the bangles on her wrist, she dropped them into her jewellery box, then sat on the bed and unclipped her silver ankle bracelet. She'd just forget the whole ridiculous episode.

She hadn't even told Juno about Brody's threat. She'd forced herself to calm down before returning to the stall— her lips still red and puffy from Brody's goodbye kiss—and had put a few things in perspective. Brody could not possibly have been serious. So why bother Juno with the details?

Edging her curtain back, Daisy peeked at the windows of Brody's house. Pitch black. Thank goodness. He must be in Paris. She huffed. Good riddance.

She let the curtain drop, lay down on the bed and stared at the fairy-tale motif she'd painted on the ceiling last winter. A blue-eyed, black-haired cherub winked at her cheekily from behind a moonbeam.

She shifted onto her side and tucked her hands under her cheek—the damn cherub reminding her of someone she did not want to be reminded of.

Sunday and Monday flew by in a flurry of work and other related activities. Daisy manned the stall, ran a class on silk-screen printing at the local community centre, got stuck into her latest clothes designs and did her regular slot at the Notting Hill Arts Project—happily getting neck-deep in tissue paper, glitter and PVA glue as she helped her group of five- to ten-year-olds make their costumes for this year's Notting Hill Carnival. Just as she'd suspected, there had been no word from Brody. By Tuesday night, the events of the weekend had been as good as forgotten—give or take a few luridly erotic dreams.

Bright and way too early Wednesday morning, her three days of denial came to an abrupt end.

'Daisy, Daisy, open up, dear.' Mrs Valdermeyer's excited voice was punctuated by several loud raps on the door. 'A package has arrived for you. Special delivery no less.'

Daisy rolled over, blinking the sleep out of her eyes. Stumbling out of bed, she checked the Mickey Mouse clock on the mantelpiece and groaned. It was still shy of seven a.m.

She pulled the door open and her landlady whisked past, holding a small brown-paper parcel aloft like a waiter on silver-service duty. She laid it ceremonially on the bed. Then turned to Daisy and bounced up on her toes.

'Isn't it exciting?' She clapped her hands. 'It's from that handsome young man next door—it says so on the front.'

Daisy felt a much louder groan coming on, but bit it back.

'What's going on?' Juno stood in the doorway, wearing her Bugs Bunny pyjamas and a sleepy frown.

'Daisy has a package from a gentleman admirer. Isn't it exciting?' Mrs Valdermeyer plopped down on the bed and patted a spot next to her. 'Come in, Juno, and let's watch her open it.'

Daisy felt the groan start to strangle her. Fabulous. When had her bedroom become package-opening central?

'What gentleman admirer?' Juno asked. Walking into the room, she glanced at the package. 'Oh, him,' she scoffed.

Daisy opened her mouth to speak—and start ushering her audience out the door—when Mrs V interrupted her. 'Don't be such a grump, Juno dear.' She whisked a pair of scissors out of her dressing gown with a flourish. 'The man is positively delicious and he saved Mrs Pootles from a fate worse than death. Daisy could do a lot worse.' She offered Daisy the scissors. 'In fact Daisy did do a lot worse—remember that awful Gary?'

'Do I ever,' Juno replied, sitting next to Mrs Valdermeyer. She caught Daisy's eye. 'But I'm not sure this guy is that big an improvement.'

'Well, he's certainly a lot better looking,' Mrs Valdermeyer shot back.

'We're not dating, Mrs V,' Daisy interceded, before her landlady got totally the wrong idea. 'So there's no need—'

'Why ever not, dear? He's loaded, you know. Which, I might add, comes in very handy if the passion fades.'

Daisy grabbed the scissors, resigned to opening the package as quickly as possible before the conversation deteriorated any further.

She snipped the string and folded the paper back carefully, aware of the two pairs of eyes watching every move she made. Her heart pummelled as she opened the lid.

Please don't let him have put crotchless knickers in here. Or something equally tacky.

But as she upended the box she was surprised to see three envelopes of varying sizes and a slim, black velvet case bounce onto the bed.

'How marvellous. Jewellery. Open that last, Daisy,' Mrs Valdermeyer said, thrusting the first of the envelopes into Daisy's hand. 'Jewellery needs to be properly savoured.'

Once Daisy had opened all three of the envelopes, Mrs Valdermeyer was practically doing cartwheels around the room and Juno's frown had turned into the San Andreas fault.

Daisy slumped onto the bed, stunned. In her lap she had a first-class return ticket to JFK dated for twelve noon that coming Sunday, a carefully typed itinerary of her travel arrangements signed by someone called Caroline Prestwick and a gold credit card in her name.

Her hand shook as Mrs Valdermeyer thrust the jewellery case into her lap on top of the other booty. Daisy picked it up, and found another envelope attached to the bottom of the case.

She ripped it off, stared blankly at her name scrawled on the front in large, block letters and then tore it open. Inside was a sheet of thick textured white paper with the Brody Construction logo stamped across the top. As she scanned the contents of the letter her fingers began to tremble.

Angel Face,

I found the sparkles in Paris and thought they would suit. Get anything else you need with the card—and don't spare yourself. I want you to look the part.

There's a car booked for the airport. See you at The Waldorf.

Connor
PS: I've my solicitor on speed-dial if you don't show.

'It's all so wonderfully romantic,' Mrs Valdermeyer crooned over her shoulder. 'Two weeks at The Waldorf *and* a gold credit card. You're going to have the time of your life, Daisy.'

'What does he mean about his solicitor?' Juno said.

'I'm not going.' Daisy folded the letter and shoved it back in its envelope. She couldn't possibly go. Okay, somewhere in the last few days she'd got over her anger, and for a moment Mrs Valdermeyer's industrial-strength enthusiasm had almost blinded her to the truth. For a split second she'd seen herself on Connor's arm decked out in glitters and her best posh frock. She'd never been further than Calais on a school trip so she felt she was entitled to get momentarily carried away. But she couldn't do it. And what had he meant by 'I want you to look the part'—as if she were his personal mannequin? The cheek of the man.

'Of course you're going, my dear. Don't be absurd,' Mrs Valdermeyer said.

'I really don't think she should,' Juno piped up. 'She'd be totally at his mercy and—'

'Stop right there, Juno.' Mrs Valdermeyer got up and took Juno's arm. 'I want you out of here. Daisy and I have to talk about this in private,' she said, dragging Juno to the door.

Before Juno had a chance to say anything else, she'd been shoved over the threshold and had the door slammed at her back.

Mrs Valdermeyer brushed her hands together. 'Right, now the most unromantic woman in the Western World has gone, let's discuss this properly.'

She sat down next to Daisy, laid a hand on her knee.

'You don't understand.' Daisy fisted her fingers on Connor's perfunctory letter. 'It's not romantic at all. He just needs a girlfriend to hang on his arm for a couple of weeks. We're not even dating. It's a business thing. Or something.' She let out a trembling breath. The truth was, he thought so little of her, he hadn't even had the courtesy to tell her why exactly he needed her there.

Daisy shoved Connor's letter and the jeweller's case back in the box—ignoring the cold fingers of regret gripping her stomach.

How pathetic that she felt depressed she couldn't go. She was her own woman, she didn't need a man to complete her and she certainly didn't need some too-sexy-by-half egomaniac sweeping her off her feet only to dump her back down to earth again two weeks later.

'He may very well think that,' Mrs Valdermeyer said gently, resting her knarled hand over Daisy's. 'But I suspect there's a bit more to it.'

Tears pricked Daisy's lids—and made her feel even more pathetic. 'Like what?' she said, cynicism sharpening her voice.

'Daisy, dear. Men don't ask a woman on a first-class, all-expenses-paid trip to New York just for the sake of a business deal.'

'He didn't ask me,' Daisy said, the tears she was busy ignoring clogging her throat. 'He told me. And I think he's expecting some pleasure mixed in with his business to justify the expense.'

Mrs Valdermeyer chuckled fondly. 'He is a scoundrel, isn't he? Just like my third husband, Jerry.' She patted Daisy's leg, still chuckling. 'But once you've tamed him, my dear, you'll see they're the very best kind. Both in bed and out.'

Daisy tried to smile at the old lady's irascible tone, but somehow she couldn't muster more than a strained grimace. 'I don't want to tame him. Believe me, it would involve far too much work.'

Mrs Valdermeyer took Daisy's hands in hers. 'Look at me, dear.' Daisy lifted her eyes, saw that the old woman wasn't smiling any more. 'Don't you think you're taking this a bit too seriously? Surely, this is about a man and a woman having a marvellous adventure together. Nothing more. And you've had far too few adventures in your life to let one as spectacular as this pass you by.'

Daisy huffed. 'That's where you're wrong. I had enough adventures to last me a lifetime before I ever came here.'

'No, you didn't. Those were your mother's adventures. They don't count. This is going to be your adventure and you're going to enjoy every minute of it. You need to get out there and experience life before you can think about finding love, you know.'

A flutter of butterfly wings began to beat under Daisy's breastbone. She tired to ignore them. 'I really don't think…'

Mrs Valdermeyer held up her finger to silence her. 'Don't think, Daisy. You're a dear sweet girl who thinks far too much, mostly about everybody but herself. For once, don't think, just feel.' She patted Daisy's knee. 'Take it from me, I'm an old woman and there are a few things I've learned. You've got the rest of your life to plan things out, to do the right thing, to be cautious and careful and responsible. That's what you have to do when you start a family—that's what your mother should have done and didn't. And if you find the right man to do it with it won't be boring, let me tell you. But you're young, and free and single and you get to be spontaneous now, to live life as it comes and take whatever fun and excitement you can grab.' She picked up the velvet jeweller's case. 'Now, I want to know what sparkles your handsome scoundrel picked out for you in Paris. Don't you?'

Mrs Valdermeyer placed the case back in Daisy's lap.

Daisy stared at the embossed gold lettering on the top, ran her finger over the textured velvet. She sighed. What the heck. What harm could it do to take a quick peek? She lifted the heavy case in one hand and opened the lid.

The sight of the emeralds winking on a lattice of silver chains had her heart leaping into her throat and threatening to choke her. She took an unsteady breath and touched the precious stones.

The butterflies went haywire as the fanciful, fairy-tale images that had been hovering at the back of her mind came into sharp, vivid and all-too-real focus.

She could feel the beautiful necklace warming her cleavage, see the luminous satin of a ball gown she'd once designed in her dreams shimmering in the glow of a thousand tiny lights and sense Connor, tall, dark and far too dangerous, his blue eyes bold with appreciation as he held her close in his arms.

She slammed the lid shut like a frantic Pandora with her box.

But the giddy beating of her heart and the heat coiling in her belly told her she was already far too late to seal in the ridiculous dream.

CHAPTER NINE

IF THE days prior to the arrival of Connor's package had gone by in a flurry, the ones afterwards went by in a blur. Once Daisy had faced the fact that she'd have to go to New York—or spend the rest of her life wondering what she might have missed—she became determined to make the absolute most of the opportunity, and avoid all the pitfalls at the same time.

Daisy being Daisy, the practicalities had to be handled first. So she lined up Jacie to help Juno on the stall, finished as much merchandise as she could, rearranged all her community and charity activities and then spent every other spare minute she had working on her wardrobe for the trip. Whether this turned out to be the grandest adventure of her life—or the biggest disaster—she intended to look fabulous. She had her own distinctive style, and whether Connor approved of it or not, she planned to look the part. That would be her part—not his.

As she drew patterns and cut fabrics and stitched and pleated and hemmed and appliquéd late into the night she worked out a basic survival strategy to go with her amazing trousseau.

Whatever happened in New York she would not lose sight of what really mattered. Her life, her career—such as it was—her hopes and dreams for the future did not depend on two thrill-seeking weeks spent in the City That Never Sleeps with a man who had twice as much sex appeal as Casanova and half the depth. As long as she kept her hormones under strict supervision—and didn't succumb to any delusions about true love—she would be absolutely fine.

But despite all Daisy's preparations and pep talks, when Sunday morning arrived, and a black Mercedes with a liveried driver parked in front of the bedsit, the nerves kicked in.

While the chauffeur loaded her suitcase into the boot, she clung onto Mrs V and Juno in a goodbye hug. But as she climbed into the plush leather interior the smell of money and privilege overwhelmed her and the nerves got worse. She wound down the window and gave her friends a shaky wave as the powerful car purred to life and swept away from the kerb.

Once the only home she had ever known was out of sight, she wound the window back up, pressed the button for the air-conditioner and listened to the deafening thumps of her heart-beat over the quiet hum. What on earth had she let herself in for?

She dropped her head back and sighed.

She would be walking into a world she knew nothing about. And throwing herself on the mercy of a guy she knew even less about—not to mention her own surprisingly volatile libido.

She forced herself to take a series of steady breaths as she smoothed the bias-cut sheath dress she'd finished the night before over her knees and felt the pearly silk whisper under her fingertips.

She watched the terraced houses of west London whisk past.

Fine, maybe this would turn out to be the stupidest thing she'd ever done—but at least she'd be doing it in style.

* * *

Daisy Dean had never coveted the lifestyles of the rich and famous. She'd never worried about how much money she had, only that she had enough—and she'd been more than happy to work as hard as she had to have the stability she'd always craved.

But as she stepped out of the royal blue limo onto Park Avenue and gazed up at the art deco frontage of The Waldorf Astoria, its gilded-gold filigree glinting in the mid-afternoon sunshine, Daisy had to concede that being rich beyond your wildest dreams might have its uses.

For a girl who'd only ever been on the cheapest of short-haul flights, the journey across the Atlantic—in a leather seat that folded down into a bed bigger than the one she had at home—had been like a dream. She'd cruised above the clouds at thirty thousand feet, sipping champagne and snacking on cordon bleu cuisine—or as much as her nervous tummy would allow—and made herself savour the experience and enjoy it for what it was—a once-in-a-lifetime adventure.

'Ma'am.' The Waldorf's doorman interrupted Daisy's thoughts to hand her a blue ticket. 'Give this to the desk clerk when you check in and we'll have your luggage sent right up to your room.'

'Thank you.' Daisy pulled a ten-dollar bill out of her purse, glad she'd changed some of her own money. But as she offered the tip to the doorman he simply shook his head.

'No need for a gratuity, ma'am. You're Mr Brody's guest. He's already taken care of it.'

'Oh.' Daisy slipped the money back into her purse, her cheeks colouring.

In the last few days she'd been careful not to dwell on her position as 'Mr Brody's guest'. But somehow not even being able to tip the doorman made her feel a bit cheap.

She pushed her uneasiness aside as she made her way up the carpeted stairs to the lobby area. Brody needed her here for his business thingy. She was doing him a favour, so why shouldn't he foot the bill? And she hardly needed to create more problems—she had quite enough on her plate already.

Her breath caught as she took in the huge chandelier hanging over The Waldorf's marbled forecourt and heard the tinkling strains of a Cole Porter song being played on a grand piano in the cocktail bar.

Portobello Road and the Bedsit Co-op suddenly felt a lot more than half a world away.

All leather sofas, vaulted ceilings and dark wood panelling with an ornate carriage clock as its centrepiece, the reception area was no less intimidating. Feeling hopelessly out of place, Daisy approached the desk.

A woman with perfect make-up and an even more perfect smile greeted her. 'What can we do for you today?'

'My name's Daisy Dean. Mr Connor Brody has booked me a room.' The minute the words were out of her mouth, the blush coloured her cheeks again. At least she'd assumed he'd booked her a room. In all the hurried preparations of the last few days and the glamour of the flight, it hadn't even occurred to Daisy to wonder about it. The thought of the kiss they'd shared in Gino's came blasting back to her and the crack he'd made about this not being a 'fake date' and she realised she should have contacted him and clarified their sleeping arrangements. She tried to ignore her pummelling heartbeat. *Don't be silly, Daze, he couldn't possibly be arrogant enough to assume you'll be sleeping together.*

The receptionist tapped a few buttons on her console and smiled. 'You're booked into The Towers Suite with Mr Brody.'

The bottom dropped out of Daisy's stomach. 'Are you sure?' she stuttered.

'Why, yes, of course, Mr Brody made the arrangements personally,' the receptionist continued, apparently oblivious to Daisy's distress. She handed Daisy a thin plastic card in a paper envelope. 'The Towers Suite is on the twenty-first floor,' she said chirpily, pointing to the lifts at the end of the lobby. 'You have a special penthouse elevator for your exclusive use. Mr Brody left a message to say he's in meetings downtown this afternoon, but we're to contact him when you get here and he'll be back at about six o'clock to escort you to dinner.' She smiled again, her teeth so white they gleamed. 'If you have the ticket for your luggage, I'll have it taken to the suite.'

Daisy reached into her bag and handed over the ticket, her mind whirring. She wanted to demand the receptionist get her another room, but how the heck could she do that when she had a grand total of one hundred dollars in her purse? She'd have to have it out with Brody first, and then insist he get her another room. But the thought of that altercation filled her with dread. She hadn't seen him for over a week, but just the mention of his name had made her thigh muscles clench and her nipples pebble beneath the thin silk of her dress.

'Thanks for your help,' she said, taking the key card in shaking fingers.

She walked to the lift lobby, keeping her back ramrod straight.

Forget feeling cheap, she might as well have had a huge scarlet letter A pasted on her breast.

When Brody finally turned up, she was going to have serious words with him.

After having inspected The Towers Suite, Daisy felt even more intimidated—and like a naive fool.

Taking up most of the twenty-first floor, the suite's rooms were all enormous and luxuriously appointed. Daisy walked through it, her eyes widening until they were the size of dinner plates. Leading off the palatial entrance lobby was a sitting room which boasted a grand piano, a plasma TV the size of a small cinema screen and a lavish balcony with a breathtaking view of the Upper East Side. There were also two walk-in wardrobes and a dressing room, but—surprise, surprise—only one bedroom.

Done out in cream silk wallpaper and matching uphol-stered furnishings, the bedroom had an en-suite bathroom containing a circular whirlpool tub big enough to house an entire rugby team. Daisy had particular trouble breathing though when she got a load of the obscenely large bed. Raised on a dais and covered in a gold satin quilt, it had enough pillows to put a harem to shame.

Of course Brody had just assumed they'd be sleeping to-gether. Why wouldn't he? The man obviously had more money than God, and the arrogance to match. And when you factored in his devastating good looks and that bad-boy Irish charm, she'd bet her bottom dollar no woman had ever said no to him.

She strode back into the bathroom, her annoyance chok-ing her. Twisting the gold-plated taps, she watched the steaming water gush out. Sprinkling in a generous helping of flakes from a heavy glass jar on the vanity, she breathed in the lavender mist and tried to focus on the scent's calming properties. She had a few hours till he arrived at six o'clock. She'd soak out the kinks from the flight, try to relax a little and go over exactly how she was going to handle Brody when he showed up.

CHAPTER TEN

DAISY glanced at the clock on the wall. Still only four-thirty. She closed her eyes, slid into the lavender-scented bubbles and let her mind drift over the classical music coming from the state-of-the-art console in the wall. Despite the battle that loomed large in her future, all the muscles in her body melted into blissful oblivion. When was the last time she'd been able to indulge herself like this? In a place as luxurious as this? Never, that was when.

Ten more minutes of nirvana, that was all she asked, then she'd get ready to face Brody.

She heard a small clicking sound beneath the music and frowned.

'Welcome to New York, angel.'

She shot upright, her eyes flying open as water cascaded onto the floor. 'What are you doing here?' she yelped, wrapping her arms around her naked breasts.

'I live here,' Connor Brody said, the lazy grin spreading as his eyes drifted down.

He stood by the tub, looking tall and gorgeous and intimidating, his hands sunk into the pockets of a charcoal-grey designer suit, a few wisps of chest hair visible above the open collar of his white shirt. She'd never seen him in anything but sweats and jeans and a T-shirt before now. The formal business-wear should have made him look tamer and more sophisticated, but somehow the perfectly tailored fabric had exactly the opposite effect—accentuating the rough, raw masculinity that lay beneath the veneer of civilisation.

And to make matters worse, she was stark naked.

Daisy swallowed heavily, the blast of heat flooding through her coming from more than just the hot bath. She was in serious trouble here.

Those deep blue eyes wandered to her bosom. 'Glad to see you made yourself at home.'

Daisy sank down sharply, splashing more water over the rim, until her chin hit the bubbles. Keeping one arm tight across her breasts, she used the other to shield her sex.

'If you don't mind,' she squeaked, equal parts outrage and mortification, 'I'm having a bath.'

'So I see.' He grinned some more. Then, to her astonishment, he took off his jacket, flung it on the floor, rolled up his shirt sleeves and perched on the edge of the tub.

'What are you doing?' she cried, still squeaking, as he picked up a bar of hotel soap.

Those piercing eyes fixed on her face as he ripped off the soap wrapper, dipped his hands into the water and began lathering the soap in long, tanned fingers. The glint of mischief in his gaze did nothing to diminish the desire.

'Giving you a hand,' he said casually, too casually. The deep husky tone of his voice reverberated across her nerve endings.

She pressed her palm into her sex, struggling to hold back the surge of heat that had made the muscles loosen. 'I don't want a hand.' The breathlessness of the words meant the statement didn't sound as definite as it should.

His lips quirked, as if she'd said something amusing.

He dropped the soap into its bowl and threaded soapy fingers through the hair at her nape. 'Are you sure?' he murmured, reminding her of their first night.

She gasped as his thumb stroked the rapid beat of her pulse and his hand cradled the back of her neck. She braced wet palms against his chest. Water splashed onto the floor as she soaked the front of his shirt. She could see the dark shadow of his chest hair through the damp linen, feel the hard muscles beneath and her arms shook.

He simply laughed and pulled her easily to him as his lips covered hers.

He devoured her mouth, exploring with the strong, insistent strokes of his tongue. The heat geysered up from her core as her fingers curled into the wet fabric. She wanted to shove him away, she really did, but his tongue, his lips were making her light-headed, and every single nerve in her body was throbbing with need. He let her go abruptly and stood up. She could hear the pants of her own breathing, ragged against the melodious tones of the concerto, as she watched him strip off his shirt and kick off his shoes. He reached for his belt and suddenly sanity came flooding back.

What was she doing? What was she letting him do? She wasn't his mistress. Maybe she wasn't going to be able to resist him for long, but she would not be treated like some convenient sex toy—at his beck and call whenever he felt like it.

'Stop it. We're not making love,' she said, but the words came out on a barely audible croak.

He glanced up, his hands stilling on his belt. 'What was that, now?'

She shivered under the intensity of his gaze as he stared at her, sure she was about to catch fire. 'We're not making love until we've got a few things sorted out,' she said, her arms clasped so tightly around her breasts she could hardly breathe.

'What things?' he said, sounding mildly interested.

She gulped, spotting the impressive erection tenting the loose pleats in the front of his trousers. The muscles in her thighs went liquid and her sex throbbed painfully, an instinctive reaction to the memory of how good he'd once felt inside her. It seemed absence had only made her more of a nymphomaniac.

'I'm not your mistress. You may think I'm bought and paid for. But I'm not.' She babbled to a stop. He was looking at her as if she'd taken leave of her senses. 'You don't own me,' she soldiered on regardless. 'And I won't be treated as if you do.'

He shrugged. 'Right enough,' he said, then pulled down his zipper. The crackle of the metal teeth unlocking drew her gaze down. 'Move over. I've a mind to join you in the tub.'

'I most certainly will…' But her indignant reply backed up in her throat as his trousers and boxers dropped to the floor and her eyes fixed on his groin. Unfortunately, he hadn't got any less beautiful, any less magnificent than the last time she'd seen him naked. Her whole body began to shake.

She gulped, her mouth bone-dry, and forced her eyes back to his face as he stepped into the tub. The sensual smile made it obvious he was very well aware of the effect his nakedness had on her.

He settled beside her, his big body making the water and her temperature rise. 'Now, where were we?' he said.

She lay transfixed by her raging hormones as he reached behind him for the soap.

She opened her mouth but no coherent sound came out as he lathered the soap then, nudging her arms to the side, placed his hands on her breasts. Her breath gushed out, sensation overwhelming her as he lifted the heavy orbs, his thumbs teasing swollen nipples. She arched up, closed her eyes, and groaned. Those demanding, purposeful fingers felt so good. She wanted him to touch her all over, everywhere. Her eyes jerked open, heat spiralling down to her core, when he captured her nipples and tugged.

'This is such a bad idea,' she whispered, swaying towards

him and gripping his lean waist for balance as he continued to concentrate all his attention on her breasts.

He laughed, a raw, dominant chuckle that told her he knew exactly how good an idea her body thought it was. 'I know,' he rasped as she felt his erection nudge her thigh. 'I left the damn condoms in the other room.'

She flattened one hand on his chest, felt the silky resilience of smooth flesh over bunched muscles and tried to find the will to stop him. But then his palm glided down her abdomen and found the swollen flesh of her sex under the water.

His fingers explored, brushing her clitoris with the tiniest of touches and she bucked against him, crying out. He sealed off her cries with a harsh, demanding kiss, dragging her against him with one arm as his other hand continued to play havoc, stroking and caressing, pressing her sweet spot and then retreating. Her hips moved in a siren's rhythm, her fingers clutching at the back of his neck. He fastened his lips on the pulse in her throat, suckled as she threw her head back and gave herself up to the sensations exploding up from her core, only dimly aware of the water soaking the floor.

The orgasm roared through her, each wave pulsing over her body with greater intensity. The broken sobs of her release echoed as she collapsed against him, limp and shuddering, his embrace the only thing that was keeping her from sinking into the bath water and drowning.

She felt the insistent outline of his erection against her hip as his breath whispered across her ear lobe. 'Let's finish this in bed.' The words had barely registered when he stood up, hefted her in his arms and stepped out of the tub, splashing water everywhere.

'Put me down.' She struggled, the serene moment of afterglow wiped out by acute embarrassment.

Why had she let him march in and take over like that? Why had she succumbed so easily? She was more at his mercy now than ever.

He set her on her feet and threw her a towel before grabbing one for himself. She wrapped it around herself. The drenched bathmat squelched beneath her feet and the remnants of his suit lay sodden on the marble tiles. 'Look what you've done,' she cried, knowing she wasn't talking about the mess.

He smiled, rubbing the towel across his chest, the relaxed grin casting a seductive spell. 'Don't worry, I intend to do a lot more—and soon.'

Heat scorched her insides as she realised just how far out of control things had become. He threw his towel away, then covered the fists she had anchored on hers with one large palm. 'Let go, angel. You don't need it.'

'I'm cold,' she murmured as she trembled, but she knew she wasn't.

'You won't be for long,' he said. Her fingers released of their own accord and he dragged the towel away. Lifting her against his chest, he carried her into the bedroom.

Her mind struggled to fight the sensual lethargy as he tumbled them onto the bed, trapping her beneath his body. She could feel every single inch of him, all firm muscle and lean masculine strength. She flattened her palms against his chest. 'Don't. I don't want you.' Her body screamed 'liar' as her mind struggled with the feeling of powerlessness, of being under his control.

He stiffened and something flashed in his eyes. 'I think you do,' he said, his voice strained. He took a condom from the dresser.

'You can't make me.' Her voice rose as she watched him sheath himself with single-minded efficiency.

'Make you?' He raised his head, one eyebrow bobbing up as his hand swept into her hair, cradled her head. 'I would never make you,' he said carefully, his thumb brushing her bottom lip. 'You must know that. But you're lying to yourself as well as me if you say you don't want me, angel.'

Strong hands gripped her thighs, angling her pelvis. 'Tell me again you don't want me and I'll let you go. I'll not force you,' he said.

She could feel the heat pulsing at her core, her chest heaving with longing, and knew she couldn't lie a second time. Couldn't bring herself to say the words that would deny her the pleasure he would give her.

The huge head of his erection probed. The pressure was immense as the slick folds of her sex tightened around him, but then he stopped.

The yearning to feel that one strong thrust that would force him deep, impale her, consumed her. But he didn't penetrate any further, the sinews in his neck taut as his eyes locked on hers.

'Ladies' choice, angel,' he murmured. His lips touched hers in a mocking kiss, tension vibrating through him. 'Now you tell me what it is you *do* want.'

Her hips flexed instinctively, and the delicious heat speared through her as he sank a fraction deeper. His fingers tightened, holding her still. She bit hard into her bottom lip, trapped and tortured by her own desires. Her own weakness.

'I want to hear you say it,' he said.

Her whole body clamoured for the release, for the blessed joy that only he had ever given her—and he knew it, she realised. She groaned, desperate to force the yearning back. Why was he making her beg? Hadn't she admitted enough? Hadn't she given him enough power? If she begged him now she'd be no better than a mistress—and maybe a great deal worse.

'Tell me you want me,' he demanded, his raw pants matching her own.

A staggered moan of surrender escaped her lips. 'Please… Do it. I want you. You know I do…'

A sharp dart of shame pierced her heart, but her mind disengaged as he thrust fully into her at last. He drove in up to the hilt, spearing through the tight, tender flesh and hurtling her over the edge. The orgasm burst free so much faster and stronger than before. She cried out, clutching his shoulders, clinging on as her legs locked around his waist. He pumped in and out in a furious, frenzied rhythm, filling her with an intensity, a ruthlessness that dragged her back with alarming speed and forced her over again—and again.

Finally, as she shattered into a million tiny glittering pieces, drained and exhausted from the relentless waves racking her body, he shouted out his own release—and shattered too.

CHAPTER ELEVEN

CONNOR collapsed onto his back, flung his arm across his face and struggled to draw a steady breath as his heartbeat battered his chest like a heavyweight champ's punching ball.

Where the hell had that come from?

One minute he'd been teasing her, enjoying the way her eyes darkened with desire, and the next he'd been gripped by a possessiveness, an intensity he didn't understand.

His affairs with women were always casual and fleeting. Sex was fun, fulfilling and must never be taken too seriously. He didn't do intense. So why had he turned into such a caveman when she'd told him she didn't want him?

The minute she'd said the words, he'd known she was lying. He'd seen the desire in her eyes, known all he had to do was touch her and she'd respond. But even so, he should have backed off, left well enough alone. Instead, something had welled up inside him, a bitterness, a resentment, a feeling of inadequacy he recognised from his childhood— and he'd been overwhelmed by the need to prove her wrong, to make her admit the truth.

He glanced across at her. She'd curled away from him, her shoulders trembling. He rose up on his elbow. Hell, was she crying? His heart clutched in his chest.

He pulled the quilt up to cover them both, smoothed his hand over her hip. She shifted away.

'Daisy, are you all right?'

'Of course,' she said, but her voice sounded small and fragile. He studied the sprinkling of freckles across her shoulder blades, the way her damp hair was already springing up around her head. She looked so delicate to him all of a sudden. He winced. She'd been so tight around him and yet he'd taken her like a man possessed. Had he hurt her?

'Are you sure?' he asked, not sure he wanted to hear the answer.

She didn't reply, just sat up with her back to him, and pulled the thin cotton shift she'd left beside the bed over her head. He watched her movements, jerky and tense. The urge to hold her, to comfort her, to make up for what he'd done, blindsided him.

He stiffened. What the hell was happening to him? He didn't even recognise himself. She'd done something to him. Come to mean something he didn't understand.

In the last week he hadn't been able to stop thinking about her. Getting her to New York had been a game—a way of showing her the error of her ways, and enjoying some great recreational sex into the bargain. Or so he'd tried to tell himself.

But if it was all a game, why had he bought her a ten-thousand-euro necklace without a thought when he'd been window-shopping in the Marais? Sure he was usually generous with the women he dated, but not that generous after only one date. Why had he spent over an hour outlining his plans for her trip with his PA? Why had he called the airline first thing that morning to check she'd boarded the flight? And why had he cancelled the rest of his meetings and raced back to The Waldorf as soon as he'd got the word she'd checked in?

He'd been behaving like an over-eager puppy begging for scraps. It made him feel vulnerable in a way he hadn't since he was a lad. But he hadn't been able to stop himself.

And then, to make matters worse, when he'd walked into the bathroom and seen her lush body covered in soap suds, her soft flesh pink from the heat, the expected sexual charge had been swiftly followed by a blast of euphoria and bone-deep satisfaction that made no sense at all.

Given all that, was it any surprise that when she'd told him she wanted no part of him he'd been bound and determined to prove her a liar? To prove that she did want him—because he wanted her so damn much it was starting to scare him.

'Daisy, will you look at me?' he said, his patience stretching. 'I want to see you're okay.'

She glanced over her shoulder.

Relief washed through him when he saw no evidence of tears.

'Why wouldn't I be okay?' Green fire flashed as she faced him. 'You gave me what I wanted, right? What you made me beg for. You should be pretty pleased with yourself, all things considered.'

An unreasoning panic seized him as she turned away and he leaped forward to catch her arm.

'Wait.' His fingers clamped on her wrist.

Whatever had happened, they'd have to sort it out, because he wasn't ready to let her walk—not yet. Not until he sorted out what the hell was happening to him. She'd triggered something inside him and he needed her here to make it stop.

'Let go of me,' she said, her head bowed as she tried to wrestle her hand free. 'I'm not staying. You'll have to find another fake date. The sex is great, but the subservience I can do without, thank you.'

He dropped his feet on the floor, sat on the edge of the bed and pulled her to him when she tried to resist. 'Daisy, I'm sorry.'

He'd never apologised to any woman before her—he'd

never needed to—and the words burned like acid on his tongue. He figured they'd been worth it, though, when she stopped struggling and looked at him. Anger still simmered, but behind it was something much harder to fathom.

'What are you apologising for?' she asked, her voice flat and remote. 'For giving me my first multiple orgasm?'

He had hurt her. He could see now he'd humiliated her. He knew a lot about pride and what it felt like to have it beaten out of you. Enough to know how much it hurt.

He took her other wrist and tugged her towards him, pressing his knees into her thighs, to keep her near. 'It wasn't meant as a punishment,' he said. He rested his hands on her hips, blew out a breath as he touched his cheek to the soft cotton covering her breasts. Her hands remained limply by her side, the muscles of her spine rigid beneath his fingers as she arched away from him. Lavender, underlaid with the scent of her, made blood surge into his groin, he hoped to hell she couldn't see it beneath the thick folds of the quilt. He raised his head, saw the flush of unhappiness and something else he didn't recognise on her face.

'Why did you make me beg for it, then?' she asked, accusation weighing every word. 'It was cruel and humiliating. What were you trying to prove?' Her frankness and vulnerability stunned him—and made him feel like a worm.

He shrugged, keeping his hands on her waist so she couldn't pull back any further.

'I wanted you to stay. And it seemed like a good way to persuade you.'

It wasn't the whole truth. In fact it wasn't even half of the truth. But he could hardly tell her how desperate he'd been to see her, how much he'd been looking forward to her coming over. It would make him look like a besotted idiot—and give her entirely the wrong impression.

Women always tried to romanticise sex—especially exceptional sex. And that was all this was really about. No woman had ever responded to him as she did, no woman had ever affected him quite like her before. But once he got her out of his system things would be fine.

Obviously his desire to stamp his claim on her had been brought on by sexual frustration. He'd never been this attracted to a woman in his life. But that would pass soon enough, he was sure of it. Romance had no part of it. Not for him.

'Why did you have to make me say it?' she asked, the words more confused than angry.

He choked out a half-laugh. Christ, why had he? 'I don't know.' And he was pretty sure now he didn't want to know. Best to leave that can of worms well enough alone. He'd just have to make damn sure he didn't lose his cool with her and open it up all over again.

Her eyes sharpened and he could see she didn't believe him. But then she sighed and her shoulders slumped. Finally she looked back at him and what he saw, to his amazement, was guilt.

'I know you paid a lot of money to get me here. And you didn't force me, not really. I wanted to come. I've never been to New York before.' She glanced round the room. 'And this place is incredible. But it's all so overwhelming. And I can't stay here as your mistress. It's demeaning.' Her brow furrowed. 'If you still need someone to pose as your girlfriend you can get me a cheap room, somewhere else, and I'll still do it. Then you won't be out of pocket. Okay?'

His heart contracted at the seriousness on her face. Damn. He'd known she was a Good Samaritan but this was stupid. He couldn't care less about her 'posing' as his girlfriend or the money he'd spent getting her here. Truth was he'd been showing off a little, wanting to dazzle her, trying to make sure she came. Who would have known his attempts to impress her would backfire?

He sighed. He should have guessed she'd be the first

woman to be turned off by the money instead of turned on by it. She was so contrary.

But how could he tell her how much he wanted her with him and not make it sound as if there were more going on than there actually was? He needed to lighten the mood, get things back on their proper footing, not make them more intense.

Then a vague recollection of what Danny had said about the whole Melrose problem came to him and he had his answer in a flash of divine inspiration.

'You'll stay here with me, Daisy. You didn't just come for New York or The Waldorf. You came because you want me and I want you. And after what just happened there'll be no more denying it.' That at least he intended to make very plain.

She stiffened. 'I don't care. I told you I won't be your—'

'Shush now,' he said, feeling the flutter of her pulse as he pressed his thumb into her wrist. 'I've a solution to the problem that should satisfy your pride.'

He gave her a friendly pat on the rump. 'Go get some clothes on. We've a lot to do before we can have supper and I'm famished.'

Instructing her to meet him in the lobby in twenty minutes, Connor left Daisy to get dressed in the private dressing room. As she prepared herself for the evening ahead Daisy got the distinct impression she'd just been railroaded, but she felt too bewildered to worry about it now. She needed some time alone, to make sense of what had happened. Of what she'd let happen.

She'd been so angry and humiliated after they'd made love—correction: after she'd begged him to make love to her, again—that she'd wanted to hate him.

But then he'd apologised, and she'd been forced to face the truth. He'd been honest about how much he wanted her and she hadn't. And then she'd been doubly humiliated. Not only could she not resist him, but she couldn't even claim the moral high ground now either.

As she dabbed on make-up and slipped into the vintage satin halter-neck dress she'd made she admitted that her protests that afternoon had made her seem like the worst kind of hypocritical prude. Had she really pretended to herself when she'd got on that plane—with a dazzling array of hooker underwear in her suitcase and the memory of their last sexual encounter still vivid in her mind—that she wasn't going to sleep with him?

She'd been deluding herself all along and all he'd done was point it out to her—in a rather forceful manner. The fairy-tale fantasy that had lured her onto the plane didn't just involve the glitz and glamour of a luxury fortnight in New York. She'd also been enthralled by Connor Brody and the incredible sexual chemistry they shared.

She stepped out of the penthouse lift, her pulse skittering as she saw Connor walking towards her, looking devastating in another of his designer suits. She wanted him, more than she'd ever wanted any man, and, however disturbing that might be to her peace of mind, she would have to stop denying it if she was going to learn to handle it.

Connor ushered her into the limo, and the small of her back sizzled under the warm weight of his palm. She sat back as the car sped off, watched the dizzying sights and sounds of Park Avenue roll by, and attempted to revise her survival strategy. Okay, staying out of Connor's bed was not going to be a viable option for the next two weeks. But her basic theory was still sound. All she had to do was make sure she didn't let her heart follow her hormones.

She watched as Connor leaned forward to give the driver instructions. Jet-black hair curled against the light-blue collar of his shirt; she clasped the purse in her lap and resisted the urge to run her fingers through the silky locks.

Connor Brody was a dangerous man: dangerously attractive, dangerously desirable and dangerously single-minded. When he wanted something he went after it. And at the moment he wanted her.

She gazed back out of the window, tearing her eyes away from him.

But he'd already told her this was strictly a two-week deal—and that suited her too. She wasn't going to start looking for her happy ever after with a guy who wasn't remotely interested. She wasn't her mother and this was her chance to prove it once and for all.

After their two weeks were up she would make sure she walked away from this relationship with some enchanting memories to savour and her heart one hundred per cent whole. The next fortnight would be a grand adventure that she intended to make the absolute most of, but it was not real life.

'We're here,' Connor said, taking her hand and stepping onto the sidewalk.

Daisy stared at the iconic jewellery stall as he tipped the driver. 'What are we doing here?'

'It's all part of the solution to our problem.' He cupped her elbow in his palm. 'By the way,' he said, his eyes sweeping her frame, 'that dress is deadly.'

Although the compliment pleased her, probably more than it should, she ignored the little leap in her pulse rate. He was railroading her again. And it was about time she put the brakes on. He'd called enough of the shots already.

'What solution?' she asked as he pushed the revolving door and stepped in behind her.

He settled his hand on the nape of her neck, his thumb stroking the sensitive skin. 'I'm buying you an engagement ring.'

And just like that, her senses went haywire and her calm, measured, practical approach to the whole situation went up in flames.

* * *

'I'm not wearing it. This is ridiculous.' She tried to tug her hand out of his grasp, but he simply lifted her fist and brushed his lips across the knuckles.

'Stop sulking, angel.' He sent her a teasing smile. 'Maureen will think you don't like the ring.' He nodded towards the sales lady, who was pretending to stack some of the store's signature blue and silver boxes.

'It's not that and you know it,' she snapped, hoping Maureen couldn't hear them. 'I can't wear it.'

Having endured the ten-minute charade as he and Maureen had ummed and ahhed over a selection of engagement rings until he'd finally picked out a delicate silver band studded with diamonds, Daisy wasn't sulking, she was in a state of shock.

She didn't want to wear the heartbreakingly beautiful ring.

She'd once dreamt of the moment when a man she loved and who loved her in return would put an engagement ring on her finger. Connor wasn't that man, would never be that man and this definitely wasn't that moment. She knew that. But she still didn't want him to put that ring on her finger.

'Why can't you wear it?' he asked, flattening her hand between his palms, turning it over. 'You don't want to be my mistress. Fine, I understand that. So we put the ring on. You become my fiancée for the next two weeks. Problem solved.'

She looked at him, saw the confidence, the arrogance and that devilish determination and wanted to kick him— not to mention herself. How could she explain her objections without coming across as a romantic fool? And why had she objected to being his mistress in the first place? When the alternative he'd found seemed a thousand times more disturbing. She felt as if she'd sashayed out of the frying pan and crashed headlong into the fire.

'But I'm not your fiancée. It would be a lie. I don't think

it's right. To lie, that is.' Great, now she sounded like a self-righteous prig instead.

He chuckled. 'Angel, don't take this so seriously. It's only for two weeks.' He brushed her cheek. 'We have some fun, my business deal is settled and no one's pride is compromised. Fair enough?'

It sounded so reasonable when he said it like that. Was she blowing this out of proportion? Making a big deal about nothing? Hadn't Mrs Valdermeyer also accused her of taking things too seriously? If she wanted to enjoy the next two weeks, make the most of them, didn't she have to learn to relax first?

She sighed. 'Fine, but you'll have to do all the introductions. I'm not good at lying to people.'

He smiled. 'It won't be a lie, just one of the shortest engagements on record,' he said and slipped the ring on her finger. But as the cool silver slid down she felt another band tighten around her heart.

Connor felt the slight tremble as he held her wrist to push the ring home. He steadfastly ignored the answering jump in his pulse. Sure he'd never put a ring on any woman's finger before, and never intended to again. The strange surge of pride, of satisfaction as he did it, didn't mean a thing. Not a blessed thing.

CHAPTER TWELVE

'I'VE got to tell you, it's been fabulous meeting you, Daisy,' Jessie Latimer said, her bright face brimming with enthusiasm. 'Monroe and I always knew the woman to capture Connor's heart would have to be very special. After all, he's quite a handful.'

'Yes, he is.' Daisy clutched the stem of her champagne glass and forced herself to smile back—not easy when her face ached and she felt as if she were about to throw up. Connor Brody wasn't just a handful, he was quite possibly a dead man after putting her in this excruciating predicament. Especially as it had come totally out of the blue.

The last week had gone by in a whirlwind of sights, sounds and activities. Daisy had never been anywhere as full on as New York before or with anyone as full on as Connor. And, despite all her misgivings, they'd had a wonderful time. They'd managed to pack in the Metropolitan Opera, the Met, Coney Island and the Circle Line tour, and in between times had had the best sex of Daisy's life. Because Connor was as full on a lover as he was a tour guide, but she'd soaked up every amazing sight and mind-blowing sexual experience and found she still wanted more. They'd both been determined to keep things light and non-committal. They didn't talk about the future and they didn't delve into each other's real lives and, as a consequence, she'd had very little time to dwell on the whole 'fake engagement' thing.

She thought she'd been handling it really well.

In fact, in the last six days, she'd only had two major hurdles to overcome. The worst had been the first night, when she'd tried to take the ring off in the bathroom of their suite and Connor had asked her to leave it on. He'd given her some excuse about not wanting to buy another if she lost it, a cocky smile on his lips, but when they'd made love that night and she'd spotted the ring winking at her she'd felt that funny clutch in her heart again. And it had taken her over an hour to fall asleep, despite the jet lag.

She'd handled the second hurdle much better. Being introduced to a group of Connor's business associates at an exclusive cocktail party the previous night had been a cinch in comparison. She'd decided that she'd settled into the charade now and it would be plain sailing from here on in. All she need do was think of herself as an actress playing a role.

But then they'd arrived at the opening of the brand-new Latimer Gallery twenty minutes ago, and Connor had introduced her to Monroe Latimer—a world-famous artist whose work Daisy had admired at the Tate Britain only a few months ago—and his wife, Jessie. And the subterfuge of pretending to be Connor's fiancée had become a thousand times tougher.

It had been obvious as soon as they'd been introduced that the couple were close friends of Connor. As he'd given her no warning, Daisy had assumed that Connor would simply tell them the truth. But when Jessie had spotted the ring and got excited, Connor had lied without a qualm, even talking about their wedding plans, before Monroe had dragged him off to find a beer.

Consequently, Daisy had been stuck lying through her teeth to a woman she'd warmed to instantly. A fellow Brit, Jessie Latimer had been friendly and funny and welcoming from the get-go; she'd been gracious and not at all big-headed when Daisy had gushed about the gallery and her husband's work and told Daisy some sweet and charming anecdotes about the couple's three daughters and what it was like to be an Englishwoman in New York. But the instant they'd got onto the subject of Daisy's impending nuptials, Daisy had felt as if she were being strangled by her conscience.

She wasn't a dishonest person—and she was fast discovering that she was a rubbish actress too.

'You're so different from the other women he's dated,' Jessie said. Her eyes widened and she touched Daisy's arm. 'God, I'm sorry, that sounded really gauche. But I mean it in the best possible way. Monroe and I have known him for three years now—ever since we started this project.' She glanced round the loft-style space in Tribeca which housed some of New York's most prestigious modern art. 'We hit it off with Connor right away, not just as an investment partner but as a friend,' Jessie continued. 'But Monroe and I could never get over some of the bimbos he dated.' She gave an easy laugh. 'I'm so glad he's finally found a woman who can match him. It's what he's always needed in his life, I suspect. Although it's taken him a hell of a long time to figure it out.'

Daisy felt her fake smile crack. Why had he lied to his friends like this? It was awful. The diamond ring felt like a lead weight on her finger as she lifted the champagne flute to her lips and took a fortifying sip. Her heart pounded so hard in her throat it threatened to cut off her air supply.

'Is there something wrong, Daisy? You're looking a little pale.'

Daisy's stomach took a swooping drop. This was the moment of truth. She couldn't continue lying to this woman. No wonder she looked pale—she was definitely going to be sick any moment.

'I don't know how to say this,' she said, her fingers shaking on the glass and making the champagne slop to the rim.

'What is it?' Concern darkened Jessie's eyes, making Daisy feel like even more of a fraud.

'We're not engaged. Connor and I.'

Jessie's eyebrows shot up. 'You're not?'

'No.' Daisy stared down at her hands, the glint of diamonds on her ring finger only adding to her shame. 'We're not getting married. We only met two weeks ago. He's my neighbour. He paid for me to come here so I could pose as his fiancée.'

God, the whole thing sounded so unbearably sordid. She looked up, steeling herself to deal with the disgust she expected to see on Jessie's face.

But she didn't see disgust. Jessie's shoulders trembled and then, to Daisy's complete astonishment, she started to laugh.

'You're kidding?' Jessie blurted out at last, when she could finally draw a steady breath.

Daisy shrugged, acutely embarrassed. 'No, I'm not. It's dreadful, I know. He's deceived you and Monroe. I've deceived you...' She trailed off, not sure what else to say when Jessie had to clasp her hand over her mouth to hold back her giggling fit.

As she stood there, listening to Jessie's muffled laughter and watching the beautiful people nearby craning their necks to stare at them, Daisy began to wonder what was worse—being Connor Brody's scarlet woman or a complete laughing stock.

'I'm so sorry. Don't be embarrassed.' Jessie squeezed her arm, managing to subdue her mirth with an effort. 'It's just, you have no idea how ironic this is.'

'Thanks for taking it so well,' she said tentatively.

'Don't mention it,' Jessie said, still grinning. 'Look, I hope you don't mind me asking this. But it's obvious you're not comfortable with this whole set-up. Why did you agree to do it?'

Daisy blew out a breath. 'That's a good question. And it's sort of complicated.'

'I'm sure it is,' Jessie said. 'And I don't mean to pry. But Connor's a good friend, and I'd love to know what's going on between the two of you.'

'It might take a while to explain it, from my point of view anyway,' Daisy said, realising to her surprise she didn't mind giving Jessie her answer. After all, she'd given the question a lot of thought over the last week and it was about time she came clean about her motives—to herself as well as Jessie.

'Honey.' Jessie smiled. 'We've got all evening, or at least until Monroe and Connor find a beer, which could take a while seeing as the caterers only stocked champagne for this event as far as I know.'

'All right,' Daisy said, taking a deep breath. 'First off, I should tell you I live in a bedsit in West London. I work six days a week on my stall in Portobello Market. And this whole scene…' she did a circling motion with her glass to encompass the glittering crowd of Manhattan's movers and shakers surrounding them '…is about as far from my real life as it's possible to get. I help out at the local old people's home once a week. I run the Carnival Arts project for the kids on a nearby council estate. I mentor and volunteer and I'm totally committed to my friends and my community.'

'Now I know why I liked you instantly,' Jessie said easily.

Bolstered by the appreciation she saw in Jessie's face, Daisy smiled. 'Don't get me wrong. I love my life. I love the stability and the purpose and the sense of belonging it gives me and I intend to build on that when I have my own family one day. And I'm not interested in becoming rich or anything.' She hesitated for a moment, stroked the stem of her glass. 'But I've spent my whole life being cautious, and practical and responsible until I find my Mr Right.' She looked at Jessie, saw the compassion in her eyes, but decided against bringing up her mother's misbegotten love life—that seemed a bit too personal. 'Connor, like the world he lives in, is the complete antithesis of my Mr Right. He's exciting, sexy, charming, completely spontaneous and totally unreliable.'

And the best lover I've ever had, she thought, but decided not to mention that either. After all, she didn't want Jessie to think she was a total slut.

'He's the opposite of what I'm looking for in a life partner. He's not dependable or interested in settling down and I totally understand that. So I'm not under any delusions.' Thank goodness. 'But right here, right now, I guess he's a guilty pleasure that I couldn't resist. I decided when I got his plane ticket, these two weeks were going to be my Cinderella fortnight and so far they've worked out really well.' Give or take the odd heart bump. 'But once this is over I'll be happy to go back to my real life and my real dreams.'

'I see,' Jessie said, giving her a considering look.

'I guess that sounds as if I'm using him,' Daisy said quickly, realising how it sounded now she'd spelled it out so succinctly. She started to feel a little queasy again. This woman was Connor's friend, after all, not hers, however much she might want her to be. 'But as he's using me right back,' she continued, 'I don't feel guilty about it.' Or she was trying hard not to.

'I don't think you're using him,' Jessie said staunchly.

'You don't?' The knots in Daisy's stomach loosened.

'No, I don't,' Jessie said firmly. 'And even if you were, it would serve him right.' She sent Daisy a quick grin. 'The words *hoisted* and *petard* springing to mind.'

Daisy's breath gushed out in a relieved huff. Maybe Jessie's approval shouldn't mean so much to her, but somehow it did.

'But I've got to tell you,' Jessie continued, 'I do think you might be selling Connor a little short. At least as far as you're concerned.'

Daisy's heartbeat kicked hard in her chest, her breathing becoming uneven again. She wasn't sure she liked the wistful look in Jessie's eyes. 'How so?'

Jessie stared at her for a long moment. 'The Connor you described—the handsome, reckless, unreliable charmer—is only the Connor you see on the surface. That's the face he shows to the world and that's the way he likes everyone to see him. Especially women.'

Jessie paused to pick up a canapé from the tray of a passing waiter, but her eyes barely left Daisy's. 'It's the way he came across to Monroe and I when we first met him.' Jessie bit into the salmon puff, took her time swallowing it. 'In fact when we got involved with this project we were both worried about him. He'd come recommended, but still we thought, Can we count on him? Will he bail out if the going gets tough? We were putting a lot of money on the line and as much as we liked him personally we weren't sure about him. Precisely because he seemed so relaxed, so easy-going, almost overconfident.'

'So why did you risk it?' Daisy asked, intrigued despite herself. She'd never asked Connor about his work, just as he'd never asked her about her stall. It was all part of that unwritten agreement they had that this wasn't a serious relationship, but, still, she wanted to know more.

'Originally we went ahead because I got my brother-in-law Linc, who's a Wall Street financier, to do a thorough check on Brody Construction. The company's still young, even now, but it came out with flying colours, so we signed the partnership deal with Connor.' Jessie huffed. 'Almost straight away things started to go wrong on the project. The permits took much longer to come through than originally forecast. One of the suppliers went into receivership out of the blue. The building had a structural problem that hadn't come up on the survey. Talk about a money pit. Frankly, the whole rehab was a complete nightmare.' She grinned. 'Connor, though, turned out to be our knight in shining armour, and the exact opposite of what he had first seemed. He was dedicated, conscientious, incredibly hard-working, inventive and one hundred and ten per cent reliable. He even put on a tool belt himself a couple of times towards the end of the build to get things done.'

Daisy felt her chest swell with pride at Jessie's praise—and then felt ridiculous. After all Connor wasn't even her proper boyfriend. She began to wonder if she really needed to know about this side of him. It had been so much easier to dismiss him as a feckless charmer.

'It's nice to know he's so good at his job,' she said, trying hard to sound non-committal. 'He must enjoy it, which is probably why he's so successful.'

'He does enjoy it. But I'd say what he enjoys most is the challenge. Which brings us to the fascinating subject of Connor's love life. Which has never been remotely challenging.'

Daisy sipped her champagne, but the bubbles did nothing to ease the dryness in her throat. She really didn't need to know about his past relationships with women. Especially as their relationship had a sell-by date that was fast approaching. Now would be a good time to change the subject.

'What were they like?' she asked. 'The other women he's dated?' Blast, where had that come from?

'Interchangeable and shallow,' Jessie said, before Daisy could take the question back. 'I was being a bit unfair calling them bimbos, though. Some of them have been very shrewd. The last one he dated, Rachel, being a case in point. I wasn't at all surprised when she told Connor she was pregnant.'

Daisy bobbled her glass. 'Connor has a child?'

'Of course not,' Jessie said. 'She wasn't pregnant. It was what you might call a very convenient scare. Just when he was trying to end the relationship.'

'What did he do?' Daisy asked, riveted by the topic despite everything.

'To everyone's astonishment he offered to marry her, to support the child. Even though Monroe and I both knew it was the last thing he wanted to do. When he told us she wasn't pregnant after all, he looked like a guy who had escaped the executioner's block.'

'He didn't want to be a father?' Daisy said, feeling strangely depressed, even though she already knew Connor wasn't the family man type.

'I don't think it's quite that simple. I don't know for sure, but I think he had a really tough childhood and his attitude to kids and family is very confused because of it. But one thing I do know is that he is petrified of commitment. He's a property developer but as far as I know the place he's rehabbed in London, the house next door to yours, is the first home he's ever bought for himself.'

'I see,' Daisy said, feeling even more dispirited.

Jessie sent her a knowing smile. 'Which makes it all the more bizarre that he's put his ring on your finger less than two weeks after meeting you.'

Daisy glanced at the ring, which seemed to have got even heavier while they were talking. 'Yes, but I've told you it's not a real commitment. On his part or mine.'

'Are you sure?' Jessie cut her off.

Daisy blinked. Swallowed. Of course she was sure, because anything else didn't bear thinking about. But somehow the denial got lodged in Daisy's throat.

'There are several things about this situation that don't add up, Daisy,' Jessie continued. 'First off, it's very noticeable how different you are from the other women Connor's dated. You're not shallow, or stupid, or shrewd.

Second off, he treats you differently from the way he treated them. I mean, he walked in here with you on his arm and basically staked you out as his for everyone to see. He's never done that before. He's not the possessive type. Not till now anyway.' Jessie took Daisy's hand and held up the ring. 'And this whole fake engagement thing. It seems a bit extreme. Why does someone like Connor need a fake fiancée? That I'd really like to know.'

'He hasn't said, not specifically,' Daisy replied, and decided then and there she was never going to ask him. Because everything Jessie was saying was making her feel very uneasy.

'Fine,' Jessie said. 'But I guess what I'm really saying is, I know Connor. And I think there's a lot more going on here than either he or you realise.'

Daisy gulped in a breath, felt her heart pound against her chest wall like a battering ram. Now she really couldn't breathe. This she definitely did not want to hear. Because she could see a great big chasm opening up at her feet.

One she had no intention of jumping into.

She pulled her hand out of Jessie's grasp. 'I'm really flattered that you'd think I'm special, or different,' she said carefully, 'but I'm not.'

'To which I'd have to say,' Jessie countered, 'that if you really think that, you're selling yourself short, as well as Connor.'

Daisy lifted her glass of champagne, ignored the way it trembled as she took a sip.

She couldn't do this. She couldn't afford to think for even a moment that this thing with Connor could be anything more than it was, because that way lay serious danger. She couldn't afford to fall in love with a man who was petrified of commitment, for whatever reason. And she didn't want to.

Jessie, she decided, was just a hopeless romantic, who

clearly cared deeply about Connor and wanted him to be happy. But whatever Jessie might think about their so-called relationship, it wouldn't change the outcome of their two-week fling. And Daisy was far too practical and well grounded to think it could.

'There's no big romance here, Jessie,' she said, but her voice wasn't quite as firm as it should be.

Jessie simply smiled and said, 'Don't be so sure.'

'Right, spill it, buddy, what's between you and that cute little redhead?' Monroe Latimer slanted Connor his 'you're busted' look and slugged back the last of his beer. 'And don't tell me she's your fiancée.' He dropped the empty bottle onto the bar. 'You may have got Red fooled, but I happen to know wild horses couldn't get you to propose.'

'Fair enough.' Connor lifted his hands in surrender, knowing when he'd been rumbled. He'd planned to tell Monroe the truth straight away, but, well, what with one thing and another, they'd been at the bar for twenty minutes partaking of Monroe's secret stash of beer and he hadn't quite got round to it. 'She's not my fiancée. She's my new neighbour in London. She's smart and pretty and, for reasons too boring to mention…' and way too transparent to mention to Monroe '…I needed a girlfriend while I was here and she fitted the bill. No strings attached.'

'Hmm,' Monroe said, keeping his eyes on Connor as he signalled the barman for a fresh beer. 'Which does *not* explain why you told Red and me she was your fiancée. Or why you bought her what has to be a real pricey ring.'

Connor took a gulp of his own beer. 'It's complicated.'

'I'll bet,' Monroe said, looking at him as if he were a bug under a microscope.

'And not the least bit interesting,' he countered.

'Humour me.'

Connor gave a half-laugh, although he wasn't finding being a bug all that amusing any more.

Monroe was a mate, a good mate. They'd even got drunk together one night and told each other more about their pasts than either of them was comfortable with—and their friendship had survived it. But there was one thing they'd never agreed on. And that was the subject of love and family.

That same night, when they'd been legless and overly sentimental, Connor had told Monroe that he would never fall in love. And Monroe had told him right back that he was talking a load of bull. Monroe had said that a guy didn't get to pick and choose those things, which Connor had thought then, and still thought now, was even bigger bull. Maybe Monroe had been blindsided and fallen in love with Jessie, and once Connor had got to know Jessie he could see why, but Connor knew that would never, ever happen to him.

Because what Monroe didn't know, what no one knew, was raising a family, having a home, was Connor's idea of hell. And no woman would ever be able to change that for him. Christ, when Rachel had told him she was pregnant, his whole life had flashed before his eyes—and not in a good way.

He knew Monroe and Jessie thought his reaction had been down to the fact that Rachel wasn't the right woman for him, but he knew different. He knew it had nothing to do with the woman. It went much deeper than that, and much further back. He'd offered to marry her, to support the baby, because he couldn't live with himself and know a child of his had been left to fend for itself. But that hadn't changed his gut reaction. He didn't want the child and he didn't want a wife. Any wife. And he was fine with that, fine and dandy.

He could tell by the way his friend was looking at him right now, though, that Monroe thought this little charade with Daisy was somehow significant. Sure he'd enjoyed her company in the last week. He'd got a thrill out of showing her the sights, and seeing her wide-eyed, enthusiastic re-action to everything. And in bed? Let's just say she'd exceeded his wildest expectations. He'd even got an unex-pected kick out of showing her off as his fiancée. But that was all there was to it. A week from now they'd go their separate ways and that would be that. So Connor intended to head his friend's misconception right off at the pass.

'All right,' he sighed. 'I should have been straight with you and Jessie. But after all the matchmaking advice I've had to endure from your lovely wife over the last three years, Roe. You've got to know, I couldn't resist when she spotted the ring.'

'Fair point.' Monroe saluted him with his bottle of beer. 'I'll grant you Jessie is pretty damn persistent. But I hope you realise your little joke is going to backfire on you.'

'She'll forgive me,' he said, feeling his confidence return-ing. He raised his eyebrows. 'After all, she can't resist my irresistible Irish charm.'

'Yeah, right.' Monroe laughed. 'But that's not what I meant.'

'What did you mean, then?' Why didn't he feel quite so confident any more?

'I gotta tell you, for a minute there you had me fooled as well as Jessie. You want to know why?'

Connor didn't say a word.

'Because you fit,' Monroe said, and Connor's heart stopped dead. 'You and your cute little redhead. Daisy, that's her name, right?'

Connor nodded dumbly, trying to pull himself together. This was ludicrous. Monroe was just trying to get a rise out of him. And it was working.

'She suits you, pal,' Monroe said, swigging his beer. 'Right down to the ground. I'm an artist, I happen to have an eye for these things and I'm telling you. She's the one.'

Connor growled a profanity under his breath, his stomach churning as he tried to see the joke. But why did it suddenly seem as if the joke was on him?

Monroe chuckled. 'Hey, what happened to that irresistible Irish charm, buddy?'

'Why didn't you tell me Jessie and Monroe were friends of yours before we got to the gallery tonight?' Daisy pulled out her earrings and dropped them in a bowl by the vanity.

She'd bided her time, not wanting to bring it up until she'd got a good firm grip on her own emotions. After the shock Jessie had given her it had taken a while.

'Hmm?' he said from behind her, then his hands settled on her waist. He pulled her into his arms, his naked chest warm against her back. 'You looked lovely tonight, you know,' he said, rubbing the silk of her slip against her belly as he nuzzled her ear. 'I may have to hire you for this gig again.'

The comment—and the heat drifting up from her sex at his casual caresses—couldn't have been calculated to ignite her temper quicker if he'd tried.

She turned in his arms, pushed against the muscled flesh. 'It's not funny,' she said, suddenly feeling more hurt than angry and hating herself for her weakness. 'You put me in a really difficult position. Not only not telling me you knew them, but then telling them we were getting married. And leaving me with Jessie like that. I felt awful. You knew I didn't want to lie to people. It wasn't fair.'

He stepped back, but kept his hands firmly on her waist. 'Come on, angel.' He tucked a finger under her chin, lifted her face to his. 'Don't look so upset. There was no harm done. They figured it out quick enough.'

'Jessie didn't. I had to tell her.' She turned away from him, braced her hands on the vanity.

And what Jessie had told her afterwards was still clutching at her heart, making panic clog her throat. Somehow her fantasy had changed tonight and become so much more real, and so much more frightening. She'd kept all the turbulent emotions at bay so effectively this past week, sealed herself off behind a wall of denial and sensation, but now the feel of his hands on hers, that clean, musky, masculine scent had become more intoxicating, more important to her than it was ever supposed to have been.

'I don't understand why you did that,' she said, raising her head to look at his reflection. With his shirt off and his chest bare, he looked as dark and devastating as always, but so much more dangerous now. 'Why did you introduce me to them as your fiancée?'

He shrugged. 'Just an impulse, I guess.' He had the lazy grin in place, but his eyes flickered away from hers as he said it. 'Stop worrying.' He pushed her hair back, trailed his thumb down the sensitive skin of her neck. 'Let's go to bed and forget it.' He pressed his lips to her pulse. 'I've got something much more interesting to discuss,' he whispered, one arm wrapping tight around her waist, his other hand cupping her breast, kneading the swollen flesh.

She moaned. His erection pressed against her bottom through their clothes, triggering the instant, instinctive response at her core. She angled her head to accept his harsh, demanding kiss, gave herself up to the heat, desperate to forget about everything but the feel of his body, the touch of his hands, his lips on hers.

He hadn't given her an answer. She knew that, but did she really want one?

She turned in his arms, encircled his neck with trembling hands, suddenly determined to cling onto the one thing that made sense.

'This is all that matters, angel,' he said, lifting her effortlessly in his arms and carrying her quaking into the bedroom. 'This is all that counts. Remember that.'

Yes. This is all that matters. I'm not looking for anything else.

But even as she threw herself into the moment, even as she chased that glittering oblivion, panic and an unreasonable regret gripped her heart.

CHAPTER THIRTEEN

As Daisy shielded her eyes to gaze at Belvedere Castle across the meadow, a bittersweet smile tugged her lips. With its fanciful turret and fortress ramparts, the elaborate folly could have been plucked straight out of a Grimm Brothers fairy tale and plopped into the middle of Central Park.

She sighed. No daydreaming allowed. It was their last full day in New York and somehow she'd managed to live in the moment in the last week, keep the doubts and uncertainties Jessie had unleashed at the gallery opening locked carefully away. She wasn't going to blow it all now.

The fact that Connor had turned out to be an expert at living in the moment hadn't hurt a bit. Whenever she'd found her mind drifting to more serious matters, whenever she'd found herself watching him and wondering, he'd found a way to distract her. With a ferry trip round the Statue of Liberty, or a deluxe dinner at his favourite restaurant, or in bed, where he had become an expert in making her forget everything but the heat between them.

But in the few quiet moments they shared, she had a bad habit of thinking about what might have been. If they'd been different people, if they'd needed the same things. She tried really hard not to let her thoughts go there, but right now, with the cartons from their impromptu picnic scattered around them and that damn fairy-tale castle looming on the other side of the meadow, she couldn't seem to stop herself.

After the Governor's Ball tonight and the first-class trip home tomorrow, she would be going back to her real life and, as much as she didn't want to admit it, she knew the thing she'd miss the most, much more than the glamour and the excitement, was the intimacy she'd shared with Connor. He'd be right next door, of course, but as far as she was concerned he'd be out of reach. She had to make a clean break, whatever happened; to let it drift on indefinitely would be suicidal and, anyway, they'd both known right from the start this was strictly a two-week deal.

The sun warmed the floppy hat she'd worn to hide her freckles as she observed Connor stretched out beside her in the long grass, his hands folded behind his head, and his eyes shaded by a pair of designer sunglasses. The hem of his T-shirt had risen up revealing a strip of tanned abdomen above the low waistband of his jeans.

She let her mind drift back to that first night, when she'd yearned to touch his naked body. She knew every glorious inch of it now—and she still had to fist her hands in her lap to stop herself from reaching out and running her palm over that warm, flat, lightly furred belly.

Well, that was certainly disappointing: two weeks of non-stop sexual pleasure hadn't even put a dent in her nymphomania.

She toed her sandals off, stretched her feet out in the grass and watched him. She knew he wasn't asleep, probably just thinking. About what? she wondered. Funny, they'd spent two whole weeks together and yet what did she really know about him? Apart from the fact that he wasn't looking for a long-term girlfriend, he had more charm and charisma than was feasible and he owned a very successful property development company. But as soon as she'd asked herself the question, a series of pictures flooded her mind like a living photo album.

The way he'd tucked into his hot dog at Coney Island and licked the mustard off his thumb with the same amount of relish as he gave to the meal he'd devoured at a five-star restaurant. The way he'd dropped change into the tin of every pan-handler and vagrant they passed. How relaxed he looked in both a designer suit and his favourite faded jeans. The sound of his terrible off-key whistle in the shower. Or how he never failed to compliment her on whatever she was wearing, usually before he stripped it off her. So what did that say about him? Generous to a fault, compassionate with those less fortunate than himself, definitely not a snob, great taste, completely insatiable and tone deaf.

But so much more about him was still a mystery. Their conversations had always been deliberately light and teasing and superficial. He didn't talk about his past and she didn't talk about hers. She'd thought that was the way it had to be, for both their sakes.

But now, with less than twenty-four hours left together, she wasn't so sure. Because she had to admit she was desperately curious to know more about him. Ever since she'd tended him through those hideous night terrors the first night they'd been together, she'd wondered about him, what had formed him.

She sighed. *Forget it, Daisy. You know what they say about curiosity and the cat. You'd be better off leaving well enough alone.*

She heard a shout and looked up to see a father throwing a ball to his two sons a few feet away. She concentrated on their game to stop her mind straying into more dangerous territory.

She smiled, noticing the way the older boy kept trying to push his younger brother out of the way, and how the father gently intervened. The sight made her heart squeeze. She wondered what kind of father Connor might have made if his last girlfriend had been pregnant after all. She chuckled. He'd probably have a heart attack if she asked him.

'What's so funny?'

She looked down to see Connor watching her, propped up on his elbow, his sunglasses thrown off on the grass and a curious smile on his face. She flushed and tried to think of an innocuous answer.

She nodded across the field to the man and his sons. 'I was just thinking what a wonderful dad he is.'

Connor craned his neck, leaning back on his elbows to watch. Then made a scoffing sound. 'How do you know he's a good father?'

It seemed self-evident to her, but she decided to humour him. 'Because he's being so fair with his two sons. And he really enjoys their company. When I have children, I'll want them to have a father like that. Someone as involved and committed as I am.' The words slipped out on a wistful sigh.

Connor's eyebrows lifted. '*When* you have children?'

'Well, yes.' She blushed, thinking she might have said too much, then thought, *What the heck?* This had been her dream for a long time, why should she keep it a secret? 'I've always wanted a family, a big happy family. In my opinion it's what makes life worth living.'

He watched her for what felt like an eternity, not saying a word. 'Is that what your own was like, then? Your family? Your father?'

The personal question stunned her a little. They'd both been avoiding them so carefully up till now. 'I never knew him.' She shrugged. 'But I was hardly deprived—there was never any shortage of pretend dads.'

His eyes narrowed. 'Pretend dads?'

She gave a laugh, trying for casual but getting brittle instead. 'My mother was the original born-again Bohemian—addicted to the idea of being in love. So she'd fall madly in love with some guy, we'd move in with him and then she'd discover he didn't love her—or not enough. I had a lot of what I called pretend dads as a result.' Why had she brought this up? Thinking about all those men who hadn't wanted to be her father, to be anyone's father, had always made her feel a little inadequate, and very insecure. 'None of them were horrible or anything like that. They all tried to be nice. But they weren't my father—and they didn't want to be.'

'That must have been tough,' he said gently.

His astuteness surprised her and made her feel unpleasantly vulnerable. 'I suppose it was at first,' she said, not sure she could cope with the sympathy in his eyes. 'When I was really little, I used to make the mistake of getting attached to them and then I'd be devastated when they left. But after a while I realised none of my mother's relationships would ever last. After that I forced myself not to get too attached and it was easier.'

Connor sat up, a strange tightness in his chest. She'd just given him an insight into her life he shouldn't really want. He'd been working overtime in the last week to make sure neither of them had too much time to think. He'd nearly blown things wide open at the gallery. And he still didn't know what had possessed him to introduce Daisy as his fiancée to Jessie and Monroe.

So he'd decided that night, when she'd looked so wounded, so unhappy, that the best thing to do was to keep things upbeat and not make any stupid mistakes again. Not to talk about feelings and emotions and any of that serious stuff that might complicate things.

But somehow, watching her now, hearing the hurt when she talked about all those pretend dads who'd rejected her, he felt the urge to comfort her, to make it right.

He gave his head a rueful shake as he studied her. 'Damn, Daisy, who'd have thought it?' He brushed his thumb down her cheek, felt her shiver. 'Who'd have thought my practical, steadfast little Daisy would be such a dreamer?' He forced a smile onto his lips, desperate to keep the situation light.

She took hold of his hand, pulled it down from her face. 'Why are you smiling?' she asked, and he could see the shadow of hurt in her eyes. 'What's so funny about the fact that I want a family? Just because you don't, it hardly gives you the right to laugh at me.'

'I'm not laughing. I don't think it's funny. What it is, is sweet and incredibly naive.'

'Why naive?' she said warily.

'Because you're looking for something you'll never find. There's no such thing as happy ever after. Your mother didn't find it because it was never there.' He sighed, then nodded at the spot across the meadow where the father was still playing with his sons, the old bitterness assailing him. 'How do you know yer man over there doesn't get drunk every once in a while and take his belt to those boys?'

She drew in a sharp breath. 'Why would you think that?' she whispered, her eyes wide with shock.

He shrugged but the movement felt stiff. 'Because it happens.'

'Your father did that to you, didn't he?' she said softly.

His heart slammed into his ribcage. 'How would you know that?' he said, carefully.

Seeing the compassion, the concern in her face, he wondered why the hell he'd started this conversation.

'You talk in your sleep, Connor, when you're having the nightmares.' Daisy watched his jaw tighten, the cocky smile gone from his face. And her heart bled for him. 'And I've seen the scars on your back.' But how many more scars, she wondered, did he have on his heart?

Jessie had said his attitude to family, to kids, was all mixed up in his past. She knew she shouldn't pry, that she really had no right to pry, but suddenly she just wanted to know. She'd accepted that this had to be a temporary fling, because he wasn't looking for permanent, and she couldn't change that. But suddenly she wanted to know why. Why would he want to deny himself the one thing in life that really mattered?

'Will you tell me about it?'

He gave a half-laugh, but it had a hollow ring that stabbed at Daisy's chest. 'There's nothing much to tell,' he said. 'My mother died. Left my Da on his own with six kids.' His Adam's apple bobbed as he swallowed. 'He came home that night from the hospital, cried like a baby and got blind drunk. And after that everything changed.' He plucked some grass up, rubbed it between his fingers.

She waited, a part of her scared to hear what he had to say, a part of her desperate to know so she could understand. 'How did it change?' she said gently.

He dropped the grass, rubbed his hands on his jeans. 'First off it was no more than a back hand to the head, or a punch now and again you weren't expecting. But then it was the flat of his belt, the heel of his boot, until you passed out. The drink changed him and he couldn't control it.'

Tears spilled over Daisy's lids, but she wiped them hastily away; from the monotone of his voice she could tell he didn't want her sympathy.

'My brother Mac and me, we'd wait at the window, watch for him. Mac would make the tea, and I'd bathe the girls, get them fed and tucked in before he got home. On a good night, he'd be so locked he could barely walk, so we'd feed him and pour him into bed and that would be the end of it. But on a bad night...' He paused. His eyes met hers. 'That's not happy families, Daisy. That's barely living.'

She cradled his cheek in her palm, desperate to give what little comfort she could. 'I'm so sorry, Connor.'

He pulled away, instantly defensive. 'There's nothing to be sorry for.'

'No child should have to endure that. Not ever.'

He caught a tear on his thumb, wiped it away. 'Don't,

Daisy. It's not a bad story, not really. I got out. I made a life for myself apart from all that. A life I'm happy with.'

But it's only half a life, she wanted to say. Couldn't he see that? 'What happened to Mac and your sisters?'

'My…' He stopped, and for the first time since he'd started talking she saw the raw flash of remembered pain. But he collected himself quickly and it was gone. 'The authorities found out what had been going on. We got separated… Fostered and adopted.'

'Did you manage to keep in touch?'

'No. I've not seen them since. But Mac's a movie actor now. Goes by his full name of Cormac.'

'Cormac Brody?' Daisy blinked. She couldn't believe it. 'Your brother's Cormac Brody?' His brother was the Irish actor who'd taken Hollywood by storm in the last few years? Now she thought about it, she could see the resemblance. Both Connor and his brother had the same piercing blue eyes and dark good looks—and that devil-may-care charm. 'But if you know that why haven't you contacted him? Surely his agent would—'

'Why would I?' he interrupted her. 'He's not part of my life and I'm not part of his. I missed him for a while.' He shrugged, his apparent indifference stunning her. 'Just like I missed all of them, but they were better off without me and I was better off without them.'

'But that's not true,' she said, unable to bear the brittle cynicism in his voice. 'Everyone should have a family. You need them. They're part of you.'

'Daisy, don't,' he said, lifting her chin between his thumb and forefinger. 'It is true. It's the way I want it. Sure, when I was little I used to lie awake nights, praying to Our Lady that my mammy would come back. That my Da would stop drinking. That everything would go back to how it was and we could all be a happy family again. But I learned a valuable lesson. You can't go back, you can only go forward.

And you can't rely on anyone. Nothing's certain. Nothing lasts. Life gets in the way, good and bad. Like you got in my way. So we enjoy it while it lasts and take everything we can grab. And that's enough.'

But it wasn't enough, she thought. Not nearly enough. Not for anyone.

He put his arm around her shoulders as they walked back across the park. As the sun dipped towards dusk, giving the fairy castle a golden glow, Daisy considered all the things he'd told her and felt her fantasy collapse and reality come flooding in.

So now she knew. Connor lived in the moment, shunned responsibility and had persuaded himself that family wasn't for him, not because he was selfish, or shallow, or self-absorbed, but because of that abused traumatised little boy who had been forced to grow up too soon, and shoulder a responsibility that should never have been his.

He wasn't scared of commitment, she realised. He was just scared of taking a chance, scared of wanting something that could blow up in his face all over again.

What a couple of cowards they both were.

Because while he'd been scared to take a chance, she'd been so scared of making her mother's mistakes she'd side-stepped, and avoided and denied the obvious all along.

That she was falling hopelessly in love with him.

She bit into her lip, determined not to let her emotional turmoil show as the enormity of what she'd just admitted to herself sank in.

Oh, God, what on earth was she going to do now?

CHAPTER FOURTEEN

As CONNOR stood beside her in a perfectly tailored tuxedo like her own Prince Charming, Daisy let her eyes wander over the magnificent ballroom and began to wonder how much more surreal her life could become. Chandeliers cast a shimmering light on the assembled throng. Women preened like peacocks in their latest designer plumage and men looked important and debonair in their dark dinner suits. The ball was an annual event hosted by the New York Governor for some deserving charity, but according to Connor it was really just an excuse for the state's most prominent citizens to show off.

The necklace he'd given her felt cool against her cleavage, matching the emerald satin gown she'd hastily put together on her second-hand sewing machine a lifetime ago. Daisy took a deep breath, and rested her hand on Connor's sleeve, trying to get her balance. Ever since they'd got back from the park her emotions had been in uproar, her senses reeling. But she had managed to make one important decision this evening. She planned to live the last of her grand adventure tonight to the max. She'd have time enough tomorrow to panic about her wayward heart.

'Daisy, that dress is sensational.'

Daisy turned to see Jessie Latimer, a champagne flute in her hand and a friendly grin on her face. 'Where ever did you get it?' she said. 'Enquiring minds want to know.'

'I...' She hesitated, wondering if it was the done thing to admit you'd made your own ball gown.

'She made it herself.' Connor smoothed his hand over the ruched satin at her hip and hugged her to his side, his gaze darkening with appreciation. 'Not just gorgeous but talented too,' he murmured against her neck.

Daisy could feel the pulse hammering in her throat as Jessie gave her a pointed look over Connor's shoulder.

'That's amazing,' she said. 'Listen, Daisy, I've told my sister Ali all about you and I'd love you to meet her. Actually, it's sort of a mercy mission.' She took Daisy's hand. 'She found out yesterday she's expecting again and she's in a state of shock. I need you to help take her mind off it.'

Daisy acknowledged the little prickle of envy and ignored it. She'd have her big happy family one day. She'd make sure of it. 'I'd love to meet her,' she said, and meant it. A little time spent away from Connor wouldn't necessarily be a bad thing. It might help her get her heart rate under control in preparation for the night ahead.

Connor gave a mock shudder. 'Ali's pregnant again? What's that? Number four?'

Jessie nodded, giving Daisy's hand a tug. 'Actually the doctor said it may be number four and five. She's so huge already. Hence the shock.'

Connor frowned as Daisy stepped out of his arms. 'Wait a minute. Why don't I come over? I can congratulate her.'

Jessie pushed her finger into his chest. 'This is strictly girls only, big boy. Linc and Monroe are over by the bar trying to finesse a couple of beers out of the barman. Go play with them.'

As Jessie led her through the crowd of Manhattan's elite Daisy couldn't resist a glance over her shoulder at Connor. Her heartbeat slowed and her stomach tightened. He still stood where she'd left him, looking impossibly dashing in the middle of the crowded ballroom in his black tuxedo with an irritated frown on his face and his hands thrust into his pockets as he watched her go.

She heaved out a breath. Okay, she was falling in love, but that didn't mean she had to get stupid. All she had to do now was keep the brakes on, enjoy tonight and then confront him tomorrow. See where she stood. Maybe she'd fallen for her romantic fairy tale, but it didn't mean she couldn't still be practical, sensible. Love might be blind, but it didn't have to turn you into an idiot. She still knew what she wanted out of life and, whatever Connor's reasons, he'd made it very clear that afternoon he didn't want the same things. Unless he was falling in love with her too, that wasn't going to change.

'There's definitely something to be said for a bad boy in a tux,' Jessie said quietly, interrupting Daisy's latest strategy briefing.

Daisy's head whipped round. The considering look in Jessie's eyes spoke volumes: Daisy had been staring at Connor for far too long. 'Yes, I suppose so,' she said, trying for practical and getting breathless instead.

'How's it going? We don't have to meet Ali. I just thought you might like a little downtime before the dancing begins. You both look a little shell-shocked. Did something happen?'

She was certainly shell-shocked, she thought. But she wasn't so sure about Connor. She'd caught him watching her, a wary, cautious look in his eyes when they'd been in the cab coming back from the park. That look was the reason she'd decided not to blurt out how she felt. Why ruin the mood before she was absolutely sure? And anyway, she'd wanted to have tonight to add to her memories before it all went belly up, as she was fast suspecting it would. He might need a family, but he didn't necessarily need her. What on earth did she really have to offer him that he couldn't get from a hundred other, much more sophisticated women?

'Don't be silly,' Daisy said, almost choking on the fake bonhomie. 'Nothing's wrong.' Well, not yet. 'This is all just a bit much for a girl from Portobello Road, that's all.'

'Yes, the Americans do excess so well, don't you think?' Jessie smiled back, but Daisy could see she was being kind and letting her off the hook. 'Oh, good grief!' Jessie said, her eyes lighting on something over Daisy's shoulder. 'That woman is a complete menace. Poor Lincoln had to peel her off him ten minutes ago and now she's got Connor in her sights.'

Daisy looked round. All the colour drained out of her face and then pumped back into her cheeks. Wrapped around Connor like a second skin was a pneumatic blonde with a skirt that barely covered her butt and boobs that could poke someone's eye out.

He still had his hands in his pockets, and his body language didn't suggest he was enjoying the encounter all that much, but as the woman leaned closer to whisper something in his ear he took one hand out and rested it on her waist.

A red haze blurred Daisy's vision. 'Who is she?' she asked, her voice calm despite the volcanic eruption bubbling beneath her breastbone.

Doesn't she know he's engaged? she almost added. Then realised her mistake. The molten magma got hotter.

'Mitzi Melrose, the biggest flirt on the planet,' Jessie said. 'Her husband's Eldridge Melrose, billionaire financier, and I don't think he's got what it takes to satisfy our Mitzi if her relentless poaching is anything...' Jessie's voice slowly receded until all Daisy could hear was the buzzing of a thousand chainsaws, her gaze transfixed on her fake fiancé and the floozy.

The Botoxed bimbo was leaning into him now, her pillarbox lips practically touching his ear lobe and her gravity-defying cleavage as good as propped on his forearm.

And, as far as Daisy could tell, Connor wasn't doing a damn thing about it. He'd taken his hand off her hip, sure, stuck it back in his pocket, but he hadn't moved away, had he? She'd never been the jealous type, even with Gary, who'd been an inveterate flirt. Daisy, being the practical, sensible, focussed woman she was, had always thought that possessive women who couldn't trust their partners were creatures to be pitied. But right at this moment she could sympathise with them completely.

She had Connor's ring on her finger. Maybe it was a temporary ring and a fake engagement, but, still, she'd worn it because he'd asked her, she'd let him introduce her to everyone as his bride-to-be and now he had another woman glued to his torso. And if that weren't bad enough, he'd made her fall in love with him, the stupid dolt.

'Jessie, you'll have to excuse me for a minute,' she said, still glaring at her non-fiancé.

'Go for it,' she heard Jessie say with a suspicious lift in her voice. But Daisy didn't have time to process it as she sailed back through the crowd propelled on a wave of righteous anger, the surge of adrenaline making her heartbeat pound in her ears and her skin flush red.

She'd been an idiot. She'd lived in the moment, soaked up every single speck of excitement and in the process lost a crucial part of herself. She was her own woman. And yet, somehow or other, she'd ended up letting Connor call all the shots. He'd got her to New York, he'd got her back in his bed, he'd put his ring on her finger and what had she got? Quite possibly a broken heart, that was what. Fine, she'd deal with that if she had to, but he was not going to get away with pawing another woman in public when he was supposed to be engaged to her. The engagement might be fake, but her feelings were real. She might not have his love, but she intended to have his respect.

His head lifted as she walked towards him, as if he'd sensed her approach, those magnetic eyes fixed on her face and he smiled.

He might as well have pulled out a red bandanna and waved it in front of her nose. What, she'd like to know, was so flipping amusing?

Connor tuned out Mitzi's breathy whisper. His heart pounded as he watched the satin gown Daisy had made shimmer, spotlighting those provocative curves to perfection. He couldn't make out her expression in the muted lighting, but the vision of high cheekbones, fine, alabaster skin and glossy red curls made all his senses stand up and pay attention. His annoyance and impatience dimmed, to be replaced by a rush of longing that he didn't understand—and didn't want to understand.

Even though she was still several feet away he could have sworn he could smell that spicy, erotic scent of hers, and feel the soft swell of her breasts beneath his fingertips.

The truth was, he'd never been a fan of networking, of getting all spruced up and showing himself off. But ever since Daisy had walked out of their bedroom earlier decked out in the ball gown, the green satin hugging her curves and making him ache in some very interesting places, the thought of going to the Governor's Ball and mingling with people he didn't give a hoot about had become considerably less appealing.

What he'd wanted to do was stay in their suite and make love to her for the rest of the evening, then listen to her talk—he adored how she drifted from topic to topic without pausing for breath in that practical, no-nonsense way she had—and then he'd planned to fall asleep with her head pillowed on his chest.

But after all the things he'd told her in the park, he'd been forced to dismiss the idea. He'd let things get too serious again without intending to, telling her things he shouldn't about his past, and then, to top it all, he'd seen the tenderness, the longing in her eyes when he'd put his arm on her shoulders and he wasn't sure what to make of it. She hadn't challenged him about what he'd said, she'd simply accepted it—but he'd been waiting for the axe to fall ever since. For her to tell him how wrong he was for her. For her to throw his past back in his face. For her to demand more from him than he could ever give. But she hadn't done it, and it was making him crazy.

But once they'd been in the limo, her seductive scent tantalising him, he'd finally had to face the fact that he wasn't going to be able to let her go when they returned to England tomorrow as he'd planned. He'd thought that if he sated himself on her during these two weeks in New York, he'd be well over his infatuation by now, but she still captivated him as much, if not more, than she had the first time they'd made love.

She was less than five paces away from him when the chandelier illuminated her face at last. He could see anger and determination swirling in those expressive emerald eyes, and his stomach pitched. Had the penny finally dropped? Was she about to give him the boot?

He clamped down on the sudden surge of panic, the strangling feeling of pain and regret closing his throat. That was too bad. Because whatever was going on between them, it wasn't over. He still had unfinished business with her and if she thought he was going to let her dump him, she'd have to think again.

'Hi, Connor, why don't you introduce me to your new best friend?' Daisy said sweetly. Sweetly enough to cause tooth decay.

The bimbo had her hand on his lapel now. Daisy's fingers clenched into a fist. She resisted the urge to slug the woman. But only just.

Connor looked momentarily confused, then glanced at the bimbo. 'Oh, yeah, Mitzi, this is Daisy Dean, my fiancée. Do you think you could leave us be for—?'

Mitzi cut off whatever he was going to say with an ear-splitting giggle. 'Your fiancée? You've got to be kidding me.' Her high-pitched voice piped out like Marilyn Monroe on helium. 'You never said you were getting married, sweetie.' She pressed one of her scarlet-tipped talons against Connor's cheek and giggled again before sending Daisy a smile filled with enough malice to make Mussolini look like a pussycat. 'Why, I guess it must have slipped his mind, we were having such a good time and all.' She shoved her expertly moulded breasts forward. 'But then men get distracted so easily, don't they, honey?'

Screw restraint. Daisy wasn't taking *that* lying down. 'Yes, they do.' She smiled sharply. 'Especially when they're being smothered in enough cheap perfume to fell an ox.'

Mitzi's jaw dropped comically. 'Huh?'

'Daisy, what's got into you?' Connor said, gripping her arm and stepping to her side.

She thrust her chin up, willing her bottom lip to stop quivering. 'Oh, I don't know, Connor. Maybe it's that you're wrapped around her when you're supposed to be engaged to me.'

He looked at her as if she were talking in tongues. 'Whoah?'

And she lost it. So this was what it boiled down to, she thought, as her fury—with herself as well as him—raged out of control.

He whisked her off to New York, he told everyone they were a couple, he said things to her she was sure he'd never said to anyone else and he made love to her with a power and a passion that made her lose her grip on reality. But when push came to shove, it had all been a game—at least for him. She was just another of the women he'd charmed into bed.

'You heard me, Connor. Either you respect me. Or you don't. You can't have it both ways.'

'I paid a grand a bottle for this stuff, you little bitch,' Mitzi shrieked.

'Shut up, Mitzi!' he snarled.

'I'm gonna tell my husband about this,' Mitzi squeaked as she shrank back. 'Don't you think I won't and you can kiss that damn deal goodbye.'

'Be my guest, now get lost.' He threw the words over his shoulder, his eyes still fixed on Daisy's face.

The woman flounced off with an audible huff and Daisy became aware of the silence around them. At least twenty pairs of eyes were fixed on their little theatrical display.

'Now why don't you tell me what the hell is going on here?' Connor announced, as if she were a naughty child, completely oblivious to their audience.

Daisy tried to step away from him, humiliation swamping her. But he was still holding her arm.

Oh, God, what had she done? She'd let her anger and uncertainty take over and now she'd made a complete spectacle of herself. But as if that weren't bad enough, Connor was looking at her as if she'd lost her marbles. She felt the tears sting her eyes and pushed them back. It was so grossly unfair. Why did she have to be the one to fall in love?

She bit the sob back. Forget it, she wasn't going to cry over him. And definitely not with all these people watching. 'Let go of my arm. I want to go back to the hotel,' she whispered. 'We're making a scene.'

'The hell with that.' He took her other arm, pulled her close despite her struggles. 'You're going to tell me what you meant. Of course I respect you—how could I not?'

'I'm not talking about this. Not now.' Not ever. It would just humiliate her more. He wasn't going to make her break.

'Oh, yes, you are. I'm sick of waiting for you to say it.'

Waiting for her to say what? But before she could figure out what the heck he was talking about, he clamped his hand on her wrist and started dragging her through the crowd. A sea of heads turned to stare at them both as he marched her out of the ballroom. She'd never been more mortified in her life. But what was worse, much worse, was the thought that he might make her crack and reveal everything—and then she'd be completely at his mercy.

He slammed into the ladies' powder room. The elderly matron busy fluffing her hair in front of the ornate mirror glanced up.

'Why, Connor Brody,' she said. Daisy blinked. Had the old dame just batted her eyelids at him? 'What are you doing in the Ladies' Lounge, you bad boy?'

Connor smiled back, giving her the full blast of his lethal Celtic charm. Daisy barely resisted the urge to kick him. First Mitzi and now a woman three times his age. Did he never know when to turn it off?

'Mrs Gildenstern, it's a pleasure.'

Good God, she'd fallen for the playboy of the Western World. Daisy snorted indignantly, but they both ignored her.

'I need a moment with my fiancée in private,' he said.

'So this is the lucky girl?' the woman purred, fluffing her hair some more and sending Daisy a flirtatious wink. She got up and touched Connor's arm. 'You go right ahead, my boy,' she said. 'I'll make sure no one disturbs you.' Her paper-thin skin crinkled as she grinned. 'But don't you two get up to anything I wouldn't,' she finished as she left the room, chortling like a naughty schoolgirl.

'Sure, thanks, Mrs G,' Connor finished distractedly. He turned to Daisy, all traces of that industrial-strength charm wiped out by a dark scowl. 'Now I want to know what's going on.'

'I don't need to tell you a thing.'

'Oh, yeah.' He pressed her back against the vanity unit, hard thighs trapping her hips, hot hands clamping on the exposed skin of her back and the smell of soap and pheromones overwhelming her. 'Think again. Because you're not getting out of here till you do.'

The warm spot between her legs pulsed hot. She slapped

her hands against his chest, and shoved. He barely budged. She glared at him some more. He didn't even flinch.

'I didn't like seeing you paw that floozy,' she said grudgingly. 'But now I'm over it.' *Almost.*

'What floozy? You mean Mitzi?' he said, sounding so astonished the old red rag popped out again and ruined all her best intentions.

'Yes Mitzi. I mean, I know this relationship is a sham. I know we're only pretending to be engaged.' When exactly had she lost sight of that? 'But if you could refrain from smooching with other women in public I'd appreciate it. I happen to have some pride, you know.' Although she'd lost sight of that too somewhere. 'Just because I don't have mile-long legs and breasts that will still be perky when I'm dead. As far as everyone here is concerned I *am* your fiancée and that ought to entitle me to a tiny iota of your respect.'

Now she sounded pathetic too. She wanted to kill him. How had he managed to turn her into a desperate, grasping, needy nutcase that she didn't even recognise?

His scowl deepened momentarily and then his eyebrows kicked up. 'Jesus. You're jealous,' he murmured incredulously.

'I am not jealous,' she shot back. 'That would make me an imbecile.' Wouldn't it just?

'Yes, you are,' he said, flashing her that megawatt grin. The satisfied gleam in his eyes lit Daisy's temper up like a Chinese firecracker.

'That does it. I'm out of here.' She struggled, but he simply grabbed her waist and held her still. Then his thumbs slipped under the satin of her gown, trailing goosebumps in their wake. She gasped.

'I've got to tell you,' he murmured, his fingers caressing bare skin as his hands wrapped round her, 'you're magnificent when you're mad, angel.' He chuckled, the sound throaty and self-satisfied and wholly male.

Fury engulfed her. She was not going to get sidetracked, not again.

'Don't you dare laugh at me,' she said, 'or I'll slug you.'

She freed her arm and tried to take aim, but he caught her fist in his, laughing as he kissed her knuckles. 'Now, now, angel. Don't get nasty.'

Then she felt it, the solid length of his arousal, outlined against the soft swell of her belly. Heat spiralled from her core and she struggled in earnest. 'No. No way,' she yelped, staring into his eyes and seeing the intent on his face. 'Forget it. We are not making love. If you haven't noticed, we're having an argument.'

'Pay attention, angel,' he said as his clever fingers whisked down the zip on her dress. 'We've had the argument.' The bodice fell away, baring her lacy push-up bra. 'And we're about to have the make-up sex.'

'But we're in the powder room. We can't,' she shouted, frantic and afraid and already so turned on she was sure she was about to explode.

This wasn't possible. It couldn't be happening. She'd never made love in a public place before. 'We can't, anyone could walk in,' she said, her voice rising in panic as he pushed her bra up.

'Don't worry, no one messes with Mrs G,' he said, weighing her breast in his palm.

'But what if Mrs Gildenstern dies of a heart attack?' she blurted out, her voice rising in panic as his fingers played havoc. 'What if the fire alarm goes off? What if the SAS storms the building?'

He fastened hot lips on her nipple, suckled strongly. She choked out a sob as he teased and bit the engorged peak— and every single coherent thought flew right out of her head.

She threaded her fingers through his hair, held on as her head bumped the mirror and she gave herself up to the fireball of sensations.

He lifted her panting onto the vanity unit, brushed his hands up her legs under the billowing satin and plunged his fingers into the heart of her.

'I want you, Daisy. More than I've ever wanted any woman.' He stroked the slick folds of her sex as she bucked against his hand. Then his lips took hers in a kiss so passionate, she could taste his vicious arousal matching her own.

She stared dumbly, her body trembling with need as he pulled the condom out of his breast pocket with unsteady fingers and freed himself from his trousers.

She whimpered as he held her hips, pushed her panties to one side and entered her in one long, relentless thrust. As she clung to him all her thoughts, all her feelings, centred on the exquisite joy pulsating through her. She rode on the crest for an eternity as his powerful strokes took him deeper. She heard his low groan, felt his shoulders stiffen as she took that last wild leap into oblivion.

Her fingers trembled on the damp curls at his nape, her senses spinning as she listened to the ragged pants of their breathing and her thundering heartbeat, the sounds harsh and uncivilised against the soft strains of music from the ballroom beyond.

He lifted his head and his eyes met hers—determination making the deep blue of his irises glow with purpose.

'This isn't over. Not yet.' His hands stroked her thighs, squeezed. 'You know that, right?'

She could hear the urgency in his voice, the yearning, and her heart swelled with hope. 'I know,' she whispered.

She felt herself plunging into the chasm—but knew she wasn't falling in love any more, she'd fallen.

CHAPTER FIFTEEN

DAISY slept fitfully on the flight home, despite the flat bed, the world-class service and the fact that she was physically and mentally exhausted from the emotional roller-coaster ride her life had somehow become. She couldn't even get a good firm grip on all the 'what ifs' whirring about in her mind, let alone answer any of them.

What if she told him she loved him and he looked angry? What if she told him and he looked bored? What if he thought she was delusional? What if she was?

She resigned herself to the fact that whatever happened she would have to tell him, because the 'what ifs' would drive her completely doolally if she didn't. And then she started stressing over the 'When'. Eventually she fell asleep over Nova Scotia, Connor's hand resting on her hip, knowing that when she got home she would have to face one of the toughest conversations of her life. But she promised herself, whatever happened, she would not wimp out—and she wouldn't let Connor wimp out either. He was going to have to come up with something a bit more substantial than, 'Not Yet'.

'Wake up, angel. We're home.'

The minute he'd said the H word, Connor felt the little spurt of panic.

Don't be an idiot, it's an expression. It doesn't mean a thing.

He shook Daisy again, leaned down to kiss her cheek. Her lids fluttered open, her eyes fixing on his face. He felt the twist in his chest as he stared into the mermaid green, and the spurt got worse.

Why couldn't he let her go?

He'd been awake during the whole of their transatlantic flight, her lush body curled up next to his, trying to figure it out. She hadn't gone the route of most females and tried to pin him down. That had to be it. As soon as she did the honeymoon period would be over. But a moment ago, when the car had pulled up at the house in Portobello, and he'd turned to see Daisy by his side, he'd begun to wonder if he wasn't in serious trouble. She'd snuck under his guard somehow—and he didn't like it.

'Mmm…' She stretched, giving him a peek of the purple lace of her bra through the buttonholes of her blouse. He felt the familiar punch of lust.

And why did he still want her? All the damn time? Had she put some kind of spell on him?

'Are we home?' she asked around a jaw-breaking yawn.

And there was that H word again. He didn't like it.

'Yeah.' He pushed back, stepped out of the limo. Maybe he needed to get away from her for a while, take a time-out. But even as he thought of letting her go, even for just one night, her hand clasped his as she stepped out of the car and he knew he couldn't do it. The spurt became a flood.

The chauffeur deposited their luggage on the kerb, tipped his hat. 'Would you like me to take them into the house, sir?'

'No, that's grand,' he said, dragging a roll of bills from his pocket and flicking out a tenner. 'Thanks for your help, Joe.'

He watched the long black Mercedes drive away and settled on his course of action. He'd keep her with him for the next little while. He wanted her with him, in his house. But he'd make damn sure she didn't get any closer. She was too close already.

He shoved one of the smaller suitcases under his arm, picked up the two larger. 'Let's take these up to mine. We need to talk.'

She blinked lids still heavy with sleep, her cheeks coloured. 'You know?' she said.

'Know what?' he asked.

Then she looked past him, her eyes widening, and all the pink leached out of her face. The small carry-on bag she carried clattered onto the pavement.

'What's that?' she asked, pointing past him.

He glanced over his shoulder and spotted the For Sale sign. He'd forgotten all about his conversation with the estate agent three weeks ago. He turned back and saw the horror on her face and the sparkle of unshed tears. Something fierce and protective clasped his heart—and not for the first time.

'You're moving out?' she said, her voice so quiet he could barely hear it.

His first instinct was to tell her he wasn't. He didn't want to any more. But the minute the need to calm and to nurture welled up inside him, the panic closed around his throat. What was wrong with him? He didn't want anything permanent. He didn't need the responsibility. He'd had permanent before, he'd had responsibility and he'd failed at it spectacularly. He couldn't risk it again. This was his get-out clause. He couldn't afford to throw it away.

He shrugged, forced himself to ignore the misery in her eyes. 'Sure. But with the market as it is, it'll take a while to sell.' Long enough, he hoped, for him to get over this infatuation once and for all. 'Until then we can continue to enjoy each other. It's been fun so far,' he said, struggling to keep the seductive smile in place.

* * *

Daisy felt as if she'd been punched in the gut.

He was selling the house, moving out, and he hadn't even bothered to tell her? And he was looking at her now, his face calm and nonchalant, as if to say, 'Why would I?' It was the same stubborn look he'd had on his face when she'd asked him why he had never contacted his movie-star brother. She looked down at the ring he'd given her and realised just how delusional she'd allowed herself to get.

She gulped down the tears tightening her throat, straightened her spine. 'No, thanks. I'd rather make a clean break,' she said. 'Here.' She tugged the silver band loose and held it out to him. 'I should give this back to you.'

His jaw tightened as he looked down at the ring. He put the suitcases down, but made no move to take it. 'Come on, angel. Don't overreact. This isn't a big deal.'

Maybe not to him, she thought, her heart shattering inside her. Her fingers curled around the ring and she felt the tiny diamonds cut into her palm.

'Actually it is a big deal. Because I've fallen in love with you, you stupid moron.' It wasn't exactly how she'd planned to tell him, but even so his reaction was worse than any she could have imagined.

His mouth dropped open and his skin paled beneath the tan. 'Whoah, what's that now?'

Horrified. He looked horrified. Well, at least she had the answer to her 'What if'.

Biting down on her lips so hard she tasted blood, she lifted his hand and slapped the ring into it. 'It's okay, Connor. It's my mistake. I'll go quietly. I'm not even going to make a scene.'

She thought of all the scenes her mother had made, all the scenes she'd had to witness over the years, and forced the vicious pain back, buried it deep. The only thing she had left was pride—and she couldn't afford to throw it away, because she had a feeling she was going to need it.

She picked up her bag to leave, but he took her arm, pulled her round to face him.

'What's this now? You don't love me. That's rubbish. Since when?'

He didn't sound horrified any more; he sounded angry. He wasn't the only one.

'Don't tell me how I feel. I do love you, Connor. But you know what? I'm not asking for anything in return. Especially as it's pretty obvious you don't want to give it to me.'

She yanked her arm out of his, but he grabbed her back. 'Hold on a minute. You can't tell me you love me then storm off. That's madness.'

'Yes, I can, because you don't love me back,' she shouted, then realised she was making a scene after all. Damn it. 'Well, do you?' she whispered.

He flinched and she felt nausea churn in her stomach.

'I don't love anyone,' he said. 'I'm no good at it.' Was that supposed to make her feel better? 'I don't want this. I told you that.'

She shook her head, the tears choking her. 'I know you did, Connor.' And he had, he had told her. And it was her own stupid fault that she hadn't listened. Or rather, she'd listened with her heart, instead of her head, and she'd got it wrong.

Daisy sighed, suddenly desperately weary, and sick to her heart as well as her stomach.

'Don't worry, Connor. I'll survive. I'll see you around.'

She turned but he called after her. 'Daisy, don't go. Let's at least talk about this some more.'

Didn't he know there was nothing else to say?

She waved over her shoulder. 'I'll be around, maybe later,' she said. Knowing full well that she'd be conveniently absent if he came to call. She'd do whatever she had to do to avoid him over the coming weeks—until he lost interest and moved on to his next conquest—and in the meantime she'd try to repair her heart.

As she walked the few short steps to her home, the sound of her suitcase wheels rolling on the pavement matching the click-click of her heels, she felt her stomach pitch—and refused to look back. She had never felt more bitterly ashamed of herself in her life.

Despite all her care over the years, despite all her caution. She'd got caught in the same foolish trap as her mother—of falling in love with the wrong guy, and hoping against all the odds that he might love her back. And he hadn't.

Connor dropped the suitcases on the floor and slammed the door shut. Well, that hadn't exactly gone according to plan. And where the hell had she got the stupid idea she loved him? It was insane.

He dumped his keys on the hall table, saw the stack of post, left it where it lay and walked down the hallway.

She'd get over it soon enough. Things had got too hot and heavy over the last fortnight. They'd been living in each other's pockets, after all. A little while cooling off would be all for the best. And then they could pick up where they'd left off.

But as he entered the open-plan kitchen, the sunlight pouring through the windows and shining off the polished oak, his gut tightened with dread and the sense of being trapped closed over him like a shroud.

What if she wouldn't come back?

He stared at the bright airy space, the gleaming glass cabinets, and felt as if they were mocking him. He fished the ring out of his pocket, dropped it on the counter top, then gazed out into the garden where he'd first spotted her three long weeks ago.

And for the first time since he'd been a boy, he wanted to pray for something he knew he could never have.

He heaved out a sigh, pushed the ring into a drawer. This was madness. He was just jet-lagged and a little shaken by how devastated she'd looked. But she'd get over it. He'd told her the truth, after all. He didn't love her. He couldn't. He'd always sworn he would never fall in love and that would never change. But he'd get her back, because he wanted her and he knew damn well she still wanted him.

But even as he tried to persuade himself there was nothing to worry about he had the niggling feeling that he'd let something irreplaceable slip through his fingers and there would be no getting it back, no matter how hard he tried.

CHAPTER SIXTEEN

DAISY stifled her tears as she opened her suitcase and saw all the mementoes she'd saved so carefully sitting on the top. The sweetly tacky tourist photo of her in Connor's arms atop the Empire State. The ticket stub from her first and no doubt last Broadway show. A napkin from the Rainbow Room. She also held firm as she folded away the cocktail dress and the ball gown and wondered when she'd ever get the chance to wear them again.

Having showered and changed into her work uniform of jeans and a Funky Fashionista T-shirt, she walked to the stall. Buffeted by the tide of tourists flowing through Portobello Market on a sunny Sunday morning, she ignored the ropey feeling in her stomach and the foggy feeling of exhaustion and still refused to let a single tear fall.

She'd been a fool—that was all. She could cope with this, as she'd coped with every other disappointment in her life. Her throat felt raw now, as if a boulder had got jammed down it, but this wasn't really so terrible. She'd allowed herself to get carried away. When she looked back on this, years from now, she'd see it as a valuable learning experience. Almost certainly.

She sucked in a tremulous breath, returned the wave of a stallholder she knew.

She still had her dream. One day she'd find the right man

for her. Connor had never been that man. She'd allowed the stardust and the glamour and the magic of the moment to blind her to the truth. She strolled up the busy thoroughfare, loaded with stalls selling everything from plaintains to paper-chains, crossed her arms over her chest and held in the tearing pain.

She'd get past this, and when she did she'd be able to remember her time with Connor as a dazzlingly exciting and wonderful romantic adventure and nothing more. So a tiny part of her heart would always be lost to him, would always wish that maybe things might have been different, that he might have wanted what she had to offer. But he hadn't and she'd be a fool to think she could change him. Wasn't that the mistake her mother had always made?

As she spotted her stall up ahead, the rainbow of cotton dresses and silk scarves she'd made and designed flapping in the breeze, a small smile quivered on her lips. This was her real life. And she loved it. This was what made her different from her mother. She'd sampled the drug that had driven her mother to find love in the wrong places and for two glorious weeks she'd ridden the high. But she could live without it if she had to. Steady, dependable, reliable was what she needed in her life—and she was the only one who could make that happen.

She stepped up to the stall, a brave smile firmed in place. 'Hey, got a blouse you can sell me?'

Juno's head came up. 'Daisy, you're back.' Her best friend dived round the stall, a welcoming grin on her face and her arms open wide. 'How did it go?'

But as Juno's arms folded around her, the emotions she'd been holding back so beautifully rose up like a summer storm and burst out of her mouth in a soul-drenching sob.

'Daisy, what is it? What happened? What's wrong?' She could barely hear Juno's frantic questions over the gulping cries ripping her apart.

Juno held on, patting her shoulders, whispering calming words until the sobs subsided, the wrenching pain tightening into a ball of misery. Daisy drew back, scrubbed an impatient hand across her cheeks. 'God, I'm sorry.'

Jacie stared at her over Juno's shoulder, wide-eyed with concern. 'Blimey, Daze. What's the matter? I've never seen you cry like that. Never.'

Juno gripped her upper arms, stood back, her eyes hard. 'He did this, didn't he?'

Daisy hiccoughed, the crying jag not quite done with. 'I fell in love with him, Ju.' A final tear slipped over her lid. She brushed it away. 'What a plonker, eh?'

'Oh, Daze,' Juno said, and hauled Daisy back into her arms for another hard hug. Then she pushed her back, fixed her eyes on Daisy. 'Did you tell him how you feel?'

'Yes, I did. And he doesn't feel the same way,' Daisy said, the admission, spoken out loud, making the depression suffocate her. 'So that's the end of it.' She walked round the stall and accepted Jacie's quick hug.

'Are you sure?' Jacie questioned, ever the optimist.

'Positive,' she murmured, her voice cracking on the finality of it all.

Jacie looked ready to question her some more, but Daisy was saved by a customer eager to buy a shawl.

Juno drew her to one side. 'He's not worthy of you,' she said. 'I thought he was a total scumbag the moment I laid eyes on him. And this confirms it.'

But he wasn't a scumbag, Daisy thought. He was a good man, not the right man maybe, but still a good man. Daisy pressed her fingers to Juno's lips. 'It's okay, Juno. I'll get over him.' She sighed. 'Eventually. We just weren't right for each other. I knew that from the start and I was a fool to think anything else. Anyway.' Daisy paused, blew out a breath. 'He's selling his house, moving on, so at least I won't have to be constantly reminded of my stupidity.'

Why didn't the thought make her feel any better, though?

In fact… She slapped a hand over her mouth as the nausea rose up to gag her.

'Quick, Juno, hand me a bag,' she cried, her voice muffled. 'I'm going to be sick.'

Juno thrust one of the stall's recycled plastic shopping bags into her hand and Daisy lost the contents of her stomach.

'Daze, are you okay?' Juno rubbed her back and took the bag out of her hands. 'Here, I'll go dump this.'

Daisy groaned. She was never ill. The events of the last hour had been fairly shattering, but, honestly, wasn't it about time she started pulling herself together?

'Gosh, Daisy, how do you feel?' Jacie remarked from beside her.

Daisy put her hand to her stomach. 'Not great, actually.' How could she still feel nauseous? She'd thrown up everything she'd eaten in the last twelve hours. 'I guess it's the emotional overload.'

'Either that or you're pregnant.'

Daisy's head shot up. 'That's not even funny, Jace. Not to mention a physical impossibility.' She sighed; at least she hadn't been stupid enough to sleep with Connor without protection.

'Are you on your period, then?' Jacie's eyes dropped to her chest. 'Because your boobs look enormous.'

Daisy glanced down. Her cleavage *was* looking rather more spectacular than usual, even accounting for her push-up bra. 'It's nothing. I'm due any day now, that's all.'

Wait a minute. When was her last period? In all the excitement of the last few weeks she'd forgotten about it. But… 'What's the date?' she asked.

'The twenty-fifth,' Juno said carefully, having returned from her trip to the bin.

Daisy's blood rushed out of her head and slammed straight into her heart. She couldn't breathe. She wasn't pregnant. She couldn't be; her period was just a couple of weeks late, that was all. Even though it had never, ever been late before. She looked up into Juno's concerned face. 'I can't be pregnant. It's simply not possible. Connor always used a condom, every time.'

Juno frowned. 'You do know they're only about ninety-nine per cent reliable, right? They're not a hundred per cent.'

'I know that, but…' Daisy stopped. But what? 'We never had one break or anything like that.' She couldn't possibly have got pregnant.

'They don't necessarily have to break.' Juno sank down in the chair next to her. Her brow furrowed into ominous rows.

'Of course they do—his sperm can't get through rubber, for goodness' sake.' Daisy jerked a shoulder. 'Not unless it's supersonic or something. Can it?'

'Oh, Daze.'

Daisy swivelled round to see Jacie wearing the same worried frown as Juno.

'What? What is it?' Why were they looking at her like that?

'How late *are* you?' Juno asked gently.

'Only…' She did a quick calculation. Oh, God, she'd been due for over two weeks.

'I think we better get you a home pregnancy test,' Juno said without waiting for her answer. 'Just to be on the safe side,' she finished hopefully.

'You have to tell him, Daisy.'

Daisy's fingers fisted on the plastic stick, her whole body trembling. She had to be dreaming this, surely. Or having a nightmare. She could not be expecting Connor Brody's baby.

Juno's hand squeezed her shoulder. 'You know that, right?'

'It's not true. Maybe we should do another. There must be some mistake. He'll never believe me if I tell him. I don't believe me.'

'We've done three tests already,' her friend said. 'There's no mistake. And unless it's the immaculate conception, Mr Superstud is the father.' Juno took a weary breath. 'You should go over there now and tell him, get it out the way. Then you can start thinking about what you're going to do.'

Daisy dropped the plastic stick on top of the others in her waste-paper bin, her mind whizzing like a Catherine wheel. The three pink plus signs floated in front of her eyes like something out of a Salvador Dali painting.

'I'm going to call Maya,' Juno whispered, her hand still gripping Daisy's shoulder. 'So you can discuss your options.'

Daisy placed her hand on her abdomen, rubbed. Her heart rate finally calmed down enough so that she could grasp one wonderful, impossible truth. 'Juno.' She looked up at her friend, tears of joy pricking her lids. 'I'm going to be a mummy.'

Tears welled in Juno's eyes too, to match the ones now flowing freely down Daisy's cheeks. 'So you're going to have it?'

Daisy nodded. 'Yes. Yes, I am. I know the circumstances are a total disaster, but I could never do anything else.'

Juno clasped her hand over Daisy's. 'Whatever happens, I'll be here to help and so will Mrs V and Jace and everyone else you know. And that's a lot of people. You're not alone.'

'I know.' Daisy nodded and sniffed. Why had she ever thought she didn't have a family?

Juno wiped the moisture away, slanted Daisy a wobbly grin. 'Enough hearts and flowers. When are you going to tell Brody?'

Daisy's heart stopped. The moment of euphoria faded to be replaced by a terrible wave of grief. 'I'm not.'

'Don't be silly. You have to tell him. He has a right to know.'

'I can't tell him,' she said dully, the awful reality of what that meant finally dawning on her.

'Are you worried he'll try and make you have an abortion?' Juno said carefully.

Daisy shook her head. 'No, he wouldn't do that.' She stared at her hands, the knuckles whitening as she twisted them in her lap. 'Actually I think he'd do the opposite.' She remembered what Jessie had told her about the pregnancy scare with his last girlfriend. 'There's a core of honesty, of goodness in him. He'll feel responsible and he'll want to do the right thing. I couldn't bear that.'

'But, Daisy, in this case he is responsible. Partly responsible. You didn't get pregnant on your own.'

'But he doesn't want to be a father.' She pictured the way he'd looked when he'd told her about his own family, that sunny day a million years ago in Central Park. 'He had a miserable childhood, Juno. His father was violent, abusive. But he didn't blame his dad for what he did to him and to his brother and sisters. Honestly, when he was telling me about it, reading between the lines, it was like he blamed himself. I think that's why he's so scared of making a commitment. I'm not going to force it on him. I love him, how could I?' she said, placing her hands on her belly.

Juno stood up and paced across the room. 'That is such a load of total rubbish.' She stabbed an indignant finger at her friend. 'Stop being such a martyr. It's not your fault you got pregnant.'

'I know, but I want this baby.' She caressed her stomach, felt the jolt of emotion. 'Whatever the problems, the challenges, the difficulties I'll have to face. This is like a dream come true for me.' Maybe not the whole dream, but a good part of it. 'I think it could well be Connor's worst nightmare.' And then another thought occurred to her.

'Plus, I spent my whole childhood around men that didn't want to be my dad. I know how inadequate that can make you feel. I'm not going to put my own child through that. I couldn't.'

Juno gave a deep sigh. 'Okay, fine, have it your way, Daisy. But I still think you're wrong.' She sat back on the bed. 'And if he finds out, there could be hell to pay.'

'He's not going to find out. He looked horrified after I told him I loved him. I don't think he's going to go to any great lengths to seek me out. Plus he's moving soon. All I have to do is be careful and keep a low profile.'

Juno slanted her a rueful look. 'Yes, and we all know how good you are at that,' she muttered.

CHAPTER SEVENTEEN

'I'LL kill ye little bastards.'

Connor flinched at the slurred shout, scrambled back at the angry thud on the door. The sharp crack as the thin plywood splintered had flop sweat trickling down beneath his T-shirt, stinging the welts from two nights back.

'He means it, Con. He really means it this time,' came Mac's panicked whisper.

Connor flung an arm round his brother's shoulder. 'Soon as he gets in, you go on. Get the girls to Mrs Flaherty's. I'll hold him off.'

They jumped together as another loud crack ripped the air. Connor's gaze was riveted to the tiny latch, hanging by the last two screws. Queasy fear gripped his stomach, the memory of the pain so vivid his muscles tensed, his back throbbed. The thundering in his ears cut out the crash as the door fell forward in slow, silent motion. Connor raised his arms, the thin whimper of Mac's crying piercing the mute terror as the dark shape stumbled towards them. Vicious pain sliced across his shoulder as the belt tore into tender flesh.

Connor bolted forward into darkness, his hands reaching for something that wasn't there.

His chest screamed as he struggled to breathe, his ears ringing with the sound of leather cutting flesh, his shoulders livid with the phantom pain.

He choked down a gulp of air.

Just a nightmare. Just a nightmare. Get a grip, Brody.

Gradually his eyes adjusted to the dim light, saw the plush drapes, the shadows cast by moonlight in the garden beyond. He braced his hands on the bed, let his chin drop to his chest, waited for his mind to adjust, to yank him out of the horror.

But as he waited an eternity to draw that first steady breath the silence echoed around him. The emptiness, the loneliness taunted him.

Why wasn't she here? He needed her.

As his breathing evened out at last he covered his face with his hands, pushed shaking fingers through his hair. Two whole days. Two long, miserable days. And the yearning, the desperation hadn't faded; they had only got worse.

He blew out a breath and finally accepted the truth. He'd mucked everything up.

How could he have been so stupid? What the hell had he thrown away? All this time he'd been running away from the one thing he should have been running towards.

He lifted the sheet, damp with his sweat, settled back into the bed. The residue of the nightmare rippled through him, making his muscles quake.

He shut his eyes and swore that tomorrow he'd make it right. He'd do whatever he had to do, to get Daisy back where she belonged.

'We need to talk.'

Daisy stared in shock as the very last man she'd expected to see, or wanted to see, stood in her doorway.

'Go away.' She went to slam the door.

He slapped his hand against it. 'I will not.' He shoved the door open and strode past her into the tiny bedsit.

'You can't come in here.' Outrage was closely followed

by panic. She'd been sick twice already since waking up an hour ago and could feel the stirrings of a new bout of nausea in the pit of her stomach.

'Too bad. I'm in already.' He stood in the middle of the room, his broad shoulders and determined scowl making the small space look a great deal smaller.

'Please leave, Connor. Our fling's over.' She tried to keep the quiver out of her voice. She had to get him out of here, before he saw her vomit. What if he put two and two together? She'd wrestled with what she had to do for two whole days. She hadn't seen hide or hair of him and, while her heart had yearned for even a quick glimpse, she knew she'd made the right decision not to tell him about the baby.

Trust Connor to turn up unexpectedly, though, and ruin her best intentions.

'I've got nothing more to say to you,' she said. 'And this is just embarrassing us both.'

'As if I care about embarrassing,' he shouted back. 'It so happens, I've got a piece to say to you and I'm going to say it. You had your say, two days ago, when you stormed off in a huff. Now I'm having mine.'

'I don't care what you have to say…' She stopped in mid-shout, clasping her hand over her mouth, the sick waves heaving up her abdomen.

He was beside her in a second, gripping her arm. 'What's wrong? You look sick.'

'Get out!' she shouted, then shot out of the room and dashed down the hall to the bathroom.

Connor stood stock-still and listened to Daisy's feet fly down the corridor. So that was the way of it? She loved him so much, he made her retch.

He sat on the bed, dropped his head in his hands.

Damn, what was the matter with him? He was handling this all wrong. You didn't turn up on a woman's doorstep to tell her you loved her and straight off start yelling. What the hell had happened to all the easy charm he'd used on women so effortlessly in the past?

He heaved out a breath. Stood up, hopelessly restless and confused.

He'd be gentle when she got back. She was obviously poorly. Problem was, he'd never done anything like this before and had no practice whatsoever at it. Was he supposed to get down on one knee? Make an idiot of himself? Probably.

He glanced round the small, cluttered room, noticed the fanciful scene she'd painted on the ceiling and sighed.

This could well be the most important moment of his life and he'd mucked it up beautifully. He knew he had a lot of making up to do, after his knee-jerk reaction two days ago, but he didn't have an idea in his head how to do it. What did he know of romance? For sure, he'd talked women into bed before, but he'd never once had to bare his soul to one. He'd spent all morning practising what to say. But in the end he'd got so frustrated he'd come storming in here like a hurricane and blown it completely.

He paced up to her vanity, picked up the little vial of perfume, sniffed. The familiar scent filled him with the same bone-deep longing he'd had in the night, after waking up from his nightmare, and in the past two days as he'd waited like a fool for his feelings to level, to change.

He put the vial down carefully. Scowled when he saw something next to it on the edge of the sink. He picked the small plastic bottle up, squinting at the label.

'Pregnacare Vitamins,' he said aloud. 'What the…?'

'Oh, no.' He heard the pained whisper, looked round to see Daisy standing by the door, a panicked look on her face. His heart began to pound, but it wasn't panic clawing up his throat as he would have expected, but hope blossoming. Bright, beautiful, glorious hope.

He held the bottle up. 'What are these, now?'

She walked towards him, whipped the bottle out of his hand and buried it in the pocket of her bathrobe. 'Nothing, now go away.'

She turned her back on him, her shoulders rigid with tension, and wrapped her hands around her waist.

He stepped up to her, went to touch her, but pulled his hands away. He wanted to hold her, just hold her for ever. But he knew he didn't have the right. Not yet. The lump in his throat made it hard for him to speak. 'You weren't going to tell me?'

She didn't look round, but her shoulders softened, and he heard her weary sigh. 'Please go away, Connor. Pretend you never saw those. Your life can go on as you want it. And so can mine.'

He rested his hands on her shoulders, unable to hold back any longer, and turned her to face him. She had her eyes downcast but he could see a silent tear running down her cheek. It pierced his heart. He tucked a thumb under her chin, forced her gaze to meet his. 'Is that really how you want it? Don't you trust me? Don't you trust your own feelings?'

She let out a soft sob, bit hard into her lip. 'What if I told you it's not even yours?' she said, desperation edging her voice.

'I'd know you were lying.' He brushed the tear away with his thumb. 'You're a terrible liar, Daisy, you know.' He pressed his lips to hers. 'I love you, Daisy. That's what I came to tell you. Although I've made a mess of it so far. Tell me it's not too late.'

Daisy had thought her heart couldn't feel any more pain, that she couldn't possibly cry any more tears, but hearing him say the words she had dreamed of hearing the last few days and knowing they weren't true felt like the worst pain yet. More tears welled over her lids.

'Don't, Connor. I don't believe you.'

'You're kidding.' He gave a brittle laugh, then frowned. 'I've never told a living soul I loved them before. And now when I do you don't believe me? Talk about Murphy's Law. Why don't you believe me?' He sounded annoyed and exasperated, but then his fingers touched her cheek. The tenderness, the understanding in his eyes shocked her. 'This is because of your mother, isn't it?' he said softly. 'Because she looked for love and didn't find it, you won't believe it when it's standing right here in front of you.'

She searched his face, desperate to believe him, desperate to take what he offered. He was right, her experiences as a child had made her wary of love. But as she looked at him all she could see was his frustration, and his determination.

She drew back, remembering only too well the look on his face two days ago, when she'd told him she loved him. She shook her head.

She couldn't let herself hope for the impossible. She knew the truth. She'd worked it all out, sensibly and rationally. People didn't change. They didn't. Her mother had proved that with every man she'd fallen in love with.

'I knew you'd do this,' she whispered. 'I knew you'd feel responsible. You didn't love me two days ago, and you don't love me now. You don't want to be a father and you don't want me, not really.' She held his forearms, tried to push him away, but he wouldn't let her go. 'I knew if I told you about the baby you'd want to do the right thing. Just like you did for your brother and your sisters. You took a belt for them, Connor. You let him beat you rather than see them get hurt, didn't you? But I'm not going to be another belt. Because that's what I'd be if I let you do the thing that was right for me and not for you.'

He dragged her closer, rested his forehead on hers.

'Daisy, that's so sweet.' He lifted his head and sent her a

tentative smile that made her insides feel all shaky. 'But it's also total rubbish. I want you. I need you. I love you. And I loved you two days ago but I was too stupid to see it. And I'm over the moon that by some miracle I got you pregnant.' He cocked his head, the smile widening. 'Although we'll have to have a little talk about how that happened. Because for the life of me I'm sure I used condoms the whole time.' He was grinning at her now. 'And if I can get you pregnant through bonded latex we may have to be a lot more careful if we don't want to end up with twenty kids. But first things first. How am I going to get it into that thick head of yours that I love you?'

She pushed away from him, her anger rising. Why was he making this so hard? 'All right then, tell me why you reacted the way you did two days ago. When I told you I loved you, you looked absolutely horrified.'

Connor swore softly and felt the joy, the hope fade.

So it was all going to boil down to this. He'd have to tell her his darkest shame and hope against hope that she could still love him afterwards. 'Are you sure you want to know this?'

Her lips firmed into a grim line of determination. She nodded.

He let her go, sat on her bed. He'd hurt her, when he hadn't meant to; now he could destroy everything—but it was a risk he'd have to take.

'If I tell you, you might change your mind about loving me,' he said, hoping to give her a get-out clause.

She didn't take it. 'No, I won't,' she said with complete certainty.

He took a deep breath, but he couldn't look at her and tell her, so he gazed down at his hands, fisted in his lap. 'You're right. I took the belt if I could. Mac and me both. But I wasn't being brave, or noble particularly. It was just, they were so little, my sisters, and they loved me. And Mac, he looked up to me, thought I knew all the answers. They all depended on me to keep them safe, to keep us together.' He shrugged, shame thickening his voice. 'But one night, I sneaked out. Maeve Gallagher had promised me heaven the last time I'd seen her. I'd fresh scars from his last drinking session and he'd come home and fallen straight into his bed. I thought they'd be safe, that no harm would come to them. I swear it.'

She sat beside him, put her hand over his. But he still couldn't look at her, couldn't bear to see her contempt at what he'd done. 'But when I got home, there was a commotion outside. The neighbours were crowded about the house. There were lights flashing.' He could still picture it all so clearly even now, hear the murmur of curious voices, smell the scent of peat fires and winter frost and feel the chilling fear that had had him scrambling head first through the crowd. 'The Garda had my Da, he had his head bent, his hands cuffed behind his back. And then I saw the ambulance and Mac.' He gulped down air, tried to steady himself. 'He was lying on a stretcher. He looked so small, his face battered, his arm all crooked. I thought he was dead.' He forced himself to meet her eyes. 'He wasn't dead, but I never saw him again. Him or the girls. I told the social worker I didn't want to. But the truth is I couldn't bear to face them.'

'Why couldn't you?' she asked, her love clear on her face despite all that he'd told her. It gave him the courage he needed to tell her the last of it.

'Because I'd let them down. It was my job to protect them and I'd failed. I didn't deserve to be their brother, not any more.'

Daisy cupped Connor's face in her palms. Seeing the pain in his eyes, the regret, the guilt, she realised she loved this man more than life itself. She tried to speak, but emotion closed her throat.

He gripped her wrists, drew her hands down. 'When you told me you loved me,' he said, 'I was so scared. Scared to love you back. Because after that night, I promised I'd never love a living soul again and risk letting them get hurt. Risk losing them.'

'Connor, it wasn't your fault,' she whispered, the tears flowing freely down her cheeks. 'You were a boy trying to do something even a grown man couldn't do. You didn't let them down. And as long as you love me as much as I love you, you could never let me down either.'

He threaded his fingers through hers, held on. 'I do love you. More than you know. But are you sure that's enough?' he asked.

She pressed her palm to his cheek. 'Of course it is. You silly idiot.'

He blew out a breath, the relief plain on his face as he lent into her palm. 'That's a fine thing to call the man that loves you and is the father of your baby,' he said, emotion deepening his voice.

She smiled, for what felt like the first time in a millennium, and threw her arms round his neck. She clung onto him so tightly she wasn't sure he could breathe.

He chuckled. 'So does this mean you believe I love you now?' he said, his voice muffled against her hair.

She nodded, the joy coursing through her making it hard for her to breathe too.

His arms banded round her waist. 'And there'll be no more doubting it?'

She nodded again, even more vigorously, then whispered, 'I'd like my engagement ring back, now. Please.'

His breath tickled her ear lobe as he laughed. 'I'll think on it,' he said, but she could hear the teasing note in his voice. He lifted his head, framed her face in warm palms, his eyes shining with love. How could she ever have doubted him?

'But first I need you to do something for me,' he murmured.

'What's that?' she asked.

His thumb caressed the pulse in her throat as his hands settled on her shoulders. 'Come home,' he said as his gaze remained locked on hers. 'Come home with me where you belong.'

She thrust her fingers into his hair, brought his lips to hers and gave him his answer in a kiss bursting with love, heat, hope and commitment—and pure, unadulterated joy.

EPILOGUE

'FOR goodness' sake, let me look, you meanie. I've waited weeks already,' Daisy ordered, her fingers grappling with the immovable hands covering her eyes.

'Hold your horses now.' Connor's deep chuckle next to her ear sounded both amused and a bit too smug for her liking. 'I'll let you loose when I'm good and ready and not a moment before. Juno, get the lights,' he shouted past her as his chest pressed into her back. 'There now. What do you make of it?'

His hands lifted and Daisy blinked, the dazzle of fluorescent light blinding her. As the sleek, beautiful lines of glass and wood came into focus through the smell of fresh paint and sawdust she gasped. She slapped her hands over her mouth as tears welled in her eyes and emotion clogged her throat. 'Oh,' was the only word she could utter.

'That bad, eh?' Connor said beside her, sounding a lot less smug.

She turned, bounced up on her toes and flung her hands round his shoulders, nearly knocking him over with her belly in the process. 'Oh, my God, Connor. It's exactly the way I envisioned it. Exactly what I wanted. How did you do it? And how did you do it so fast?'

He'd given her another of her dreams, she thought, her heart bursting with love and excitement. And this was one she hadn't even realised she'd wanted. In fact she'd needed quite a lot of persuading to start with.

Six months ago when he'd walked into the bathroom after she'd just finished puking and informed her he'd bought her a shop at auction that morning, she'd had the distinct urge to throttle him, if she recalled correctly.

Was he insane? Why hadn't he discussed it with her first? He might enjoy being impulsive, reckless even, but she didn't. How was she going to organise refurbishing a shop? Then manage it and supply it while she was suffering from the worst case of morning sickness known to woman? And how would she handle all the extra responsibility when the baby was born?

But over the months her doubts had faded along with the morning sickness, and the excitement of having her own proper space to display her designs, her own workshop in the back to manufacture them, had built to impossible proportions.

And through it all Connor had been there, by her side. Encouraging her ideas, offering suggestions about the refurbishment, organising the construction, insisting she hire a manager so she could devote her time to designing, overseeing his crew with calm efficiency through all the inevitable hiccups—and on one memorable evening strapping on his tool belt to put up the shelving in the workshop and then letting her seduce him in the newly installed bathroom afterwards.

The experience had brought them even closer together. They weren't just a couple any more, they were a unit, with a shared dream.

In the last month though, with her approaching the end of her pregnancy he'd insisted she stay at home as he and the crew installed the cabinets and counters, finished the fitting rooms and did all the painting and decorating. And she had to admit she'd been a little miffed by his high-handedness. But she still couldn't believe how he had transformed that empty shell from four short weeks ago into the dream come true she saw before her now.

'I didn't do it on my own,' he said, smiling down at her.

'Oh, I know, you must thank all the crew. Are we going to have a proper opening, with champagne? We'll have to invite them all. I was thinking we could have it in a month if we get our skates on and—'

'We'll be doing no such thing,' he said firmly, interrupting her excited babble. He slung his arm round her shoulder and drew her close. 'The grand opening will have to wait a while.' He stroked his palm across her huge belly and she felt the heat right down to her toes. 'You're going to be busy for the next little while, looking after yourself and my child. This place is to be off limits until Junior's out and you're up and about. We'll schedule the opening for July, but only if you behave.'

'But that's ridiculous, that's months away,' she sputtered, starting to feel a little miffed again.

'And Juno here is under strict instructions to make sure you do as you're told.' He winked at Juno. 'Is that right, Juno?'

'Aye aye, Connor.' Juno gave a mock salute, grinning at Connor. The sight warmed Daisy's heart, despite her frustration with the two of them. How could it not?

Connor had gone out of his way to win Juno over since Daisy and he had started living together. It hadn't been easy at first, Juno's hostility towards him making her prickly and tense. But he'd worn her down over time, first getting her to accept him, then getting her to let go of her suspicion of good-looking men, at least as far as he was concerned, and finally engineering an easy friendship between them that had sprung from their mutual love for Daisy.

He treated Juno like a little sister, advising her and looking out for her and teasing her, while she treated him like an older brother, only taking the advice she felt she needed, and teasing him mercilessly right back.

But right now, as Daisy watched the silent communication between them, she was beginning to wonder if they weren't like brother and sister after all. But more like evil twins.

She could feel herself pouting. She hated being ganged up on. 'The baby's not due for two whole weeks.' She scowled at them both. 'Surely I can get a bit done in here before then.' She waddled over to the beautifully carved walnut counter tops, ran her palm lovingly across the smooth, vanished wood. 'We can't just leave it sitting here empty all that time.'

Connor stepped up behind her, wrapped his arms round her enormous waist and hugged her close. 'We can and we will,' he murmured, his breath feathering her ear. 'And from the size of you I'd say two weeks is optimistic, angel.'

She stuck an elbow in his ribs. 'Thanks a bunch. I know I look like a barrage balloon but you don't have to keep reminding me.'

'Stop fishing for compliments.' He chuckled. 'You know right well you're gorgeous.'

Daisy felt herself softening at the compliment. The man's charm was deadly.

He placed his hand over hers on the wood, brought her fingers to his lips. 'There's no rush, Daisy. We've all the time in the world, you know.'

Daisy gave a resigned sigh, the huge rush of love making her chest ache, and knew he'd got her, again. Then she heard a loud choking sound from behind them.

'If you two are going to get all drippy, I'm off,' Juno said, her voice light.

The deep rumble of Connor's laugh reverberated against Daisy's back. 'You best go, then, because drippy's definitely on the cards right enough.'

'You don't have to ask me twice,' Juno shot back, sounding more carefree than Daisy had ever known her. 'I'll be round tomorrow, Daze,' she called across to her. 'To stand guard.'

Daisy leaned round Connor. 'You traitor,' she said and grinned.

'Absolutely.' Juno gave a jaunty wave and left, slamming the shop door behind her.

'Right.' Connor pulled her back into his embrace. 'Now little Juno the killjoy's out the way and I've got you all to myself, there's one other thing we need to talk about. And I want this settled before the baby's born. So you can cut out the delaying tactics.'

'What's that now?' Daisy said in her best Irish brogue, although she had a pretty good idea what he was referring to. After all he'd been banging on about it for months.

'You know full well what. We've yet to set the wedding date.'

'I told you, I don't want to get married looking like a beached whale.'

'And, while you look nothing like a beached whale,' he said, sounding pained, 'I agreed to that bit of fancy, didn't I? You've a few months once Junior's born to get yourself together, but then we're doing it. I found a place in France that would be perfect. It's available for the third Saturday in August. We can party there with all our pals for a week and be back in time for Carnival. I've a mind to book it tomorrow. What do you say?'

She wanted to say yes, there was nothing more she wanted to do than marry this man and claim him as her own for everyone to see. But something had been bothering her for months about their wedding. Something that had nothing to do with her figure. And she still hadn't found the best way to broach the subject.

'I thought you said we had all the time in the world,' she said lamely.

He huffed and turned her in his arms. Keeping his hands on her hips, he dipped his head to look into her face. 'Is there another reason you won't set the date? Because if there is you best spit it out now.'

She swallowed hard, could see the stubbornness in the hard line of his jaw and knew this was it. She would have to say it now, or for ever hold her peace. And that she couldn't do. Connor needed closure on the horrors of his childhood, and he would never have it unless he took this next step.

She took a deep breath. 'I want to contact Mac,' she blurted out. 'I want to invite him to the wedding.'

His eyebrows shot up. 'You… What?'

'He's your brother, Connor. We're having a baby in a few weeks and he'll be its uncle. And when we get married we'll be saying vows that will make us a family for ever. I want him there to witness them with us. Don't you?'

His hands fell from her waist. He looked shocked. But at least he didn't look angry or defensive, which were the two reactions she'd feared the most.

'What…?' His voice broke. He cleared his throat. 'What if he won't come?'

She took his hands in hers, squeezed. 'If he's your brother, he can't possibly be that much of a coward.' She was counting on it. 'You need to forgive yourself for what happened that night—and to do that you need to see Mac again, to make things right with him. He's your family which makes him my family too.' She paused, willing him to understand. 'If you don't want to contact him, I'll accept your decision and we'll never talk about it again. But I had to ask.'

He sucked in a long breath, raised his eyes to the ceiling, and slowly let it out. 'You are the most contrary woman…' he muttered, but there was no heat in the words.

His eyes met hers. 'Okay, you go ahead and contact Mac. But I hope he's ready for what's about to hit him.'

She wrapped her arms around his neck and smacked a

kiss on his lips. 'Thank you, Connor. It's the right thing to do, I know it is. And if everything goes well with Mac, we could start trying to trace your sis—'

He slapped his hand over her mouth before she could say another word. 'Stop right there. There'll be no more meddling until we're married, the shop's up and running and the baby's at least five. Do you understand?'

She nodded behind his hand, her heart swelling at the rueful grin on his face. He wasn't mad. He didn't seem upset. He might even be a little pleased about the plan to contact his brother. Everything was going to work out, she was sure of it.

'Now, when I lift my hand,' he said carefully, the mischievous twinkle in his eyes belying the severity in his voice, 'I want you to say you'll make an honest man of me on August eighteenth. No more excuses. You got it?'

She nodded. He lifted his hand.

'Aye, aye, Connor,' she chirped, feeling as if all the happiness in the world had just exploded in her heart.

'And none of your cheek either,' he said, then took her in his arms and kissed her into complete submission to seal the deal.

Three days and fourteen excruciating hours of labour later, and Daisy held another of her dreams in tired arms. As little Ronan Cormac Brody suckled ferociously at her breast, and his father stared down at the two of them, his arm tight around Daisy's shoulders and his eyes filled with awe, Daisy knew she had the happy ever after she'd once only dreamed of in some secret corner of her heart.

Now all she had to do was start living it.

TYCOON'S RING OF CONVENIENCE

JULIA JAMES

For JW and CE – with thanks.

CHAPTER ONE

THE WOMAN IN the looking glass was beautiful. Fair hair, drawn back into an elegant chignon from a fine-boned face, luminous grey eyes enhanced with expensive cosmetics, lips outlined with subtle colour. At the lobes of her ears and around her throat pearls shimmered.

For several long moments she continued to stare, unblinking. Then abruptly she got to her feet and turned, the long skirts of her evening gown swishing as she headed to the bedroom door. She could delay no longer. Nikos did not care to be kept waiting.

Into her head, in the bleak reality of her life now, came the words of a saying that was constantly there.

"'Take what you want," says God. "Take it and pay for it."'

She swallowed as she headed downstairs to her waiting husband. Well, she had taken what she'd wanted. And she was paying for it. Oh, how she was paying for it...

Six months previously

'You do realise, Diana, that with probate now completed and your financial situation clearly impossible, you have no option but to sell.'

Diana felt her hands clench in her lap, but did not reply.

The St Clair family lawyer went on. 'It won't reach top price, obviously, because of its poor condition, but you should clear enough to enable you to live pretty decently. I'll contact the agents and set the wheels in motion.'

Gerald Langley smiled in a way that she supposed he thought encouraging.

'I suggest that you take a holiday. I know it's been a very difficult time for you. Your father's accident, his progressive decline after his injuries—and then his death—'

He might have saved his breath. A stony expression had tautened Diana's face. 'I'm not selling.'

Gerald frowned at the obduracy in her voice. 'Diana, you must face facts,' he retorted, his impatience audible. 'You may have sufficient income from shares and other investments to cope with the normal running and maintenance costs of Greymont, or even to find the capital for the repairs your father thought were necessary, but this latest structural survey you commissioned after he died shows that the repairs urgently needed—that *cannot* be deferred or delayed—are *far* more extensive than anyone realised. You simply do not have the funds for it—not after death duties. Let alone for the decorative work on the interior. Nor are there any art masterpieces you can sell—your grandfather disposed of most of them to pay his own death duties, and your father sold everything else to pay *his*.'

He drew a breath,

'So, outside of an extremely unlikely lottery win,' he said, and there was a trace of condescension now, 'your only other option would be to find some extremely rich man with exceptionally deep pockets and marry him.'

He let his bland gaze rest on her for a second, then resumed his original thread.

'As I say, I will get in touch with the agents, and—'

His expression changed to one of surprise. His client was getting to her feet.

'Please don't trouble yourself, Gerald.' Diana's voice was as clipped as his. She picked up her handbag and made her way to the office door.

Behind her she heard Gerald standing up. 'Diana—what are you doing? There is a great deal more to discuss.'

She paused, turning with her hand on the door handle. Her gaze on him was unblinking. But behind her expressionless face emotions were scything through her. She would *never* consent to losing her beloved home. Never! It meant everything to her. To sell it would be a betrayal of her centuries-old ancestry and a betrayal of her father, of the sacrifice he'd made for her.

Greymont, she knew with another stabbing emotion, had provided the vital security and stability she'd needed so much as a child, coping with the trauma of her mother's desertion of her father, of herself... Whatever it might take to keep Greymont, she would do it.

Whatever it took.

There was no trace of those vehement emotions as she spoke. 'There is nothing more to discuss, Gerald. And as for what I am going to do—isn't it obvious?'

She paused minutely, then said it.

'I'm going to find an extremely rich man to marry.'

Nikos Tramontes stood on the balcony of his bedroom in his luxurious villa on the Cote d'Azur, flexing his broad shoulders, looking down at Nadya, who was swimming languorously in the pool below.

Once he had enjoyed watching her—for Nadya Serensky was one of the most outstandingly beautiful of the current batch of celebrity supermodels, and Nikos had enjoyed being the man with exclusive access to her. It had sent a clear signal to the world that he had arrived— had acquired the huge wealth that a woman like Nadya required in her favoured men.

But now, two years on, her charms were wearing thin, and no amount of her pointing out what a fantastic couple they made—she with her trademark flaming red hair, him with his six-foot frame to match hers, and the darkly saturnine looks that drew as many female eyes as her spectacular looks drew male eyes—could make them less stale. Worse, she was now hinting—blatantly and persistently—that they should marry.

Even if he had not been growing tired of her, there would be no point marrying Nadya—it would bring him nothing that he did not already have with her.

Now he wanted more than her flame-haired beauty, her celebrity status. He wanted to move on in his life, yet again. Achieve his next goal.

Nadya had been a trophy mistress, celebrating his arrival in the plutocracy of the world—but now what he wanted was a trophy *wife*. A wife who would complete what he had sought all his life.

His expression darkened, as it always did when his thoughts turned to memories. His acquisition of vast wealth and all the trappings that went with it—from this villa on exclusive Cap Pierre to having one of the world's most beautiful and famous faces in his bed, and all the other myriad luxuries of his life—had been only the first step in his transformation from being the unwanted, misbegotten 'embarrassing inconvenience' of his despised parents.

Parents who had conceived him in the selfish carelessness of an adulterous affair, discarding him the moment he was born, farming him out to foster parents—denying he had anything to do with them.

Well, he would prove them wrong. Prove that he could achieve by his own efforts what they had denied him.

Making himself rich—vastly so—had proved him to be the son of his philandering Greek shipping magnate father, with as much spending power as the man who had disowned him. And his marriage, he had determined, would prove himself the son of his aristocratic, adulterous French mother, enabling him to move in the same elite social circles as she, even though he was nothing more than her unwanted bastard.

Abruptly he turned away, heading back inside. Such thoughts, such memories, were always toxic—always bitter.

Down below, Nadya emerged from the water, realised Nikos was no longer watching her and, with an angry pout, seized her wrap and glowered up at the deserted balcony.

Diana sat trying not to look bored as the after-dinner speaker droned on about capital markets and fiscal policies—matters she knew nothing about and cared less. But she was attending this City livery company's formal dinner in one of London's most historic buildings simply because her partner here was an old acquaintance—Toby Masterson. And he was someone she was considering marrying.

For Toby was rich—very rich—having inherited a merchant bank. Which meant he could amply fund Greymont's restoration. He was also someone she would never fall in love with—and that was good. Diana's clear grey eyes shadowed. Good because love was dangerous. It destroyed people's happiness, ruined lives.

It had destroyed her father's happiness when her mother had deserted her doting husband for a billionaire Australian media mogul, never to be seen again. At the age of ten Diana had learnt the danger of loving someone who might not return that love—whether it was the mother who'd abandoned her without a thought, or a man who might break her heart by not loving her, as her mother had broken her father's heart.

She knew, sadly, how protective it had made him over her. She had lost her mother—he would not let her lose the home she loved so much, her beloved Greymont, the one place where she had felt safe after her mother's desertion. Life could change traumatically—the mother she'd loved had abandoned her—but Greymont was a constant, there for ever. Her home for ever.

Guilt tinged her expression now. Her father had sacrificed his own chance of finding happiness in a second marriage in order to ensure that there would never be a son to take precedence over her, to ensure that *she* would inherit Greymont.

Yet if she were to pass Greymont on to her own children she must one day marry—and, whilst she would not risk her heart in love, surely she could find a man with whom she could be on friendly terms, sufficiently compatible to make enduring a lifetime with him not unpleasant, with both of them dedicated to preserving Greymont?

A nip of anxiety caught at her expression. The trouble was, she'd always assumed she would have plenty of time to select such a man. But now, with the dire financial situation she was facing, she needed a rich husband fast. Which meant she could not afford to be fussy.

Her eyes rested on Toby as he listened to the speaker and she felt her heart sink. Toby Masterson was amiable and good-natured—but, oh, he was desperately, *desperately* dull. And, whilst she would never risk marrying a man she might fall in love with, she did at least want a man with whom the business of conceiving a child would not be…repulsive.

She gave a silent shudder at the thought of Toby's overweight body against hers, his pudgy features next to hers, trying not to be cruel, but knowing it would be gruelling for her to endure his clumsy embraces…

Could I endure that for years and years—decades?

The question hovered in her head, twisting and cringing.

She pulled her gaze away, not wanting to think such thoughts. Snapped her eyes out across the lofty banqueting hall, filled with damask-covered tables and a sea of city-folk in dinner jackets and women in evening gowns.

And suddenly, instead of a faceless mass of men in DJs, she saw that one of them had resolved into a single individual, at a table a little way away, sitting on the far side of it. A man whose dark, heavy-lidded gaze was fixed on *her*.

Nikos lounged back in his chair, long fingers curved around his brandy glass, indifferent to the after-dinner speaker who was telling him things about capital markets and fiscal policies that he knew already. Instead, his thoughts were about his personal life.

Who would he choose as his trophy wife? The woman who, now that he had achieved a vast wealth to rival that of his despised father, would be his means to achieve entry into the socially elite world of his aristocratic but heartless mother. Proving to himself, and to the world, and above all to the parents who had never cared about him, that their unwanted offspring had done fine—just fine—without them.

His brow furrowed. Marriage was supposed to be life-long, but did he want that—even with a trophy wife? His affair with Nadya had lasted two years before boredom had set in. Would he want any longer in a marriage? Once he had got what a trophy wife offered him—his place in her world—he could do without her very well.

Certainly there would be no question of love in the relationship, for that was an emotion quite unknown to him. He had never loved Nadya, nor she him—they had merely been useful to each other. The foster couple paid to raise him had not loved him. They had not been un-kind, merely uninterested, and he had no contact with them now. As for his birth parents... His mouth twisted, his eyes hardening. Had they considered their sordid adulterous affair to be about *love*?

He snapped his mind away. Went back to considering the question of his future trophy wife. First, though, he had to sever relations with Nadya, currently in New York at a fashion show. He would tell her tactfully, thanking her for the time they'd had together—which had been good, as he was the first to acknowledge—before she flew back. He would bestow upon her a lavish farewell gift—her favourite emeralds—and wish her well. Doubt-less she was prepared for this moment, and would have his successor selected already.

Just as he was now planning to select the next woman in his life.

He eased his shoulders back in the chair, taking an-other mouthful of his cognac. He was here in London on business, attending this City function specifically for networking, and he let his dark gaze flicker out over the throng of diners, identifying those he wished to approach once the tedious after-dinner speaker was finally done.

He was on the point of lowering his brandy glass,

when he halted. His gaze abruptly zeroed in on one face. A woman sitting a few tables away.

Until now his view of her had been obscured, but as other diners shifted to face the after-dinner speaker she had become visible.

His gaze narrowed assessingly. She was extraordinarily beautiful, in a style utterly removed from the fiery, dramatic features of Nadya. This woman was blonde, the hair drawn back into a French pleat as pale as her alabaster complexion, her face fine-boned, her eyes clear, wide-set, her perfect mouth enhanced with lip-gloss. She looked remote, her beauty frozen.

One phrase slid across his mind.

Ice maiden.

Another followed.

Look, but don't touch.

And immediately, instantly, that was exactly what Nikos wanted to do. To cross over to her, curve his long fingers around that alabaster face and tilt it up to his, to feel the cool satin of her pale skin beneath the searching tips of his fingers, to glide his thumbs sensually across that luscious mouth, to see those pale, expressionless eyes flare with sudden reaction, feel her iced glaze melt beneath his touch.

The intensity of the impulse scythed through him. His grip around his brandy glass tightened. Decision seared within him. A trophy wife might be next on his list of life ambitions, but that did not mean he had to seek her out immediately. He had been with Nadya for two years— no reason not to enjoy a more temporary liaison before seeking his bride.

And he had just seen the ideal woman for that role.

Ideal.

* * *

With an effort, Diana sheared her gaze away, heard the speech finally ending.

'Phew!' Toby exclaimed, throwing Diana a look of apology. 'Sorry to make you endure all that,' he said.

She gave a polite smile, but in her mental vision was the face of the man who had been looking at her across the tables. The image was burning in her head.

Darkly tanned, strong features, sable hair feathering his broad forehead, high cheekbones, a blade of a nose and a mouth with a sculpted contour that somehow disturbed her—but, oh, not nearly so much as the heavy-lidded dark, dark eyes that had rested on her.

Eyes that she still felt watching her, even though she was not looking at him. Did not want to. Didn't dare to.

She felt her heart give a sudden extra beat, as if a shot of pure adrenaline had been injected into her bloodstream. Something that she was supremely unused to—unused to handling. She was accustomed to men looking at her—but not to the way she had reacted to *this* man.

Urgently she made her eyes cling to Toby. Familiar, amiable Toby, with his pudgy face and portly figure. In comparison with the man who'd been looking at her, poor Toby seemed pudgier and portlier than ever. Her eyes slid away, her heart sinking. She was feeling bad about what she was contemplating. Could she *really* be considering marrying him just because he was rich?

Guilt smote her that she should feel that way about him, but there it was. Had seeing that darkly disturbingly good-looking man just now made her realise how impossible it would be for her to marry a man like Toby? But if not Toby then who? Who could save Greymont for her?

Where can I find him? And how soon?

It was proving harder than she'd so desperately hoped, and time was running out…

Speeches finally over, the atmosphere in the banqueting hall lightened, and there was a sense of general movement amongst the tables as diners started to mingle. Nikos was talking to his host, a City acquaintance, and casually bringing the subject around to the woman who had so piqued his interest. The ice maiden…

He nodded in her direction. 'Who's the blonde?' he asked laconically.

'I don't know her myself,' came the reply, 'but the man she's with is Toby Masterson—Masterson Dubrett, merchant bankers. Want an introduction?'

'Why not?' said Nikos.

There had been nothing in his brief perusal to indicate that the blonde's dinner partner was anything more to her—an impression confirmed as he was introduced.

'Toby Masterson—Nikos Tramontes of Tramontes Financials. Fingers in many pies—some of them might interest you and vice versa,' his host said briefly, and left them to it, heading off to talk elsewhere.

For a few minutes Nikos exchanged the kind of anodyne business talk that would interest a London merchant banker, and then he glanced at Toby Masterson's guest.

The ice maiden was not looking at him. Quite deliberately not looking at him. He was glad of it. Women who came on to him bored him. Nadya had played hard to get—she knew her own value as one of the world's most beautiful women, and was courted by many men. But he did not think the ice maiden was playing any such game—her reserve was genuine.

It made him all the more interested in her.

Expectantly he glanced at Toby Masterson, who dutifully performed the required introduction.

'Diana,' he said genially, 'this is Nikos Tramontes.'

She was forced to look at him, though her grey eyes were expressionless. Carefully expressionless.

'How do you do, Mr Tramontes?' she intoned in a cool voice. She spoke with the familiar tones of the English upper class, and only the briefest smile of courtesy indented her mouth.

Nikos gave her an equally brief courtesy smile. 'How do you do, Ms...?' He glanced at Masterson for her surname.

'St Clair,' Masterson supplied.

'Ms St Clair,' he said, his glance going back to the ice maiden.

Her face was still expressionless, but in the depths of her clear grey eyes he was sure he saw a sudden veiling, as if she were guarding herself from his perusal of her. That was good—it showed him that despite her glacial expression she was responsive to him.

Satisfied, he turned his attention back to Toby Masterson, moving their conversation on to the EU, the latest manoeuvres from Brussels, and thence on to the current state of the Greek economy.

'Does it impact *you*?' Toby Masterson was asking.

Nikos shook his head. 'Despite my name, I'm based in Monaco. I've a villa on Cap Pierre.' He glanced at Diana St Clair. 'What of you, Ms St Clair? Do you care for the South of France?'

It was a direct question, and she had to answer it. Had to look at him, engage eye contact.

'I seldom go abroad,' she replied.

Her tone still held that persistent note of not wanting to converse, and he watched her reach for her liqueur glass, raise it to her lips as if to give her something to do—something to enable her not to answer more fully. Yet her hand trembled very, very slightly as she replaced her glass, and satisfaction again bit in Nikos. The permafrost was not as deep as she wanted to convey.

'That's not surprising,' Masterson supplied jovially. 'The St Clairs have a spectacular place in the country to enjoy—Hampshire, isn't it? Greymont?' he checked. 'Eighteenth-century stately pile,' he elaborated.

Do they, indeed? thought Nikos. He looked at her with sudden deeper interest.

'Do you know Hampshire?' Toby Masterson was asking now.

'Not at all,' said Nikos, keeping his eyes on Diana St Clair. 'Greymont? Is that right?'

For the first time he saw an expression in her eyes. A flash that seemed to spear him with the intensity of the emotion behind it. It made him certain that behind the ice was a very, very different woman. A woman capable of passion.

Then it was gone, and the frost was back in her eyes. But it had left a residue. A residue that just for a moment he thought was bleakness.

'Yes,' she murmured.

He made a mental note. He would have a full dossier on her by tomorrow—Ms Diana St Clair of Greymont, Hampshire. What kind of place was it? What kind of family were the St Clairs? And just what further interest might Ms Diana St Clair have for him other than presenting him with so delectable a challenge to his seductive powers to melt an ice maiden?

His eyes flickered over her consideringly. Exquisitely beautiful and waiting to be melted into his arms, his bed... But could there be yet more to his interest in her? Could she be a candidate for something more than a fleeting affair?

Well, his investigations would reveal that.

For now, however, he had whetted his appetite—and he knew with absolute certainty that he had made the impact on her that he had intended, though she was striving not to let it show.

He turned his attention back to Masterson, taking his leave with a casual suggestion of some potential mutual business interest at an indeterminate future date.

As he strolled away his mood was good—very good indeed. With or without any deeper interest in her, the ice maiden was on the way to becoming his. But on what terms he had yet to decide.

He let his thoughts turn to how he might make his next move on her...

CHAPTER TWO

DIANA THREW HERSELF back in the taxi and heaved a sigh of pent-up relief. Safe at last.

Safe from Nikos Tramontes. From his powerfully unsettling impact on her. An impact she was not used to experiencing.

It had disturbed her profoundly. She had done her best to freeze him out, but a man that good-looking would not be accustomed to rebuff—would be used to getting his own way with women.

Well, not with me! Because I have no intention of having anything to do with him.

She shook her head, as if to clear his so disturbing image from her mind's eye. She had far more to worry about. She knew now, resignedly, that she could not face marrying Toby—but what other solution could save her beloved home?

Anxiety pressed at her—and over the next two days in London it worsened. Her bank declined to advance the level of loan required, the auction houses confirmed there was nothing left to sell to raise such a sum. So it was with little enthusiasm that she took a call from Toby.

'But it's Covent Garden. And I *know* you love opera.'

The plaintive note in Toby's voice made Diana feel bad. She owed him a gentle let-down. Reluctantly she acquiesced to his invitation—a corporate jolly for a performance of Verdi's *Don Carlo*.

But when she arrived at the Opera House she wished she had refused.

'You remember Nikos Tramontes, don't you?' Toby greeted her. 'He's our host tonight.'

Diana forced a mechanical smile to her face, concealing her dismay. With her own problems uppermost in her mind, she'd managed to start forgetting him, and the discomforting impact he'd had on her, but now suddenly he was here, as powerfully, disturbingly attractive as before.

Then she was being introduced to the other couple present. Diana recognised the man who had brought Nikos Tramontes over to their table. With him was his wife, who promptly took advantage of the three men starting to talk business to draw Diana aside.

'My, my,' she said conspiratorially, throwing an openly appraising look back at Nikos Tramontes, 'he is most definitely a handsome brute. No wonder he's been able to hold on to Nadya Serensky for so long. That and all his money, of course.'

Diana looked blank, and Louise Melmott promptly enlightened her.

'Nadya Serensky. You know—that stunning redheaded supermodel. They're quite an item.'

It was welcome news to Diana. Perhaps she'd only been imagining that Nikos Tramontes had eyed her up at the livery dinner.

Maybe it's just me, overreacting.

Overreacting because it was so strange to encounter a man who could have such a powerfully disturbing physical impact on her. Yes, that must be it. She tried to think, as she sipped her champagne in the Crush Room, if she had ever reacted so strongly as that to any other man, and came up blank. But then, of course, she *didn't* react to men. Had schooled herself all her life not to.

The men she'd dated over the years had been good-looking, but they had always left her cold. A tepid goodnight kiss had been the most any of them had ever received. Only with one, while at university, had she resolved to see if it were possible to have a full relationship without excessive passion of any kind.

She had found that it was—for herself. But eventually not for her boyfriend. He'd found her lack of enthusiasm off-putting and had left her for another woman. It hadn't bothered her—had only confirmed how right she was to guard her heart. Losing it was so dangerous. A policy of celibacy was much wiser, much safer.

Anxiety bit at her. Except such a policy would hardly find her a husband rich enough to save Greymont. *If* she was truly still contemplating so drastic a solution.

With an inward sigh she pulled her mind away. Tomorrow she would be heading back to Greymont to go through her finances again, get the latest grim estimates for the most essential work. But for now, tonight, she would enjoy her evening at Covent Garden—a night off from her worries.

And she would not worry, either, about the presence of the oh-so-disturbing Nikos Tramontes. If he had a famous supermodel to amuse him then he would not be interested in any other women. Including herself.

As they made their way to their box she felt her anticipation rising. The orchestra was tuning up, elegant well-heeled people were taking their seats, and up in the gods the less well-heeled were packed like sardines.

Diana looked up at them slightly ruefully. The world would see her as an extremely privileged person—and she was; she knew that—but owning Greymont came with heavy responsibilities. Prime of which was stopping it from actually falling down.

But, no, she wouldn't think of her fears for Greymont. She would enjoy the evening.

'Allow me.'

Nikos Tramontes's deep, faintly accented voice beside her made her start. He drew her chair back, allowing her to take her seat, which she did with a rustling of her skirts as he seated himself behind her. Louise Melmott sat beside her at the front of the box.

His eyes rested on the perfect profile of the woman whose presence here tonight he had specifically engineered in order to pursue his interest in her. An interest that the dossier he had ordered to be compiled on her had indicated he must show. Because she might very well indeed prove suitable for far more than a mere fleeting seduction.

Diana St Clair, it seemed, was possessed of more than the exquisite glacial beauty that had so caught his attention the other evening. She was also possessed of exactly the right background and attributes to suit his purposes. Best of all about Ms Diana St Clair was her inheritance—her eighteenth-century country estate—and the fact that it *was* her inheritance, bringing with it all the elite social background that such ownership conferred.

An old county family—not titled, but anciently armigerous—possessing crests and coats of arms and all the heraldic flourishes that went with that status. With landed property and position, centuries of intermarriage with other such families, including the peerage. A complex web of kinship and connection running like a web across the upper classes, binding them together, impenetrable to outsiders.

Except by one means only…

Marriage.

His eyes rested on her, their expression veiled. Would Diana St Clair be his trophy wife?

It was a tempting prospect. As tempting as Diana St Clair herself.

He sat back to enjoy further contemplation of this woman who might achieve what he now most wanted from life.

To Diana's relief, the dramatic sweep of Verdi's music carried her away, despite her burning consciousness that Nikos Tramontes was sitting so close to her, and as she surfaced for the first interval it was to be ushered with his other guests back to the Crush Room for the first course of their champagne supper.

The conversation was led mainly by Louise Melmott, who knew the opera and its doubtful relationship to actual history.

'The real Don Carlos of Spain was probably insane,' the other woman said cheerfully, as they helped themselves to the delicacies on offer. 'And there's no evidence he was in love with his father the King's, wife!'

'I can see why Verdi rewrote history,' Diana observed. 'A tragic, thwarted love affair sounds far more romantically operatic.'

She was doing her best to be a good guest—especially since she knew Toby had no interest in opera, so she needed to emphasise her own enthusiasm.

'Elisabeth de Valois was another man's wife. There is nothing romantic about adultery.'

Nikos Tramontes's voice was harsh, and Diana looked at him in surprise.

'Well, opera is hardly realistic—and surely for a woman like the poor Queen, trapped in a loveless marriage, especially when she'd thought she was going to be married to the King's son, not the King himself—surely one can only feel pity for her plight?'

Dark eyes rested on her. '*Can* one?'

Was there sarcasm in the way he replied? Diana felt herself colouring slightly. She had only intended a fairly light remark.

The conversation moved on, but Diana felt stung. As if she'd voted personally in favour of adultery. She felt Nikos Tramontes's eyes resting on her, their expression masked. There seemed to be a brooding quality about him suddenly, at odds with the urbane, self-assured manner he'd demonstrated so far.

Well, it was nothing to do with her—and nor was Nikos Tramontes. She would not be seeing him again after this evening.

It was to her distinct annoyance, therefore, that when the long opera finally ended and she had bade goodnight to Toby, making sure she told him she was heading back to Hampshire the next day, she discovered that somehow Nikos Tramontes was at her side as she left the Opera House. It was a mild but damp night, and his car was clearly hovering at the kerb.

'Allow me to offer you a lift,' he said. His voice was smooth.

Diana stiffened. 'Thank you, but a taxi will be fine.'

'You won't find one closer than the Strand, and it is about to rain,' he returned blandly.

Then he was guiding her forward, opening the rear passenger door for her. Annoyed, but finding it hard to object without making an issue of it, Diana got in. Reluctantly she gave the name of the hotel she and her father had always used on their rare visits to the capital, and the car moved off.

In the confines of the back seat, separated from the driver by a glass divide, Nikos Tramontes seemed even more uncomfortably close than he had in the opera box. His long legs stretched out into the footwell.

'I'm glad you enjoyed this evening,' he began. He paused minutely. 'Perhaps you'd like to come with me to another performance some time? Unless you've seen all this season's productions already?'

There was nothing more than mild enquiry in his bland voice, but Diana felt herself tense. Dismay filled her. He was making a move on her after all, despite the presence in his life of Nadya Serensky. Her hopes that her disturbing reaction to him were not returned plummeted.

'I'm afraid not,' she said, giving a quick shake of her head.

'You haven't seen them all?' he queried.

She shook her head again, making herself look at him. His face was half shadowed in the dim interior, with the only light coming from the street lights and shop windows as they made their way along the Strand towards Trafalgar Square.

'That isn't what I meant,' she said. She made her voice firm.

His response was to lift an eyebrow. 'Masterson?' he challenged laconically.

She gave a quick shake of her head. 'No, but...'

'Yes?' he prompted, as she trailed off.

Diana took a breath, clasping her hands in her lap. She made her voice composed, but decisive. 'I spend very little time in London, Mr Tramontes, and because of that it would be...pointless to accept any...ah...further invitation from you. For whatever purpose.'

She said no more. It struck her that for him to have sounded so very disapproving of a fictional case of adultery in the plot of *Don Carlos* was more than a little hypocritical of him, given that he'd just asked her out. Clearly he was not averse to playing away himself, she thought acidly.

She saw him ease his shoulders back into the soft leather of his seat. Saw a sardonic smile tilt at his mouth. Caught a sudden scent of his aftershave, felt the closeness of his presence.

'Do you *know* my purpose?' he murmured, with a quizzical, faintly mocking look in his dark eyes.

She pressed her mouth tightly. 'I don't need to, Mr Tramontes. I'm simply making it clear that since I don't spend much time in London I won't have any opportunities to go to the opera, whomever I might go with.'

'You're returning to Hampshire?'

She nodded. 'Yes. Indefinitely. I don't know when I shall be next in town,' she said, wanting to make crystal-clear her unavailability.

He seemed to accept her answer. 'I quite understand,' he said easily.

She felt a sense of relief go through her. He was backing off—she could tell. For all that, she still felt a level of agitation that was unsettling. It came simply from his physical closeness. She was aware that her heart rate had quickened. It was unnerving…

Then, thankfully, the car was turning off Piccadilly and drawing up outside the hotel where she was staying. The doorman came forward to open her door and she was soon climbing out, trying not to hurry. Making her voice composed once more.

'Goodnight, Mr Tramontes. Thank you so much for a memorable evening at the opera, and thank you for this lift now.'

She disappeared inside the haven of the hotel.

From the car, Nikos watched her go. It was the kind of old-fashioned but upmarket hotel that well-bred provincials patronised when forced to come to town, and doubtless the St Clairs had been patronising it for generations.

His eyes narrowed slightly as his car moved off, heading back to his own hotel—far more fashionable and flashy than Diana St Clair's. Had she turned down his invitation on account of Nadya? He'd heard Louise Melmott say her name. If so, that was all to the good. It showed him that Diana St Clair was…*particular* about the men she associated with.

He had not cared for her apparent tolerance of the adultery in the plot of *Don Carlos*, but it did not seem that she carried that over into real life. It was essential that she did not.

No wife of mine will indulge in adultery—no wife of mine, however upper crust her background, will be anything like my mother! Anything at all—

Wife? Was he truly thinking of Diana St Clair in such a light?

And, if he were, what might persuade her to agree?

What could thaw that chilly reserve of hers?

What will make her receptive to me?

Whatever it was, he would find it—and use it.

He sat back, considering his thoughts, as his car merged into the late-night London traffic.

Greymont was as beautiful as ever—especially in the sunshine, which helped to disguise how the stonework was crumbling and the damp was getting in. The lead roof that needed replacing was invisible behind the parapet, and—

A wave of deep emotion swept through Diana. How could Gerald possibly imagine she might actually sell

Greymont? It meant more to her than anything in the world. Anything or anyone. St Clairs had lived here for three hundred years, made their home here—of *course* she could not sell it. Each generation held it in trust for the next.

Her eyes shadowed. Her father had entrusted it to *her*, had ensured—at the price of putting aside any hopes of his own for a happier, less heart-sore second marriage—that *she* inherited. She had lost her mother—he had ensured she should not lose her home as well.

So for her to give it up now, to let it go to strangers, would be an unforgivable betrayal of his devotion to her, his trust in her. She could not do it. Whatever she had to do—she would do it. She *must*.

As she walked indoors, her footsteps echoing on the marble floor, she looked at the sweeping staircase soaring to the upper floors, at the delicate Adam mouldings in the alcoves and the equally delicate painted ceilings—both in need of attention—and the white marble fireplace, chipped now, in too many places. A few remaining family portraits by undistinguished artists were on the walls ascending the staircase, all as familiar to her as her own body.

Upstairs in her bedroom, she crossed to the window, throwing open the sash to gaze out over the gardens and the park beyond. An air of unkemptness might prevail, but the level lawns, the ornamental stone basin with its now non-functioning fountain, the pathways and the pergolas, marching away to where the ha-ha divided the formal gardens from the park, were all as lovely as they always had been. As dear and precious.

A fierce sense of protectiveness filled her. She breathed deeply of the fresh country air, then slid the window shut, noticing that it was sticking more than ever, its paint flaking—another sign of damp getting in. She could see another patch of damp on her ceiling too, and frowned.

Whilst her father had been so ill not even routine maintenance work had been done on the house, let alone anything more intensive. It would have disturbed him too much with noise and dust, and the structural survey she'd commissioned after he'd died had revealed problems even worse than she had feared or her father had envisaged.

A new roof, dozens of sash windows in need of extensive repair or replacement, rotting floorboards, collapsing chimneys, the ingress of damp, electrical rewiring, re-plumbing, new central heating needed—the list went on and on. And then there was all the decorative work, from repainting ceilings to mending tapestries to conserving curtains and upholstery.

More and yet more to do.

And that was before she considered the work that the outbuildings needed! Bowing walls, slate roofs deteriorating, cobbles to reset... A never-ending round. Even before a start was made on the overgrown gardens.

She felt her shoulders sag. So much to be done—all costing so, *so* much. She gave a sigh, starting to unpack her suitcase. Staff had been reduced to the minimum—the Hudsons, and the cleaners up from the village, plus a gardener and his assistant. It was just as well that her father had preferred a very quiet life, even if that *had* contributed to his wife's discontent. And he had become increasingly reclusive after her desertion.

It had suited Diana, though, and she'd been happy to help him write the St Clair family history, acting as secretary for his correspondence with the network of family connections, sharing his daily walks through the park, being the chatelaine of Greymont in her mother's absence.

Any socialising had been with other families like theirs in the county, such as their neighbours, Sir John Bartlett and his wife, her father's closest friends. She herself had been more active, visiting old school and university friends around the country as they gradually married and started families, meeting up with them in London from time to time. But she was no party animal, preferring dinner parties, or going to the theatre and opera, either with girlfriends or those carefully selected men she allowed to squire her around—those who accepted she was not interested in romance and was completely unresponsive to all men.

Into her head, with sudden flaring memory, stabbed the image of the one man who had disproved that comforting theory.

Angrily, she pushed it away. It was irrelevant, her ridiculous reaction to Nikos Tramontes! She would never be seeing him again—and she had far more urgent matters to worry about.

Taking a breath, anxiety clenching her stomach, she went downstairs and settled at her father's desk in the library. In her absence mail had accumulated, and with a resigned sigh she started to open it. None of it would be good news, she knew that—more unaffordable estimates for the essential repairs to Greymont. She felt her heart squeeze, and fear bite in her throat.

Somehow she *had* to get the money she needed.

But not by marrying Toby Masterson. She could not bring herself to spend the rest of her life with him.

She felt a prickle of shame. It had not been fair even to think of him merely as a solution to her problems.

Wearily, she reached for her writing pad. She'd have

to pen a careful letter—thanking him for taking her out in London, implying that that was all there was to it.

As she made a start, though, it was quite another face that intruded into her inner vision, quite different from Toby's pudgy features. A face that was dramatic in its looks, with dark eyes that set her pulse beating faster—

She pushed it from her. Even if Nikos Tramontes were *not* involved with his supermodel girlfriend, all a man like that would be after would be some kind of dalliance—something to amuse him, entertain him while he was in London.

And what use is that to me?

None. None at all.

Nikos slowly made his way along the avenue of chestnut trees, avoiding the many potholes as Greymont gradually came into view.

With a white stucco eighteenth-century façade, a central block with symmetrical wings thrown out, its aspect was open, but set on a slight elevation, with extensive gardens and grounds seamlessly blending into farmland. The whole was framed by ornamental woodland. A classic stately home of the English upper classes.

Memory jabbed at him, cruel and stabbing. Of another home of another nation's upper class. A chateau deep in the heart of Normandy, built of creamy Caen stone, with turrets at the corners in the French style.

He'd driven up to the front doors. Had been received.

But not welcomed.

'You will have to leave. My husband will be home soon. He must not find you here—'

There had been no warmth in the voice, no embrace from the elegant, couture-clad figure, no opening of her arms to him. Nothing but rejection.

'That is all you have to say to me?'

That had been his question, his demand.

Her lips had tightened. *'You must leave,'* she'd said again, not answering his question.

He had swept a glance around the room, with its immaculate décor, its priceless seventeenth-century landscapes on the walls, the exquisite Louis Quinze furniture. *This* was what she had chosen. *This* was what she had valued. And she had been perfectly willing, to pay the price demanded for it. The price *he* had paid for it.

Bitterness had filled him then—and an even stronger emotion that he would not name, would deny with steely resolve that he had ever felt. It filled him again now, a sudden acid rush in his veins.

With an effort, he let it drain out of him as he drew his powerful car to a momentary halt, the better to survey the scene before him.

Yes—what he was seeing satisfied him. More than satisfied him. Greymont, the ancestral home of the St Clairs, and all that came with it would serve his purpose excellently. But it was not just the physical possession he wanted—that was not what this visit was about. Had he wished. he could easily have purchased such a place for himself, but that would not have given him what he was set upon achieving.

His smile tightened. He knew just how to achieve what he wanted. What would make Diana St Clair receptive to him. Knew exactly what she wanted most—needed most. And he would offer it to her. On a plate.

His gaze still fixed on his goal, he headed towards it.

CHAPTER THREE

'MR *TRAMONTES*?'

Diana stared blankly as Hudson conveyed the information about her totally unexpected visitor. What on earth was Nikos Tramontes doing here at Greymont?

Bemused, and with an uneasy flutter in her stomach, she walked into the library. She found her uninvited guest perusing the walls of leather-bound books, and as he turned at her entrance she felt an unwelcome jolt to her heart-rate.

It had been a week since she'd left London, but seeing his tall, commanding figure again instantly brought back the evening she'd spent at Covent Garden. Unlike on the two previous occasions she'd set eyes on him, this time he was in a suit, and the dark charcoal of the material, the pristine white of his shirt, and the discreet navy blue tie, made him every bit as eye-catching as he had been in evening dress.

It annoyed her that she should feel that sudden kick in her pulse again as she approached. She fought to suppress it, and failed.

'Ms St Clair.' He strode forward, reaching out his hand.

Numbly, she let him take hers and give it a quick, businesslike shake.

'I'm sorry to call unannounced,' he went on, his manner still businesslike, 'but there is a matter I would like to discuss with you that will be of mutual benefit to us both.'

He looked at her, his expression expectant.

Blankly, she went and sat down on the well-worn leather sofa by the fireplace, and watched him move to do likewise. He took her father's armchair, and a slight bristle of resentment went through her. She leant over to ring the ancient bell-pull beside the mantel and, when Hudson duly appeared, asked for coffee to be served.

When they were left alone again, she looked directly at her unexpected visitor. 'I really can't imagine, Mr Tramontes, that there is anything that could be of mutual benefit to us.'

Surely, for heaven's sake, he was not going to try and proposition her again? She devoutly hoped not.

He smiled, crossing one long leg over the other. It was a proprietorial gesture, and it put her hackles up. The entrance of Hudson with the coffee tray was a welcome diversion, and she busied herself pouring them both a cup, only glancing at Nikos Tramontes to ask how he took his coffee.

'Black, no sugar,' he said briskly, and took the cup she proffered.

But he did not drink from it. Instead, he swept his gaze around the high-ceilinged, book-lined room, then brought it back to Diana.

'This is an exceptionally fine house you have, Ms St Clair,' he said. 'I can see why you won't sell.'

She started, whole body tensing. What on *earth*? How dared Nikos Tramontes make such a remark to her. It was *none* of his business.

He saw her expression and gave a smile that had a caustic twist to it. 'It wasn't that hard,' he said gently, not letting her drop her outraged gaze, 'to discover the circumstances of your inheritance. And I have eyes in my head. I may not be that familiar with English country houses, but a pot-holed drive, masonry that is crumbling below the roofline, grounds that could do with several more gardeners...'

He took a mouthful of coffee, setting the cup aside on the table her father had used to lay his daily newspaper on. Looked at her directly again.

'It makes sense of your interest in Toby Masterson,' he told her. 'A man with a merchant bank at his disposal.'

Again, outrage seethed in Diana—even more fiercely. Her voice was icy. 'Mr Tramontes, I really think—'

He held up a hand to silence her. As if, she thought stormily, she was some unruly office junior.

'Hear me out,' he said.

He paused a moment, studying her. She was dressed casually, in dark green well-cut trousers and a paler green sweater, with her hair caught back in a clip, no jewellery, and no make-up he could discern—a world away from the muted elegance of her evening dress. But her pale, breathtaking beauty still had the same immediate powerful impact on him as it had when she'd first caught his eye. Her current unconcealed outrage only accentuated his response.

'I understand your predicament,' he said.

There was sympathy in his voice, and it made her suspicious. Her expression was shuttered, her mouth set. Her own coffee completely ignored.

'And I have a potential solution for you,' he went on.

His eyes never left her face, and there was something in their long-lashed dark regard that made it difficult to meet them. But meet them she did—even if it took an effort to appear as composed as she wanted to be.

He took her silence for assent, and continued.

'What I am about to put to you, Ms St Clair, is a solution that will be a familiar one to you, with your ancestry. I'm sure that not a few of your forebears opted for a similar solution. Though these days, fortunately, the solution can be a lot less…perhaps *irreversible* is the correct term.'

He reached for his coffee again. Took a leisurely mouthful and replaced the cup. Looked at her once more. She had neutralised her expression, but that was to be expected. Once he had put his cards on the table she would either have him shown the door—or she would agree to what he wanted.

'You wish—extremely understandably—to retain your family property. However, it's quite evident that a very substantial sum of money is going to be required—a sum that, as I'm sure you are punishingly aware, given the current level of death duties and the exceptionally high cost of conservation work on listed historic houses, is going to stretch you. Very possibly beyond your limits. Certainly beyond your comfort zone.'

Her expression was stony, giving nothing away. That didn't bother him. It made him think how statuesque her beauty was. How much it appealed to him. The contrast of her chilly ice maiden impassivity with Nadya's hot-blooded outbursts was entirely in Diana St Clair's favour. She was as unlike Nadya as a woman could be—and not, he thought with satisfaction, just in respect of the ice maiden quality, but in so much more—all of which was supremely useful to him.

'As I say, you've clearly already considered—and rejected—Toby Masterson as a solution to your problem, but now I invite you to consider an alternative candidate.'

He paused. A deliberate, telling pause. His eyes held hers like hooks.

'Myself,' he said.

Diana's intake of breath was audible. It scraped through her throat and seemed to dry her lungs to ashes.

'Are you *mad*?' came from her.

'Not in the least,' was his unruffled reply. 'This is what I propose.' His mouth tightened a moment, then he went on. 'I should make it clear immediately, however, that my relationship with Nadya Serensky is at an end. She was a woman I wanted two years ago—now I want something, and some*one*, quite different. *You*, Ms St Clair, suit my requirements perfectly. And I,' he continued, ignoring the mounting look of disbelief on her face, 'suit *your* requirements perfectly, too.'

She opened her mouth to speak, to protest, but no words came. What words could possibly come in response to such a brazen, unbelievable announcement? He was continuing to talk in that same cool manner, as if he were discussing the weather, and she could only listen to what he said. Even while she stared at him blankly.

'What I want now, at this stage of my life,' he was saying—perfectly calmly, perfectly casually, 'is a wife. Nadya was quite unsuitable for that role. You, however...'

His dark eyes rested on her, unreadable and opaque, and yet somehow seeing right into her, she felt with a hollowing of her stomach.

'You are perfect for that part. As I,' he finished, 'am perfect for you.'

She could only stare, frozen with disbelief. And with another emotion that was trying to snake around her stunned mind.

'We would each,' he said, 'provide the other with what we currently want.' He glanced once more around the library, then back to her. 'I want to be part of the world you inhabit—the world of country houses like this, and those who were born to them. Oh, I could quite easily buy such a house, but that would not serve my purpose. I would be an outsider. A *parvenu*.'

His voice was edged, and he felt the familiar wash of bitterness in his veins, but she was simply staring at him, with a stunned expression on her beautiful face.

'That will not do for me,' he said. 'What I want, therefore, is a wife from that world, who will make me a part of it by marrying her, so that I am accepted.' Again, his voice tightened as he continued. 'As for what *you* would gain...' His expression changed. 'I am easily able to afford the work that needs to be done to ensure the fabric of this magnificent edifice is repaired and restored to the condition it should enjoy. So you see...' he gave his faint smile '...how suitable we are for each other?'

She found her voice—belatedly—her words faint as she forced them out.

'I cannot believe you are serious. We have met precisely twice. You're a complete stranger to me. And I to you.'

He gave the slightest shrug of his broad shoulders. 'That can easily be remedied. I am perfectly prepared for our engagement to provide sufficient time to set you at your ease with me.'

He reached to take up his coffee cup again, levelled his unreadable gaze on her.

'I am not suggesting,' he continued, 'a lifetime together. Two years at the most—possibly less. Sufficient for each of us to get what we want from the other. That is, after all, one of the distinct advantages of our times— unlike your forebears, who might have made similar mutually advantageous matches, we are free to dissolve our marriage of our own volition and go our separate ways thereafter.'

He took another draught of his coffee, finishing it and setting down the cup. He looked directly at her.

'Well? What is your answer?'

She swallowed. There was a maelstrom in her head: thoughts and counter-thoughts, conflicting emotions. Swirling about chaotically. This couldn't be real, could it? This almost complete stranger, sitting here suggesting they marry?

Marry so I can save Greymont—

She felt a hollowing inside her. That had been exactly what she herself had contemplated—had told Gerald Langley that she would do. She had seriously contemplated it with Toby, then balked at making a life-long commitment to a man she would never otherwise have considered marrying.

But Nikos Tramontes only wants two years.

Two brief years of her life.

Sharply, she looked at him.

'You say no longer than two years?'

He nodded, concealing an inner sense of triumph. That she had asked the question showed she was giving his offer serious consideration. That she was tempted.

'I think that will suffice, don't you?'

It would for him—he was confident of that. Not just because when they parted he would be secure in the social position that marriage to her would give him, but because he knew from his liaison with Nadya that he was unlikely to be bored with the woman in his life before then. For two years, therefore, having Diana St Clair in his life, his bed, would be perfectly acceptable.

He let his gaze rest on her, absorbing her pristine beauty, the pallor in her cheeks from her reaction to his proposition. She was still looking dazed, but no longer outraged. Again, triumph surged in him. He knew he was most definitely drawing her in.

'Well?' he prompted.

'I need time,' she said weakly. 'I can't just—' She broke off, unable to say more, feeling as if a tornado had just scooped her up and whirled her about.

'Of course,' Nikos conceded smoothly.

He got to his feet. His six-foot-plus height seemed to overpower her.

'Think it over. I'm flying to Zurich tomorrow, but I will be back in the UK at the end of next week. You can give me your answer then. In the meantime, if you have any further questions feel free to text or email me.'

She watched him extract a business card and lay it on her father's desk before turning back to her.

Suddenly, he smiled. 'Don't look so shocked, Diana. It could work perfectly for both of us. A marriage of convenience—people made them all the time in the past. They still do, even if they don't admit it.'

He turned on his heel, leaving her sitting staring after him as he left the room. She heard his swift footsteps, the front door opening and closing again. The sound of a car starting. Her heart was pounding like a hammer inside her. And it wasn't just because of the bombshell he'd dropped in her lap.

When he smiles and calls me by my name...

She felt her pulse give a quiver, and deep inside her she felt danger roil. For reasons she could not understand Nikos Tramontes, of all the men she had ever known, seemed to possess an ability to...to *disturb* her. To make her hyper-aware of his masculinity. Of her own femininity. She didn't know where it was coming from, or why— she only knew it was dangerous.

I don't want to react to him like that—I don't want to!

Her features contorted. Nikos Tramontes had walked into her life out of nowhere and put down in front of her what could be the best hope she had of getting exactly what she wanted—the means to save Greymont. As easily and as painlessly as it was possible to do so outside of a lottery win.

Yes, he was a complete stranger—but, as he'd said, they could get to know each other during their engagement. Yes, his announcement had initially shocked her. But, as he'd also said, such marriages for mutual advantage had been perfectly unexceptional to her ancestors. And theirs would be brief—a year or two at most. Not the life-long commitment that Toby would have required...

And yet for all that she heard a voice wail in her head. *Why can't he look like Toby? Overweight and pug-faced! That would be so, so much better! So much safer.*

So much safer than the dangerous quickening of her blood that came whenever she thought of Nikos Tramontes.

Deliberately, she silenced her fear. Dismissing it. There was no need for such anxieties. None! That quickening of her blood was irrelevant—completely irrelevant. It had nothing to do with what Nikos Tramontes was offering her.

The formality of a marriage of convenience, for outward show only—a dispassionate, temporary union to provide him with an assured entrée into her world and her with the means to preserve her inheritance. Nothing else—nothing that had anything to do with that quickening of her pulse.

It was because she owned Greymont and came with the social position and connections he wanted to acquire that he was interested in her. Nothing more than that. Oh, he would want her to grace his arm, be an ornament for him—that was understandable. But that would be in public. In private their relationship would be cordial, but fundamentally, she reassured herself, it would be little more than a business arrangement at heart. He got a society wife—she got Greymont restored. Mutually beneficial.

We would be associates. That's a good word for it.

With a little start she realised she was giving his extraordinary proposition serious consideration.

Her mind reeled again.

Could she really do this? Accept his offer—use it to save Greymont?

It was all she could think about as the days went by. Days spent in visits from the architect, and from the specialist companies that would undertake the careful restoration and conservation work on Greymont that would have to be carried out in accordance to the strict building regulations for historic listed buildings, adding to the complexity—and the cost.

With every passing day she could feel the temptation to accept what Nikos was offering her coiling itself like a serpent around her. Tightening its grip with every coil.

Nikos settled himself into a seat in first class. His mood was good—very good. His decision to select Diana St Clair as the means of achieving his life's second imperative goal might have been made impulsively, but he'd always trusted his instincts. They'd never failed him in business yet, enabling his rise to riches to be as meteoric as it had been steep.

A faint frown furrowed his brow as he accepted a glass of champagne from the attentive stewardess.

But marriage is not a business decision...

He shook the thought from him. His liaison with

Nadya hadn't been a business decision, but it had proved highly beneficial to both of them while it had lasted, with each of them gaining substantially from it. There was no reason why his time with Diana St Clair should not do likewise. As well as gaining the restoration of her home, she would gain an attentive husband and a *very* attentive lover.

What more could she—or he—want?

Certainly not love.

His mouth twisted. Love was of no interest to him. He'd never known it, did not want it. And nor, clearly, did Diana St Clair, or she would have sent him packing when he'd set out his proposal in front of her. But she hadn't—and she would accept it, he knew, his expression changing to one of confident assurance.

What he was offering suited her perfectly. And not just as the means to save her home. On a much more personal level too. Oh, she might not yet realise that her inner ice maiden had finally met a challenge it could not freeze off, but when the time came—and come it would!—she would accept from him all the exquisite sensual pleasure that he would ensure she experienced, all the pleasure that he was so hotly anticipating for himself.

It would be his gift to her—opening the door for her to accept the admiration and desire of men at last. Frozen as she was within, he would ignite within her that flare of sensual awareness he'd seen so briefly, so revealingly in her eyes when he'd first looked upon her.

He would not hurry her—he would give her time to get used to him—but in the end... His smile deepened and he took a mouthful of champagne, easing his shoulders as an image of her pale, exquisite beauty formed in his mind's eye, lingering over the fine-boned features, the silken line of her mouth.

In the end she would thaw.
And melt into his waiting arms.

Diana stared at the vast bouquet of exotic, highly scented lilies that sat on the Boule table in the hall, fragrancing the air. Then she stared down at the cheque she was holding in her slightly shaking hands, and the note accompanying it.

An advance, sent in good faith.

She stared at the numbers on the cheque. A quarter of a million pounds. She felt her lungs tighten. So much money—

With a stifled noise in her throat she marched back into her office. But the scent of the lilies was in her nostrils still. Beguiling. Enticing.

Can I do it? Marry Nikos Tramontes?

The cheque in her hand demanded an answer. Accept or reject it. Accept or reject the man who'd signed it.

The phone on her desk rang, startling her. It was her architect, politely, tactfully enquiring whether she was yet in a position to set a start date for the work that needed to be done. Work that could not start without Nikos to pay for it.

Her hand clenched, her signet ring with the St Clair crest on her little finger catching on the mahogany surface of the desk. Emotion bit into her, forcing a decision. The decision she had to make *now.* Could postpone no longer. If she did not restore Greymont it would decay into ruins or she would have to sell. Either way, it would be lost.

I can't be the St Clair who loses Greymont. I can't betray my father's devotion and sacrifice. I can't!

The offer that Nikos Tramontes had put in front of her was the best she could ever hope to find. It was a gift from heaven.

Nothing else can save Greymont.

She could feel her heart thumping in her chest, her mouth drying, suddenly, at the enormity of what she was doing.

It will be all right—it will be all right...

She heard the words in her head, calming her, and she clung to them urgently.

Slowly—very, very slowly—she breathed out. Then she spoke. 'Yes,' she said to her architect. 'I think we can now make a start.'

CHAPTER FOUR

THE WEDDING VENUE WAS the ballroom of an historic London hotel, with impeccable upper-crust ambience and timelessly stylish art deco décor, and it was packed with people.

Apart from the guests who were Nikos's business acquaintances, Diana had rounded up everyone from her own circles whom Nikos Tramontes was marrying her in order to meet: those people who represented upper-class English society, based on centuries of land ownership and 'old money', who had all gone to school together, intermarried over the years, and would socialise together for ever. It was a closed club, open only to those born into it. Or to those who, like her new husband, had married into it.

She was glad so many had accepted her invitation— it made her feel she was definitely keeping her side of the bargain she'd struck with the man she was marrying. He wanted a society wife—she was making sure he got one, in return for funding the repairs now actively underway at Greymont.

The ongoing work had been her main preoccupation during the three months of their engagement, but she had made time to meet up with Nikos whenever he was in London, including attending a lavish engagement party at his newly purchased town house in Knightsbridge. The fact that his business affairs seemed to require his continuous travel around the globe suited her fine.

All the same, he'd taken pains to allow her to get used to him, to come to terms with being his fiancée, just as he'd promised he would. He'd taken her out and about to dinner, to the theatre and the opera, and to meet some of her friends or his business acquaintances.

He was no longer a stranger by any means. And, although she had been unable to banish that unwanted hyperawareness of his compelling masculinity that made her so constantly self-conscious about him, she had, nevertheless, become far easier in his company. More comfortable being with him. His manners were polished, his conversation intelligent, and there was nothing about him to make her regret her decision to accept marriage to him as a solution for Greymont.

Becoming engaged to Nikos had proved a lot more easy than she had feared. He'd certainly set aside her lingering disquiet that her disturbing awareness of his sexual magnetism might cause a problem. He seemed oblivious to it, and she was grateful. It would be embarrassing, after all, if a man to whom she was making a hard-headed marriage of convenience were to be inconvenienced by a fiancée who trembled at his touch.

Not that he did touch her. Apart from socially conventional contact, such as taking her arm or guiding her forward, which she was studiously trying to inoculate herself against, he never laid a finger on her. Not even a peck on the cheek.

It was ironic, she thought wryly, that her friends all assumed her sudden engagement was a *coup de foudre*…

She'd let Toby Masterson think so, out of kindness for

him, and he'd said sadly, 'I could tell you were smitten, from the off,' before he wished her well.

The only dissenting voice against her engagement had come from Gerald, the St Clair family lawyer.

'Diana, are you sure this is what you want to do?' he'd asked warningly.

'Yes,' she'd said decisively, 'it is.'

As she'd answered that old saying had come into her head. *'Take what you want,' says God. 'Take it and pay for it.'*

She'd shaken it from her. All she was paying was two years of her life. She could afford that price. Two years in which to grace the arm of Nikos Tramontes in their marriage of convenience, a perfectly civil and civilised arrangement. She had no problem with that.

And no problem with standing in the receiving line beside him now, greeting their guests as his wife. She stood there smiling, saying all that was proper for the occasion, and continued to smile throughout the reception.

Only when, finally, she sank back into the plush seat of the vintage car that was to take them to the airport, from where they would fly off on their honeymoon in the Gulf—where Nikos had business affairs to see to—did she feel as if she'd come offstage after a bravura performance.

She could finally relax.

'Relieved it's all over?'

Nikos's deep voice at her side, made her glance at him.

'Yes.' She nodded decisively. 'And I'm glad it all went flawlessly.'

He smiled at her. 'But then, you were flawless yourself.'

'Thank you,' she said, acknowledging his compliment. She was getting used to his smiles now. Making herself get used to them. Just as she would make herself get used to the fact that he was her husband for the time being. Theirs might be a marriage of convenience, but it could be perfectly amiable for all that. Indeed, there was no reason why it shouldn't be. The more time she spent with him, the easier it would get.

Even on a honeymoon that was actually a business trip.

'It's been pretty strenuous,' she went on now, easing her feet out of the low-heeled court shoes that went with her cream silk 'going away' outfit—considerably more comfortable than those that had gone with her thirties-style, ivory satin bias-cut wedding dress, which had been four-inch heeled sandals. 'But, yes, I think I can agree it's all gone extremely well. And, of course—' and now there was real warmth in her voice '—the work at Greymont is making wonderful progress. I can't thank you enough for expediting matters in that respect!'

'Well, that *is* my contribution,' he agreed.

It had been a long day, and she'd been on the go from the moment she'd woken in the bridal suite at the hotel, ready to receive the ministrations of hair stylists and make-up artists, to this moment of relative relaxation now, and maybe that accounted for the tightening of her throat, the rush of emotion in her voice.

'It means so much to me—restoring Greymont. It's my whole world. '

Was there a flicker in his eyes? A sudden shadowing? But he said nothing, only smiled before getting out his phone with a murmured apology about checking emails.

She let him get on with it. He was a businessman. And global business ran twenty-four-seven. It didn't stop for weddings.

Or honeymoons.

Yet when they arrived in the Gulf—Diana having managed to get some sleep during the flight—it was to discover that the incredibly lavish hotel they were staying at was most definitely putting the honeymoon into their arrival with a capital H.

As they were conducted to their suite by a personal butler, Diana could not suppress a gasp. The walls seemed to be made of gold, as did most of the furniture, a vast sweep of glass gave a view out over the vista beyond, and the floor looked to be priceless marble. Huge bouquets of red roses stood on just about every surface, scenting the air richly.

'Oh, my goodness...' she said weakly.

Did she really lean slightly against Nikos, half in weariness, half in amazement at the utterly over-the-top gilded lavishness of their surroundings? She didn't know—knew only that for a moment his strength seemed to be supporting her. And then he was leading her forward, to where their butler was opening a bottle of vintage champagne.

'Is it giving you ideas for improving the décor at Greymont?'

Nikos's low voice was at her ear. She cast him a look, then realised that there was a hint of humour at his mouth and in his eyes. She felt a strange flutter deep inside her. Even though she was getting used to his smiles, he should not smile at her like that. Not so intimately. Not in a marriage like theirs—a marriage in which intimacy was not in the terms and conditions.

'It's perfect for *here*,' she allowed.

She took the glass of champagne proffered to her and Nikos did likewise, dismissing the butler.

He raised his glass. 'Well, Mrs Tramontes, shall we drink a toast to our marriage?'

That smile was still in his eyes, but now she was more composed as she met his gaze.

'Definitely,' she said brightly, lifting her glass to his.

It was odd to hear him call her that. She'd heard it a few times at the wedding reception, but it hadn't seemed real then. Now, coming from Nikos, it did.

Well, yes, on the surface I suppose it is real, in the legal sense. But it's not really real—it's simply...

Convenient.

That was what it was. Convenient for both of them. Almost a kind of business partnership.

Mutually beneficial, perfectly amicable.

She clinked her glass against his lightly. Smiled back at him. Brightly, civilly, cheerfully. OK, she wasn't yet *totally* used to being in his company, but the next few days would see to that.

She just had to get used to him, that was all.

'To us...'

Nikos's voice was deep, but if she'd thought for a second she'd heard something in it that smacked of some kind of intimacy, well, she was sure she was mistaken. He was, she reminded herself, a formidably attractive man, and he would have an impact on any woman without even intending to.

'To us,' she returned, and took a dutiful mouthful.

Nikos slid open the door to the huge balcony and they stepped out to take in the vista of the hotel's gardens and azure swimming pools, and the glittering waters of the Gulf beyond.

She gave a sigh of pleasure and leant against the glass balcony rail. Nikos moved beside her, not too close, but almost in a companionable fashion, looking down with her, taking in the scene below.

His mood was good—exceptionally good.

The wedding had gone superbly, achieving just what he'd wanted to achieve—his entry by marriage into the world that his bride took for granted as her birthright. A flicker of dark emotion moved in his mind—the bitter memory of being ejected from that Normandy chateau, unwanted and unwelcome, rejected and refused, reminding him that *he'd* had no such auspicious start.

His mouth tightened. Well, he did not need what his own mother had denied him! He had achieved it without her acceptance! Just as he'd made himself as rich as the father who'd repudiated him, denied any claim to paternity.

He shook the dark thoughts from him. They had no place in his life—not any longer. They had no more power to haunt him.

His gaze dropped to the woman at his side and his good mood streamed back. For three months—long, self-controlled months—he'd held himself on a tight leash. For three endless months he'd held himself back, knowing that above all the woman he had chosen for marriage was not a woman to be rushed. He must thaw the ice maiden carefully.

This moment now, as he leaned companionably beside her, was the reward for his patience. And soon he'd be reaping the full extent of that reward.

But not quite yet. Not until she was fully at ease with him, fully comfortable with him. The first few days of their honeymoon should achieve that. It would take more immense self-control on his part, this final stage of the process, but, oh, it would be worth it when she finally accepted his embraces. When she accepted the passion that would, he knew with masculine instinct, flare between them when the time was right.

He hauled his mind back to the present. For now it was still necessary for him to exercise patience. Self-denial.

He turned his head towards her with an easy smile, his voice casually amiable. 'What would you like to do for lunch?' he asked. 'We've flown east, so although you may feel as if it's only early morning, here the sun is high.'

She glanced at him, returning his easy smile, glad that it felt natural to do so. Glad that standing here beside him, side by side, seemed quite effortless. She could see how much more relaxed he was—just as she was. It might not be a honeymoon in the traditional sense, and he might have business affairs to conduct, but there was a holiday atmosphere all the same. She was enjoying the easy feeling it brought. Enjoying just being here.

'I don't mind,' she said. 'Whatever you prefer. And Nikos...' her voice changed slightly '...please don't feel you have to keep me company while we're here. I know you have business appointments and, really, in an ultra-luxurious hotel like this I'll be more than happy to lounge around lazily. And if I feel like anything more energetic I can always take a formal tour and go exploring. You know—souks and whatever. Even the desert, maybe. I'll be perfectly OK on my own, I promise.'

She said it quite deliberately, and was glad she had. She wanted to set the right tone, make it clear that she understood the unstated but implicit conditions of their marriage right from the off.

But he was looking at her strangely. Or so she thought. She gave an inner frown of puzzlement.

'Yes, I do have some business appointments,' he said, 'but I believe I can still find time for my bride on our honeymoon.' His voice was dry.

Her expression flickered, then recovered. 'Well, lunch together now would certainly be nice,' she said lightly. 'Do you think there's anywhere suitable to eat poolside? I must say, that water looks tempting.'

'Let's find out,' he returned. 'We'll take our swim-suits—be sure to apply enough sun cream. Your pale skin will burn instantly in these latitudes.'

They made their way down, bringing the cham-pagne bottle with them, and emerged into the hotel's vast atrium, in the centre of which an enormous crystal fountain cooled the already air-conditioned air and the fragrance of frankincense wafted all around.

She gazed openly at the opulence, and then Nikos was guiding her outdoors. The heat struck her again, and the sun's glare, and automatically she fished out her dark glasses from her tote bag. Nikos did likewise.

As she glanced at him she felt her tummy do a quick flip.

They'd both changed into casual gear—she into a floaty sun dress and he in chinos and an open-necked short-sleeved shirt—but somehow, from the moment he put on his sunglasses, there really was only one word to describe him.

Sexy.

It was such a cheap word—so redolent of dire TV re-ality shows or girlish banter in the dorm. Not a word for a grown-up woman like her.

But it was the only word for him, and that was the problem. He just...*radiated* it. Whatever 'it' was. He had it in jaw-dropping amounts.

She tore her gaze away, grateful that her eyes were veiled with sunglasses too, berating herself silently for her illicit thoughts as they took their places at a shaded table in the open-air restaurant near the pools.

She gazed around in pleasure as Nikos recharged their champagne glasses. 'This really is gorgeous,' she said. 'Completely over the top, but gorgeous.'

He gave a laugh, taking the menu proffered by a

waiter. He sounded relaxed, at ease. 'Well, be sure to
mention that to the Prince when we meet him tomorrow.'

Diana stared. *'Prince?'* she echoed.

'Well, not the ruling Prince, but one of his nephews.
He's the main driver behind development here—and I
have an interest in various of his ventures—but he has
to proceed carefully. Several of his cousins oppose him,
and several more want to push for a Dubai-style future.
As it happens, we've been invited to his palace tomorrow for—of all things—afternoon tea.'

'Afternoon tea?' Diana echoed again.

'Yes, Sheikh Kamal's sister, Princess Fatima, is a big
fan, apparently, and she welcomes any opportunity to
partake of it.'

'Good heavens!' Diana exclaimed. 'Well, I dare say
to an Arabian princess afternoon tea is as exotic as a
desert banquet would be for me.' She frowned slightly.
'You'll have to guide me as to etiquette. I'm not at all *au
fait* with royal protocol in the Middle East.'

'We'll get a briefing tomorrow morning from a palace official,' said Nikos. 'But I have every confidence
in you, Diana.' He paused, then disposed of his dark
glasses. His expression was serious. 'It's thanks to *you*,
you know, that we've been invited to the palace. Were I
here on my own I would only be receiving a brief audience on a strictly business basis, in his office. Whereas
with you to accompany me it has become a social engagement and, as you are probably aware, that takes things
to a completely different level in places like this. It will
open doors for me.'

She met his gaze. 'I'm happy to be of use, Nikos. It
makes me feel I'm...well, pulling my weight, I suppose.'
Her tone altered as she inserted a lighter note. 'I'd bet-

ter ensure I don't do anything to shock the Sheikh or his sister. '

'You'll be perfect,' he assured her. 'It comes naturally to you—knowing the correct way to behave in any social situation.'

She gave a self-deprecating moue. 'I can't claim any personal credit, Nikos. I've had a very privileged existence. It's people like *you*, you know, who didn't have those advantages and yet are where they are today by their own efforts and determination, who deserve credit. All of us are who we are completely by accident of birth—and none of us is responsible for that.'

Was there a sudden veiling of his eyes? A sense of withdrawal behind a mask? If so, it made her conscious of just how little she knew about him. He had never spoken of his own background—only those few dismissive remarks about Greece. Other than that she'd gathered that he'd been brought up in France, spoke the language fluently, and he had made a passing reference to studying economics at one point.

As for his relationship with Nadya Serensky—she knew no more than what he had told her and that she did not have to feel any concern over his discarded trophy mistress. Nadya had married a Hollywood A-lister within weeks of Nikos finishing with her and was now queening it up in LA. Diana could not help but be relieved that she did not need to feel bad about helping herself to Nikos Tramontes.

For her own part, Diana had said very little about herself either. Nikos had asked no questions of her—and nor had she of him. After all, with their marriage being little more than a mutual business deal, there was no need for them to know anything much. All that was required was for them to be civil—friendly. Nothing more than that.

They enjoyed a leisurely lunch, and as it had during their engagement when they'd spent time together, Diana found the conversation flowing easily. Again, there was nothing personal in it—it was mostly about the Gulf, with Nikos briefing her as necessary to supplement what she already knew and then moving on to other parts of the world that her widely travelled husband was acquainted with.

It made for a perfectly pleasant meal, and after coffee they repaired to a poolside cabana. Diana changed in the private tented cubicle to the rear, emerging wearing a sleek turquoise one-piece and a cotton sarong in a deeper blue. The sarong revealed no more of her than her sundress had, and yet for all that she was aware of a sense of self-consciousness.

She sat herself down on a lounger, and was starting to anoint herself with sun cream when Nikos strolled up. He'd clearly changed elsewhere, and now dropped his bag on the lounger beside hers.

Diana tried hard not to stare—and failed dismally.

Oh, dear God...

She'd known in her head that he must have a good physique—his wide shoulders, broad chest, and absolutely no sign of any flab on him anywhere was an indication of that. But there was a difference between knowing it and seeing it in the flesh.

Taut, muscled flesh was moulded like an athlete's, each pec and ab sculpted to perfection. She wished she'd jammed her concealing sunglasses back on her nose. Wished she could make her head drop. Wished she could just stop *staring* at him.

Her only saving mercy was that he didn't appear to notice her fixed gaze. Instead, he dropped down on his lounger and reached across in a leisurely fashion to help himself to one of the large selection of magazines that lay on a side table. Diana could see that it took him no effort at all to use simply his ab muscles to take the reaching weight of his body.

Urgently she pulled her gaze away, made a play of putting down her sun block.

Nikos settled back to read. His mood was even better than it had been before. He could see she'd also taken one of the magazines—not a glossy fashion one, he wouldn't have expected her to, but a popular history title. Satisfaction eased through him—and not just because he was very comfortably settled in a poolside cabana at an ultra-luxury hotel in the Gulf.

Because the woman he'd made his wife less than twenty-four hours ago was trying to pretend she was unaware of him right now.

He smiled inwardly. He'd been right to follow his instincts—to stick to his strategy of thawing the ice maiden Diana slowly before he moved in to melt her. He wanted her to relax in his company, lower her guard, become used to his constant presence.

So he gave no sign that he was perfectly aware of how aware she was of him, stripped to the waist, wearing only dark blue swim shorts, his long legs extended, feet bare. Instead he immersed himself in various articles in the financial magazine he'd helped himself to, while she read as well.

Their studied relaxation was only interrupted by intermittent enquiries from their personal butler as to whether they required anything.

He asked for mineral water, so did she, and then a glass of iced coffee, and both of them picked idly at a heaped plate of freshly cut fruit.

Eventually, with sun lowering and the heat of the day

easing as the afternoon wore on, he tossed his reading aside.

'OK,' he announced, 'time for some exercise.' He threw a smile at her and limbered to his feet. 'Fancy a dip?' he asked.

'I'd better, I think,' Diana agreed. 'Otherwise I'm going to snooze off…it's so restful here. And that will screw up my sleep patterns—jet lag's kicking in.'

He held out his hand and she took it, because to do otherwise would look pointed in a way she did not wish it to. He drew her up as though she weighed only a feather, and then loosed his grip as they walked towards the pool.

The sun, starting to lower behind the hotel to the west, shed a deep golden light over the water, which was shimmering in the heat. The main pool was relatively empty and Nikos strolled to the edge of the deep end, executing a perfect dive into the azure water, sending up a shower of diamond drops.

Diana couldn't help but watch him—watch the way his powerful, muscled body drove through the water, demolishing the length in seconds, only to double under in a tumble turn and head back towards her.

He surfaced, dark hair sleek around his face. 'Come on!' he instructed. 'It's warm as milk.'

To her relief, he didn't wait to watch her slip her sarong from her, and moments later she was in the water, dipping under the surface to get her head and hair wet. It was glorious—refreshing and cooling despite the ambient temperature of the pool.

She began a rhythmic traverse, contenting herself with breaststroke, enjoying the feeling of her long hair streaming behind her in the water, aware of Nikos steadily ploughing up and down only from the splashing of his arms in a strong, rapid freestyle. Having done the number of laps she was content with, she came to a halt at the far end and realised Nikos had also paused.

'Call it a day?' he asked. 'Shall we head back up and think about dinner?'

They got out of the water, put on the towelling gowns their butler had laid out for them, and headed back into the hotel. Diana was very conscious of her dripping hair, now wrapped in a turban. It would take a while to get ready.

It did, but Nikos left her to it, using the bathroom in the ancillary bedroom, obviously set aside for a child or a personal servant, leaving Diana in possession of the bridal bedroom and its palatial en suite bathroom. She was grateful for the unspoken tact with which Nikos had appropriated the other bedroom for himself.

By the time she emerged, over an hour later, she was ready for whatever demonstration of extreme opulence awaited her next. It proved to be an ultra-lavish bridal banquet, served to them in a private alcove off the main restaurant which was cantilevered out over the Persian Gulf.

The dress code, judging by the other diners, was formal, so she was glad she'd come prepared. Her silk gown, with its very fine plissé bodice, was in the palest eau-de-nil, and the soft folds of her long skirts brushed her legs as she walked in on Nikos's arm—an extended kind of body contact she was schooling herself to get used to now that she was his wife. With practice, she would soon lose her self-consciousness about it, she knew.

Her face lit up as they approached their table. 'Oh, how beautiful!' she could not help exclaiming.

Over the top it might be, but the table décor was exquisite. Huge bouquets of flowers flanked it on either side, and the floor was strewn with rose petals. More covered the table, which was also set with exquisite flowers, little candles, and napery constructed into swans—an image echoed on the side table, where stood an ice sculpture of two swans, their necks entwined in a heart shape, a feast of fresh sliced fruit and champagne chilling in a silver ice bucket.

With a low murmur of an appreciative *'Shukran!'* to the bevy of waiting staff now ushering them into their chairs, she was aware that they were drawing the eyes of the other diners as they took their places.

Nikos had opted for the restaurant's speciality—a tasting menu. Tiny portions of exquisite and extraordinary concoctions that went on and on...and on.

'More?' Diana all but gave a mock groan as the waiting staff gathered to bestow upon them yet another tender trifle for their delectation.

'Keep going,' Nikos advised her, 'or the chef will be out here, brandishing his knives in rage at your lack of appreciation for his genius.'

She laughed, and got stuck in to yet another delicious morsel filled with flavours that were impossible to identify but which created a fantasy inside her mouth. She gave a murmur of intense appreciation and closed her eyes.

From across the table Nikos's gaze flickered over her. That little moan she'd given in her throat...that look of pleasure on her face...

He dragged his mind away. First their visit to the palace tomorrow, and then... Ah, *then* the honeymoon proper could begin. And how very much he was looking forward to that.

CHAPTER FIVE

'YOUR HIGHNESS.' DIANA dropped her head to the correct degree as she was formally presented to Sheikh Kamal and then his sister, Princess Fatima, who was at his side, also greeting their guests.

The Sheikh was, she had instantly appreciated, extremely handsome, with dark Arabian looks, a hawk-like nose, and piercing dark eyes from which, she suspected, little was hidden. But his manner to his guests was urbane in the extreme, and that of his sister fulsome.

Having been comprehensively briefed by one of the palace officials that morning in their hotel suite, Diana was confident she was not making any mistakes in protocol, and that her outfit of a long-sleeved, high-collared, ankle-length dress, worn with a loose but hair-concealing headscarf, was acceptable, and she found herself beginning to relax, encouraged by the warmth of their illustrious hosts' welcoming attitude.

'Afternoon tea' turned out to be an exact replica of what might be found in the UK, of the very highest standard, and she was not slow to say so. Her praise drew a giggle from Princess Fatima.

'My brother flew in the pastry chef from London this morning, and he brought all the ingredients with him to bake the scones just as you arrived!' Her dark eyes twinkled. 'Now, tell me,' she said confidentially, 'as an Englishwoman, what *is* the correct order in a cream tea? Jam first or clotted cream first?'

Diana gave a laugh. 'Oh, that's an impossible question, Your Highness. In Devon, I believe it is one way, and in Cornwall the other—but I never remember which! I'm afraid I do jam first.'

'So do *I*!' cried the Princess delightedly. She smiled warmly. 'I do hope, my dear, that we can take tea together when I am next in London?'

'I would be honoured and delighted,' Diana said immediately.

Nikos smiled. 'If it pleases the Princess,' he said, 'afternoon tea at Greymont would be our pleasure.'

Diana's fingers tightened on the handle of the priceless porcelain tea cup she was holding. A small but distinct sense of annoyance flared in her that Nikos had presumed to offer *her* home in his invitation to the sister of the man whose approval he needed to make money out of doing business here. Greymont was *hers*—and *she* would choose who to invite to it.

But he'd clearly said the right thing, and it obviously *did* please the Princess. Her eyes lit up. 'I *adore* English country houses,' she exclaimed in her enthusiastic manner.

'So much so that I bought my sister one only last year,' her brother interposed dryly.

'And so he did—he is the most generous of brothers,' Fatima acknowledged.

A chill replaced the flare of annoyance that Diana had been feeling.

If I hadn't married Nikos then Greymont might have been snapped up as the latest amusement for an Arabian princess.

It was a sobering reminder of just why she was sitting here, in a royal palace in the Persian Gulf, next to the man who was legally her husband, but in name only, making small talk with an Arabian princess about her latest acquisition.

The Princess rattled on in her bubbly manner, asking Diana about how great houses used to be run and how best to furnish them in a style to look authentic. Diana contributed as best she could, making several suggestions which the Princess seemed to value.

As she talked to the Princess, all the while taking delicate bites of the lavish cream tea laid before them, she became aware that the Sheikh and her new husband had moved their own conversation on to matters concerning the economic development of this particular Gulf state.

After a while, with the final sliver of Dundee fruit cake consumed, the final cup of Darjeeling taken, the Princess got to her feet.

'We shall leave the men to their tedious affairs,' she announced smilingly to Diana.

Nikos and the Sheikh immediately got to their feet as well, as did Diana, who was then swept off by the Princess. When they were in the Princess's own apartments Fatima cast aside her veiling, then turned to show Diana that she could do likewise with her headscarf.

'My dear, *what* a handsome husband you have.' She gave a theatrical sigh, her dark eyes gleaming wickedly. 'I'm going to tell my brother that he must lend you his…' She giggled even more wickedly. 'His *love-nest* in the desert. It's actually *quite* respectable—our great-grandfather had it built for his favourite wife, so they could escape together, away from his jealous older wives.'

'Oh, my goodness!' Diana exclaimed weakly, not knowing what to say.

'You must demand of your oh-so-handsome husband that he declares his love for you every morning. And even more importantly...' she cast a knowing look at Diana '...every *night*.'

Diana's expression was a study. It was impossible for her to comment, but fortunately for her the Princess took her silence as embarrassment.

'Oh, you English,' she cried laughingly. 'You are always so frozen—so...what is that word? Ah, yes—repressed. Well, I will not tease you—you are a bride. You are allowed to blush.' She took Diana's arm. 'Now, come and see my wardrobe. I am dying to show it to you.'

She led her off into a chamber which made Diana's eyes widen. It was like, she realised, a museum of costume, for along the walls were a parade of gowns arrayed on mannequins set on pedestals, each and every one a priceless haute couture number, a work of art in its own right. Entranced, Diana let the Princess guide her around, enthusing volubly to the Princess's evident delight.

Then, to her dismay, the Princess exclaimed, '*This* one will be my wedding gift to you.'

She clapped her hands and one of her hovering servants hurried forward to receive instructions in rapid Arabic. Diana immediately demurred—a gown like this would cost thousands upon thousands. She couldn't possibly accept.

The Princess held up a hand, imperious now. 'To refuse it would be to offend,' she instructed regally.

Diana bowed her head. 'You do me too much honour, Highness,' she said formally, knowing she must concede.

'And *you* will do it justice,' the Princess returned warmly, adding for good measure 'The colour is all wrong for me. It makes my skin sallow. But you, with your fairness—ah, that shade of palest yellow is ideal.' She smiled.

'I will have it delivered.' The dark eyes gleamed with a wicked glint. 'Make sure you wear it at the *love-nest*.'

Again, Diana had no idea what to say—could only hope that the Princess would forget to speak to her brother about any such thing as a desert love-nest, which was the last place she wanted to go with Nikos. Meekly she let the Princess lead the way into another exquisitely decorated room, this time with a balcony overlooking a beautiful ornamental pool in a pillared courtyard.

'Tea,' the Princess announced, lowering herself onto a silk-covered divan and indicating that Diana should do likewise, 'but this time from *my* part of the world!'

The mint tea that was served proved very refreshing, and their conversation returned to the subject of historic English country houses. Diana waxed enthusiastic, mentioning the exhaustive restoration work she was having done on Greymont.

'You love your home dearly, do you not?' the Princess observed.

'It's the most important thing in the world to me!' Diana answered unguardedly.

The dark eyes rested on her curiously. 'Not your husband?'

Diana started, not sure what to say.

The Princess was still looking at her curiously. 'But surely you are in love with him more than anything in the world? If, after all, you had to choose between your home or your husband, surely there would be no choice at all?'

Diana swallowed. How could she answer?

Then, to her relief, a servant approached, bowing, then murmuring something to her hostess, who immediately got to her feet.

'We are summoned,' she announced.

A servant was there at once, with their headscarves,

and once appropriately attired Diana followed the Princess from her private apartments back into the palace, to take her farewell of their hosts with Nikos.

As they settled back into the limousine that would return them to their hotel, she turned to him. 'How did it go? I hope the Sheikh was as gracious to you as his sister was to me.'

Nikos eased his shoulders back into the soft leather seat. 'Extremely well—just as I hoped after our having been invited socially,' he said with evident satisfaction. 'I have an agreement in principle from the Sheikh—which is essential—and clearance to talk to the relevant ministers. Exactly what I wanted.'

He looked at Diana and smiled warmly in a way that she must wish he hadn't.

'You did wonderfully. Thank you. I don't just mean all the protocol—I wouldn't insult you by implying you might not have been able to handle it—but the personal touch. The Princess clearly took to you…that was obvious—'

Diana cut across him, feeling flutteringly uncomfortable after that warm smile. 'Nikos, Princess Fatima has given me one of her couture gowns. It's worth a fortune, but she insisted. I know I couldn't refuse, but what on earth should I do now?'

'Make her a present of equal value,' he returned promptly. 'I don't mean financial—that would be crass, and anyway they have so much money it makes *me* look like a pauper, let alone you,' he said carelessly. 'I mean something matching.'

Diana furrowed her brow, and then a thought struck her. 'I know! I'll find an antique gown for her—something she can possess but not wear because it's too historic. Maybe she can display it in her English country house when it's all done up.'

'Great idea,' said Nikos. He rested his eyes on her with warm approval, in that way she wished he wouldn't. 'You impressed the Sheikh, too, I could see that—he quoted from some Persian poet about how a beautiful and intelligent wife is the ultimate jewel a man can possess.' He paused, keeping that look on his face. 'And he was right about you being a jewel, Diana, both in beauty and intelligence. You are, indeed.'

For one long, endless second it seemed to her there was no breath in her body. Then, as if urgently grabbing a towel after emerging naked from the shower, she forced a little laugh to her lips.

'Well, I'm glad I came in useful this afternoon,' she said, and now her face was deliberately bright. 'And thank you for the opportunity to see inside a royal Arabian palace. It was like something out of a fairytale, and with a real-life prince and princess inside it too.'

Determinedly she went on to recollect with admiration some of the architectural details that had impressed her, even more determined *not* to mention anything about the Princess's talk about desert love-nests.

Hopefully Princess Fatima would forget all about it. A desert love nest was the last place that could be relevant to a marriage such as theirs.

A marriage in name only had no need of such a place.

'What do you say we dine up here tonight?'

Nikos's voice was casual as they walked into their huge suite and Diana's reply was immediate.

'Oh, yes, let's. I feel today has been quite a strain, and to be honest I could do with an evening just vegging.'

She rolled her head on her shoulders, rubbing at the nape of her neck.

'Need a massage?' Nikos gave a laugh and crossed towards her. He rested his hand on her neck and kneaded it gently with his fingertips.

It was a casual gesture, lasting only a few moments, but Diana froze. There was something about the weight of his large hand on her nape…something about the soft pressing of his fingers into her skin, the brush of his hand against the loosened tendrils of her hair caught into its habitual chignon…something that made her feel suddenly weak. Breathless.

'Better?' he murmured, and she realised that somehow he seemed to have stepped close to her, so that he stood just behind her. Close—so close.

Despite her frozen muscles, she seemed to be feeling a wash of intense relaxation easing through her—an impulse to roll her head forward and let free the low moan in her throat as she succumbed to the seductive touch of his fingers working at her neck.

Seductive?

With a scrambling of her senses she pulled herself together, made herself shake her head. *Seductive?* Was she mad to think such a thing?

She took a step away, freeing herself, and turned towards him with a bright smile. 'Lovely,' she said lightly. 'Thank you.'

She headed towards her bedroom. She needed a bit of sanctuary right now.

'I'm going to freshen up, then maybe order some fruit juice. The terrace looks very appealing at this time of day.'

Chattering brightly, she didn't look at him, just got inside her bedroom. She felt breathless. Determinedly, she inhaled. This had to stop. All this nonsense with her making such a fuss just because Nikos touched her. He hadn't meant anything by it—not a thing. And especially nothing *seductive*, for heaven's sake.

Yet a few minutes later, as she stood under the shower, warm water plunging like rainfall over her body, sluicing over her shoulders, her breasts, down over her flanks and legs, she felt a kind of restlessness inside her. An awareness of her own flesh and blood that was as rare as it was disturbing. As she smoothed the rich, foaming shower gel over herself, running her hands along her arms, her shoulders, her breasts and abdomen, there was a kind of sensuality about it...

As if it were not her own hands running over her body...

For one vivid, overpowering moment she had a vision of Nikos standing beside her in the steamy enclosure, the water sluicing over both of them as she stood in front of him, his strong arms enveloping her, his hands on her body, soothing, easing, smoothing...caressing her as he washed her then turning her towards him, his arms sliding around her waist, drawing her to him...

She cut off the water. Furious with herself. What on *earth* was she thinking of? Nikos might be the man she'd married two days ago but he wasn't her husband in anything but name. It was totally out of order to think of him in any other way.

Determinedly she stepped out of the shower, towel-dried herself vigorously without the slightest hint of sensuality at all, deliberately not looking at herself in the glass as she did so, and got dressed as quickly as possible.

Friendliness—that was the only atmosphere she wanted between them, and that was what she was set on ensuring.

To her relief, that seemed to be Nikos's idea as well for the evening. So it was in an atmosphere of relaxed congeniality that they dined on their terrace, she wearing a simple cotton print dress with a thin lacy shawl around her shoulders, he in chinos and a polo shirt, feet in leather flip-flops, both of them casual and comfortable.

Unlike the elaborate tasting menu of the previous evening they chose more simple fare—grilled fish for herself, a steak for Nikos, followed by ice cream. Their conversation centred on chatting through the events of the afternoon, then Diana asked about his plans for the next day.

'If you're meeting those government ministers I'll either laze by the pool or go and browse in the souks. Maybe both.' She smiled at Nikos, reaching for a piece of fruit to chase down the last of her wine.

He smiled at her in return, the lamp on the table softening his features. In the dim light, Nikos looked less formidable than he so often did.

'You're a very complaisant wife—do you know that, Diana?' he observed. 'How many other brides would be so undemanding?'

She gave a laugh. 'Good heavens, I'm perfectly capable of entertaining myself for a day, Nikos. So you go off and get your business done. Anyway, it's not like I'm a *real* bride, after all,' she finished lightly.

Was there a strange look in his eyes suddenly, or was it just the flickering candlelight?

His voice was lazily amused when he replied. 'That very swish wedding seemed real enough to me.'

She made a face. 'Oh, you know what I mean!' she exclaimed, taking another piece of fruit.

'Do I?' he replied, in that same lazily amused tone.

'Of *course* you do!' she said in mock exasperation.

She made herself look straight at him. She had to put it behind her—*right* behind her—that stupid, totally inappropriate mooning that had come over her when she'd been showering. There was no place for it—*none*, she told herself sternly.

I have to crush it down if it ever strikes again. Blank it and ignore it until it no longer exists.

He didn't answer, only continued to hold her gaze a moment longer with that same quizzical, amused look in his eye which she was making herself meet in a determinedly unaffected fashion. Then he broke contact, reaching for the bottle of wine and moving to refill her glass.

She covered it with her hand. 'I'd better not. I'm starting to yawn already,' she said.

She didn't want any more discussion about the nature of their marriage. It didn't need to be discussed. Let alone questioned. It was useful to both of them. Nothing more than useful. End of, she told herself firmly.

He accepted her decision. 'Well, it's been quite a day,' he said.

'It certainly has,' she said lightly.

Light—that's the way I have to be. Keeping everything nice and light. Or composed and businesslike. And friendly. Easy-going. Bright and cheerful. Or—

She ran out of adjectives that described the kind of behaviour that she needed to demonstrate for the next two years of marriage with Nikos.

A yawn started in her throat and she was unable to prevent it. She made another face. 'That's it, I'm calling it a day,' she said, and started to get to her feet. 'I'm off to bed.'

He stood up, helping her with her chair. He seemed very tall beside her suddenly.

'Goodnight, then,' he said. There was still that lazy note in his voice. 'Enjoy your bridal bed.'

There was nothing but amusement in his voice, Diana was sure, because obviously there couldn't be anything else. Not in a marriage like theirs.

So she answered in the same vein. 'Indeed I shall,' she agreed. 'I wonder if it's been deluged in rose petals again?'

An eyebrow tilted. 'Shall I come and check for you?'

'Thank you, no. I'm sure I can sweep them away with my own fair hand,' she said, lightly but firmly.

Then she beat a retreat. Any banter, however light-hearted, about bridal beds and rose petals was best shut down swiftly. Any banter at *all* between her and Nikos about anything that could have the slightest sexual connotation should not even be acknowledged. It had no place in their marriage. None at all.

And she had to make sure it stayed that way. Absolutely sure.

The following day passed very pleasantly for Diana. Nikos went off to his business appointments and she went browsing in the tourist souks, lunched at the hotel, then had a lazy afternoon poolside.

Nikos returned early evening, just as she got back up to their suite, his mood excellent.

'Good meetings?' she enquired.

'Highly satisfactory,' he said.

He disappeared down to the pool to cool off, and by the time he came back up Diana was ready. They'd agreed to try out one of the other restaurants at the hotel, less formal than where they'd dined their first night. Tonight she wore a cocktail dress in pale blue had used minimum make-up and wore low-heeled shoes. Nikos looked relaxed and casual in an open-neck shirt, turned-back cuffs and no tie.

He looked devastatingly attractive, but she refused to pay attention to that fact. Instead she chattered on about her adventures in the souks as they tucked into the Italian-style dishes.

'Buy any gold?' he asked, with a lift of his eyebrow.

'A few bits and pieces,' she conceded. 'I know it's not hallmarked, but I couldn't resist. And,' she added, 'I bought a carpet! I saw it and thought it would be perfect for the library at Greymont—the one there is very moth-eaten now. I'm having it shipped home directly.' She made a moue. 'I probably got diddled over the price, because I'm not much good at haggling, but it seemed good value to me all the same. Cheaper than a dealer in London, at any rate.'

'A good morning's work,' he said, and smiled.

His mood was excellent, and not just because he'd had a very productive meeting with one of the Sheikh's key people, but also because Diana was clearly considerably more relaxed with him this evening. His careful strategy was working—get her comfortable with him, let her lower her guard, so she would be ready to accept what was inevitable between them. Ready to accept her own desire for him and his her for her.

The ice maiden melted in passion. Made mine at last...

And now, thanks to the Prince and Princess, he was going to be presented with the absolutely perfect setting in which to do so.

'Oh, desperately strenuous!' she laughed. 'So I rewarded myself with lazing by the pool all afternoon.'

He looked her over. 'You're starting to tan,' he said. 'It suits you.'

There was nothing particularly provocative in the way he was inspecting her, but she had to steel herself all the same.

'How sweet of you to notice,' she said, making her voice lightly humorous. 'I'm still using huge amounts of sun cream all the same!'

He smiled. 'Well, make sure you take plenty with you when we head off into the desert tomorrow.'

She looked at him. 'Desert?' Had he planned an expedition? Dune-bashing perhaps?

But it was not dune-bashing.

'Yes. I've had a communiqué from the palace.' He paused, letting his eyes rest on Diana. 'Apparently it has pleased the Princess to request that her brother the Sheikh lends us the use of his…ah…"desert love-nest", I believe is the term the Princess used, since we are here on our honeymoon…'

Dismay filled Diana's face. 'Nikos, we can't *possibly* accept!'

She'd deliberately not told him what Princess Fatima had said to her—had hoped the Princess would forget all about it, or that her brother would turn down any request she might make. But in vain…

His expression changed. 'Diana, we can't possibly *not*.' His tone was adamant. 'It would cause grave offence to do so. It's a singular honour, and an indication of how the Princess has taken to you.'

'To refuse would be to offend…' Diana echoed in a hollow voice.

'Exactly,' Nikos confirmed in that same steely voice. Then his expression softened, and there was a humorous glint in his eye now. 'Think of it as an adventure. You'll be able to dine out on it in years to come.'

She gave a disheartened sigh. 'I suppose so,' she said reluctantly.

Her mood had plummeted. For a start, she felt a total hypocrite. A complete fraud. Here was Princess Fatima, bestowing upon her what she fondly imagined would be a fantastically romantic interlude, when it was the very last thing that was appropriate for her and Nikos.

But there was more to her dismay than the consciousness of being a hypocritical fraud. The thought of being wafted off to a desert hideaway, all on her own with Nikos…

Sternly, she rallied herself. There was nothing she could do to evade this, and it would, after all, be very good schooling for her to get more and more used to being with Nikos. It would help her to get over this ridiculous overreaction to him she had.

It was an instruction she kept repeating to herself as they set off the next day, heading out into the desert in a luxurious leather-seated, air-conditioned SUV with jacked-up wheels that would clear the desert sand, shielded from the burning heat outside.

It was a heat that deepened as they left the coast and drove along black metalled roads that glistened in the sunshine, first across scrubby flat land and then snaking amongst towering sand dunes that signalled the start of the fabled Empty Quarter.

Diana gazed rapt at the desert scenery which was gradually becoming rockier. The road wound through deep gullies and past oases of palm trees, with few signs of habitation and an occasional glint of murky-looking water. Camels—some being herded along in a chain, some merely wandering on their own, presumably either wild or having been let out to graze as and where they could—wandered along the roadside sometimes, but otherwise there was little visible sign of life.

Though they'd set out early in the morning, in order to catch what amounted to the coolest part of the day, it was nearing lunchtime when they finally arrived. They had been through a village of sorts, and what looked to Diana's eyes like some kind of military base, and now, about half an hour's drive thereafter, a building hove into view that at first she thought merely to be an outcrop of rock.

But she realised as they approached that it was a small, square building, made of the same sand-coloured stone as the earth, two storeys tall against the surrounding desert. Only a perimeter fence indicated that there was something special about the place—and the guards standing to attention as they drove through the metal gates to approach the building itself. High, arched double doors opened wide, and the four-by-four drove through with a flourish to enter what was soon revealed to be an outer courtyard.

Along with Nikos she climbed down. Palace servants were running forward to help. At once the heat struck her, clamping around her like a vice. Immediately she felt perspiration bead on her spine, despite the loose cotton shirt she was wearing. The glare of the sun after the tinted windows of the vehicle made her reach for her dark glasses.

'We need to get inside,' Nikos murmured, putting his arm around her waist and guiding her forward.

She craned her head as she walked towards the ornately carved inner doors that were opening as if controlled by a magic genie, and entered what she realised was the inner courtyard—the palace itself.

The love-nest.

CHAPTER SIX

DIANA GAVE A gasp of pleasure.

'Oh, how absolutely beautiful!' she exclaimed spontaneously.

The courtyard was an exquisite garden—an oasis with trickling fountains in stone basins, little channels that wound about bordered by greenery, the whole edged with vine-covered columns creating shady arbours under which marble benches were set.

They were ushered forward by bowing servants into the interior of the bijou palace, and Diana gazed in pleasure at the delicate fretwork archways and the inlaid marble columns as they went up to the upper floor where the royal apartments were. There might be only one bedroom, huge though it was, but the day room—or whatever it might be called in Arabic—contained plenty of silk-swathed divans, which would, she hoped uneasily, solve the sleeping situation.

Quite how she would cope she didn't know, but somehow she would. She must.

For now, though, what she wanted was a bathroom to freshen up in, and she was relieved to discover it was western in style. Even so, as she took a cooling shower she kept her water usage to the minimum, mindful that they were in the middle of a desert. Then she donned a calf-length, floaty, fine cotton flower-printed dress, draped a chiffon scarf over her hair and bare shoulders.

She found Nikos, also showered and changed, waiting for her by an arched colonnade that looked out on the wide room-length balcony. Lunch had been set out for them, and as they took their places, soft-footed servants unobtrusively waiting on them, Diana resolved that however inappropriate being in an Arabian love-nest might be for her and Nikos, they might as well make the most of this privileged stay.

Lunch passed congenially while they chatted in what had now become quite a comfortable fashion, on subjects roaming from the journey they'd had that morning to more intellectual consideration of the geopolitics of the region and the impact on world affairs and global economics.

Nikos was, as Diana already knew, very well informed, and she found it stimulating to discuss such matters with him. It struck her that he was a far more interesting person to talk to than most of her friends and acquaintances. He had a world view that they lacked, a broadness of opinion and a highly incisive intelligence. No wonder he'd come so far in his life.

I never find his company tedious, she found herself thinking.

So often when she was talking to people socially she was conscious of simply going through the motions—saying what was proper, most of it trivial but socially acceptable, anodyne, appropriate to the occasion. She could do it in her sleep, but it was hardly a mental workout. Exchanging views and arguments with Nikos was quite the opposite, and she found that she really enjoyed trying to keep up with him.

We get on surprisingly well.

The thought was suddenly in her head, lingering a moment, and then, as the leisurely meal ended, Nikos brought the subject round to themselves again.

'So, how do you want to spend the afternoon?' he asked her. His tone was easy, relaxed, his glance at her the same.

'Camel riding?' she suggested, with a hint of humour in her voice.

He nodded. 'We must most definitely do so while we are here—but not in the main heat of the day. However, there's a pool if we want it—though for me...' Nikos flexed his long legs '... I wouldn't mind a good workout after our long drive and this highly delicious lunch—there's a gym here too.'

'Well, why don't you?' Diana smiled amiably, then smothered a yawn. 'I have to say that our early-morning start and that large lunch is making taking a siesta very tempting!'

And that was what she did, dozing peacefully for a good couple of hours or more.

The palace had been built long before air-conditioning, and used the ancient Arabian technique of maximising the up-draught of air through cleverly positioned open archways and slatted wooden windows to create a cooling effect.

When she finally arose, much refreshed, it was to be served with mint tea and tiny pastries, before going to change into her swimming costume and sarong and being shown down to the pool. It was situated in the gardens that stretched beyond the palace, away from the entrance they'd arrived at, bordered by a high stone wall and fronted by palm trees for total privacy.

The heat was beginning to ebb, she fancied, and once she was wet it was much cooler as she swam lazily around, feeling her loose hair streaming sleekly behind her. A sense of well-being eased through her. This really was a magical experience, and however inapplicable it was for her and Nikos to be here in the Sheikh's love-nest it was not an experience she would ever have again.

'So this is where you are.'

Nikos's voice penetrated her consciousness and she looked up from her lazy circling of the pool to see him standing at the water's edge. He looked even taller from this low perspective, and he'd clearly done a vigorous workout indeed. His T-shirt was damp, so were his shorts, and his muscles were pumped.

A moment later she saw even more than his shoulders, biceps and quads. He peeled off the damp shirt and chucked it, then yanked off his trainers. A moment later he was in the pool beside her, under the water, then surfacing in a flurry of diamond droplets, shaking the water from his eyelashes and grinning.

'Wow! That feels good!' he exclaimed feelingly. He looked at Diana. 'Apparently the temperature will start dropping once the sun has set, and for that I shall be grateful.' He quirked an eyebrow in his characteristic manner. 'Do you fancy some star-gazing later on? There's a very fancy telescope up on the roof, I'm told, but even without that the show should be spectacular.'

As he spoke, he found himself thinking about Nadya for a moment. He'd never have made such a suggestion to *her*. She'd have looked at him as if he were mad, and then counter-suggested going to a fashionable nightspot instead, where she could enjoy being seen and admired.

He frowned inwardly. Had he really never noticed how limited Nadya was? She was a professional to the hilt in her work, but when it came to anything else—from astronomy to geopolitics—her eyes would glaze over.

Diana's eyes brightened and sharpened—she listened

and responded, sometimes agreeing, sometimes arguing a counterpoint, putting a different perspective and engaging vigorously, holding her corner, but open to new views as well.

She was open to the prospect of studying the night sky too. She was smiling enthusiastically at his suggestion, as he'd thought she would.

'Oh, yes please!' she said eagerly.

'Great,' Nikos returned, banishing the memories of Nadya's time in his life, utterly irrelevant to him now that he had Diana.

Diana, who was opening the door to the next stage of his life with her impeccable background, her very own stately home, the upper-class world she had been born into and which he would now enjoy as her husband, the world she took for granted, the world he himself had had no right to. Diana would give him that and more.

Diana was the woman he desired for her cool pale beauty, the woman he was so close to making his own in the most intimate way.

Soon...so very soon now.

With a flexing of his muscles he executed a perfect duck-dive and disappeared under the water completely, swimming strongly to the end of the pool and back several times before needing to surface.

Diana watched him admiringly. 'That's amazing breath control,' she told him as he finally broke the water.

He grinned again. 'It's just practice,' he said. 'And good lung capacity.'

Diana's eyes went to the smooth, muscled expanse of his chest, with its perfectly honed pecs and taut solar plexus in the flat between his hard-edged ribs. She looked away hurriedly. Feasting her gaze on his near naked body was no way to behave.

She waded to the steps and clambered out, wrapping a towel around herself. 'I'm heading indoors,' she announced. 'Time to shower. What's the drill for this evening?' Her voice held the light, bright tone she was determined to keep with him.

'Sunset drinks on the terrace,' he informed her. 'No rush.'

It was just as well he'd said that, Diana discovered, for when she returned indoors she was immediately swept away by what seemed to be a whole posse of waiting women who, with a flurry of soft-footed, smiling attention, proceeded to get her ready for the evening.

For a brief moment she resisted—then relented. After all, never again would she be staying in a royal hideaway in the Arabian desert—so why not indulge in what was being so insistently offered to her?

With murmurs of *'Shukran!'* she gave herself up to their ministrations.

Nikos stood on the wide upper-storey terrace, edged by a balustrade in the red sandstone that the whole building was constructed with, smooth and warm to the touch still, though the sun was close to setting. To the east, colour was fading from the sky, and soon stars would be pricking out in the cloudless sky. There would indeed be a spectacular show later on.

Ruminatively he sipped his drink, a cool, mint-flavoured concoction that went well with the ambience. There was champagne on ice awaiting Diana's eventual emergence. His eyes narrowed slightly as he recalled that moment in the pool, when she'd made no secret of being oh-so-aware of his body. Finding it pleasing to her.

Anticipation thrummed softly through him. Finally... *finally* he was losing the ice maiden! It had taken him this long, but the thaw was underway. He felt the tug of a caustic smile at the corner of his mouth as his eyes rested on the desert vista beyond. In this heat, how could she help but thaw?

And here, now, in this the ultimate hideaway, she would melt completely, he knew.

Mentally he sent a message of thanks to the Sheikh and his romantic-souled sister. This place was absolutely ideal. The hotel might have been designed to convey the impression of *Arabian Nights*—but this was the real thing.

His smile lost its caustic edge and widened into one of true appreciation. An appreciation he knew Diana shared too. There was an authenticity to this place that appealed to her—it had a history, a cultural heritage. Generations had passed through it, leaving the echo of their presence, and that made it similar in essence to her own country house home. He felt it was a good omen for their stay.

A sound behind him made him turn. And as he did every thought about the edifice he was in vanished. Every thought in his head vanished except one.

It was Diana—and she looked...

Sensational.

She was walking towards him slowly. Slowly, he realised, because she was in very high heels and her dress was very tight. It must, he realised instantly, be the couture gown gifted to her by the Princess. And, oh, the Princess had chosen well!

The superbly crafted gown contoured Diana's figure like a glove, fitting her almost like a second skin. There was nothing at all immodest in the fit—it simply skimmed over her flawlessly, the smooth, pale yellow material creating a sheen that glistened in the fading light, aglow from the setting sun reflecting off the golden dunes.

He gazed at her, riveted, as she approached, the short train of the dress swishing on the marble floor, the delicate beading rustling at her bodice and hem.

She stopped as she came up to him. 'The Princess had this delivered here!' she announced.

She'd been half dismayed to discover that Princess Fatima had kept to what she'd promised, and half dazzled by wearing so exquisite a gown, far in excess of what her own wardrobe ran to.

Nikos's eyes swept over her. 'You look fantastic,' he breathed.

His whole body had tensed, tautened, and he could not take his eyes from her. The incredible gown—haute couture at its most extravagant best—needed no jewellery. The beading served as that, and all that had been added was a kind of narrow bandeau of the same material, embroidered all over with the delicate beading that had been woven through the elaborate coiffure of her hair. Her make-up was subdued, but absolutely perfect for her, her lips a soft sheen, her skin unpowdered, her eyelashes merely enhanced, and a little kohl around the eyes themselves. It made her look sensual and exotic.

'It's incredible,' he murmured, still sweeping his gaze over her. He found himself reaching for her hands—their nails were pearlescent, with a soft sheen like her lips. Slowly he raised them to his mouth. His eyes met hers. 'You were always beautiful,' he said, 'but tonight—tonight you surpass the stars themselves!'

For a moment their eyes met and mingled. Held. Something seemed to pass between them…something that she could not block—did not wish to. Something that seemed to keep her absolutely motionless while Nikos beheld her beauty.

Then, with a little demur, she slipped her hands away

and gave a tiny shake of her head. 'It's the gown,' she said. 'It's a work of art in its own right.'

'Then it needs a toast of its own!' Nikos laughed.

A servant was hovering, waiting to open the champagne, and Nikos nodded his assent. A moment later he was handing Diana a softly beaded flute and raising his own.

'To your gown—to its exquisite beauty.' He paused. A smile lurked at his mouth, and his eyes were not on the gown. They were on Diana. 'And to you, Diana, my most exquisitely beautiful bride.'

She gazed up at him, her own glass motionless, and met his dark, lustrous eyes, so warm, so speaking...

And suddenly out of nowhere, out of the soft desert night that was slowly sweeping towards them from the east, as the burning sun sank down amongst the golden dunes, she felt a sense of helplessness take her over. She hadn't wanted to come to this place—this jewel-like desert hideaway, this royal love-nest dedicated to sensual love—but she was here. Here and now—with this man who, alone of all the men she had ever encountered, seemed to have the ability to make her shimmer with awareness of his overpowering masculinity.

She simply could not bring herself to remember that he was the man who was saving Greymont for her, to whom she was to be only a society wife, playing the role that he wanted her to play at his side.

How could she think of things like new roofs for Greymont and rewiring, restoring stonework and all the bills that came with that? How could she think of being just a useful means for Nikos Tramontes to move in circles he had not been born into? And how could she think of things like marriages of convenience that were nothing more than business deals?

It was impossible to think of such things! Not standing here, in this priceless precious gown, with a glass of vintage champagne between her fingers as she stood looking out over the darkening desert, miles and miles from anywhere, alone with Nikos.

So she raised her glass to him, took a first sip, savouring the delicate *mousse* of the champagne.

'To you, Nikos,' she said softly. 'Because I would not be here were it not for you.' Her eyes held his still. 'And, as you say, this is an experience of a lifetime…'

Something changed in his eyes—a fleck of gold like flame, deep within. 'It is indeed, my most beautiful bride.'

A frisson went through her and she was powerless to stop it. Powerless to do anything but look back at him and smile. Drink him in. Her eyes swept over him. He was wearing narrow-cut evening trousers, but not a dinner jacket. His dress shirt, made of silk, was tieless, open at the neck, his cuffs turned back and fastened with gold links that caught the last of the setting sun and exposed his strong wrists.

He looked cool, elegant and—she gulped silently—devastatingly attractive. His freshly shaved jawline, the sable hair feathering at his nape and brow, the strong planes of his features and those dark, deep-set, inky-lashed eyes that were meeting her gaze, unreadable and yet with a message in them that she could not deny.

Did not wish to deny…

Emotion fluttered in her again. How far away she was from the reality of her life—how immersed she was, here, in this fairytale place, so remote, so private, so utterly different from anything she had known.

It's just me and Nikos—just the two of us.

The real world seemed very far away.

She felt a quiver in her blood, her pulse, felt sudden

breathlessness. Something was happening to her and she did not know what.

Except that she did…

She took another mouthful of the rare-vintage champagne, feeling the rush of effervescence in the costly liquid create an answering rush in herself. She felt as light as air suddenly, breathless.

She became aware that the silent-footed servants were there again, placing tempting delicacies on golden platters on an inlaid table, bowing and then seeming to disappear as noiselessly as they had appeared.

'How do they do that?' Diana murmured as she leant forward to pick at the delicate slivers of what, she did not know—knew only that they tasted delicious and melted in her mouth like fairy food.

'I suspect a magic lamp may be involved,' Nikos answered dryly, and Diana laughed. Then he smiled again—a smile that was only for her—and met her eyes. He raised his glass again. 'To an extraordinary experience,' he said, his slight nod indicating their surroundings.

She raised her own glass and then turned her attention to the darkening desert. 'I shall certainly remember this all my life,' she agreed. Her gaze swept on upwards. 'Oh, look—stars!'

'There'll be a whole lot more later on,' Nikos said. 'For now, let's just watch the night arrive.'

She moved beside him, careful not to lean on the balustrade lest the work of art she was wearing was marked or creased in any way. Her mood was strange.

She had given herself over to the murmuring attentions of what she could only refer to as handmaidens, letting them do what they willed with her. It had started with them bathing her, in water perfumed with aromatic oils, and gone on from there until she'd walked out on to the terrace feeling almost as if she were in a dream.

Because surely it *must* be a dream—standing here beside Nikos, watching the night darken over the dunes, hearing the strange, alien noises of night creatures waking and walking, feeling the air start to cool, the air pressure change. How far away from the real world they seemed. How far away from everything that was familiar. How far away from everything that was not herself and Nikos.

Her eyes went to him again, seeing his elegantly rakish garb, the absence of a tie, the open-necked shirt, the turned-back cuffs, all creating that raffish look, looking so *sensual*.

She felt a ripple of ultra-awareness go through her like a frisson. As if every nerve-ending were suddenly totally alert—quivering. And as she stood beside him she caught his scent—something musky, sweet-spiced and aromatic, that went perfectly with this desert landscape, matching the oh-so-feminine version of the perfume with which she had been adorned. It caught her senses, increasing the tension that was vibrating silently through her as she stood beside him, so aware of his presence close to her, knowing she only had to lean a little sideways for her arm to press against his. For his arm to wrap around her, pull her to him as they stood gazing out over the darkening desert.

From somewhere deep within her another emotion woke. One she should pay heed to. One that called to her to listen. But she would not listen. She refused to listen. Refused to heed it. She would only go on standing here, nestled into the strong, protective curve of Nikos's arm, gazing out over the desert that surrounded them all about, keeping the world beyond far, far away.

She sipped her champagne, as did he, and they stood in silence until the night had wrapped them completely and the dunes had become looming, massy shapes, darker than the night itself. Overhead, stars had started to blaze like windows into a fiery furnace beyond. Behind them torches were being lit by unseen hands along the length of the terrace, and several braziers, too, to guard against the growing chill of the desert night, and the flickering firelight danced in the shadows all around them.

She turned, and realised that through the archways that pierced the inner border of the terrace more light was spilling—softer light—and the characteristic sweetly aromatic scent of Middle Eastern cuisine.

'Ready to dine?' Nikos asked her with a smile, and she nodded, suddenly hungry.

Lunch seemed a long time ago. Her everyday reality a long time ago.

Because this surely wasn't real, was it? Nikos as her very own desert prince, dark-haired, dark-eyed, and she, gliding beside him like a princess, in a gown fit for royalty, her train swishing on the inlaid marble floor.

Servants were guiding them forward, smiling and bowing, ushering them into yet another room. She gave a soft cry of delight as they entered. It was a dining room, the interior constructed out of wood, fretted and inset with tessellations which glinted in the light of the dozens of candles that were the only illumination, burning in sconces on the walls and pillars all around, and on the table set for them with golden dishes, golden plates—golden everything, it seemed. The air was heavy with the fragrance of frankincense from hidden burners.

'*Jamil jaddaan*—very beautiful!' Diana exclaimed, clapping her hands in delight and indicating the exquisite room.

The servants bowed and smiled, and the steward pulled back huge carved wooden chairs, lined with silk cushions, for her and Nikos. She took her place carefully, and Nikos sat opposite her.

The meal that followed was as exquisite as the room they dined in—dishes of rich, fragrant Middle Eastern food, with delicately spiced charcoal-baked meats as familiar as lamb and as unfamiliar as goat and camel, and who knew what else besides, as tender as velvet, all served with rice enhanced with nuts and dates and raisins, sweet and savoury at the same time.

As a mindful precaution for her priceless gown Diana had called for a shawl to be brought, which she'd swathed around her upper body while she ate.

'I couldn't bear to mark this dress!' She shuddered at the thought. 'I doubt it could ever be cleaned—and even if it could the cost would be terrifying!' She looked at it musingly. 'I wonder when I'm ever going to have an opportunity to wear it again.'

He answered instantly. 'When we entertain at Greymont,' he said. 'Once all the work is complete we can give a grand ball—and you shall wear the Princess's gown for it.'

A vision leapt in her mind instantly. Greymont, thronged with guests, and she and Nikos descending the stairs to the hall, her hand on his arm—man and wife, side by side. As if their marriage was a true one.

For a moment longing fired within her. So fierce she felt faint with it.

What if my marriage to Nikos were real?

The thought wound its way around her senses, enticing, beguiling, sweet and fragrant—just as the fragrance of the frankincense was winding its way around her senses, along with the glowing effervescence of cham-

pagne, the deep, rich sensuality of the wine, her physical repletion after the delicately spiced foods, the soft
golden light of the candles, reflected a million times in
the golden dishes...

The light was setting off the man she had married a
few short days ago with a golden sheen, softening the
contours of his face, giving him glints like flecks of gold
in his dark, long-lashed eyes.

Eyes that were resting on her.

With a message in them that was as old as time.

'Diana.'

He said her name in a low voice, setting down his wine
glass slowly, paying it no attention. All his focus was on
her, now, as she sat there, held in his gaze.

'Diana...'

He said her name again. His voice was husky now.
How beautiful she was! Like a rare, exquisite jewel, shining in this jewel box of a room. For him alone.

He got to his feet, oblivious of the servant who was
instantly there, drawing back the heavy, carved cedar-
wood chair. He held out a hand towards Diana. Slowly,
very slowly, she got to her feet. Unnoticed, her swathing shawl fell to the floor. Unnoticed, a servant stooped
to pick it up, drape it gracefully around her shoulders.

Wordlessly she took Nikos's hand. It closed over hers,
warm and strong. She felt faint suddenly, and filled with
a subliminal sense of anticipation. His eyes smiled at
her—warm, like his handclasp.

'Shall we look at the stars?' he said softly.

Still wordless, she nodded. There was a breathlessness
in her—a headiness that had nothing to do with the con-
sumption of champagne and wine and everything to do
with Nikos holding her hand, leading her away.

They went back out on to the wide marble terrace and

down to the far end where, Diana realised, there was a
flight of steps that would take them upwards to the roof.

As they gained the flat surface she gave an audible
gasp. Only a very dim torch, low down, lit the top of
the steps. Beyond there was velvet darkness. A darkness that was pierced only above their heads by a forest
of stars, the incandescence of them burning through the
floor of heaven.

She lifted her hand. 'It's as if I could reach up and
pluck one down, they seem so close!' she said in wonder.

Nikos tucked her hand into the crook of his arm, leading her carefully, mindful of her high heels, into the centre of the wide flat rooftop, which was carpeted like a
roofless open-air room. Roofed by stars.

The sky was like a bowl, inset with stars down to the
horizon, or so it seemed—a horizon marked only by the
rounded edges of the dunes, the jagged outlines of rocks
and outcrops. She gazed about her, lips parted, awestruck,
tilting back her head.

She dimly was aware that she was leaning against the
strong column of Nikos's body to give herself balance.
He was gazing upwards too, his gaze sweeping in wide
arcs to take it all in. He started to name the constella-
tions that were visible at these latitudes, at this season,
raising his arm to guide her.

'It's the most glorious thing I've seen in my life!' She
sighed, still breathless with awe.

'Do you want the telescope set up?' he asked her, but
she shook her head.

'No, for tonight this is enough—I can't take it all in
as it is.' She turned to face him. 'Oh, Nikos, this is the
most wonderful sight!'

'It is indeed,' he said. 'And we can see them better
still if we lie down...'

He gestured to something that had not at first been visible to Diana, but now, with her darkness-adjusted eyes, she saw that—incongruous as it might appear—there was what seemed to be a king-sized divan in the centre of the rooftop, presumably set there for the very purpose of lying down to see the stars. Already her neck was aching with tilting her head upwards, and her feet in their high heels were scarcely prepared for long standing.

Gratefully she let Nikos guide her, help her to ease down, to take off her shoes—not needed now—and then lie back on the myriad cushions piled on the silk-covered divan.

'Oh, that's better,' she said gratefully, able now to gaze straight up at the night sky.

She felt the divan dip slightly as Nikos's heavy form came down on the other side. With half her mind she felt a flicker go through her—maybe she and Nikos lying virtually side by side like this, all alone under the desert night sky, was not the wisest thing. Then she brushed it aside. This was an experience to be made the very most of. They were here to star-gaze—nothing else.

For a while they simply lay quietly, gazing upwards. Speech seemed not just superfluous, but intrusive. The cushion beneath Diana's head was soft, but because of her elaborate coiffure it was not entirely comfortable. She shifted position slightly, and then heard Nikos speak beside her in the dark.

'What is it?'

'It's my hair,' she said. 'This style is designed to be vertical, not horizontal.' She propped herself up, reaching with her other hand behind her head, patting it to see where the pins were.

'Let me help,' said Nikos.

He levered himself to a sitting position and turned

her shoulders slightly, to give him greater access to the back of her head. For reasons she did not want to explore, Diana let him. It was easier for him to do it than for her.

But there was more about this than ease of access. She dipped her head slightly. And as his fingers worked gently over the intricate plaits and coils, seeking pins and grips, she felt a great sensuous languor creep over her. His touch was delicate, feathering through her hair, and as each pin was removed she felt its loosening go through her. Felt a slow surge of blood start to pulse through her.

'Oh, that feels so good...' She sighed as coil after coil was released, easing the tension on her skull. She felt her locks cascading loose to her shoulders, nothing restraining them at all but the beaded bandeau threaded through them.

'Does it?' said Nikos softly.

Her hair was loose now, all the pins and grips discarded—presumably, she thought absently, on the carpet surrounding the divan. But the thought was vague, inchoate. Irrelevant in comparison with that oh-so-sinuous languor that was stealing over her.

Nikos's fingers were still threading through her hair, softly smoothing her locks, gently kneading her scalp, just above her nape. Instinctively she dipped her head further, giving a little sigh of pleasure. She heard his low laugh again, felt his sensuously working fingertips move to the tops of her ears. Then, with another silvered quickening of her pulse, she felt his thumb idly tease at a lobe. A million quivers of sensation went through her. It felt *so* good...

There was a haze inside her, around her. Above, the stars were blazing in their glory, but she felt her eyelids dip, made a little sound in her throat.

As she did so, she felt Nikos's hand stroke down her

throat, its slender column caressed by his long, sensitive fingers. She felt her face being turned towards him, felt her eyelids fluttering open—to see him looking down at her.

And in his eyes, in the starlight, was what she could not deny.

Did not want to deny.

She said his name. Just his name. Breathed it like a sigh.

Who was there to hear it but him and the empty desert? The desert and the night. The night and the stars. The stars and Nikos.

Nikos—who, alone of all the men in all the world, seemed to possess what no man had ever possessed before.

The power to enthral her. Entice her. Tempt her. Tempt her to do what she was doing now—what she *must* do, it seemed, here, now, on this soft silken divan under the burning desert stars, where nothing else existed but themselves and the night and their desire. His for her, hers for him.

I want him so much... So much...

She did not know why—did not care—only knew that her hand was lifting to feather at his temple, to graze the sable hair and drift down the planed cheek to edge along the roughened outline of his jaw.

Her eyes were still half closed, her body still filled with that incredible heaviness. And as she touched him she made that little sound in her throat again, felt as if in a dream that her breasts were tightening, quickening under the second skin that was her precious, priceless gown. The gown given to her by a princess—a princess who'd asked for this desert love-nest to be theirs. For now. For tonight.

It wasn't what their marriage was about—she knew that—but she couldn't think of it now. Could only think and feel what was happening to her here, beneath the desert night burning with myriad stars.

Yearning filled her, and an instinct so powerful she could not resist it. She had no wish to resist it—not here, not now, not under these burning desert stars, not under the heavy-lidded gaze of the man whose mouth was now lowering slowly, infinitely slowly, to meet hers.

His kiss was like silken velvet—infinitely soft, infinitely sensuous. Infinitely arousing. That little sound came from her again, deep in her throat. She felt her neck arch, her loosened wanton hair sliding like satin, felt the hot pulse at her throat strengthen. She felt her hand slip around the nape of his neck, draw him down to her as she rested slowly backwards, moving down upon the waiting cushions, her hair now spilling out across them.

He came down with her, his kiss starting to deepen. She felt her breasts cresting, straining against the bodice of her gown, and still he kissed her as if he would never release her. Desire was sweeping up inside her. A desire whose power she had never known, had only glimpsed in brief glances, crushed thoughts, whenever she'd looked at the man she had married—who was not hers to glance at like that, not hers to think about, not hers to desire…

Except for this night.

She could have him for this night only! Here, where the rest of the world had ceased to exist, seemed as if it might never exist again, might never have existed at all. For only the stars were burning in their own eternity. An eternity she could share for this one night only…

Nikos—the only man to arouse her, awaken her. The only man to whom she was a woman—a woman who could feel what other women felt.

Never... Never have I felt this desire before! Never!

But now she did—now she knew its power, its force and strength. It was arousing and inspiring her, sweeping her along with its tide so that she could not resist, taking her to a new land—a land she had thought was not for her, had never found before.

But she had found now...with him...with Nikos.

The land of sweet desire.

Desire that was mounting in her now, quickening in her blood, in her heating body, in her shallow, hectic breath. She felt her fingers mould his nape, spear into his hair, felt her body turn towards him like a magnet.

Bliss was seeping up inside her at the drowning sweetness of feeling his lips grazing hers—lips that were slowly, remorselessly, teasing from her a deeper response now, a response that began a restlessness inside her, a sense of going over the edge, giving up all control. Giving it up to the feelings filling her body, her mind, her very being.

Of their own volition, in their own mounting need, her lips parted and she gave that low moan in her throat again—of relief, of pleasure, of wonder and bliss as she tasted to the full all that Nikos was offering, all that he was doing, giving to her, with a touch so skilled, so arousing, that she was blind with it.

He was murmuring her name even as he kissed her, tasted her, his hand slipping down, sliding slowly and sensually over the bodice of the dress to mould the contours of her body. Her spine arched into his caress. She was aching for his hand to close over the straining mound of her breast, and when it did, his palm grazing the straining crests, she felt another surge of unbearable desire. And yet another. And another. Each one stronger, more urgent than the last.

She wanted this with all her being. Madness though it was. She didn't care—could not care—could only go on yielding endlessly, urgently, to the hunger that was growing in her with every passing moment, every yearning press of her body into his.

And then suddenly, abruptly, his hand was lifted from her—and his mouth. With a muffled cry of loss she tried to reach for him again, her eyes blind to all but the overpowering need for him that had brought her to this point. But he resisted her reach and instead, with a gasp of shock, he flipped her over so her face was pressed into the pillows.

She tried to raise herself.

'Lie still.'

There was a growl in his voice—a growl that melted her bones. For she knew at a level so deep she did not understand it that this was a command that was for her, not him. And a moment later she realised why.

His hands were at the back of her dress and his fingers were working assiduously, steadily, at slipping free the myriad tiny hooks that fastened the exquisite gown. It seemed to take for ever, and she felt herself grow restless, filled with a sense of frustration that it was taking so long for him to ease the delicate fabric from her skin, exposing, hook by hook, the long line of her spine. She felt her fingers clutch at the silk of her pillow, felt a heat building in her—a heat she could not cool, did not want to cool.

She wanted only to feel as she did when finally the fabric fell aside, and then his long velvet fingertips were easing beneath, splaying out with the most leisurely arousing touch, so that her fingers clenched more tightly, the restlessness in her mounting, wanting more of him, more of his feathered touch, more of the way his mouth was now lowering to her spine, grazing each sculpted contour as swirls of pleasure began to ripple through her.

As his lips grazed down her spine, teasing those swirls of exquisite sensation from her, she felt his hands spread out, easing the gown completely from her until it was all but falling off. Gently, but with a strength that made it effortless, he lifted her from the gown so that it lay like a discarded thing beside her. Gently he lowered her back upon the silken divan, turning her towards him.

She was naked—completely naked. For an endless moment he gazed down at her. Incapable of more. Incapable of anything except letting his eyes feast on the incredible beauty of her naked body. She was everything he'd known she would be—everything and more. Oh, *so* much more!

Her slender frame, the narrow waist, the perfect contours, the sweet lushness of her breasts, bared now for him alone. The swell of her hips, the deep vee below, her long legs, her loosening thighs…

Then with a sudden movement he sat up, seizing the priceless gown. She did not even remark when he dropped it to the floor—her eyes were only for him. Urgently he hauled his own clothing from him—so much more swiftly than he'd just freed her from the gown that had done its job so well—had made her aware of her own beauty, of how precious it was to her, to him, and was now no longer necessary.

Nothing was needed now. Now they had everything they wanted. They had the silken couch, the night sky, the warmth of the desert, the silence and the darkness, the stars their only witness.

They had each other.

It was all that he wanted now. All he had wanted from the first moment he had set eyes on her. This exquisitely beautiful woman, so different from any he had known, offering him so much...

Offering him now the greatest gift of all—the gift that he had waited so many months to claim.

Herself.

She was his at last. The ice maiden was gone for ever. His self-control, his self-denial was finally needed no longer and she was melting in his arms. Melting and then catching fire at his touch, his kiss, his absolute caress.

With a sense of absolute liberty he lowered himself down beside her. Smoothed her golden hair from her forehead. Gazed down at her with a look that told her everything she needed to know, that sent the blood flushing through her, hot and urgent.

'And now,' said Nikos as he started to lower his mouth, his voice rich with anticipation, satisfaction, 'we can begin our wedding night.'

CHAPTER SEVEN

THE SUN WAS RISING, swelling over the rim of the eastern-most dune, bleaching the sky, quenching the stars one by one by one. Rose-gold lit up the horizon, a long, rich line of colour as the sky above turned to azure blue.

In Nikos's arms, Diana slept—as he slept in hers. Her head and torso rested on his chest, that strong, muscle-sculpted wall that could take her weight as if she were feathers drifting from a passing eagle. And around her waist his arm was clamped, heavy upon her, but it was a weight she'd gloried in, holding her to him even as sleep had swept over them in the long, late reaches of the night.

A wedding night that had burned hot as the distant stars whose light had illuminated their bodies—bodies moving in passion, in desire, in endless, boundless need and satiation. Her voice had cried out time after time, each note higher with an ecstasy that had ripped her mind from her body then melded them back, fusing them with the same heat that had fused her body to his. Fusing them as if they were one body, one flesh. They had clasped each other, their tangled limbs impossible to separate.

The sun crept higher now, spilling into the day. It shafted the world with brilliant radiance. Washing up over their naked bodies, covered only by the silken cloths with which the divan was strewn.

Diana stirred. There was warmth moving along her legs now, and she wondered why, her eyes flickering feebly open, blinking at the day. The sun had gained its final clearance of the dunes and now blazed out over the rooftop, instantly heating them. She felt Nikos stir too, his limbs tensing as he moved upwards out of deep sleep.

The arm around her tightened automatically. But he did not wake.

Breathless, Diana eased herself from him. Her body was stiff, unyielding, but move she must. Carefully, very carefully, she stood up. Every muscle in her body ached. She cast her gaze about. She could not stand here naked, exposed on the rooftop. She dipped down, seizing up her cashmere shawl and hurriedly swathing it around herself as consciousness increasingly came back to her.

With a smothered cry she pressed the tips of her fingers against her mouth.

What have I done? Oh, what have I done?

But she knew what she had done. The evidence was there, spread out beneath her gaze—a gaze that could not help but instantly go to the powerful male glory of Nikos's naked his body. An amazed delight leapt in her. Flaring through every cell in her body. Firing every synapse in her dazed brain.

I never knew... I just never knew how it could be!

But she knew now. Knew that Nikos had taken her to a place she had never understood, never realised existed. She felt dazed with the knowledge. Stunned by it.

But it was not knowledge that she could possess freely. She felt her stomach plummet. Dear God, what she had done she should never have allowed herself to do. How *could* she?

This was not what she had married Nikos for.

It was not what he'd married *her* for.

That was the blunt truth of it. The truth that crushed her as she hurried barefoot back down to the interior rooms, rushing into the bathroom. Maybe water would sluice away the madness of what she'd done.

But when she finally emerged from her shower, wrapped in a huge towel, it was to find Nikos waiting for her. He didn't speak—not a word. He was wearing a cotton dressing gown now, and he simply strode up to her. Wrapped her to him.

His bear hug was all-enveloping. Impossible to draw back from.

But I don't want to! I don't want to pull away from him.

The cry came from deep within, from a place she had not known existed. Not until last night.

It seemed an age before he let her go, but when he did he simply said, his eyes alight, his smile wide, 'Breakfast awaits.'

He scooped up a silken robe that was lying draped across the unused bed. It was in sea-green, vivid and vibrant, and he threw it around her and slipped the towel from her.

'You must keep covered,' he growled, and there was an expression in his eyes that she did not need a dictionary to describe. 'Or we'll never get to breakfast.'

His arm around her shoulder, he led her out. She went with him, as meekly as a lamb. For it was the only thing in the world she wanted to do.

Out on the terrace the silent army of servants had set a lavish breakfast table, shaded by an awning, and they took their places. Beyond the terrace and beyond the outdoor pool glittering in the morning sun, the palm trees guarding it, the desert stretched to infinity. All the world was here, in this one place.

In this one man.

Nikos raised his glass of orange juice to her, his smile wide and warm. His eyes warmer still.

'To us, Diana,' he said.

To us? she echoed silently. There was no 'us'—there was only an empty shell of a marriage, designed to make use of each other, with no future in it. None.

But, as she raised her own glass defiance and a reckless daring surged up in her. Beyond this desert hideaway there could be no 'us' for her and Nikos.

But while we are here there can.

And for that… Oh, for that she would seize it all.

'All strapped in?' Nikos said, checking her seat belt. He nodded at their driver. 'OK, let's go.'

With a roaring gunning of the engine the driver grinned and accelerated the four-by-four almost vertically up the perilous slope of the dune.

Within seconds Diana discovered why it was called 'dune-bashing'. She shrieked and covered her eyes as the skilled driver performed manoeuvres that took them to the top, then slid them down the other side, then careered up again to totter precariously at an impossible angle before plunging down in a huge flurry of sandy and sideways sliding.

Nikos hoped that she was, despite appearances, enjoying herself.

By the time the driver finally screeched to a juddering halt, turning back to Nikos with a triumphant grin on his face, he believed she was.

'Oh, good *grief*!' she cried, half-laughing, half-shaking as she finally let go her death grip on the door strap. 'I was absolutely *terrified*!'

'Me too,' Nikos admitted ruefully.

He turned to the driver, exchanging comments on how

he'd performed those almost impossible and certainly potentially lethal manoeuvres on the steep soft sand.

Diana caught at his arm. 'No, Nikos, you are *not* to try doing it yourself!' she exclaimed feelingly.

He turned towards her. 'Worried for me?' he asked, grinning. His eyes glinted. 'How very wifely of you.'

It was lightly said, but it was like a sudden sword in her side, reminding her of just how little right she had to be 'wifely'. But she could not, *would* not think of that now. Not here in the desert, cocooned in this world so distant from their own.

And then Nikos was announcing his need for lunch—for breakfast had been long ago, before they'd set out to try their hands at the ship of the desert, mounting camels as the patient beasts lay on the sand, clambering up with a serpentine grace and starting to move with their slow, swaying gait.

Diana had found the experience unforgettable as her camel trod silently along the way, feeling only the desert wind playing across her heated cheeks, her head shaded by a wide-brimmed hat, the blown sand off the tops of the dunes catching in the light, the burning azure bowl of the sky arching over them, and the endless ocean of sand stretching boundless and bare all around. She'd felt as if she were in a different world. Ancient and primeval, timeless and eternal.

Far, far away from the real world beyond.

But this world here, now, timeless and primeval, was the world she was giving herself to—and she was giving herself to the man here with her, to this time together. She would not think of the world beyond, would not remember it. Not now.

Elation seared through her—a kind of reckless joy as she seized this moment, this time out of time that had come to her unasked-for, unsought, but which she had taken all the same, bestowed upon her like a gift of all gifts.

The gift of this time with Nikos, the man who, out of all men that existed, had taken her to a place she had not believed could ever be for her.

But it is—it is! It's real for me—passion and desire. It's real and now I have it—here, with Nikos, in this timeless place.

That was all she cared about, all she would let herself care about, feel and believe. This time *now*, with Nikos, alone in the desert.

She could see the camels again now, lying down in the shade of high rocks, resting, as their four-by-four descended to the level dirt track again, taking her and Nikos to where a canopy had been set up over carpets laid on the sand.

There they were offered moistened, cooling cloths to wipe their dusty hands and hot faces, before tucking into an array of spiced and fragranced dishes whose delicious aroma quickened her appetite.

And not just for food.

Her eyes slid to the man she was with and she felt that rush of amazement and wonder that came every time she looked at him, feasted on him. He caught her open gaze and smiled—a warm, intimate smile that brought colour flushing to her cheeks. He said nothing, though, only let his long lashes sweep down as he urged her to try yet another dish.

Around them servants stood, pouring cool drinks from tall silver jugs, removing empty dishes, replacing them with yet more food that seemed to be arriving in a procession from the open-air cooking station some way downwind of where they lounged.

Eventually, sated and replete, Diana felt her eyelids start to drift down.

'I'm falling asleep,' she heard herself say as the heat and drowsiness of midday took their soporific toll.

'Then sleep,' said Nikos.

He made a gesture for the servants to clear the last of the bowls and glasses, which they instantly did, then reached across to Diana, drawing her down on the cushions beside him, letting her head loll on his lap. Idly he stroked her hair, plaited into a confining ponytail, but feathering in soft tendrils around her face. Her beautiful, fine-boned face, flushed now with the sun, her hair bleached even paler.

He felt desire stir in him, but held it at bay. It would wait until they were private again.

A slow smile slid across his features and there was reminiscence in his eyes. Their eventual consummation had been everything he'd wanted. Everything he'd intended. Leisurely he replayed in his head that first night—melting her under the stars, seeing the revelation in her starlit eyes as realisation had swept over her, as she'd felt the full intensity of the sensations he'd drawn from her, using all his skills and experience, knowing just what would most sate the desire burning in her like a flame. A desire *he* had kindled, against her own long-held assumption that men were of no sexual interest to her.

His smile deepened, took on a sensual twist. Well, he had made an end of *that*! From now on she would burn for him—burn for however long it took before his desire for her began to wane and the day came when he woke and knew their time together was done with.

Until that time came she was his…

He felt his own lids grow heavy in the somnolent heat. To lie like this, with Diana supine in his lap, her arm across his limbs, warm and close and intimate, was so very good.

Would he *ever* not want her?

The question hung like an eagle over the desert sand, motionless and unanswered, as his eyelids closed and he, too, succumbed to sleep.

'I hate to say this…' Nikos's voice sounded regretful '…but our idyll here is over.'

Diana looked across at him as they sat taking their breakfast in the beautiful inner courtyard, the trickling fountain cooling the air beside them, verdant greenery all around them in the private, enclosed space.

Nikos set down his phone. 'That was the Minister for Development's office. There's another meeting this afternoon with the minister and several other bigwigs. I'll need to be there.'

Diana blinked. The world beyond the desert had seemed so very far away, and yet here it was intruding, downloaded from the ether, summoning them back to reality. She tried to count the days since they'd arrived here from the coast, and failed. One day had segued into the next—indolent, lazy, luxurious, self-absorbed and self-indulgent. A time of passion and desire—a time of bliss.

A fantasy of *Arabian Nights* made real…

And now it was to be ended.

A kind of numb dismay filled her—a sense of dissociation, loss.

Nikos was already getting to his feet. 'I need my laptop,' he said. 'There are some things I must check. Finish your breakfast, though. There is no immediate rush. They're sending a helicopter to take us back to the city.'

The helicopter, when it arrived, was a huge, noisy, angry wasp, churning up the sand, landing just beyond the perimeter fence. It seemed like an invasion to Diana. As Nikos helped her aboard, ducking under the sweeping rotors, it was as if the twenty-first century was crashing back into her.

The machine took off with a deafening roar, wheeling up into the steel-blue sky, casting its wrinkled shadow over the dunes as it headed back to the coast. It took them back to their hotel, but Nikos was not there long—only long enough to shower, change into his business suit, take up his briefcase and depart again, leaving Diana alone and feeling dislocated and bereft in their suite.

Her head was all in pieces. The abrupt change was jarring. From the emptiness of the desert—the absolute privacy of their time there and all that that had brought—back now into the modern world, busy and crowded, demanding and bustling.

Here, time existed. Other people existed. Other priorities. Other realities.

Realities that now forced themselves upon her.

She did not want to face them—but she must.

Restlessly she paced about, netted by tension. There was a deep disquiet within her. A deep, fearful unease.

Danger was lapping at her feet...

CHAPTER EIGHT

NIKOS THREW HIMSELF into the back of his car, his face set. That meeting had *not* gone well. The damned internal politics of the sheikdom were raising their heads again. Sheikh Kamal's cousin, Prince Farouk, who was against *all* development, was leaning on the minister to block him, Nikos, favoured as he was by Sheikh Kamal. So, although the minister had been urbane, he had also been regretful. And adamant.

There would be problems. Difficulties. Delays. It was unfortunate, but there it was.

He gave a frustrated sigh. Sheikh Kamal, shrewd and far-seeing, would, he knew, outmanoeuvre his cousin in the long term, and until then he would have to exercise patience—though it went against the grain to do so. All his life he'd targeted what he wanted, gone after it and achieved it. Wealth, a trophy mistress, and now a trophy wife.

Immediately his mood improved. After all, there was an upside to this delay in his business affairs here. It would give him more time with Diana…

He felt himself start to relax and his body thrummed with anticipation. She would be waiting for him in their suite, no longer the ice maiden but the warm, ardent, passionate woman of his desires, fully awakened by *him*, as by no other man, to the rich glory of her sensuality.

A sensuality that had swept him away.

Oh, Nadya had been a passionate woman—fiery and tempestuous—and he'd always chosen women for their passion. But with Diana... His expression changed, became wondering. With Diana it had been more than passion, that incandescent union with her beneath the stars.

He tried to understand it, to comprehend it. Was it because he'd had to wait so long to claim her? Was that the reason that those days with her in the desert had been so...so *special*? So different from any other days he'd known? Was it because she'd been that untouchable ice maiden, yielding to him only after so long a wait? An ice maiden only he could thaw, who only melted in *his* arms, no other man's?

A frown drew his brows together as he tried to work it out. Work out why it was that those nights he'd spent with her had been so overwhelming.

Because it wasn't just passion or desire—that was why. There was more than that. Oh, yes, there was a sense of triumph that she'd finally yielded to him and his patience had been so lavishly rewarded. But still there was more than that.

It was the sense of companionship they'd shared. Whether it had been watching the stars, knowing she was as beguiled by their majesty as he was—something that Nadya would have found incomprehensible and irrelevant—or laughing as they'd swayed on those poor camels, bearing the load of riders who were rookies, or leaning back into each other's arms as they lounged on the divans by the poolside, under an awning out in the desert heat.

And talking—always talking. Sometimes about world affairs, sometimes just about anything or nothing. Stimulating and energising, or easy and uncomplicated—they could segue from one to the other effortlessly, seamlessly.

I like her company—I enjoy being with her—whether she is in my arms or just spending time with me.

Was it really that simple? If it was, then there was something else, too. Something basic, fundamental—something he'd never thought about before.

She is happy to be with me. She likes my company... enjoys being with me. As I enjoy being with her—for her company, for just being together...

That seemed an odd thing to think, in many ways, because it wasn't something he'd ever considered before when it came to women. It made him realise that the time he'd spent with Nadya, with all of her predecessors had been entirely superficial. It had been about sex—nothing more than that. Nadya had been specifically chosen to be a trophy mistress—showing the world he could have so lauded and beautiful a woman in his bed, on his arm.

Memory flickered in him. He'd thought of Diana as the next step on from that. Did he still think of her that way? Merely as a trophy wife? Or could the woman he'd made his own beneath the desert stars mean something more to him?

Maybe I'll never get bored with her! Maybe I'll never tire of her?

The thought hovered in his mind. It was something that he'd never felt about any woman before and he did not know the answer—not yet. For now all he wanted was what he had had in the desert—Diana in his arms, clinging to him in ecstasy.

Arriving at the hotel, he strode across the vast atrium, hastening up to the honeymoon suite. To Diana—warm and ardent with all the passion he had awakened in her, all the desire he had released in her.

My bride. My wife!

Emotion washed through him—strange and unfamiliar. It was desire for her, yes—strong and powerful—but more than that too. He didn't know what, but it was there, just as strong, just as powerful. He wondered at it, for he did not recognise it, had no experience of it.

Then the elevator doors were opening, and with eager steps he strode along the plush corridor to reach their suite, swiping the key card and going in.

She was there, by the window of the balcony, a coffee tray set out on the dining table in the embrasure where she sat with her tablet, studying the screen. She looked up with a startled expression as he walked in, carelessly tossing aside his briefcase.

'Oh!' she exclaimed.

For a moment there was a panicked look on her face, but Nikos didn't register it. He walked up to her, loosening his tie as he did so, as if it were constricting him.

'Thank God that's over,' he said feelingly. 'That damned meeting!'

Diana looked at him, alarmed. 'It didn't go well?'

Was there strain in her voice? He hardly knew. Instead he answered directly.

'A set-up by Sheikh Kamal's rival for power,' he expostulated. 'I'm being blocked—and it's because of an internal power struggle in the royal family.'

'Oh, I'm sorry...' Diana's voice was concerned, but distracted.

He shook his head. 'Well, it's not that bad. Things will come about. I put my money on Kamal—he's a smart guy and won't be outmanoeuvred. But I'll have to hold fire for a while.' His expression changed. 'In a way,' he said, and there was a glint in his eye now, 'it has its advantages. Gives me more free time while we're here. We can enjoy ourselves all the more. Starting...' there was a growl in his voice '...right now.'

He drew her upright, made to slide her into his arms, into his waiting embrace. It was good, *so* good to have her here for him. So good to feel her slender body, so pliant, so beautiful, to see her upturned face, her mouth waiting for the kisses which she had come to yearn for in their desert idyll, returning them as ardently as he bestowed them. Diana, his beautiful, exquisite Diana—*his*, all his, completely, all-consumingly.

'I've been aching for you,' he said, his voice a low, husky growl, his eyes alight with sensual desire. 'Aching…'

His mouth lowered to hers, his arms around her tightening. But there was something wrong—something different. She was tensing her body, straining back from him.

'Nikos—'

There was something wrong in her voice, too.

He drew back a moment, loosening his clasp but not relinquishing her. 'What is it?' he said. Concern was in his voice, in the searching frown of his eyes.

She slipped her hands from her sides to rest them against his shoulders—to brace herself against them. Hold herself away.

'Nikos—we…we can't!'

His frown deepened, as did his expression of concern. 'What is it?' he asked again. 'What is wrong?'

She did not answer, then carefully she drew away from him. He let her go and she walked to the far side of the dining table, as if to put it between them.

'We need to talk.'

He stared at her. There was distress in her voice, in her face—her eyes.

His brows drew together in a frown. 'What is it?' he said, and now his voice was different too. Edged.

She took a breath. Cowardice bit within her. And temptation. Sweeping, overpowering temptation! The temptation not to say what she was steeling herself to say. To keep silent. To hold out her arms to Nikos and let him sweep her against him. To carry her through to that preposterous bridal bed smothered in rose petals and take her to the place they had found in each other's arms, each other's ecstasy.

But if she did…

Emotion devoured like the jaws of a wolf. If she succumbed, as she so longed to succumb, then what she had tried to keep at bay out in the desert, what she had denied, refused, would happen.

And I cannot let it happen. I dare not!

All her life she had kept intimacy at bay, kept herself safe from what she had seen destroy her father. The hurt he'd suffered that she dared not risk for herself! So now she must say what she must say. Do what she must do.

Nikos's voice was cutting across her anguished thoughts.

'Diana—speak to me. What is it?'

There was steel in Nikos's voice now. He wanted answers, explanations. Something was going wrong, and he wanted to know what it was. *Why* it was. So that he could fix it. Whatever it was, he could fix it.

Her breath caught—then she forced herself into words. Words she had to say. *Had* to…

'Nikos—what happened in the desert…it shouldn't have happened!'

Disbelief flashed across his face. 'How can you say that?'

His voice was hollow. As if the breath had been punched from his body by a blow that had landed out of nowhere. His mind was reeling, unable to comprehend what she had just thrown at him. It made no sense. *No sense.* How could she possibly be saying what she had just said?

'And how can you *not* see that?' she cried in response. 'It's not what our marriage is about! It never was—it was never anything more than…than convenience! A marriage that would suit us both, provide us both with something that was important to each of us—restoring Greymont for me, an *entrée* into my world for you! And then we'd go our separate ways! You *said* that, Nikos— you said it yourself to me. It was what you proposed!'

She took another ragged breath.

'And that's what I agreed to. *All* I agreed to.'

He was staring at her. Every line in his face frozen. Disbelieving.

'Are you telling me,' he said slowly, 'that you actually believe our marriage should be *celibate*?'

Now it was Diana looking at him as if he were insane. Her eyes flared. 'Of *course*!' she said. 'That's what we signed up to. Right from the start.'

An oath sprang from him. 'I don't believe I'm hearing this!' he said.

His voice was still hollow, but there was an edge to it that made her blench.

He took a heaving breath. Lifted his hands. 'Diana, how can you possibly have thought our marriage should be celibate? When did I *ever* give you cause to think so?'

Consternation filled her features. 'Well, of course I thought you thought that! You gave me every reason to believe so. Nikos, you never laid a finger on me in all the time of our engagement. Nor when we first arrived here!'

He ran his hand agitatedly through his hair. He still could not believe what he was hearing. It was impossible—just impossible—that she should have thought what she *said* she'd thought. Impossible!

'I was giving you *time*, Diana. Time to get to know me,

to get used to me. Of *course* I wasn't going to be crass enough to pounce on you the moment we'd signed the marriage register. I wanted the time to be right for us.'

He made no reference to ice maidens—what help would that have been? She probably hadn't even been aware that she *was* one—that she'd radiated *Look but don't touch* as if it had beamed from her in high frequency.

The very fact that she was talking now, in this insane way, of celibacy—dear God, when they were *married*, when they'd just returned from that burning consummation under the desert stars—was proof of how totally unaware she was of how unaroused, how frozen she had been. It was a state she'd thought was normal.

His mind worked rapidly. Was that why she was being like this now? Was this just panic—a kind of delayed 'morning after the night before' reaction as she surfaced back in the real world, away from the desert idyll that had so beguiled her—beguiled them both? That must be it—it was the only explanation.

His mood steadied and he forced himself to stay calm. Reasonable. He took a breath, lowering his voice, making it sound as it needed to now. Reassuring.

'And we *have* come to know each other, haven't we, Diana?' he went on now, in that reassuring tone. 'We've got used to one another now that we've finally had time to be with each other, now we're married—and we've found each other agreeable, haven't we? We get on well.'

His expression changed without him being aware of it. It was vital that she understood what he was saying now.

'Maybe if we hadn't had that invitation from the Sheikh to stay at his desert palace it might have taken longer for our relationship to deepen. To reach the conclusion that it has. A conclusion, Diana, that has *always* been inevitable.'

He took a step towards her, unconscious of his action, only of his need to close the distance between them. To make everything all right between them again. The way it had been in the desert.

His voice was husky. He had to tell her. He had to make things clear to her, cut through the confusion that must be in her, the panic, even, which was the only way he could account for what she was saying.

'It's always been there, Diana, right from the start. That flame between us. Oh, it was hardly visible at first—I know that—but I know, too, that you were not indifferent to me, however much you might have been unaware of it at a conscious level. And, Diana...' his voice dropped '...believe me, I was the very opposite of indifferent to you from the very moment I first saw you. But it took the desert, Diana, to let that invisible flame that has always run between us flare into the incandescent fire that took us both.'

He strode around the table. Clasped his hands around her shoulders. Gazed down into her face. Her taut and stricken face. He ached to kiss her, to sweep her up into his arms and soothe the panic from her, to melt it away in the fire of his desire—of *her* desire.

'We can't deny what's happened, and nor should we. *Why* should we? We're man and wife—what better way to seal that than by yielding to our passion for each other? The passion you feel as strongly as I do. As powerfully. As irresistibly.'

His voice was low, his mouth descending to hers. He saw her eyelids flutter, saw a look almost of despair in them, but he made himself oblivious to it. Oblivious to everything except the soft exquisite velvet of her lips.

He drew her to him, sliding his hand around her nape, cradling the shape of her head, holding her for his kiss—

a kiss that was long and languorous, sensual and seductive. He felt the relief of having her in his arms again, of making everything all right. It was a kiss to melt away her panic, her fears. To soothe her back into his embrace.

He heard the low moan in her throat that betokened, as he now knew, the onset of her own arousal—an arousal he knew well how to draw from her, to enhance with every skilled and silken touch. His hand slid from her shoulder to close his over her breast, which ripened at his touch, the coral peak straining beneath his gentle, sensuous kneading. He groaned low in his chest, feeling his own arousal surge. Desire soared in him—and victory. Victory over her fears, her anxieties. He was melting the ice that was seeking to freeze her again, to take her from him. To lock her back into a snow-cold body, unfeeling, insensate.

He would never let her be imprisoned in that icy fastness again! In his arms he would melt away the last of her fears. The ice maiden was never to return.

He heard again that low moan in her throat and he deepened his kiss, drawing her hips against him, letting her know how much he desired her and how much *she* desired him.

The low moan came again—and then, as her head suddenly rolled back, it became a cry. Her face was convulsing.

'Nikos! *No!*'

He let her go instantly. How could he hold her when she had denied him?

She was backing away, stumbling against the edge of the mahogany table, warding him off with her hand. Her face was working…she was trying to get control of her emotions. Emotions that were searing through her like sheet metal, glowing white-hot. Emotions she had to quench now—right now.

*He talks of a flame between us as if that makes it better—
it doesn't! It makes it worse—much, much worse! It makes
it terrifyingly dangerous! Just as I've feared all my life!*

So whatever it took, however much strength she had
to find—desperately, urgently—she had to keep him at
bay. *Had* to!

'I don't want this,' she said. Her voice was thin, almost
breaking, but she must not let it break. 'I don't want this,'
she said again. 'What happened in the desert was a…a
mistake. A *mistake*,' she said bleakly.

There was silence—complete silence. She took another razoring breath, then spoke again, her voice hollow. Forcing herself to say what she *had* to say.

'Nikos, if I had thought…realised for one moment that
you intended our marriage to be anything but a marriage
in name only, that you intended it to be consummated, I
would never have agreed to marry you.'

Her jaw was aching, the tension in her body unbearable, but speak she must. She had to make it crystal-
clear to him.

'It wasn't why I married you.'

She forced herself to hold his gaze. There was something wrong with his face, but she could not say what.
Could do nothing but feel the emotions within her twisting and tightening into vicious coils, crushing the breath
from her.

The silence stretched, pushing them apart, repelling
them from each other.

As they must be.

There was incomprehension in his eyes. More than
that. Something dark she did not want to see there that
chilled her to the bone.

Then he was speaking. The thing that was wrong in
his face, in his eyes, was wrong in his voice, too. It had

taken on a vicious edge of sarcasm that cut into her with a whip-like lash.

'I thank you for your enlightening clarification about our marriage,' he said, and coldness iced inside him. 'In light of which it would therefore be best if you returned to the UK immediately. Tonight. I will make the arrangements straight away.'

He turned, and with a smothered cry she made to step after him.

'Nikos! Please—don't be like that. There's no need for me to leave. We can just be as we were before...'

Her voice trailed off. The words mocked her with the impossibility of what she was saying.

We can never be as we were before.

His face had closed. Shutting her out as if an iron gate had slammed down across it.

'There is no purpose in further exchange. Go and pack.'

He was walking away, picking up the house phone on the sideboard, uttering the brief words necessary to set in motion her departure.

'I have work to do,' he said.

His voice was as curt as it had been to the person at the front desk. He walked over to where he'd tossed his briefcase, picked it up. Walked into the spare bedroom.

She heard the door snap shut.

Then there was silence.

Silence all around her.

CHAPTER NINE

BLACK, COLD ANGER filled Nikos. Like dark ink, it filled his veins, his vision. His gaze, just as dark, was fixed on the blackening cloudscape beyond the unscreened porthole of the first-class cabin of the jet, speeding into the night as far and as fast as it could take him.

Australia would do—the other side of the world from Diana.

Diana whom he had made his wife in good faith. Concealing nothing from her, having no hidden agenda.

Unlike his bride. His oh-so-beautiful ice maiden, his look-but-don't-touch bride, who'd never intended, even from the start, to make their marriage work.

Over and over in his head, like a rat in a trap, he heard that last exchange with her. Telling him what she thought of him. What she wanted of him.

What she did not want.

Not him—no, never that.

'It wasn't why I married you.'

Her words—so stark, so brutally revealing—had told him all. All that she wanted.

Only my money, in order to give her what she wants most in all the world.

His eyes hardened like steel, like obsidian—black and merciless. Merciless against him. Against her.

And what she wants most in all the world is not me.

It was her house—her grand, ancestral home—and the lifestyle that went with it. That was all that was important to her. Not him. *Never* him.

Memory, bitter and acid, washed in his veins, burning and searing his flesh. A memory he could not exorcise from his mind. Driving up to that gracious Normandy chateau bathed in sunlight, so full of hope! Hope that now he was no longer a child, and now he had been told who his parents were by the lawyer who had summoned him to his offices on his eighteenth birthday, he had found the mother who had given him away at birth.

He had been hoping he would discover that there was some explanation for why she had disowned him—something that would unite them, finally, that would see her opening her arms to him in joy and welcome.

His mouth twisted, his face contorting. There had been no joy, no welcome. Only cold refusal, cold rejection. He'd been sent packing.

All I was to her was a threat—a threat to her aristocratic lifestyle. To the lifestyle that came with her title, her grand ancestral home. That was all she wanted. All that was important to her.

The revelation had been brutal.

As brutal as the revelation his wife, his bride, had just inflicted upon him.

He tore his mind away as anger bit again, and beneath the anger he felt another emotion. One he would not name. Would not acknowledge. For to acknowledge it would infect his blood with a poison he would never be able to cleanse it from. Never be free of again.

The jet flew on into the night sky.

Out of the brightness of the day into the dark.

* * *

The taxi from the train station made its slow way along the rutted drive that led up to Greymont. The state of the drive was still on her 'to-do' list like a great deal else—including all the interior décor and furnishing work, conserving curtains and restoring ceilings. But the majority of the essential structural work was nearing completion, and work on the electrics and the plumbing were well underway.

Yet the very thought of them burned like fire on Diana's skin.

How could I have got it so wrong? So disastrously, catastrophically wrong!

The question went round and round in her tired, aching head as she walked into her bedroom, collapsed down upon her bed. It had been going round and round ever since she'd walked out of the hotel and into waiting car waiting to take her to the airport, her suitcase having been packed by the maids, her ticket all arranged.

Nikos had stayed immured in his room, the door locked against her. Refusing to have anything more to do with her. Sending her away.

She'd walked out of the hotel like a zombie, feeling nothing. Nothing until she'd taken her seat on the plane and faced up to what the reality of her marriage was.

Completely and utterly different from what Nikos had thought it would be.

That was what she could not bear. That all along Nikos had assumed their oh-so-mutually convenient marriage was going to include oh-so-mutually convenient sex…

He'd assumed that from the start! Intended it from the start!

And she'd blinded herself to it. Wilfully, deliberately,

not wanting to admit that right from that very first moment she'd seen him looking at her it had been with desire.

I told myself he was just assessing me, deciding whether I would fit the bill for his trophy wife, if had the right connections, the right background—the right ancestral home.

Bitter anger at herself writhed within her. How could she have been such a fool not to have realised what Nikos had assumed would be included in their marriage deal? What he'd taken for granted would be included right from the start.

But it was easy to see why. Because she'd wanted to believe that her only role in his life would be to give him an entrée into her upper-class world. Because that had meant she would be able to yield to the desperate temptation that he'd offered her—the means of saving Greymont.

It meant I could take his money and get what I wanted. Easily and painlessly. Safely.

Without any danger to herself.

A smothered cry came from her and she forced her fist into her mouth to keep it from happening again.

Danger? She had wanted to avoid danger—the danger she'd felt from that very first moment of realising that of all the men she had ever encountered it was Nikos Tramontes who possessed the power she had feared all her life.

I walked right into the lion's den. Blindly and wilfully.

And now she was being eaten alive.

The smothered cry came again.

What have I done? Oh, what have I done?

But she knew—had known it the moment she'd surfaced on that rooftop, in the arms of the man she should never have yielded to. She had committed the greatest and most dangerous folly of her life.

Into her head that old saying came: *Take what you want, says God. Take it and pay for it.*

Her eyes stared out bleakly across her familiar childhood room, where she had learned to fear what she must always fear... Well, now she was starting to pay.

Tears welled in her eyes. Anguish rose in her heart.

Nikos was back in London. He'd spent three weeks in Australia, returning to Europe via Shanghai, and then spent another week in Zurich. He had, he thought grimly, been putting off going to London. But he could not put it off for ever.

When he arrived at his house in Knightsbridge his expression darkened. He'd imagined bringing Diana here after their honeymoon, carrying her over the threshold, taking her to bed...

Well, that would not happen now. Would never happen. The black, dark anger that he was now so familiar with, that seemed always to be there now when he thought of her—which was all the time—swilled in his veins. His mouth set in a hard line.

He reached for his phone. Dialled her number. It went to voicemail, and he was glad of it. He did not want to hear her voice.

His message was brief. 'I'm in London. I require you. Be here tomorrow. We have an evening party to go to.'

He disconnected, his expression masked. Diana—his wife, his bride—might have made clear what she thought of him, what she thought of their marriage, but that was of no concern to him right now. She had duties to perform. Duties he was paying her to perform.

However reluctant she might be to do so.

* * *

Diana arrived, as summoned, at the end of the following afternoon. The housekeeper admitted her. Nikos was
still at his London offices, but he arrived shortly afterwards. She had installed herself in a bedroom that was
very obviously *not* the master bedroom. She'd brought
a suitcase with her and was hanging up her clothes—including several evening dresses.

As he walked in she started, and paled.

'Nikos—'

There was constraint in her voice, in her face—in her
very stance. Yet the moment her eyes had lit upon him
she had felt the disastrous, betraying leap of her blood.

He ignored her, walked up to the wardrobe she was
filling with her gowns and leafed through them, extract-
ing one and tossing it on the bed.

'Wear this,' he instructed. 'Be ready to leave in an hour.'

He walked out again.

Behind him, Diana quailed. She had dreaded coming
up to town, dreaded seeing him again, but knew she had to.
Could not evade it. Could not hide at Greymont any longer.

*I have to talk to him—stop him being like this. Try to
make it like it was originally between us—civil, friendly...*

The words mocked her. Agitation and worse, much
worse, churned inside her.

Joining him in the drawing room, changed into the
gown he wanted her to wear, steeling herself, she felt
them mock her again. He was wearing evening dress,
tall and dark and devastating, and as her eyes lit on him
a ravening hunger went through her, blood leaping in her
veins. She almost ran towards him, to throw herself into
his arms, to hold him tight.

Memories exploded in her head of herself in his arms,
he in hers...

She thrust them from her.

I cannot let myself desire him.

Desperately she schooled herself to quench that perilous leaping of her blood, the flood of memories in her head. Too dangerous.

He turned his head at her entry, and for just a second she thought she saw the briefest flaring of his eyes as they alighted on her. Then the light was extinguished. He let his gaze rest on her.

'Very suitable,' he said.

His voice was flat, his face closed. She made herself walk towards him, his chill gaze still upon her, feeling the swish of her silken gown around her legs, the low coil of the chignon at her nape, the cool of her pearl necklace around her throat. On the little finger of her left hand her signet ring glinted in the lamp light—the St Clair family crest outlined. A perpetual reminder of why she had become his wife—to keep the house that went with this armorial crest.

She fancied she saw Nikos's shuttered gaze flicker to it, then away.

'Nikos…' She made herself speak, lifting her chin to give her courage—courage she did not feel, feeling only a hollow space inside her. 'Nikos, we have to talk.'

He cast her a crushing look. 'Do we? Have you yet more to tell me, Diana?'

There was a harshness in his voice she had never heard before. An indifference. Absently he busied himself adjusting his cufflinks, not looking at her.

She swallowed again, her throat tight. 'Look, Nikos, our marriage was a mistake. A misunderstanding. I'm sorry—so very sorry—that I got it so wrong in understanding what you…' She swallowed again. 'What you expected of it.'

She couldn't look him in the eyes. It was impossible. He wasn't saying anything, so she went on. Making herself continue. Say the next thing she had to say.

'I've stopped the work on Greymont.'

She said it in a rush, her eyes flying to him, but he gave no indication that he had heard, only went on inspecting his cuff. If she'd thought she saw a nerve work in his taut cheek she must have been mistaken.

She took another breath.

'I've made a tally of all that has been done so far, and anything I'm contracted for. But everything else has been halted. As for what has already been done—the total sum it amounts to...' She faltered, then made herself go on. 'I will do my best to repay you. It will take time—a lot of time, because if I had been able to raise the capital myself I would have done so. And if I realise all my capital, sell my stocks and shares, I'll lose the income from them that I need for maintenance. That's always been the problem—trying to find money both for the restoration and simply keeping Greymont going. The maintenance costs are high—from local taxes to utilities, to just keeping everything ticking over. The place has to be heated in winter or damp gets in, and rot. And I can't throw the Hudsons out on to the street...'

She was rambling, trying to make him understand. He simply went on not looking at her.

'But I will repay you, Nikos. However long it takes me.'

He looked at her then. Finally spoke. 'Yes, you *will* repay me, Diana, of that I am certain.'

She paled. There was something in his voice that felt like a blow. Her lips were dry, but she made herself speak. Tried to reach him.

'Nikos, I'm sorry! I'm sorry this has gone so wrong. I

blame myself—I was naïve, stupid. I really thought you wanted a marriage in name only—'

'What I *want*, Diana—' his voice cut across hers like a guillotine '—is for you to honour your agreement with me. To make your repayment in the only way you can. The only way I want you to.'

The blood drained from her face and she seemed to sway. He saw it and wanted to laugh. A savage, baiting laugh. Emotions were scything through him, slicing and slicing. She was standing so close. A single step would take him to her. Crush her to him.

But she was beyond him now. Beyond him for ever.

His expression changed. Became mocking. Savagely mocking. Mocking himself.

'It's what you signed up for, Diana. To be—what did you call yourself? Ah, yes. My "society wife". At my side, graceful and poised, beautiful and elegant—the envy of other men, a trophy on my arm, with your impeccable background, your absolute self-assurance in how to conduct yourself, whether in palaces or in stately homes, or anywhere else I take you. Opening a door for me into your upper-class world. And that's what you will do, Diana, my chaste and beautiful bride.'

His face was set, grim now.

'It will be your full-time job. If you've halted restoration work on Greymont, so much the better. It will give you all the time you require to do your work here, at my side. Starting…' he glanced at his watch '…right now.'

He crossed to the door and opened it, pointedly waiting for her to walk through. As she did so she strained away from him, and he saw that she did. Saw that she was as tense as a board, her features taut. He didn't care. Would not care. Would do nothing at all but steer her to the front door.

As he opened it he turned to her. 'I'll brief you in the car about where we are going, who our hosts are and why they are important to me.'

His tone was businesslike, crisp. And as remote as a frozen planet.

She could not look at him. Could only feel a stone forming in her throat, like a canker growing inside her. Melding to her flesh. Choking her.

The house in Regent's Park was lit up like a Christmas tree, but for Diana it was dark and cheerless. She stood, wine glass in hand, her drink untouched and a stiff smile on her face, and forced herself through the ritual of polite chit-chat that the occasion required.

Nikos was standing beside her. Occasionally his arm would brush against hers, and she had to try not to flinch visibly.

He was no longer the person she'd thought she had come to know. He'd become a stranger—a stranger who spoke to her with chilly impersonality, looking at her but not meeting her eyes, withdrawing behind an expressionless mask. She'd had no option but to do likewise and play the part he wanted her to play—Mrs Nikos Tramontes, the oh-so-elegant, oh-so-well-bred, oh-so-well-connected society wife, with her impeccable background and her magnificent stately home—the home her husband's vast wealth had saved for her.

Exactly the marriage she had wanted.

Take what you want...take it and pay for it.

The words mocked her with a cruelty that she had never thought they could possess.

I brought this on myself! I did it to myself! Fool that I am!

A memory as blazing as the desert stars sought entry,

but she held it at bay with all her remaining strength. To remember… No, no, she could not bear it! Could not bear to think of what she should never have permitted herself to have.

It had left her here, now, in this hollow shell of a marriage she should never have made, mocking her with bitter gall. Demanding a price from her that was anguish in every way. And she must go on paying, go on enduring…

Over the weeks that followed—weeks that were spent at Nikos's side, at his direction, on his requirement, she played her part. Performing her social role as Mrs Nikos Tramontes, immaculately dressed whatever the occasion, behaving just as the situation demanded, whether it was luncheon parties at Thames-side mansions, cocktail parties in Mayfair, dinners in top restaurants in London or attending the theatre or opera at Nikos's side. Always she was there, always perfect, always smiling. The perfect wife.

Trapped in a marriage that had become a torment and an agony.

Nikos was angry. He was angry all the time now. With the same dark, cold anger that had possessed him when he'd sent Diana—his beautiful, enticing wife, his beautiful, *untouchable* wife—back to what she loved most of all in her privileged world. Her grand house and the gracious lifestyle that went with it, all that was important to her.

As the weeks passed a kind of pall settled over him. Outwardly he went through the motions of life, but it was only for show. Deadness was filling him. Numbing him. With part of his mind he knew he should let Diana go, that it was achieving nothing but torment keeping her in their impossible marriage, and yet letting her go seemed even worse.

He could not face it.

It wasn't supposed to be like this!

His marriage should have given him everything that he wanted! *Everything.* Diana, his trophy wife, would grant him the place in the world his mother's rejection of him had denied him. Diana, so elegantly beautiful, so perfect a wife, would show him off to the world.

And Diana, his ice maiden, would melt for him and him alone...

And now she had brutally, callously rejected him—refused him.

He felt that perpetual anger bite again. Oh, he had his trophy wife, all right, chained to his side, but it was like dust and ashes in his mouth.

She melted in my arms, burned in my embrace under the desert stars! I thought that it was me that she wanted! How could I not have thought that after what we were to each other those precious days? Those days that seemed to bring us so close together—in body and in even more than that.

Into his head came the memory of what he'd felt that day he'd rushed back to her from that disastrous meeting with the Minister for Development, and the question that had formed in his head of what Diana might be to him...more than he had ever envisaged. What she might yet be to him...

He had not answered the question. But now he knew the answer for the savage mockery that it was.

A silent snarl convulsed in his throat. Fool—arrant fool that he'd been! Fool to think he'd melted her. There was nothing in her to melt—not at the core of her. Nothing at all. At the core of her being was only one thing, the only thing she wanted and the only thing she valued.

And it was not him.

All she wanted was to preserve her precious lifestyle, her grand ancestral home—that was all that was important to her!

It's all she values.

Just as it was all his mother had valued.

Not me.

And his wife—his glitteringly beautiful, icily cold, frozen-to-the-core trophy wife Diana—was the same. The same as the woman who had thrust him from her chateau, ordering him away. Rejecting him.

Just as Diana had.

That was the truth slamming into him day after punishing day. It burned in him like acid in his throat, in his guts. Eating him alive.

He could feel it now, biting invisibly as it always did, by day and by night, as he stood, an untouched glass of champagne in his hand, at this reception at the headquarters of a French investment bank in Paris by whom he was being wooed as a prospective client.

The valuable business he might potentially bring guaranteed that he had the full attention of one of the top directors, but as they talked about business opportunities his mind had scarcely been on the conversation.

He tore his thoughts away. Forced himself to focus on what the director was saying to him.

With a flicker in his eyeline he became aware of someone else coming up to them. A man older than himself by a few years, obviously French, and… Nikos felt his eyes narrow suddenly. He looked vaguely familiar. Did he know him?

The man came up to him, politely but pointedly waiting while the bank's director finished speaking. Then he interjected.

'Monsieur Tramontes, I wonder if I might have a word with you?'

He must be someone notable, for immediately the bank director made a murmuring conclusion and took his leave.

Nikos turned his attention to the man who had addressed him, trying to place him. 'Have we met?' he asked, with an enquiring look and a slight civil smile.

The man did not smile in return. 'No,' he said with a shake of his head.

Nikos frowned. 'Forgive me, you seem familiar…'

The man nodded, acknowledging the comment. He reached inside his jacket pocket, took out a silver card case and extracted a card. He proffered it to Nikos.

'This may account for it,' he said.

Nikos took the card, glanced down at it.

And froze.

All thoughts of Diana, his cold, frozen trophy wife, vanished.

CHAPTER TEN

DIANA WAS IN the rose garden, cutting blooms. Summer sun slanted through the trees that sheltered Greymont from the world beyond, birdsong twittered overhead, and a woodpigeon pecked hopefully nearby. Warmth enveloped her—and peace.

But not in her heart. Not in her soul. Only torment filled her.

How long can I bear this?

Two years, Nikos had told her, holding her to the damning contract she had made—made when she had not known the price she would have to pay, when she had not realised the danger in which she stood, deluding herself, never dreaming she would not be able to bear to pay, but must. Two endless years to endure this hideous, bitter existence. Chained to a husband she had once thought a gift from heaven, who was now keeping her in this hell.

Her only respite was the time she could spend here, at Greymont, when Nikos went abroad and did not want her at his side. Then and only then was she allowed to flee back here, take consolation in the refuge it offered her.

The irony was biting—it was *because* of Greymont that she was trapped in her tormented mockery of a marriage to Nikos. A marriage she could not escape for it was the price she was paying to keep Greymont, to keep it safe.

And safe it was. That was her only comfort. Yes, she had halted all the repairs, but the most critical work had already been completed. The structure of the house was secure, and that was her greatest relief. As for the rest of it—well, she could not even think that far...not yet, not now. Perhaps in the distant future, when she had finally freed herself from Nikos, she would be free...

Free?

The word mocked her, sliding a knife into her flesh.

She could never be free of him.

It was too late.

With a smothered cry she went on cutting, placing the scented blooms—their petals so perfect, so fragrant, so beautiful—into the willow basket at her feet, then, sufficient gathered, she headed indoors. She would arrange them for the drawing room, a task she always found solace in.

But as she left the rose garden and glanced down the long driveway curving far away along the rising ground towards the distant lodge gates she paused, frowning. Two cars were heading along the drive. She could just make them out through the lime trees bordering the avenue. Both cars were long and black, with tinted windows.

Who on earth...? She wasn't expecting anyone.

She made her way indoors, through the garden room door, hastily depositing the blooms in water but not pausing to arrange them. Then she washed her hands and went out into the hallway to open the front door, not troubling to call for Hudson to do so.

She stepped out on to the wide porch. As she did so the two cars drew up in front of the house and immediately the one behind disgorged a handful of dark-suited men, looking extremely businesslike. A moment of fear struck Diana, then astonishment. One of them came up to her, and as he spoke she realised they were all of Middle Eastern appearance.

'Mrs Tramontes?'

She nodded, and then, with another ripple of astonishment, saw that one of the men was opening the passenger door of the first car, and someone was emerging. A woman who was sailing up to her, imperiously dismissing the dark-suited men who backed away dutifully, still scanning the environment as if sharpshooters might be lurking on her roof.

A gasp escaped Diana—she could not help it. 'Your Highness!' she heard herself exclaim, with open astonishment and incredulity in her voice.

'My dear Mrs Tramontes!'

Princess Fatima greeted Diana warmly. Then she turned to another woman, who had now emerged from the huge dark-windowed car, saying something to her in rapid Arabic. The other woman—chaperon, maid, lady-in-waiting? Diana wondered wildly—glided up to the front door, pressed it open, and then stood aside to admit the Princess.

Helplessly Diana followed suit, wondering what the bodyguards—as she now realised these men must be—would do. Her attention was all on the Princess, who was now addressing her again.

'I hope you will not mind my unexpected arrival, my dear Mrs Tramontes,' Princess Fatima was saying, 'but I could not resist paying you an afternoon call!'

Diana gathered her manners. Seeing the Princess again was overwhelming—releasing a storm of memories and emotions. With an effort she made herself say what had to be said, while inside her head everything seemed to be falling into a million pieces.

'I'm honoured and delighted, Your Highness,' she said mechanically, forcing a welcoming smile to her lips. Then she shook her head. 'But, alas, I am quite unprepared—you will find my hospitality very poor.'

The Princess waved an airy hand, dismissing her apology. 'The fault is mine for not giving you notice,' she said.

She was looking around, gazing up at the marble staircase, the walls lined with paintings, the cavernous hall fireplace.

'Your house is as beautiful as you told me it was,' she said, her voice warm. 'I am eager to see it all.'

'Of course, Your Highness,' Diana assented faintly.

'But first, would it be too much to hope that I might partake of afternoon tea with you?'

Immediately calling on all her training to behave impeccably, whatever tumult was inside her, Diana assured her it would not be too much to hope at all, and ushered the Princess into the drawing room. Hudson was hovering in the doorway and Diana instructed that tea must to be served by Mrs Hudson, and, please, she was to bake fresh scones.

Back in the drawing room, Princess Fatima was settling down on a sofa. The other woman was standing by the windows looking out, almost as if on guard.

The Princess turned to Diana. 'How very good it is to be here,' she said warmly. 'Please do be seated,' she invited.

Diana sat down on the sofa opposite, her limbs nerveless, and Princess Fatima launched into an enthusiastic panegyric of the charms of Greymont, then graciously accepted the arrival of Mrs Hudson with the tea tray.

'Ah, scones. Delicious!' she exclaimed enthusiastically, and Diana murmured her thanks to the housekeeper for having baked them in record time.

The Princess ate as enthusiastically as she praised, chattering all the while—to Diana's abject relief, for she felt utterly unequal to conversing. She told Diana about the progress being made on the English country house that her brother the Sheikh had bought for her, and expressed absolute delight in the gift Diana had made to her of a historic costume—a mid-eighteenth-century heavily embroidered silk gown with wide panniers—that she planned to display in her private sitting room.

As she expressed her delight shadows fleeted across the polite expression on Diana's face. Memory as vivid as poison stung through her, of she and Nikos discussing what gift she should make the Princess as they returned from the royal palace.

Pain twisted inside her. It was hard, brutally hard to see the Princess again, to be reminded with bitter acid in her veins of the wedding gift she and Nikos had been given. The gift of the Sheikh's desert love-nest.

More memory seared inside her—unbearable yet indelible.

Had the Princess caught that fleeting shadow? All Diana knew was that as they finished their repast the Princess gave a brief instruction to the veiled woman—servant, lady-in-waiting, chaperone, female bodyguard?—and the woman bowed and left the room.

Only then did the Princess turn to Diana and, in a voice quite different from her gay chatter, asked, 'My dear, what is wrong?'

Diana tensed. 'Wrong, Your Highness?' She tried to make her voice equable, as it had been during their social chit-chat just now.

But Princess Fatima held up an imperious hand, her rings and bracelets flashing in the afternoon sunlight. 'There is a sadness in your face that should not be there. It was not there when we first met. What has put it there?'

Her dark eyes held Diana's grey ones, would not let them go.

'Tell me,' she said. It was half an invitation—half a command. 'I insist.'

And Diana, to her horror and mortification, burst into tears.

Nikos's expression closed like a stone as he stared down at the gilt-edged card in his hand, read the name on it.

'We have nothing to say to each other,' he bit out.

He made to walk away, but his arm was caught.

'But *I* have much to say to *you*!' the other man said.

There was hauteur in his voice, but there was something else as well. Something that made Nikos stop.

The man's eyes—almost as dark as Nikos's, and as long-lashed—bored into his. Refusing to let Nikos go. The next words the man spoke turned him to stone.

'Our mother wishes to see you—'

Instantly Nikos's face contorted. 'I have no mother.' The savagery in his voice was bitter.

Emotion flashed in the other man's eyes. This man who was his half-brother—son of the woman who had given birth to Nikos, a bastard child, unwanted and unacknowledged, thrust away from her unloving arms, given away to foster parents, spurned and discarded.

The other man was implacable. 'That may soon be truer than you know,' he said, his voice grim. He took a breath, addressed Nikos squarely. 'She is about to have an operation that is extremely risky. She may well not survive. For that reason…' Something changed in his voice—something that Nikos recognised but would not acknowledge. 'For that reason I have agreed to seek you out. Bring you to her.'

Nikos's expression twisted. 'Are you *insane*?' he said, his voice low, enraged. 'She threw me out when I tried to see her. Refused to accept me. Refused even to admit that she *was* my mother!'

Pain flashed across the other man's face. His own half-brother. A stranger. Nothing more than that.

'There are things I must tell you,' he said to Nikos. 'Must make clear to you. Mostly they concern my father.' He paused. 'My *late* father.'

Dimly Nikos's mind clicked into action. The card that this man—this unknown half-brother—had given him.

He lifted it to glance at it again. Read what it said in silvered sloping engraved script.

Le Comte du Plassis

He frowned. But if this man was the Count—?

'My father is dead,' his half-brother told him. 'He died three months ago. And that is why…' He paused, looked at Nikos. 'That is why everything has changed. Why there are things I need to tell you. Explain.' He took a breath. 'Where can we talk in private?'

He took another breath—a difficult one, Nikos could tell.

'It is essential that we do so.'

For a long, timeless moment Nikos looked at him. Met the dark eyes that were so familiar in the face that was as familiar as his own. Slowly, grimly, he gave his assent.

Inside his chest his lungs were tight, as if bound in iron bars.

* * *

Diana was still sobbing. She was appalled at herself, but could not stop. The Princess had crossed from her sofa to plump herself down beside her, pick up her hands and press them.

'Oh, my dear friend—what is wrong?' She patted Diana's hands, her dark eyes huge with sympathy and concern.

Helpless to stop herself, Diana let all her anguish pour out in a storm of weeping. Gradually it abated, leaving her drained, and she reached for a box of tissues from a magazine holder by the fireplace, mopped at her face mumbling apologies.

'I'm sorry. *So* sorry!' Dear God, how could she have burst into tears like that in front of the Princess? Was she insane to have done such a thing?

But Princess Fatima did not seem either offended or bemused. Only intensely sympathetic. She leant back, indicating that Diana must do the same. Then poured her a new cup of tea with her own royal hands and offered it to Diana, who took it shakily.

'You must tell me everything,' the Princess instructed. 'What has gone wrong between you and your handsome husband? No, don't tell me it hasn't. For I will not believe you. No new wife weeps for any other reason.'

Yet still Diana could not speak. Could only gulp at her tea, then set it down again with still shaky hands. She stared at her royal guest with a blank, exhausted stare.

The Princess took a delicate sip of her own tea and replaced the cup with graceful ease on the table. Then she spoke, slowly and carefully, looking directly at Diana, holding her smeared gaze.

'Here in the west,' she began, her tone measured, but meaningful, 'I am well aware that it is the custom for marriages to be based on emotion. Love, as you would call it. It is the fashion, and it is the expectation. But for all that it is not always the case, is it?'

Her eyes were holding Diana's fixedly.

'You will forgive me for speaking in a way that you Europeans with your propensity for democracy might find old-fashioned, but for those who are born into responsibilities greater than the acquisition of their own happiness such a custom may not always be appropriate.'

She smiled, exchanging another speaking glance with her hostess.

'Perhaps we are not so unalike, you and I? At some point I must make a marriage for reasons greater than my own personal concerns—and perhaps that is something that you yourself can understand? Something you have also done?'

She patted Diana's hand again, holding her gaze questioningly as she did so.

'I teased you when you visited me,' she reminded Diana, 'about having so handsome a husband that surely he must be the most important aspect of your life—more important than anything else. But perhaps...' She paused, then went on, glancing around her. 'Perhaps that is not so? You gave me reason to suppose that when you answered me...'

Diana's eyes dropped and she stared into her lap. Spoke dully as she replied. With heaviness in her voice.

'I thought I was saving my house...my home. It is dearer to me than anything in the world. I thought—' she gave a little choke '—I thought I would do anything to save it.'

She lifted her eyes, met those of the Princess who, perhaps alone of anyone she knew, would understand.

'Even marry for it.' She took a breath, felt it as tight

as wire around her throat. 'So that's what I did. I married to save my house, my home, my inheritance. To honour what my father had done for me.'

She gave the Princess a sad, painful smile.

'My mother left my father when I was a child, but he chose never to remarry. It was for *my* sake. You will not need me to tell you that in England it is the tradition for sons to inherit family estates, not daughters—unless there is no son. My father knew how much I loved Greymont, how important it had become to me. It gave me the sense of security, of continuity, I so desperately needed after my mother abandoned and rejected me. So he gave up his chance of happiness to ensure mine.'

She sighed.

'When he died, and I found I needed so much money to honour his sacrifice for me, I made the decision to marry money. Forgive me,' she said tightly, 'for such vulgar talk—but without money Greymont would eventually decay into a ruin. You know that, Your Highness, from your own house that you are saving.'

The Princess nodded. 'So you married the handsome man who just happened to have the wealth that you required for this?' She gestured all around her. She paused, then, 'It does not sound so absurd a decision. It was a marriage that made sense, no? Your husband ensured the future of your home and you, my dear Mrs Tramontes, provided the beauty that any husband must treasure!' She paused again, her eyes enquiring. 'So, what is it that has gone so very wrong?'

She searched Diana's face.

Diana, filled with misery, crumpled the sodden tissue in her hands, meshing her fingers restlessly.

'I thought… I thought he married me out of self-interest. Just as I had married him! Because we were *useful* to each other. I—I thought,' she said, her voice faltering, 'that was the only reason and that it would be enough. But then—' She broke off, gave a cry. 'Oh, Your Highness,' she said in anguish, 'your kindness, your brother's generosity, worked magic that was disastrous for me! Disastrous because—'

She felt silent. Incapable of admitting what had happened out under the scorching desert sun in the *Arabian Nights* fantasy she had indulged in so recklessly. So punishingly stupidly...

The Princess took her writhing hands. Stilled them. 'Tell me,' she said. 'Tell me why it was so disastrous for you.'

There was kindness in her voice, and command as well—but not the command of a princess, but that of a woman, knowing the ways of women. The mistakes they made—mistakes that could ruin lives. Devastate them.

And with a faltering voice, stammering words, Diana told her.

There was silence. Only the sound of birdsong through the open window and the sound, very far off, of a lawn being mowed beyond the rose garden.

'Oh, my poor friend.' The Princess's voice was rich with sympathy, with pity. 'My poor, poor friend.'

The small café was all but deserted. Nikos sat with an untouched beer, his half-brother likewise.

'My father,' said Antoine, 'was not an easy man. He was considerably older than our mother. A difficult, demanding man whom she should never have married. That *no* woman should have married,' he said dryly. 'But there it was—too late. She was his wife. His *comtesse*. And required to behave in a manner he considered appropriate. Which demanded, above all, her producing an heir.'

Antoine's voice was dryer still.

'Myself. And so I duly made my appearance.' His eyes grew shadowed. 'Did my mother love me? Yes—but she was not allowed to spend much time with me. I had nurses, nannies, a governess—eventually a tutor, boarding school. Then university, military academy—the usual drill.'

He shrugged with an appearance of nonchalance.

'In the meantime my mother was lonely. Her life sterile. When she met your father...' his eyes went to Nikos's now, unflinching '...despite his philandering reputation she believed she had met the love of her life. His betrayal of her—his repudiation of any loyalty to her after their affair had resulted in the disaster that was your conception—broke her. And then...'

His voice hardened, with a harshness in it that Nikos recognised—recognised only too well.

'And then my father broke what was left of her.'

Antoine reached for his drink now, took a long swallow, then spoke again. The harshness was still in his voice.

'He made her choose. Choose what she would do with the remainder of her life. She was entirely free, he told her, to fly to Greece that same day—to throw herself at the feet of the philandering seducer who had amused himself with her. Or, indeed, she was entirely free to raise her bastard child as a single parent on her own, anywhere in the world she wanted. But if she did then consequences would follow.'

He looked at Nikos, with dark, long-lashed eyes.

'She would never set eyes on me again and I would be disinherited of everything but the title. My father could not take that from me when the time came, but everything else would be sold on the day of his death. My entire inheritance—the chateau, the ancestral lands, all the property and wealth of our name. I would be landless, penniless.'

Nikos saw his half-brother's hands clench, as if choking the life-force from an unseen victim.

'She would not do it. Would not leave me to the tender mercies of my father…' His voice twisted. 'To grow up knowing that nothing but an empty title would be his legacy to me. Knowing that she had abandoned me.'

A shadow went across his eyes.

'She felt her responsibility was to me rather than you. That you would be better off raised in a foster home, never knowing her. Thought it would give you some form of stability at least, however imperfect.'

Nikos watched him take another deep draught of his beer, feeling emotion swirl deep within him, turbid and muddied, as if sediment that had long sunk to murky depths was being stirred by currents sweeping in from unknown seas.

Antoine was speaking again, his glass set down.

'When you came to see her all those years ago, as a young man, she knew that nothing had changed and nothing *could* change. Oh, I was an adult then myself, of course, and even my father could not have kept me apart from her, but still he held the threat of disinheriting me over her head. She knew you were financially protected— that your biological father had settled a large amount of money on you, to be given to you when you came of age.'

'He can rot in hell too!' Nikos heard his own voice snarl. 'I never took a penny of that money. He'd disowned me from birth!'

For a moment Antoine held his half-brother's gaze. 'We have not had good fathers, have we?' he said quietly. 'But…'

He held up a hand, and in the gesture Nikos saw a thousand years of aristocracy visible in the catching of light on the signet ring on his brother's finger.

'But I do not think that of our mother.' He was silent a moment, then spoke again. 'Come to her, Nikos.'

It was the first time he'd used his half-brother's name.

'She has a serious heart condition. This operation is risky, and requires great skill from a top surgeon. She deferred the operation deliberately for years, waiting for her husband to die. Only now, with my inheritance assured, can she take the risk.' He took a breath that was audibly ragged. 'The risk that she might die before seeking to make what peace she can with you.'

Antoine gave a long sigh.

'You blame her—I can understand that. I too would be bitter. But I hope with all my heart that perhaps you can at some point bring yourself if not to forgive her, to understand her. To accept the love she has for you despite all she did.'

Nikos closed his eyes. He could not speak. Could not answer. Could only feel, deep in that part of him he never touched any longer, where the sediment of bitterness, of anger, had lain for so long, that there could now be only one answer.

His eyes flashed open. Met those of his half-brother.

'Where is she?' he said.

Diana stood at the wide front entrance to Greymont, with the lofty double doors spread to their maximum extent. Dusk was gathering in the grounds and she could hear rooks cawing in the canopy, an early owl further off, and she caught the subliminal whooshing of a bat.

The warmth of the evening lapped around her, but she could not feel it. Her eyes were watching the slow progress of the two-car cavalcade driving away, down towards the lodge gates.

Princess Fatima was leaving.

But not without leaving behind a gift that was price-less to Diana.

A gift she had immediately, instantly demurred over.

'Highness, I cannot! It is impossible. I cannot accept.'

An imperious raised hand had been her answer. 'To refuse would be to offend,' the Princess had said. But then her other hand had touched the back of Diana's. 'Please…' she'd said, her voice soft.

So, with a gratitude she had been able to express only falteringly, Diana had taken the Princess's gift. And now, as she watched her uninvited but oh-so-kind guest take her leave, the same profound gratitude filled her.

The black cars disappeared down the long avenue and Diana went back indoors. Went into the estate room—her office—sat down at the desk and withdrew her cheque-book. With a shaky hand she wrote out the cheque she had longed with all her being to be able to write for so many long, punishing months.

The cheque that would set her free.

Free of the one man in the world she could never be free of.

However much money she repaid him.

Nikos sat in his seat on the jet, curving through the air-space that divided France from England. He stared out over the broken cloudscape beyond the window, his thoughts full. Emotions fuller.

She had been so frail, that woman in the hospital bed. So slender, so petite, it had hardly seemed possible that she had given birth at all—let alone to the two grown sons now standing at the foot of her bed. The son she had chosen over her baby, who had now brought that lost child back to her. And the son who had hated her all his life.

Who could hate her no longer.

Her eyes had filled with tears when they had gone to him. Silent tears that had run down her thin cheeks so that her older son had started forward, only to be held at bay by the veined hand raised to him. Nikos's half-brother had halted, and she had lifted her other hand with difficulty, lifted it entreatingly, towards the son she had abandoned. Rejected.

'I am so sorry.' Her voice had been a husk, a whisper. 'So very, *very* sorry.'

For an endless moment Nikos had stood there. So many years of hating. Despising. Cursing. Then slowly he had walked to the side of her bed, reached down, and for the first time in his life—the first time since his body had become separate from hers at his birth—he'd touched her.

He had taken her hand. For a second it had lain lifeless in his. And then, with a convulsion that had seemed to go through her whole frail body, she had clasped his fingers, clutching at him with a desperation that had spoken to him more clearly than words could ever do.

Carefully, he had lowered himself to the chair at her side, cradled her hand with both of his, pressing it between them. Emotion had moved within him, powerful, inchoate. Impossible to bear.

'Thank you.'

The voice had been weak and the eyes had flickered—dark, long-lashed, sunken in a face where lines of illness had been only too visible—moving between them both.

'Thank you. My sons. My beloved sons.'

She'd broken off, and Nikos had felt a tightening in his throat that had seemed like a garrotte around his neck.

Antoine had come forward on jerky legs, sitting himself on the other side of the bed, taking her other hand, raising it to his lips to kiss.

'Maman…'

In his brother's voice Nikos had heard an ocean of love. Had felt, for one unbearable instant, an echo of the word inside himself. An echo that had turned into the word itself. An impossible word…an unbearable word. A word he had never spoken in all his life.

But it had come all the same. The very word his brother had spoken.

Maman.

He heard the word again now, sitting back in his seat as the plane banked to head north. He felt again the emotion that had come with that word. Felt again the spike of another emotion that had stabbed at him—at his half-brother, too—as their heads had turned at the entry of a man in theatre scrubs.

'Monsieur,' the cardiologist had said, 'I regret, but it is time for you to leave. Madame la Comtesse is required in surgery.'

Fear had struck him—a dark, primitive fear. A blinding, urgent fear.

A fear that had one cry in it.

Too late.

In his head the cry had come—primitive, urgent.

Let it not be too late! Let me not have found my mother only to lose her to death.

And now, as the powerful twin engines of the private jet raced him back across the Channel, he heard that cry again. Felt that fear again.

But this time it was not about his mother.

Let it not be too late. Dear God, let it not be too late.

Not too late to learn the lesson that finding his mother

had taught him. The lesson that meant he must now take a risk—the essential, imperative risk that was driving him on. Taking him back to England.

To Diana.

But as he opened his laptop, forcing his mind to a distraction it desperately needed, his eyes fell upon the latest round of emails in his inbox, and he realised with a hollowing of his guts that it was, indeed, too late.

The first email was from his lawyers.

His wife was filing for divorce.

And the money he had spent on Greymont—the money that she owed him—had been repaid. Every last penny of it.

CHAPTER ELEVEN

DIANA STARED AT Gerald across his desk. 'What do you mean, he says no?'

Memory thrust into her head of how she had sat here in this very chair, in this very office, after her father's death, refusing to sell her beloved home. Telling Gerald she would find a husband with deep pockets.

Well, she had done that all right. She'd done it and she'd paid for it.

But not with money. She was abjectly grateful that Princess Fatima had insisted on lending her the money—however long it took her to pay it back over the years ahead.

No, she had paid for what she'd wanted with a currency that was costing her far more. That would never be paid off. Try as she might by breaking the legal bonds that bound her to her husband. They were the least of the bonds that tied her to him. That would always tie her to him...

Her lawyer shifted position and looked at her directly. 'I'm afraid he says he has no wish to agree to a divorce.'

Diana's expression changed to one of consternation—and a whole lot more.

Gerald shook his head. 'I did warn you, Diana, about this rash marriage. And as for that disgraceful pre-nup he insisted on—'

She cut across him. 'This has nothing to do with the pre-nup. I don't want a penny from him. Just the opposite. That's why I've paid off the sum of every last invoice he settled, direct to his account. He has no *reason* not to agree to a divorce.' Her mouth set in a tight line. 'He has no grounds for refusing me.'

'Except, my dear Diana,' Gerald said in his habitually infuriating manner, 'the law of the land allows him to do so, irrespective of any grounds you might imagine you have. And you don't have any, do you? He hasn't been unfaithful. He hasn't inflicted any cruelty upon you—'

She blenched. Cruelty? What else had it been, these past nightmare months since he'd insisted on having his pound of flesh from her?

Oh, not in a physical sense—her thoughts shrank away from that; it was forbidden territory and must always remain so—but in requiring her at his side, as the perfect society wife. Beautiful, ornamental, decorative, the envy of all who knew him. The immaculately groomed society wife who could move in any circles he chose to take her, always saying just the right thing, in just the right way, wherever they went.

Outwardly it was a wealthy, gilded life—how could that possibly be considered cruel?

How could anyone have seen how she bled silently, invisibly, day after day, drained of all hope of release in the frozen chill of his obvious anger with her?

Anger because she'd refused to have the kind of marriage that he'd expected, had assumed they would have—taking it for granted that it would be consummated and then refusing to see why it was impossible...*impossible*!

She dared not think *why* such a marriage as Nikos had wanted was so impossible! She must not let in those memories that made a lie of all her insistence that she did not want a marriage such as Nikos had wanted.

She couldn't afford to let those memories surface. Memories that haunted her…memories that were a torment, an agony of loss…of their bodies entwined beneath the burning stars, bringing each other to ecstasy.

Gerald's dry voice sounded in her ears, making her listen. 'Well, Diana, if you have no grounds for divorce then you will simply have to wait until you can divorce him without his agreement. That will take five years.'

She stared aghast, disbelieving. *'Five years?'*

'Unless you can persuade him to consent to end your marriage.'

He shifted position again, leafed through some papers in a fashion that told Diana he was looking for a way to say what he had to say next.

He glanced across his desk at her. 'You may be able to change his mind, Diana,' he said. 'Your husband has indicated that he will discuss the matter with you personally.'

'I don't want to see him!' The cry came from her. 'I couldn't bear to see him again.'

'Then you will have to be prepared to wait five years for the dissolution of your marriage,' he replied implacably.

She closed her eyes again, emotion tumbling through her. To see him again—it would be torment, absolute torment! But if it was the only way to plead with him to end this nightmarish façade of a marriage—

She looked across at her lawyer. 'Where and when does Nikos want to meet me?' she asked dully.

The uniformed chauffeur who was waiting for her at Charles de Gaulle Airport gave no indication of where he was driving her, but she could see it was not into Paris, but westwards into the lush countryside of Normandy. There was no point asking. Nikos had demanded this meeting and she was in no position to refuse—not if she wanted to be free of the crushing chains of her torturous marriage.

Apprehension filled her, and a clawing dread—knowing she must face him, plead with him for her freedom. She could feel her stomach churning, her breathing heavy, as the car drove onwards.

The journey seemed to last for ever, longer than the flight had, and it was past noon before they arrived at their destination, deep in the heart of the countryside.

She frowned as she got out of the car, taking in the turreted Norman château in creamy Caen stone, grand and gracious, flanked by poplar trees and ornamental gardens, and the little river glinting in the sunshine, winding past.

It was a beautiful house, like something out of a fairytale, but she was in no frame of mind to appreciate it. Its beauty only mocked the tension in her, her pinching and snapping nerves. Why was she here? Did Nikos own it? Was he renting it? Simply staying here? It could be a hotel for all she knew.

A man was emerging from the chateau, tall and dark-haired, and for a moment, with a tremor of shock, Diana thought it was Nikos. Then the rush to her bloodstream that had come just with thinking she was seeing Nikos again subsided.

'Welcome to the Chateau du Plassis,' he said. 'I am Antoine du Plassis. Please come inside.'

Numbly she followed him, having murmured something in French, she knew not what. Inside, the interior was cool, and there was an antiquity about the place that was immediately was familiar to her. It was a magnificent country house like Greymont—but in another country.

'Is Nikos here?' Her voice broke the silence as she followed her host.

The tall, dark-haired man, who for that heart-catching moment she had thought was Nikos, glanced back at her.

'Of course,' he said.

He threw open a pair of double doors, standing aside to let her enter first. She saw a beautiful salon, much gilded, and a huge fireplace with the characteristic French chimneypiece. But she took in little of it. Nikos was getting to his feet from his place on a silk-upholstered Louis Quinze sofa, and her eyes went to him with a lurch of her stomach.

He said something in French to her host—something too low, too rapid for Diana to catch—and nor could she catch Antoine's answer.

Her eyes were only for Nikos, and she was wishing with all her heart that her pulse had not leapt on seeing him, that her eyes were not drinking him in like water in a parched desert. He was looking strained, tense, and she found herself wondering at it.

Then, as her eyes went back to her host, Diana's eyes widened disbelievingly.

The Frenchman was slightly less tall than Nikos, less broad in the shoulder, less powerfully made, with features less distinct, less strongly carved, and there was more of a natural Gallic elegance in his manner. His hair was slightly longer than Nikos's, less dark, as were his eyes, but the resemblance was immediate, unmistakable.

Her gaze went from one to the other.

'I don't understand…' Her voice was faint.

It was Nikos who answered. 'Antoine is my half-brother,' he said. 'The Comte du Plassis.'

A faint frown formed between Diana's brows as she tried to make sense of what she did not understand—that Nikos had a half-brother she had not known existed. It was the Count who spoke next, his voice with a similar timbre to Nikos's, but his accent decidedly French, lighter than Nikos's clipped baritone.

'I will leave you to your discussion.'

Antoine gave a little bow of his head and strode from the room. As he closed the double doors behind him the large room suddenly felt very small. A great weariness washed over Diana and she folded herself down in an armchair, overwhelmed by tension, by all the emotions washing through her, swirling up with her being here.

'I don't understand,' she said again.

The three words encompassed more than just the discovery that he had a half-brother. Why had she been summoned here? To what purpose?

She gazed at Nikos. It hurt to see him.

It will always hurt to see him.

That was the truth she could not escape. She could escape their marriage—however long it took her to do so—but it would always hurt to see him. Always hurt to think about him. Always hurt to remember him.

For a moment he was silent, but beneath the mask that was his face a powerful emotion moved. He stood by the fireplace, one hand resting on the mantel, and his gaze targeted Diana.

'I have to talk to you,' he said. He took a ragged breath. 'About things I have never talked about. Because I need you to understand why I have been as I have been towards you these last difficult months. Why I have been so harsh towards you.'

She stared at him, her insides churning. She was here to beg him to end their marriage, beg him to release her from the misery of it all. She did not need to hear anything from him other than agreement to that.

'You don't need to explain, Nikos,' she bit out bleakly. 'It was because I didn't want sex with you. And since you'd assumed right from the off that, contrary to what *I'd* been assuming, sex was going to be on the menu, my refusal didn't go down well.'

There was a brusqueness in her voice, but she didn't care.

Dark fire flashed in his eyes—anger flaring. Her jaw tightened. So he didn't like her spelling it out that bluntly? Well, tough—because it was true, however much it might offend him.

But his hand was slashing through the empty air, repudiating her crude analysis. 'That is *not* why. Or not as you state it like that! Hear me out.' His expression changed suddenly, all the anger gone. Instead, a bleakness that echoed her own filled his face. 'Hear me out, Diana—please.'

His voice was low and his eyes dropped from hers. His shoulders seemed to hunch, and it struck her that she had never seen him like that before. Nikos had always been so sure of himself, so obviously in command of every situation, never at a loss. Self-confident and self-assured. And in the last unbearable months of their marriage he'd steeled into his stony, unrelenting determination to keep her at bay, yet chained inescapably to his side.

Was the change in him now because she had finally broken free of him?

No, far more had shaken him than the repayment of her debt to him, her demand for a divorce. And as she let her gaze rest on him she felt emotion go through her— one that she had never in all her time with him associated with him.

She tried to think when *she* had ever felt such an emotion before, and what it might be. Then, with a shiver, she realised—and remembered.

It was for my father—when my mother left him.

Pity.

Shock jagged through her as she looked across at Nikos, at the visible strain in his face. Was she feeling *sorry* for him? After all his harshness to her?

She couldn't bear to feel pity! Couldn't bear to see such painful emotion in his eyes. Why was it there? There was no need for it—no cause.

He was speaking again and she made herself listen, fighting down the emotion she did not want to feel for him. She was here to end her misery of a marriage, that was all. Nothing he could say or do would alter that.

'It was because, Diana, your reaction after we came back from the desert showed me that I had never realised just what kind of a person you truly are.'

He paused and she felt his gaze pressing on her, like a weight she could not bear.

'A woman like my mother.'

She stared and saw his gaze leave her, sweep around the room.

She frowned—felt confusion in her mind, cutting through her tortured emotions at his accusation. Why was Nikos here, in the home of a half-brother she hadn't known he possessed?

Her confusion deepened as she remembered how Nikos, when he'd proposed their stark marriage of convenience, had told her that he wanted to marry her for her social background, in order to give him an entrée into her upper-class world of landed estates and stately homes.

But he has that already, here with his brother the Comte. So why—?

His sweeping gaze came back to her. Unreadable. Masked. He moved suddenly, restlessly, breaking eye contact with her. Looking instead somewhere else. Into a place she knew nothing about.

His past.

She heard him start to speak. Slowly. As if the words were being dragged from him by pitiless steel-tipped hooks...

'My mother, Comtesse du Plassis. Wife of Antoine's father.' He paused. His eyes were on her now. 'Who was not *my* father.'

He shifted again restlessly, his hand moving on the mantel, lifting away from it now as if he had no right to rest it there.

'The man who fathered *me*,' he said, and Diana could hear a chill in his vioce that made her quail, 'was a Greek shipping magnate—you would know his name if I told you. He was notorious for his affairs with married women. He liked them married, you see.' Something moved in his eyes, something savage, and her chill increased. 'Because it meant that if there were any unfortunate repercussions there would be a handy husband on the scene to sort them out.' He paused again, then, 'As Antoine's father duly did.'

Restlessly he shifted his stance again, his eyes sliding past her.

'I was farmed out when I was born. Handed over to foster parents. They were not unkind to me, merely... uninterested. I was sent to boarding school, and then university here in France. At twenty-one, after I'd graduated, I was summoned to a lawyer in Paris. He told me of my parentage.'

An edge came into his voice, like a blade.

'He told me that my father would settle a substantial

sum on me, providing I signed documents forbidding me from ever seeking him out or claiming his paternity.' The blade in his voice swept like a knife through the air. 'I tore up the cheque and stormed out, wanting nothing from such a man who would disown his own son. Then I drove out here to find my mother—'

He stopped abruptly. Once again his eyes swept the room, but this time Diana could sense in his gaze something that had not been there before. Something that made her feel again what she had felt so unwillingly when he had first started speaking. The shaft of pity.

His face was gaunt, his mouth twisted. 'She sent me away. Saw me to the door. Told me never to come here again—never to contact her again. Then she went back inside. Shutting me out. Not wanting me. Not wanting the child she had cast aside.' He paused. His voice dropped. 'Rejecting me.'

That something moved again in his eyes, more powerfully now, and it hurt Diana to see it. It was that same look her father had had in his eyes when he'd remembered the wife who had not wanted him, who had rejected him.

'I drove away,' Nikos was saying now, piercing her own memories with his, 'vowing never to contact her again, just as she wished, washing my hands of her just as I had my father, as both of them had washed their hands of *me*. I took a new name for myself—my own and no one else's. Cursing both my parents. I was determined to show them I did not need them, that I could get everything they had on my own, without them.'

There was another emotion in his voice now.

'I've proved myself my father's son,' he ground out, his eyes flaring with bitter anger. 'Everything I touch turns to gold—just as it does for him! And, having made as much money as my father, I gained all the expensive baubles that he possesses, the lavish lifestyle that goes with such wealth—and, yes, the celebrity trophy mistress I had in Nadya! But it wasn't enough. I wanted to get for myself what my mother had denied me in her rejection. My place in the world she came from—the world *you* come from, Diana.'

He paused, his eyes resting on her, dark and unreadable.

'By marrying you I would take my place in that world—but I would also obtain something else. Something I wanted the very first moment I saw you.'

He shifted his position restlessly, and then his gaze lanced back to her. And in it now was an expression that was not unreadable at all. It blazed from him openly, nakedly. It made her reel with the force of it.

'I could get *you*, Diana. The woman I've desired from my very first glimpse of you. The woman I thought I had finally made my own—the woman I transformed from frozen ice maiden to warm, passionate bride, melting in my arms, burning in her desire for me!'

His voice changed, expression wiped clean. There was harshness in his voice now—a harshness that had become all too familiar in these last hideous months while she had been chained to his side.

'Only to discover that after all we had together in the desert it meant nothing to you. *Nothing!* That to you all I was good for was supplying the money that would save Greymont for you. That only your precious ancestral home was important to you, your privileged way of life. You did not want me disturbing that with my *inconvenient* desire for you.'

She stared at him. The bitterness in his voice was like gall.

He spoke again. 'Just as my mother valued above all

else her privileged way of life here at this elegant chateau, undisturbed by the *inconvenient* existence of an unwanted bastard son.'

Diana felt her face pale, wanted to cry out, but she couldn't. He was speaking again, his words silencing her.

'All these months, Diana, I have blamed you for being like her. For valuing only what she valued. For rejecting me.' He paused. Drew breath. 'It made me angry that you should turn out to be like her. Valuing only the privileged lifestyle you enjoy.' His mouth twisted. 'Nothing else. No one else.'

She could read bitterness in the stark lines of his face, savage and harsh, but there was something else beneath it. Something that seemed to twist her up inside.

He was speaking again, and now there was a tension in his voice, like wire strung too tight, and his strong features were incised with that same tension.

'And *that* is what I need to know! Was I right to be so angry with you? Right to accuse you of being no better than my mother, who only valued all of this?'

His hand swept around the room, condemning in a single gesture all that it represented. His gaze was skewering her, nailing her where she sat. She saw his mouth twist again.

'Are you the same, Diana? Is Greymont all that you are capable of wanting, valuing? Is Greymont and all that goes with it all you care about?'

His eyes were dark—as dark as pits. Pits into which she was falling.

Her voice was shaking as she answered him. Inside her chest her heart had started to pound, like a hammer raining blows upon her. 'You...you knew I married you to protect Greymont, Nikos. You *knew* that—'

A hand slashed through the air. 'But is that all you

are, Diana? A woman cut from the same cloth as my mother? Caring only for wealth and worldly status and possessions?'

She reeled. Suddenly, like a spectre, she saw her father, shaking his head sorrowfully, looking at her with such desolation in his face she could not bear to see it. Nor to hear his words.

'I wasn't rich enough for her...your mother—'

She felt her insides hollowing as the echo of her father's words rang in her ears.

She stared at Nikos, eyes distended. There was a spike in her lungs, draining the air from her, and his bitter accusation was stinging her to the quick, the echo of her father's words like thorns in her soul.

Words burst from her as she surged to her feet. His words had been blows, buffeting her. In agitation and self-defence she cried out at him.

'Nikos, I'm sorry—*so* sorry!—that your mother hurt you so much! Because I know how that feels. I know it for *myself.*'

She took a hectic breath, feeling her heart pounding inside her, urgently wanting to defend herself—justify herself. Protect herself from what he'd thrown at her.

'When I was ten my mother walked out on my father. And on me!' Her expression changed, memory thrusting her back into that long-ago time that was searing in her heart as if it had only just happened. 'Like your mother, Nikos, she didn't want me. She only wanted the huge riches of the Australian media mogul she took off with. A man twice her age and with a hundred times my father's wealth!'

She could hear the agitation in her own voice, knew why it was there. She saw that Nikos had stilled.

Her gaze shifted, tearing away from him, shifting

around the elegant salon in this beautiful chateau. Shadowing. Taking another breath, she made herself go on. It was too late to stop now.

'She cut all contact. I ceased to exist for her. Was not important to her. So I made her not important to me.'

Her eyes came back to Nikos. He was standing stock-still, his eyes veiled suddenly.

Shock was detonating through him. He had summoned her here to find the truth. The truth he had to discover. The truth on which so much rested. So much more than he had ever dreamt.

Well, now he had the truth he'd sought.

I thought she rejected me because she was like my mother—as I thought my mother to be.

But it was himself. All along it was himself. That was who she was like. Like him she had been abandoned, rejected, as he had felt himself to be, by the one woman who should have cherished her.

A chill swept through him.

She was speaking again.

'My father became my world—he was all I had left. And Greymont—'

A low ache was starting up in her, old and familiar, from long, long ago. Without realisation, her arms slid around herself. As if staunching a wound.

With a dry mouth she forced herself on.

'It was the same for my father. We—Greymont, and myself—became his reason for going on after my mother left him. And it was because...' Her voice changed. 'Because he saw how desperately I loved Greymont—how I clung to it, to him—he vowed to make sure I would never lose it.'

She shut her eyes a moment, her jaw clenching. Then her lids flew open and she looked straight at Nikos. He was stock-still, his face unreadable, his eyes unreadable. It didn't matter. She had to say this now. *Had* to.

'And to ensure that I did he gave up all hope of ever finding anyone else to make him happy. Gave up all thoughts of marrying again. For *my* sake. Because...' She gave a sigh—a long, weary sigh. 'Because he would not risk having a son who would take precedence over me—inherit Greymont, dispossess me of the home I loved so desperately.'

There was a heaviness inside her now, like a crushing weight, as she lifted her eyes to his, made herself hold them, as impossible as it was for her to do so.

'His sacrifice of any chance of happiness for himself made it imperative for me to honour what he'd done. He ensured I'd inherit Greymont—so I had to save it, Nikos, I had to! I *had* to make it the most important thing in the world to me. Saving Greymont. Or I would have betrayed his trust in me. His trust that I would keep Greymont, pass it on to my descendants, preserve it for our family.'

She looked about her again, at the elegant salon with its antiques, its oil paintings on the walls, the vista of the grounds beyond, the sense of place and history all about her—so absolutely familiar to her from Greymont.

Her lips pressed together. She had to make him see, understand...

CHAPTER TWELVE

HER GAZE WENT back to him, with a pleading look on her face.

'It's something those not born to places like this can never really comprehend—but ask your brother, Nikos, whether he would ever want to part with his heritage, to be the Comte du Plassis who loses it, who lives to see strangers living here, knowing it's not his any longer, that's he's had it taken from him?' She shook her head again. 'But places like this demand a price. A price that can be hard to pay.'

She did not see the expression on Nikos's face change, the sudden bleakness in his eyes. He knew just what price had been paid for his brother to inherit. And who had paid it.

There was a hollowing inside him. Yes, he had paid the price, had been farmed out to foster parents. But his mother had paid too. Had stayed locked in an unhappy marriage in order to preserve her son's inheritance. Her husband had been pitiless, refusing to release her, punishing her for not wanting him whilst chaining her to him.

As he, Nikos, had kept Diana chained to his side, punishing her for not wanting him.

Again a chill swept through him.

No! I am not like him!

Denial seared in him. And memory—memory that flamed in his vision.

Diana in my arms, with the desert stars above, her face alight with passion and ecstasy. Diana laughing with me, her face alight with a smile of happiness. Diana asleep in my embrace, my arms folding her to me, her head resting on me, her hair spread like a flag across me.

Each and every memory was telling him what he knew with every fibre of his being, every cell in his body.

She wanted me just as I wanted her. That desire that flamed between us was as real to her as it was to me. So how could she deny it—how?

A 'mistake', she'd called their time in the desert. The word mocked him, whipped him with scorpions.

But she was speaking again, her voice heavy.

'And so I married you, Nikos, to keep Greymont safe. That's why I married you—for that and only that.'

His gaze on her was bleak. 'A man whose touch you could not tolerate? Would not endure? Despite all we were to each other in the desert?'

A cry broke from her—high and unearthly. '*Because* of it! Nikos, are you so blind? Can you not *see*?'

Her arms spasmed around the column of her body, as if she must contain the emotion ravening through it. But it was impossible to contain such emotion, to stop it pouring from her, carrying with it words that burst from her now.

'Nikos—when you came to Greymont and put down in front of me your offer of marriage I wanted to snatch it with both hands! But I hesitated—I hesitated because—'

Her eyes sheared away. She was unable to look at him directly, to tell him to his face. But emotion was tumbling through her, churning her up, and she had to speak—she *had* to! Her arms tightened about herself more fiercely.

'I'd seen the way you looked at me at that dinner. Seen the way you looked at me at *Don Carlo*, and in the taxi back to my hotel. I saw in your eyes what I'd seen in men's eyes all my adult life. And I knew I could not...' Her voice choked again. 'I could not have that in our marriage!'

She did not see his expression change. His face whiten. She plunged on, unable to stop herself.

'But I was desperate to accept your offer and so I persuaded myself that it wasn't there. I believed what I wanted to believe—confirmed, as I thought, by the way you were during our engagement.' She gave a high, hollow laugh, quickly cut short. 'And all the while you were just biding your time. Waiting for the honeymoon to arrive.'

She shut her eyes, not able to bear seeing the world any longer. Not able to bear seeing *him*.

'And arrive it did,' she said, her voice hollow.

Into her head, marching like an invading army that she had so long sought to keep at bay, came memories. Images. Each and every one as fatal to her as a gunshot.

Her eyes sprang open, as if to banish those memories that were so indelible within her. But instead of memory there was Nikos, there in front of her. So real. So close.

So infinitely far away.

As he must always be.

Nikos—the man who had caused her more pain than she had ever known existed!

'Oh, God, Nikos!' The words rang from her. 'You think me an ice maiden. But I've had to be—I've *had* to be!'

Slowly, very slowly, she made the crippling clenching of her arms around her body slacken, let her hands fall to her sides, limp. She was weary with a lifetime of exhaustion, of holding at bay emotions she must not let herself feel or they would destroy her.

'Being an ice maiden kept me *safe*. Having a celibate marriage to you kept me *safe*.'

There was silence. Only the low ticking of the ormolu clock on the mantel.

'Safe,' she said again, as if saying it could make it so.

But the word only mocked her pitilessly. *Safe?* It had been the most dangerous thing in the world, marrying Nikos—the one, the only man who had set alight that flare of sexual awareness inside her with a single glance. That single, fateful glance that had brought her here, now, to this final parting with him.

Pain seared inside her—the pain she had feared, so much all her life. A wild, anguished look pierced her eyes as she cried out.

'I *needed* to be an ice maiden! I didn't want to feel anything for any man. I had to protect myself! Protect myself from what I saw my father go through! Because what if what happened to my father, happened to *me*? He broke his heart over my mother! Because she never loved him back—'

She broke off, turning away. She had to go—flee! However long Nikos made her wait for her divorce. The divorce that would free her from the chains he held her by.

But he holds me by chains that I can never break! Never!

The anguish came again, that searing pain. A sob tore at her throat and her arms were spasming again, as if she would fall without that iron grip to hold her upright.

And then suddenly there was another clasp upon her. Hands folding over hers. Nikos's strong, tall body right behind her. Slowly, deliberately, he was turning her around to face him.

His hands fell away from her, and she suddenly felt so very cold. She stood, trembling, unable to lift her head to look at him. He spoke. His voice was low, with a resonance in it that had never been there before.

'Diana...' He spoke carefully, as if finding his step along a high, perilous path, 'Your fears have haunted you, possessed you—you must let them go.'

She lifted her head then. Stared at him with a wide, stricken gaze.

'That isn't possible, Nikos,' she answered, her voice faint. 'You, of all people, should know that.' Her expression contorted. 'Those nights we had in the desert... You could not understand why I so regretted them—why I told you it should never have happened. But now you know why I said that to you. Just as I, Nikos...' her voice was etched with sadness '...know why my rejection of you made you so angry. Because it made you think me no better than your mother—the mother who rejected you so cruelly.'

His expression was strange.

'Except that she did not.' He saw the bewilderment in Diana's eyes. 'Antoine came to me—the half-brother I never even knew I had took me to her,' he said. 'He told me the truth about why she had to do what she did.'

Sadly, he told her the bleak, unhappy tale—and then the miracle of his reconciliation with her.

'It was realising how wrong I had been about her, how I had misjudged her, that made me fear I had misjudged *you*, too!' His expression was shadowed. 'And fear even more that I had not.'

His expression changed, his voice becoming sombre now.

'We've both been chained by our past. Trapped. I was trapped in hating the mother who had rejected me, only to find that she had been trapped by her need to protect my brother. And you, Diana, were trapped by the wounds your mother's desertion inflicted on you—trapped by your gratitude to your father, your guilt over his sacrifice for you, your pity for him—the fear you learnt from him. The fear I want so much to free you from.'

'But that fear is *real*, Nikos!' she cried out. 'It's real. It was real from the first moment I set eyes on you, when I knew, for the first time in my life, that here was a man to make me feel the power of that fear. And it was terrifyingly real after our time together in the desert!'

There was a wild, anguished look in her eyes.

'Oh, God, Nikos, that time we had there together only proved to me how *right* I was to be so afraid. You thought I rejected you afterwards because our time in the desert meant so little to me. But it was the very opposite!'

Her voice dropped.

'So I can't be safe from such fear—it's impossible.' She closed her eyes, felt her hands clench before her eyes flew open again. 'I can only try to insulate myself from it, protect myself.'

Even as she spoke she knew the bitter futility of her words. It was far too late. But she plunged on all the same, for there was no other path for her. None except this path now, lined with broken glass, that she must tread for the rest of her life.

'Just give me my divorce, Nikos,' she said wearily. 'It's what I came here to beg for.'

'So you can be free of me?' He paused. 'Safe from me?'

Her eyelids fluttered shut. It was too much to bear.

'Yes,' she whispered. 'Safe from you.'

She could not see his face. Could not see his eyes, fastened upon her. She could only hear him say her name. The words he spoke.

'Diana—what if you could be safe? Not *from* me, but safe *with* me?'

Emotion was welling inside him. An emotion that he scarcely recognised, for he had never felt it in all his life, had never known until he had seen it in his mother's eyes, as she lay so frail, so pitiful, awaiting the operation that might take her from him for ever.

He felt it again now, fresh-made, rising up in him like a tide that had been welling, invisible, unseen and un-stoppable, for so, so long.

Since he had held Diana in his arms beneath the burn-ing desert stars.

'Safe *with* me, Diana,' he said again.

That strange, overpowering emotion welled again. It was an emotion full of danger—a danger that the woman he spoke to now, whose clenched hands he was reaching for, knew so well.

Yet it was a danger he must risk. For all his future lay within it. All *her* future.

All our future.

Urgency impelled him, and yet he seemed to be mov-ing with infinite slowness. Infinite care. So much de-pended on this.

Everything that I hold precious.

That emotion seared him again, rising like a break-ing wave out of that running tide within him, so power-ful, so unstoppable.

He felt her hands beneath his touch, her pale fingers digging into the sleeves of her jacket. He gently prised them loose, slid them into his hands, drew them away from her body into his own warm, strong clasp.

'Diana…' He said her name again, softly, quietly. Willing her to lift her sunken head, open the eyes closed against him.

'Safe *with* me. *Safe.*'

He took a breath—a deep, filling breath that reached to his core, to his fast-beating heart, and with his next word he risked all—risked the fear that had crippled her for so long, wanting to set her free from it.

'Always.'

Her eyelids were fluttering open...her head was lifting. His hands pressed hers, clasping them, encompassing them. Drawing her towards him, closer and yet closer still.

She came, hesitant, unsure, as if stumbling, as if she could not halt herself, as if she were walking out across a precipice so high she must surely fall, catastrophically, and smash herself on rocks. Her eyes were wide, distended, and in them he saw emotions flare and fuse. *Fear.* And something else. Something she tried to hide. Something that was not fear at all—something that filled him with a rush, an urgency to speak. To say what must now fall from his lips.

The most important, the most vital, the most essential words he would ever say. Words that he had never dreamt in all his life would be his to say. They were filling his whole being, flooding through him, possessing him and transforming him. Fulfilling him.

They could never be unsaid.

They *would* never be unsaid.

'Safe, Diana, in my love for you.'

They were said! The words that had come to him now, burning through all the doubts and fears, all the turbulent emotions that possessed him, burning through like the desert sun burning over the golden dunes.

Love—bright love.

Love that blazed in the heavens.

Blazed in *him*.

Now and for ever.

He folded her to him, releasing her hands, and as his strong arms came around her he felt the sweet softness of her body against his, felt her clutch at him, heard the choking sob in her throat.

He let her weep against him, holding her all the while, smoothing her hair, his cheek against hers, wet with her tears.

'Do you mean it? Oh, Nikos, do you mean it?' Her voice was muffled, her words a cry.

'Yes!'

His answer was instant, his hugging of her fierce. That wondrous emotion was blazing through his whole being now, illuminating the truth. The truth that had started to form out in the desert, under the stars with Diana—so beautiful, so passionate, so precious to him!—whose rejection of him had caused him so much pain.

Pain he had masked in anger. Pain that he no longer had to mask. No longer had to feel. Because now he knew the emotion blazing in him by its true name.

'I love you, Diana. I love you. And with all my heart I hope and pray that you will accept my love. That you do not fear it or flee it! The love,' his heart was in his voice now, heaved up to her, 'I hope that you can share with me, together. '

She pulled away from him, leaning back into the strength of his hands at her spine, her tear-stained face working. At last she was free to say what she had so feared to say—even to herself. What she had kept locked within her, terrified that she had brought about the very fate she had guarded herself against for so long. The tormented and tormenting truth she had admitted to no one—least of all herself—denying it and rejecting it until that fateful day when, with a simple question, it had been prised from her.

One simple question from the Princess—*'What is wrong?'*

And Diana had told her. The truth pouring from her. As she was telling Nikos now, the words choking her.

'I do! Oh, Nikos, I fell in love with you out in the desert. I could not stop myself—could not protect myself. You swept away every defence, every caution. But I knew that I'd condemned myself to heartbreak!' Her eyes were anguished, her voice desolate. 'Because when our marriage ended—as end it must, just as we'd agreed it would—you would move on and then I would become like my father, mourning the loss of a love I should never have let myself feel, but which it was far too late to stop.'

Sudden fear smote her, ravaging her.

'And you *will* move on, Nikos! Whatever you say now, you'll move on. One day you'll be done with me—'

An oath broke from him and all self-control left him. He hauled her back into his arms.

'I will love you *always* Diana.' His voice changed and he cradled her face between his hands. 'I have never known what love is—never experienced it in all my life. Until I found my mother's love for me, learnt the truth about her, about how I had misjudged her. And I feared then that I had misjudged you, too. And I recognised at the very moment you were demanding a divorce what it was I felt for you—what I feared *you* did not feel, *could* not feel, were incapable of feeling.'

She silenced him. With a smothered cry she pressed her mouth to his. Sealing his lips with hers, her love with his. Only drawing back to say, her eyes full, tears still shimmering on her lashes, 'Oh, Nikos, we both bear scars from wounds that nearly parted us, but love has healed them and that is all we need!'

Joy, and a relief so profound it made her weak, was flooding through her. She hugged him close against her, letting her cheek rest on his chest, feeling his strength, his arms fastening around her again. How much she loved him—oh, how much! And she was *safe* to love him—always.

She gave a sigh of absolute contentment. Felt his lips graze her hair, heard him murmuring soft words of love. Then he was drawing a little apart from her, smiling down at her. She met his gaze, reeling from the love-light blazing in his eyes. She felt her heart turn over, joy searing through her more fiercely yet.

And then the expression in his eyes was changing, and she felt her pulse give a sudden quickening, her breath catching, lips parting, breathless with what she saw in his face. She felt her body flush with heat.

'How fortunate,' he was murmuring, 'my most beautiful beloved, that we are already man and wife. For now I do believe a second wedding night must fast be approaching.'

She gave a laugh of tremulous, sensuous delight, and it was a sound he had not heard for so many long, bitter months. Not since they had found their paradise in the deserts of Arabia—a paradise that now would be in their hearts for ever.

'It's only midday!' she exclaimed, her hands looping around his neck, her fingertips splaying in the feathered softness of his hair. Glorying in the touch of her palms at his nape.

Her eyes were alight with glinting desire. Hunger for him was unleashed within her. And all the memories that she had barred were freshly vivid in her mind, heating her bloodstream. How achingly long it had been since she had held him in her arms!

'Then we shall have an afternoon of love,' he proclaimed, his voice a husk of desire, his gaze devouring her.

There was a cough, discreet, but audible, and a voice spoke from across the room.

'Indeed you shall.' The voice was cool and accented, and very obviously amused.

They turned instantly. Antoine, Comte de Plessis, was standing in the open double doorway, his light gaze resting on them, the slightest smile on his mouth.

'But not, I implore you, until *after* lunch!'

His smile widened, and in his gaze Diana could see fond affection as well as humour.

'I am delighted beyond all things,' the Comte continued, his voice more serious now, 'that the reconciliation which I know my brother longed for has successfully been accomplished.' He bestowed a slight nod upon Nikos, and then Diana, and again that amused smile was flickering at his mouth. 'And I am even more delighted that I may now properly welcome you, *ma chère* Madame Tramontes.'

And now he was walking towards them, as Nikos changed his stance so that Diana was at his side, his arm around her waist and hers around his, drawn close against each other. With Gallic elegance he possessed himself of Diana's free hand, raising it to his lips.

'*Enchanté, madame,*' he murmured as he lowered it again, released it. 'I can see,' he said, and now his smile was warm, 'that it is quite unnecessary for me to say that you have made my brother the happiest of men. I profoundly hope that it is within his capabilities to make you the happiest of wives.'

His smile deepened.

'And with that concluded…' he raised his hands in another very Gallic gesture and turned to walk back to the doors '… I must, I fear, warn you that your presence in the dining room is required *tout de suite*, for the culinary genius of my chef—upon which he has called in measures previously unsurpassed to present us with a celebratory *dejeuner du midi*—is exceeded, *hélas*, only by the volatility of his temperament. In short, I beg you not to arouse his wrath by a tardy appearance.'

He flung open the doors in a dramatic gesture, infused still with humour.

'*Venez,*' he invited. 'Love can wait—luncheon cannot!'

Laughingly, their arms still entwined around each other, as their hearts would be entwined all their lives, Nikos and Diana followed him from the room.

From now on, all their days—and all their nights—would be with each other.

For each other.

EPILOGUE

DIANA SAT AT the dressing table in her bedroom at Greymont, putting the finishing touches to her appearance, ensuring she looked her best for her beloved Nikos. And for his brother, and his mother, recovered now from her operation, who'd both arrived this evening to celebrate with herself and Nikos their wedding day on the morrow.

Our real wedding, thought Diana, feeling a wash of love and gratitude go through her. *Which will take place in the little parish church.*

There would be no guests but Antoine and the Comtesse, who would be their witnesses. Witnesses to the union that would not be the empty marriage of convenience that had brought herself and Nikos together, but a marriage of their hearts that would bind them, each to the other, all their lives.

The marriage she longed to make.

She left her bedroom—*their* bedroom, hers and Nikos's—and paused for a moment at the top of the stairs, wondering how she could be so happy. How she could be so blessed. Her beloved home, her beloved Nikos...

But it's the other way round! It's my beloved Nikos and then my beloved home! And it is ours together—and our children's after us.

She descended the marble staircase, glancing in approbation around her. Everything at Greymont was now fully restored as it should be. And now, its beauty renewed, she and Nikos could make plans to open Greymont to the public for periods during the summer. How pleased her father would have been at that!

And at her married happiness. She sent a wish towards him, full of love and gratitude, then smiled at Hudson as he waited benignly at the foot of the stairs.

She walked into the drawing room, her silken skirts swishing. Nikos and his brother rose immediately, and Nikos came to take her hand, walking with her to the woman sitting by the fireside. So petite, so frail, but despite the lines of fatigue around her eyes her gaze on Diana and her son was filled with an emotion Diana knew only too well—for it was in her own eyes too, whenever she gazed at Nikos.

Diana stooped to kiss her, welcoming her to Greymont. It was the first time Nikos's mother had been strong enough to make the journey, and Diana knew that both Nikos and Antoine were treating her like precious porcelain. It was a cherishing kind of care that drew the two brothers ever closer together, and Diana rejoiced in it. They had so many years to catch up on.

She rejoiced, too, that shortly after her *belle mère* and her brother-in-law had returned to Normandy Greymont would be host again—to royalty this time.

Princess Fatima had wasted no time, on receiving payment in full of the loan she had made to Diana, paid by Nikos, in discovering what had transpired to bring this about—and she was thrilled at what she had discovered. She wanted to see for herself, she informed Diana, and therefore she would honour them with a visit—'to take afternoon tea!' she had exclaimed gaily.

And in the early spring, when the weather would be

perfect in the Gulf, the Princess was insisting that Nikos and Diana visit again. *Especially* to take a trip to her brother's love-nest.

'It is where you fell in love with your husband,' she had said, looking sternly at Diana. 'To refuse would be to offend,' she'd warned. But there had been a glint of humour in her eyes as she'd spoken. And there had been a glint of answering humour in Nikos's face as he'd bowed his grateful assent.

'Only a madman would refuse to take the woman he loves more than life itself to the place where the stars themselves blessed their union,' he'd said.

The Princess had sighed in romantic satisfaction.

And taken another scone.

* * * * *

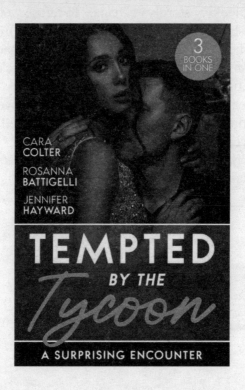

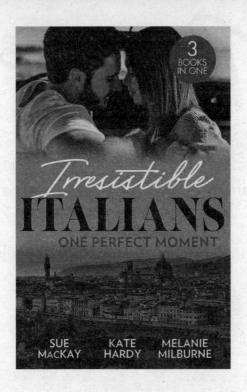

MILLS & BOON

THE HEART OF ROMANCE

A ROMANCE FOR EVERY READER

MODERN
Prepare to be swept off your feet by sophisticated, sexy and seductive heroes, in some of the world's most glamourous and romantic locations, where power and passion collide.

HISTORICAL
Escape with historical heroes from time gone by. Whether your passion is for wicked Regency Rakes, muscled Vikings or rugged Highlanders, awaken the romance of the past.

MEDICAL
Set your pulse racing with dedicated, delectable doctors in the high-pressure world of medicine, where emotions run high and passion, comfort and love are the best medicine.

True Love
Celebrate true love with tender stories of heartfelt romance, from the rush of falling in love to the joy a new baby can bring, and a focus on the emotional heart of a relationship.

Desire
Indulge in secrets and scandal, intense drama and sizzling hot action with heroes who have it all: wealth, status, good looks…everything but the right woman.

HEROES
The excitement of a gripping thriller, with intense romance at its heart. Resourceful, true-to-life women and strong, fearless men face danger and desire - a killer combination!

To see which titles are coming soon, please visit

millsandboon.co.uk/nextmonth